Match Penalty

TEAGAN HUNTER

For the ones who have ever felt like they aren't enough, even when they are.
Your brain is lying to you. Tell it to shut the fuck up.

And to Conrad Fisher, the boy who reminded us all what yearning truly means.

DEAR READER

This book depicts a struggling marriage. It shows that sometimes, even if you love someone more than anything in the world, you still have to put yourself first. You still have to make hard choices. It's a glimpse at two people who have been together a long time, who may have let themselves get too comfortable and have forgotten what brought them together to start with—love.

Please know that while there are some hard conversations had in this book, there is *no* cheating.

However, this book does mention bullying regarding weight and some pushy parents.

For a list of all potential triggers for my books, please visit my website.

Your mental health matters while reading.

KELLER

Lawson: Still meeting at Top Shelf tonight to ring in the New Year, right?

Lawson: Just say yes, or I swear I'll cry.

Hayes: I kind of think I'd like to see that.

Hayes: You crying, just so we're clear.

Hutch: I have. It's not pretty. You're better off just agreeing to whatever it is he's trying to cook up.

Fox: Aww. Why'd you cry, buddy?

Locke: I'm guessing it was one of the times Keller was mean to him.

Me: I'm not mean. I just say what everyone else is thinking.

Lawson: In the worst way possible.

Lawson: And no, Keller did NOT make me cry.

Hutch: It was at his brother's wedding. Dude was slinging snot all over the place and everything.

Lawson: That's because weddings are beautiful. You're just cold-hearted!

Hutch: I am not. I cry.

Lawson: Oh, really? Name one time.

Hutch: Uh, when my BABY was born.

Lawson: Ha ha what a loser!

Hayes: Shit, Hutchy. That's kind of sweet.

Fox: Awww

Locke: I mean, how could you not? She's adorable.

Lawson: WAIT

Lawson: WTF

Lawson: You guys really aren't going to make fun of him for CRYING?!?!

Locke: Nah

Hayes: No, dude. His girl just had his freakin' BABY.

Fox: I would never!

Lawson: Keller? Anything?

Me: I got nothing. Like Hayesy said, he had a baby. Tears are expected.

Lawson: WHAT IN THE ACTUAL HELL

Lawson: If Daisy had a baby and I cried,
I would NEVER hear the end of it!

Me: That's because Daisy is your DOG.
Why would you cry??

Lawson: Because it's beautiful! Just like
Jacob's wedding, which is why I cried.
Do you know how much of a love-hater
that guy was before he met his wife?
And how now he's all sappy and in love
and shit? It's romantic as fuck.

Hayes: He was pretty bad.

Hutch: Worse than Keller?

Hayes: Is ANYONE worse than Keller?

Locke: Yeah, not sure that's possible.

Fox: Come on, guys. Kells isn't that bad.

Lawson: Foxy Baby, I love you, but
you're full of shit.

Fox: I love you, too, buddy.

Hayes: Yeah, sorry, but you're delusional
if you think that. He's very clearly
that bad.

Locke: Didn't he block us all on
Christmas because he didn't want to see
our family photos?

Hutch: To be fair, I think that was because Lawsy wouldn't stop sending pictures of all twenty of his dogs in pajamas.

Lawson: It's not twenty! I only have three...and one cat, though Hades is technically Rory's. He hates me.

Lawson: And those matching pajamas were fucking adorable! Rory and I had them on, too. She even cracked a smile in one photo!

Lawson: He blocked us because he's sad he's the only single guy in the Serpents Singles Club now.

Me: He's also in this godforsaken group chat and can see you assholes talking about him.

Me: And he's not sad. He just doesn't have the patience for anyone else's bullshit.

Lawson: Soooo...you're jealous.

Me: The fuck I am.

Lawson: J-E-A-L-O-U-S

Me: Congrats. You can spell. Want a sandwich?

Lawson: A sandwich? Aren't you supposed to offer me a cookie?

> Me: A knuckle cookie doesn't sound
> nearly as appealing as a knuckle
> sandwich.

Lawson: See? All he does is resort to
violence. I bet it's all that pent-up rage
he has because he's jealous we're all
happy and in love, and he's probably
sitting on his couch like some lonely
loser with nobody to hang out with on
New Year's Eve.

Hutch: Whoa

Hayes: Damn, Lawsy. You're brave.

Lawson: Brave or just honest?

Locke: Definitely brave.

Fox: Or dumb.

Lawson: Hey, what the fuck, man?

Fox: Sorry, but you're on your own with
this one. Messing with Keller is like
unleashing a barely restrained rabid dog.

> Me: Thanks, Foxy. That might be the
> nicest thing you've ever said about me.

> Me: As for you, Lawsy, you can go fuck
> yourself.

Lawson: Oh, so YOU can be honest, but
I can't? How is that fair?

> Me: Life isn't fair.

Lawson: You're the worst.

Lawson: Are you coming to the damn party or not?

Fox: Lilah and I are in.

Hutch: We'll be there.

Locke: Yeah, man, wouldn't miss it.

Hayes: Quinn is more than ready to let loose after this semester, so we'll definitely be there.

Lawson: …Keller?

Me: What?

Lawson: *eye roll emoji*

Lawson: Are you coming to Top Shelf, or are you going to sulk alone all night while we have fun?

Me: Why should I?

Lawson: You shouldn't. I don't care what you do.

Me: Then fine. I won't go.

Lawson: OH MY GOD ARE YOU SERIOUS WHY ARE YOU BEING SUCH A BUTTHOLE RIGHT NOW

Fox: …butthole?

Hutch: I won't lie, I laughed.

Hayes: I did too.

Locke: We're all a bunch of twelve-year-olds.

Lawson: Except you. You're still an old man, Lockey Poo.

Locke: I swear I'll rescind my RSVP.

Lawson: Nooooooooooooo

Lawson: I take it back. You're not old, even if you do sound extra old saying shit like "rescind." Nope. You're not old at all.

Hayes: I could hear the sarcasm dripping from every word.

Locke: Me fucking too.

Lawson: Who? Me? Never! 😇

Locke: Keep it up, Lawsy. It'll just be you, Keller, and that knuckle sandwich tonight.

Lawson: Rory will be there too, so I'm cool with that.

Me: Jesus fuck. Please don't start with all that lovey-dovey shit. My stomach can't handle that and tequila shots tonight.

Lawson: Then we'll hold the shots.

Lawson: And also, that means you're coming. NO TAKEBACKS!

Lawson: See you all at 10! Don't be late or I'll cry.

Hutch: What is with you and crying
today?

Lawson: Just don't be late, Hutchy.
Okay? Okay. I love you guys. Bye.

Me: Does anyone else wish Lawson was
never traded to the Seattle Serpents?

Hayes: Bro, we're number two in the
Pacific right now. Absolutely not.

Hutch: He's annoying as hell, but no.

Fox: Do you really want me to answer
that?

Locke: He's a fucking champ on the
faceoff dot AND he's on pace to score
50 goals this year. Think it's safe to say
he's an asset.

Lawson: OMG 😊 I knew you guys loved
me. I KNEW IT.

Me: Whoa. Calm down. Nobody ever
said that.

Lawson: You didn't have to. I can
FEEL it.

Me: Like you're going to FEEL my fist in
your face later, right?

Lawson: I'm gonna kiss those knuckles,
Kells. Right at midnight. 😘

Me: Touch me and die.

Lawson: Then I welcome death. 😈

. . .

"Fuck me," I grumble, tossing my phone onto the cushion next to me as it continues to vibrate with incoming texts, most likely from Lawson. I swear, that guy never knows when to shut up, which would explain the yellow-green bruise I'm rocking after sticking up for him in our win over Vegas last week.

I don't mind it. I love fighting. It makes me feel like I'm actually useful and not just a body keeping the bench warm. Because let's face it—I am not a superstar. I'm that guy they send out when they need to get some energy into the team. I'm the one with grit, the guy who sacrifices his body to block shots and get the more skilled players in a better shooting position. And I'm okay with that. I've accepted my role. I love it.

What I don't love? Filing into a crowded-as-hell bar on New Year's Eve and throwing back shots of tequila when we're in the middle of the season. Is it better than staying home and falling asleep before midnight? No, absolutely not, and I refuse to pretend otherwise. But am I going to go anyway? Un-fucking-fortunately.

I wish I could say it's solely because Lawson will annoy me to death if I don't, but that's not true. Lucas Lawson is going to do that no matter what. That's just who he is, which I've come to accept over the last few years we've been teammates on the Seattle Serpents, and even more so since he forced me to join his ridiculous

"Serpents Singles Club." The name is comical now, really. It began as a promise for all of us to stay single until we hoisted the Cup, but since that's all been blown to shit with everyone being in committed relationships, we're just a bunch of guys who like hanging out together. Not that I'd ever admit that out loud, of course.

Just like I'd never admit the real reason I'm going out to join my teammates is I don't want to sit on the couch and let the onslaught of horrible memories do a fucking jig in my head all night long. New Year's Eve is the worst day of the year—hands down, no questions asked. It's the day everything changed. The day *I* changed. The day *we* changed.

I fucking hate today.

I grab the controller I abandoned when my phone started blowing up the first time and focus my mind on taking out demons with my chainsaw shield. While it's not the best use of my time, it's better than letting the memories of what once was seep into my head. I can't let that happen. I can't let them plant themselves, and I definitely can't water them with my attention. It only leads to more of the same shit I've been living with for the last three years—heartbreak.

Eventually, my phone calms down, and so does my mind. For the next two hours, I think of nothing but taking out this demon king and being the scariest thing in all of hell. It's not until Percy yells at me from across my apartment that I realize how long has passed.

"What's up, little man?" I ask as the three-legged cat jumps onto the couch, his tail smacking me right in the face. If it weren't for the two asymmetrical patches of black around his eyes, he would be all-white.

He turns, then nuzzles his face against my chin per usual. It's his go-to move when he senses I'm about to leave him.

"It's just for a few hours," I say. "I won't be out all night. I promise."

He presses his head against me harder, almost like he's saying, *Okay, I believe you…but just this once.*

I chuckle lowly. "All right. You've convinced me. Five more minutes of snuggles, then I have to get ready. Apparently, your uncle Lucas—whom you've never met but have heard me bitch about plenty—is demanding I show up for New Year's Eve festivities."

Meow.

"I know. Sounds like a bunch of bullshit to me, too."

Meow.

I think about not going, about just sitting on the couch like this, holding Percy, and eating snacks until I pass out. Then I remember I'd have to face Lawson and the rest of my teammates tomorrow at practice, and they'll be armed with a hundred questions, just like always, and I don't want that. I'd rather bag skate for an hour straight than have to answer why I hate this day so damn much.

Meow.

"I'm going anyway, bud. I have to. You understand, right?"

Meow.

He accepts this answer—or at least that's what I tell myself—and I keep an eye on the clock as I run my hand up and down his back, loving the soft purrs he emits. When it gets close enough to ten that I know I'll have Lawson annoying the piss out of me again if I procrastinate any longer, I peel myself off the couch and head to my bedroom.

Percy jumps off, following close behind, and I grin. I was never one of those kids who begged for a puppy or a kitten. The only thing I was ever interested in was hockey. I would have taken new skates or new gloves over anything else. But with Percy, I wandered into the clinic on a whim, we locked eyes, and I knew we were meant to be. Maybe it was because we had just lost our shot at making the playoffs, or maybe it was because I was lonely. It doesn't matter. I'm stuck with him now, and he's stuck with me. I wouldn't have it any other way.

The cat hops onto my bed as I swap my joggers for jeans and my old t-shirt for a long-sleeved gray Henley. I'm sure most of the group will be dressing up more than this, but it's not like I have anyone to impress.

"All right," I say to Percy once I've finished getting ready. I stand by the front door, slipping my shoes on. "I'll be back by twelve thirty at the latest. Keep an eye on the place. If anyone breaks in, gouge their eyes out, then scream like you always do at three in the damn morning."

Meow.

I give him one last ear scratch and head out, making sure to lock the door behind me. Phone in hand, I order a rideshare on the way to the elevator. I have no plans of drinking until I'm shit-faced tonight, but I figure it's better to be safe than sorry. Because who knows? Maybe Lawson will annoy me just enough that I might need alcohol to survive until midnight.

As I wait for the elevator, I pray nobody I know is inside. With Whitlocke and his girlfriend, Vanessa, living here, I run into them far too often for my liking. I'm glad the old man is happy—truly—but do they have to make out in the elevator even when someone else is in there with them?

I'm relieved to find the car empty as the doors slide open, and I step inside. I rest against the back railing, closing my eyes as I descend, trying to extinguish the urge to march right back into my apartment and become one with my couch.

Fuck, maybe I *should* get shit-faced on tequila shots tonight. Maybe then I'll forget just how much I hate this fucking holiday.

If only I didn't know Coach Smith has a long morning planned for us tomorrow. He always makes us come into the rink early after a holiday. It's his way of keeping us all in check, making sure we don't get too rowdy. I used to hate it, mostly because I had an actual reason to celebrate, but now? I don't care. Drag me out of bed at six AM. Hell, do it at five. It's not like I get much sleep anyway. What's it going to matter to me?

My phone buzzes in my pocket, and I check it, just in case it's my rideshare.

It's not. It's my brother.

Stefan: Broooooo

Stefan: new

Stefan: shit

Stefan: HPPY NEWSPAPER YOUR

I laugh, knowing that since it's already midnight on the East Coast, where he's attending law school, he's likely drunk as hell. There's a ten-year age gap between us, and though it's easier now that he's older, it's still funny to see how differently our lives have ended up. What I was doing at twenty-one is vastly different than what he's doing.

I shoot him a quick text back, wishing him a happy New Year, then pocket my phone. It doesn't feel like a happy New Year, though, not even close.

My fingers climb their way up my chest and to the

chain that's dangled around my neck for the last couple of years. The metal is warm from resting against my skin, but it still somehow feels cold. I'm sure it's because it sits so close to my heart.

When the elevator stops on the lobby floor, I drop my hand away and shove it back into my pocket, along with all the thoughts and longing for what I've lost that come every time I close my eyes. I give a nod to security as I make my way out of the building. The ride I ordered is already waiting, and I slip into the back seat without saying a word to the driver. The low thrum of whatever's on the radio fills the silence as the driver merges in and out of traffic—another reason I didn't take my Audi R8 out on the town tonight—and we're pulling up next to Top Shelf before I know it.

"Thanks," I murmur as I climb out of the car.

I tug my phone from my pocket, rate the driver five stars, and drop them a twenty-dollar tip for leaving me the hell alone. Taking a deep breath, I steel myself as I yank open the door, where I'm hit with the smell of stale beer, loud music, and the desire to run away. I turn on my heel, ready to do just that, but I'm caught before I can get far.

"Keller!"

I wince as his hand lands on my shoulder. I try to shake him off, but—per usual—it's pointless.

"You're not trying to run away, are you?" Lawson grins at me. "Because if you were, I might have to—"

"Cry?" I finish for him with an eye roll, shrugging off his touch once again. "What is with you and crying lately?"

"What? Is it so bad for a guy to be in touch with his emotions?" Not taking the hint that I don't want him touching me, he slings his arm around my neck as he pulls me farther into the bar. "Come on. We're over here."

He leads me over to the same booth we always occupy whenever we come here, which is admittedly quite a bit, but we knew right away that Top Shelf was a safe place for us to unwind after and between games. The owner made me and the rest of my teammates feel at home from day one, and it has now turned into the Seattle Serpents' official hangout.

"Keller!" our number one goalie yells, a wide, toothy grin gracing his face. I would blame it on the free-flowing alcohol, but that's just Arthur Fox for you. In the time I've known him, I think I've seen him without a smile twice.

I nod his way. "Foxy."

"Oooh Foxy! I love that they call you that," Lilah, his girlfriend-slash-former fiancée, says with a giggle. I can see she's already taken advantage of the drink specials tonight too.

"Sit, sit." Lawson shoves me into an empty spot. "What do you want to drink? Nessa can get it for you."

"Um, excuse me. No, she cannot. Nessa is not

working tonight," says the woman in question, turning her nose up at Lawson's suggestion.

Locke reaches out and smacks Lawson's stomach. "She's not your barmaid, Lawsy. Get Keller's drink yourself since you're so dead set on playing host tonight."

"Fine. Anyone else want drinks?"

It opens a can of worms the forward clearly wasn't ready for as eleven people shout their orders all at once. We eventually get it sorted out, and Rory, his veterinarian girlfriend who is far too smart and good for him, follows behind to help.

"Is it just me or did he look like that Winona Ryder GIF where she's looking around like she's completely unsure of what's happening?" asks Quinn with a laugh.

"He did, but can we also please discuss just how hot that woman still is? Like *good grief*. I can't get over it." Auden fans herself while her fiancé, our captain, nods in agreement.

The table delves into discussions of all things Winona Ryder, and I tune out. It has nothing to do with the subject—Auden is spot on with her assessment of Winona—but because I'm still trying to figure out how exactly I'm going to slip out of here before midnight.

I could fake being sick. Or I could start a brawl. I could even pick a fight with Lawson until everyone else is uncomfortable and the best thing would be for me to leave.

But no. None of that would work. I am very clearly

not sick, and starting a fight would just land me in trouble with the team. Plus, making Lawson mad is almost impossible. I swear insults are some sort of turn-on for him.

I'm stuck here. Even worse? I'm stuck here with the reminder of everything I lost.

"And for you, my favorite grumpy bear." Lawson ruffles my hair as he sets a pint of delicious green apple cider in front of me. It's from a local cidery-slash-farm that makes one hell of a drink.

I don't even bother flipping him off or yelling at him for touching me again. I just grab my glass and down half the contents in one go.

"What?" I ask Locke when he lifts his brows my way. "It's just cider. It's practically apple juice."

He looks like he wants to say more, but doesn't.

"Your face is looking better. Less yellow than it was yesterday," Hayes comments. "Still can't believe that jackass from Vegas landed a punch like that."

I smirk, thinking of the fight that let me feel alive, even if just for a few moments. "Don't worry. I'll get him back when we play them later this month."

Hutch grunts from beside me at the mention of the asshole who almost blew up his whole life a few years back. I went toe-to-toe with him then, too, and I have no problem doing it again, especially not after last week and the cheap shot he landed on Lawson.

"How's the back, Lawsy?" Hutch asks, concern lacing his words as he leans closer to the obnoxious forward.

"Better. Still feel like I'm skating a little slow, but give it another day or two, and I'll be as good as new." He beams across the table, and if I didn't know him so well, I might believe it, but I see the wobble at the edges of his smile. He's still hurting, but he's playing through it in stride.

Say what you want about hockey players, but there is no denying the toughness these guys show. We go to war every night, and while we come out with the broken bones and bruises to prove it, we still stand tall for the next battle. It's one of the things I respect about every one of my teammates sitting around this table, even Lawson.

"You're hitting fifty goals this season. I can feel it," Rory says, running her hand through Lawson's hair. He leans into her like the golden retriever he is, looking at her like she's the only woman in the world, and I take another drink of my cider.

This is going to be a long, long night if I have to sit around and watch my teammates and their partners kissing and touching each other the whole time. They think I'm being dramatic or that I'm jealous when I'm subjected to these little gatherings of ours, but it's not that. I just know firsthand what it's like to have it and lose it all in the blink of an eye.

One day, you're living your life with no worries. You

have the career you've always wanted, the house, the nice cars, the fenced-in yard, that one person who makes you feel like you're on top of the world…it's all there. Then, suddenly, it's gone. Poof. Vanishing like it never happened at all.

So, no, I'm not being dramatic, and I'm not fucking jealous either. I'm merely trying to exist when my heart stopped beating a long time ago.

Conversations ebb and flow over the next hour and a half, and though they try to get me to join in, it's pointless when I'd rather be anywhere else. Finally, midnight sneaks closer, and when we're just five minutes from the clock ticking over into the new year, we stand and gather in the best semicircle this many people can form.

"Here's to another year and another Serpents Single down!" Lawson announces. I swear he gets a thrill out of being the center of attention.

We all clink our glasses together, everyone looking at their partner with love in their eyes. My stomach rolls at the thought of having to watch them all kiss while I stand here with nobody next to me. Maybe I could sneak off to the bathroom. With how crowded it is, it's likely they wouldn't even notice anyway.

I'm just about to step away when Lawson speaks again.

"Guys, I have an announcement." He waits for all eyes to be on him before adding, "I love you all."

I roll my eyes, finishing off my second cider of the night.

"Knock it off, Lawsy," the captain grumbles.

"What he said," Hayes agrees.

"Yep," Locke adds.

"Aww, I love you too, buddy." Fox grins, patting the forward on the back. I wish I could say his palpable excitement is due to his buzz, but he's only had one drink. It's all him.

"Finally!" Lawson throws his hands in the air. "Someone cares about me!"

I barely hold back another eye roll. Leave it to Lawson to be dramatic tonight. The guy loves an audience, and he has a big one right now. While the people who frequent Top Shelf are used to professional hockey players being here, this isn't a usual night out. The bar is packed with more people than I've ever seen before, and we're getting more stares than I'd like.

A few people try to catch my eye, but I avert my gaze before they get any ideas or think I want to talk to them, which I don't. As I'm dragging my eyes through the bar, a flash of red hair catches my eye. *Is that...*

No. I shake the thought away as soon as it enters my mind because it's not possible. There's no way it could be.

Still, I find myself squinting against the dark lighting and leaning forward. Anything to get a clearer glimpse of the woman standing across the room, partially hidden by the horde of bodies. Someone shifts to the right, giving me another peek, and I hold my breath as that same red comes into view again. It's familiar, achingly so, but I tell myself I'm overreacting. I'm imagining it. Because there is no way *she's* here in Seattle. There's just no chance of it.

Then, almost as if I've willed it to happen, the crowd parts, and every ounce of me that's felt dead for the last three years springs back to life. My breath whooshes from my lungs, and my hands shake harder than ever before.

Either this cider has hit me far harder than I anticipated, or the impossible has happened.

"What? No comment, Keller?" Lawson asks, and somewhere in the back of my mind, I'm acutely aware everyone is staring at me, but it doesn't register. Not fully. How can it when *she's* standing just a hundred feet away?

Is this…is this a dream? Did I fall asleep on my couch and imagine this?

But then she laughs, tossing her head back, and I know it's not a dream. This is real. She's here.

Finally! my mind screams as I rake my eyes over her, and fuck, I swear she's gotten even more beautiful with time. Her deep red hair is as gorgeous as ever, though shorter than the last time I saw it, now hitting just below her shoulders. She's wearing a navy dress that sparkles when she moves and hugs her curves—the same ones that felt like sin beneath my fingers—just the right way. The freckle I've run my tongue over more times than I can count still sits on her right shoulder, and the urge to touch it has my fingers buzzing.

She leans her head back, laughing again, and I wish more than anything I were closer so I could hear it. Does it sound the same as it once did? Is it raspy and just a little too loud at the worst of times?

I want to know. I *have* to know.

I take a step toward her, ready to march over there and slant my mouth over hers, then I realize she's not alone.

She's. Not. Alone.

A guy—one I already hate with every fiber of my being—leans into her, his arm linked with hers, his mouth moving as he whispers something in her ear, and now my body is vibrating for a whole different reason. I want to hit someone. More specifically, I want to punch this man who has dared to lay a hand on what belongs to me.

My eyes fall to her left hand, the one absent of the ring I slid on it ten years ago, and all it does is exacerbate the fury.

"Keller, you okay, man?"

I don't know who asks the question, but I find myself biting out a single word. "Fine."

It's a damn lie. I'm not fine. Not even fucking close. My body is thrumming with more anger than I've felt in…fuck, I'm not even sure how long. All I know is this can't be compared to how I felt last week pummeling that guy from Vegas, and that's saying a lot because I fucking loathe that team.

It's more than that. This is rage. Blinding and white, and it has me gnashing my teeth so damn hard I'm afraid they'll break.

I don't care, though. Let them. I'll happily lose them all if it means he'll stop touching her.

"Do you know her or something?" This time, I know it's Lawson who asks the question, and that's only because I don't think I've ever heard him so somber before. It's fitting for how I feel in this moment.

"You could say that," I say, unable to take my eyes off her even as the guy inches closer and her smile widens. "She's my wife."

Chapter 2

CHLOE

"Are you sure you don't mind?"

"Oh, no, of course not."

I force a smile because I do mind. I mind *a lot*. Going to a random bar on New Year's Eve sounds like my worst nightmare, but if I want a full-time writing gig at *Seattle Daily*, I need to learn to suck it up and play nice.

I can hear my mother's words from our call earlier still ringing in my head.

"I thought this was what you wanted, Chloe. It's why you gave up on the biology degree your father and I paid for. You wanted to be a writer, didn't you? Well, sometimes you have to make sacrifices for what you want."

And don't I know that better than anyone.

Even though my mother has never truly supported my decision to be a writer, she is right about this. I did ask for this career, and I gave up a hell of a lot for it, too.

So I'm going to do the damn thing, even when I don't want to.

Besides, getting the job will mean my name on the byline every day, a massive pay raise—which I desperately need—and they'll cover the relocation costs. On paper, it's the ideal job for me and everything I've been working toward, but I'm still on the fence about it.

I try to tell myself it's most definitely *not* because Dirk has paid a little too much attention to the way my dress hugs my breasts, but that would be a lie. It absolutely factors in.

For the third time, I curse myself for not insisting on taking an Uber, all because I'm trying to save money on this trip that I'm not even sure will pan out. I guess that's what I get for giving up my steady job as a lab technician and trading it for the tumultuous path of a freelance writer. Sure, I had a big surge and got good money from the two viral articles I wrote about navigating life after making bold decisions, but that's long gone. Now I'm banking on this offer from *Seattle Daily* going through so I can figure out my next move before the rest of my meager wages vanishes.

"You're going to love this place," Dirk says. "The perfect vibes." He grins at me from the driver's seat of his Volkswagen sedan, which could use a wash and vacuum, the red from the stoplight we're at casting an almost eerie glow over his face.

The light changes to green, and the second he turns

his attention back to the road, I drop my fake smile and sag lower in my seat while he navigates the rainy streets of downtown Seattle. My phone buzzes in my purse, no doubt a text from my best friend, Talia, checking in for the day, but I ignore it in an attempt to remain professional.

I try to relax as best I can with music I don't recognize playing softly in the background, watching as we pass tall buildings and various businesses, all packed with people out celebrating the holiday.

Once upon a time, that was me, too. I loved New Year's Eve more than any other day of the year, even Christmas, which just sounds ridiculous. I would drag everyone I knew out to a party or throw one myself. It meant far more to me than opening expensive gifts or stuffing my face with too much food. It was a chance for something *new*, something fresh, and that was what I loved about it—the opportunity to begin again. I really wanted to begin again, especially three years ago when I officially stopped celebrating the holiday.

"All good?" Dirk's words break through the trip down memory lane my brain is trying to take, and I'm grateful for it. The last thing I want is to spend this night reminiscing when I'm supposed to be focused on my future.

I give my head a shake. "Yes, sorry. Just…taking in the city."

"I get that." He nods. "It can be overwhelming to a

newcomer. You said this is your first time in Seattle, right?"

"Yes."

There was a time this was supposed to be my new home, but I try not to think about that now.

"It's a fun place," Dirk continues. "I love it. And don't worry—you'll get used to the rain. It's not like it's a torrential downpour or anything. Just light and nearly constant half the year. Parking is a shitshow everywhere you go, though, so we'll have to hoof it the rest of the way." He pulls the car to the curb as another drives away, then flicks his chin toward the street as he shuts the engine off. "If we hurry, we should make it in time to grab a drink before midnight."

The words might sound innocent, but I hear the impatience in his tone, and I put my hand on the door handle. I'm eager to get inside, too, but for different reasons. I want this night to be over so I can go back to my hotel, fill that gorgeous tub in my room, then sleep for a solid ten hours.

"Careful!" he yells as I push it open, and the warning comes just in time for me to yank it closed again as a car doing well over the speed limit goes sailing by us.

I give him a small smile. "Oops. Sorry again."

"Chloe…" He laughs lightly, but there's a tenseness to it that's hard to miss. "People here drive like morons and think the speed limit is about fifteen miles per hour over what is posted. You'll get used to that too, but you have to be careful, okay?"

I don't point out that he was also one of those morons on the drive over here, and this time, I make sure to check my mirror before exiting the car. I meet him on the sidewalk, where he offers me his arm. I pay no attention to the shake to my hand as I take it, linking us together as we quickly make our way to the bar he's so hellbent on going to.

"It's awesome. And they have the best drink specials, which the boss will appreciate since it's on his dime."

That was his pitch to get me to agree as he flashed me the business credit card for the third time tonight, and since I foolishly allowed him to pick me up from my hotel, I felt like I couldn't say no.

"We don't have to stay long," he promises as we hurry along. "But we can if you want."

He tosses me a wink, and I tell myself he's not flirting with me, just being polite.

We show our IDs to the security standing outside, and I wish silently that he'll find a reason to turn us away. It doesn't happen, and Dirk pulls the door open. Loud music spills onto the sidewalk, and for the hundredth time tonight, I wish I had insisted on him dropping me back at the hotel.

"Oh, I should have mentioned," he yells over the music as we step inside, "this is a sports bar, hockey mostly. The Seattle Serpents hang out here often. Maybe we'll get lucky and spot one or two of the players tonight."

It's the last thing he says before we are engulfed by the bass and the crowd, and an overwhelming sense of dread pools low in my belly. When *Seattle Daily* came knocking on my door, I was more than happy to hear them out, and it wasn't just because they pay so damn well. It was because I had a mission in Seattle. I had a history I needed to face.

A person. *The* person.

And I planned to…eventually. Just not tonight. I wanted time to settle in. I wanted a chance to sort out what it is I need to say, even if I have had years to do it.

He's not here, Chloe. He can't be. I'm sure he has other plans, grander plans.

Still, my eyes dart all over the bar, taking in what must be two dozen TVs hanging on the walls, the sports memorabilia taking up the rest of the space, and the people. Definitely the people. Because as much as I tell myself I'm not looking for him, I am.

If Talia were here, she'd give me a knowing look, then remind me for the hundredth time how important it is that I face my fears. I'd likely flip her off and order a double shot of booze, but I'm not much in the mood for drinking right now. Not with the way my stomach is doing somersaults at the idea that I could very well be in the same room as the one person who is capable of undoing me.

"Thirsty?" Dirk says in my ear, and I nearly jump out of my skin at how close he suddenly is. "Shit. Did I scare you?"

He grins down at me, and I return the gesture, though I have no doubt it's wobbly. "Maybe a little."

"My bad." He laughs, obviously not noticing how uncomfortable I am. "It's loud in here, huh?"

I nod. "Very."

"Nothing a stiff drink can't fix."

Another wink, and I force myself to laugh as he pulls me toward the bar. The whole trek, my body is humming, and it has nothing to do with the bass overpowering the small space. It's something else I can't quite place my finger on, but whatever it is, it has me on edge in a way I haven't been in a long time.

Not since…

I shove that thought away just as quickly as it enters my mind and focus on making my way through the throngs of bodies and trying not to step on anyone's toes. We force our way to the bar, and I'm relieved when he finally drops my arm, only to rest his hand on my lower back. I try to move away from his touch as subtly as I can, but he just steps closer.

Dirk huffs when his attempt to flag down the bartender goes unnoticed. "I swear it's never like this," he explains. "Must be the holiday."

A busy bar on New Year's Eve. Who would have thought?

But I don't say that out loud. Instead, I let my eyes

roam again, holding my breath for…well, I'm not even sure what it is I'm waiting for. All I know is I can't seem to shake the feeling that someone is watching me.

Of course someone is watching you. It's a packed bar. People are drunk and have no boundaries. It's expected, Chloe. Just focus on what's happening in front of you.

Still, the thought doesn't comfort me, and I force myself to let it go as the bartender makes their way over to us.

"Finally," Dirk snaps. "I'll have a whiskey on the rocks, whatever is on special tonight, and the lady here will take a white wine."

"Actually, I'll have a Diet Coke, please."

"Really?" Dirk's brows pull together. "I thought you wanted to get a drink."

No, you *wanted to get a drink,* I want to remind him.

"I'm, uh, still full from dinner. Not sure a drink would be a good idea right now."

"I'm sure you are. You finished off that pasta in record time." He squeezes my hip, and that very same pasta threatens to crawl back up my throat. I've never felt comfortable about my body, but I've been working hard to overcome that in the last few years. I am not about to let this prick undo all the work I've done.

I'm about two seconds away from telling him to fuck all the way off, the job be damned, when I hear a voice I haven't heard in months.

"Clover."

The entire room comes to a halt, or at least that's what it feels like, and my knees buckle beneath me. Dirk's hand is still on me, and he catches me. I wish it were someone else.

"Get your fucking hands off her," that same haunting voice commands. His words are snarled. Angry. Full of rage I haven't heard from him before.

I turn and look into the same eyes I once swore I loathed, then loved more than anything in the world. Even though they're shrouded in darkness, just like they did a decade ago, they remind me of looking into a bottle of whiskey, the good stuff that sits on the top shelf. My heart rate kicks up ten notches, my ears overpowered by the sudden pumping.

Thu-thump. Thu-thump. Thu-thump.

"Who the fuck do you think you are, buddy?" Dirk barks back at him, his hold tightening on me, and I try to squirm free, but I can't move. Hell, I can barely even *breathe.*

Thu-thump. Thu-thump. Thu-thump.

"Definitely not your *buddy.* Now, get your goddamn hands off her before I take them off myself." He steps closer, right under one of the dim lights. "And I really don't think you want that, now do ya, *buddy?*"

Dirk drops his hands as his eyes widen, his mouth opening as he registers just who it is he's talking to. "Holy shit. You… You're…"

Thu-thump. Thu-thump. Thu-thump.

"Callum."

His eyes snap to me, and it's like being hit by a freight train. Everything—each soft touch and sweet kiss and whispered word—comes flooding back to me all at once. The edges of my vision blur, and I rest my hand on the sticky bar top, trying to keep myself upright.

He looks good. *Too* good. He's put an easy fifteen pounds of muscle on his tall frame, and his light brown hair, which always felt like the world's softest blanket when I ran my hands over it, lies neatly on top of his head. His long-sleeved shirt is pushed up to show off his forearms, and though they've always been decorated in ink for as long as I can remember, it's obvious they're sporting new art. It extends down to the backs of his hands, over his fingers, new additions that are far more attractive than I could have imagined. And while the yellow-ish bruise on his cheek should draw more concern, all it does is make me want to reach over and trace my fingers across it, then maybe kiss it better.

He's nothing and everything like I remember, and that thought makes it hard to breathe. Or maybe it's just being near him again. Either way, I'm struggling to catch my breath, and I'm grateful when my host for the evening breaks the lingering tension.

"Wait a second," Dirk says. "You know him?"

I nod, unable to take my eyes off the tattooed man before me. The man I've known for over a decade. The one who used to mean everything to me.

The one looking at me with such contempt that I can barely stomach it.

Fuck, here comes the pasta again, I think, choking down the urge to vomit.

Dirk laughs. "Well, shit. How come you didn't tell me you know *the* Callum Keller? I told you the Seattle Serpents like to hang out here."

"I, uh, I didn't think he'd be here."

Callum works his jaw back and forth, his nostrils flaring at my words, and I know it's thanks to what they sound like: *I was hoping he wouldn't be here. I was hoping I could sneak into the city and back out again without having to see him.* The worst part is I can't even deny it. That is what I wanted. I needed this to happen on my own terms, not on New Year's Eve of all nights.

"That's certainly something you're allowed to bring up whenever. How do you guys know each other exactly?"

I swallow once, then again, and I don't miss how Callum's eyes drink me in. I don't miss how they roam over every inch of my face, the way they linger on my lips, then the necklace sitting at the base of my throat.

And I really don't miss how his jaw hardens and his lips set into a firm line, waiting for my answer.

"He's my husband."

Husband. The word feels so foreign on my tongue. I used to dream about the day I would get to call Callum that, but now? It feels…off.

I don't have to be looking at Dirk to know shock is covering his face. It makes sense. I haven't mentioned anything about a partner, let alone a husband, and I certainly didn't mention that he plays professional hockey.

I dare a peek over at my potential future co-worker, and he takes a step backward at this news. "You, uh, you didn't say you were married."

Callum scoffs, and I swing my gaze back to him just in time to see him dragging his eyes away from the very empty spot on my left hand, right where his ring should be sitting but isn't.

"I didn't leave the information out on purpose." I'm not sure whether I'm telling my husband or saying this to Dirk. "I just…"

But I don't have a good explanation for not telling him. It's not like I was trying to hide it intentionally. I just didn't know *how* to explain it.

How am I supposed to tell people I walked away from the love of my life three years ago and have hardly spoken to him since? Especially when there wasn't some big scandal to go along with it? He didn't cheat, and I didn't either. We just… Well, I'm not exactly sure what we did, but I do know what was once a solid foundation crumbled so quickly that now I don't have any idea how to put it back together.

"Well, I—" Dirk starts, but his words are cut off as

the music suddenly dies and a loud screech fills the packed bar.

"Sorry about that," someone says into a megaphone, and I turn to find someone standing atop the bar holding one. "One minute to midnight, folks!" Everyone cheers. "Grab your guys and grab your gals and get those lips ready because remember: the person you kiss at midnight is the one you'll spend the year with!"

Another roar of cheers courses through the bar, but I pay it no mind. I'm far too busy staring at my estranged husband, who looks like he's never been in more pain in his life. My fingers itch to reach out and smooth the wrinkle that seems to be etched between his furrowed brows, but I remember I don't have the privilege anymore, and worse, it's my own fault.

We stand there for what feels like years, but really, it's less than a minute before everyone begins to count.

"Ten!"

I jump at the surge of noise, taking my eyes off the man I haven't seen up close in far too long for just a second, but it's long enough because when I turn back around, he's already leaving.

"Callum!" I call after him, but the word is swallowed by the crowd continuing their countdown.

"Nine!"

"Callum, wait. I—"

But he doesn't wait, and he disappears before I'm even able to register it.

"Eight!" the crowd continues to chant, and it's enough to get me to move.

"What the… Chloe!" Dirk's hand circles my wrist, halting my movements. "Where are you going?"

I try to pull away, but he tightens his grip, his eyes darkening, and it causes my stomach to flip in the worst kind of way. "Let me go."

"But—"

"I'm sorry. Really. I'll call the paper tomorrow."

His jaw hardens, and before he speaks his next words, I know this is going to affect things with *Seattle Daily*. "This isn't how you conduct business, *Ms. Harris*."

He says my maiden name disdainfully, and I regret ever using it to begin with.

"It's *Mrs.* Keller," I hiss before yanking my hand away, turning on my heel, and shoving my way through.

I try to follow Callum, but every step I take, I swear I get swallowed by more and more bodies.

"Callum!" I call out again, even though it seems pointless.

"Four!"

No, no, no, I chant to myself, using more force as I push forward, desperate to get to him.

"Three!"

"Callum!"

"Two!"

I can see the door swinging shut just a few feet away.

"One!" the crowd hollers just as I reach it, tossing it open so hard it bounces off the wall.

"Hey! What the fuck?" the security guard shouts, but I ignore him as I look left, then right, *praying* he's still there.

Maybe this night isn't complete shit, or maybe it's because it is *technically* New Year's Day—by some miracle, there he is.

"Callum!" I bellow again, and he pauses momentarily, but it's enough to let me know he's willing to hear me out if I can catch him.

So I run. I hike up my long dress, and I push my legs harder than I ever have before. I can't let this be our reunion. I have to talk to him. I have to tell him I wasn't trying *not* to see him, just that I wasn't ready to yet.

"Callum, please," I beg as I push myself harder, my heels clacking against the sidewalk as I try to close the distance between us that feels like it's just getting bigger and bigger. "I just…" I draw in a deep breath. "Let me explain, okay? I need to talk to you. I need—"

"What?!" He whirls around so quickly I barely have time to skid to a stop.

In fact, I *don't*. I stumble into him, his arms going around me, and though I'm sure it's purely instinct, a part of me says it's because he *wants* to touch me.

I hate the way my body reacts, like it's falling into a pile of pillows as I sink into him. And I hate even more how he still smells just as he did all those years ago—like bodywash and expensive cologne and every single thing I've ever wanted.

But it's gone as fast as it comes, and I'm standing on my own, Callum's hands no longer on me. Instead he's staring down at me with dark eyes.

"What do *you* need, Chloe?"

Chloe. Not Clover. Not babe. Not sweetheart. Not any of the other nicknames he's used over the years.

Just Chloe.

I don't want to be just Chloe to him.

"I…"

But nothing else comes out. All the words I know I should say get stuck in my throat. It's like every thought I've had over the last three years seems to dissipate right before my eyes, and I say nothing. I stare up at him blankly, looking for anything that tells me we'll be okay after this. Tells me he'll talk to me again. Tells me we'll figure this thing out.

But there's nothing. No hint of the man I fell in love with during my freshman year of college, or the one I married in a rushed ceremony because I couldn't wait another day to be his wife.

He's just Callum Keller, the Seattle Serpents' most relentless and brutal power forward. He laughs, and the sound is scathing, as if he's just dumped a steaming hot cup of coffee right on my heart.

"Of course you don't have the words. You don't have an explanation. You didn't then, and you don't now. Yet you still come into my city with some fuckwad and you—"

"No," I say, shaking my head. "No, it's not—"

"Stop!" he yells, so damn loudly the word bounces off the buildings, and a few passersby turn their heads our way.

Tears spring to my eyes, and I can't tell if they're from the fact that he's never talked to me this way before, if I'm embarrassed, or if I'm just finally breaking down.

"Just stop," he continues, more quietly, but his words are just as harsh. "I don't want to hear it, okay? I don't want your excuses. Not tonight. *Especially* not fucking tonight."

I'm sure he's thinking of the last time we were together on New Year's Eve. I'm sure it's a night both of us wish we could forget for good.

"Callum, I—"

He shakes his head and shoves his hands into his pockets, putting distance between us that I want to close so damn desperately, but I don't know how. "I can't do this anymore. I just can't, okay? Go back inside, Chloe, and leave me alone."

Then he turns, doing the same thing I did to him three years ago tonight.

He walks away.

Chapter 3

An unrelenting pounding wakes me up, and it's Percy screaming at the top of his lungs that tells me it's not all in my head. It's at my door.

With a groan, I toss my sheet off my body and set my feet on the floor. About a hundred elephants dance around my skull, or at least that's what it feels like as I scrub a hand over my face. Another round of knocking reverberates through my apartment, but I don't move yet. I'm afraid if I do, I might puke. It has nothing to do with drinking either. I came home and crawled right into this bed to rot. I didn't touch another drop of booze, even though I really wanted to.

No, it's just that reality is that tough of a pill to swallow, and the reality is my wife is here in Seattle, and I had no fucking idea she was even stateside. How the hell did Chloe end up in Seattle? Why is she here? And, probably most importantly, who the fuck was that asshole she was with?

I grind my molars as images of his hand wrapped around her waist flit through my mind. I remember that waist. I got a taste of it again last night when she fell against me. She was soft, and my palm fit around her perfectly. My fingers curled into her plush curves as they've done so many times before. It felt like coming home after a long road trip. Better even.

It was the first time in years I'd touched my wife, and it wasn't nearly enough.

"Who the fuck do you think you are, buddy?"

That prick's words echo through my mind again, and I get angry all over again. Why was he holding her? Why was she laughing at whatever the douche nozzle was saying? And why didn't she tell me she was here? Things between us are strained to say the least, but not giving me so much as a phone call? Is that where we're at in our marriage?

Yes.

I hate how much that word rings true in my mind.

Another attempt to get me to open the door draws my attention, and I'm so eager to get away from the thoughts tumbling around my mind that I push to my feet. I tug on a pair of joggers, the same ones I stripped out of yesterday before heading to Top Shelf, and whatever shirt I find lying on the pile of laundry I still need to fold. Then I shuffle out of my bedroom into the living room.

"Keller?" The knock is even louder than before. "It's Locke. You in there, man?"

I want to ignore him, or better yet, tell him to fuck off and go away, but given what occurred last night, I doubt he will.

"Come on," he says. "I can hear you moving around in there."

With a sigh, I wrench open the door and find that the fucker lied. It's not just Locke. It's all of *them*.

"Serpents Singles to the rescue!" Lawson announces, pushing his way through the other guys and holding a to-go cup my way. "We brought coffee. It's black just like your soul, but only because we didn't know how you take it."

"And donuts, too," Hayes chimes in, holding up a box from B's Bakes, his girlfriend's mother's bakery.

Hutch looks between the two, then smacks them both on the back of the head. "Dumbasses."

"Hey!" Lawson protests, but Hayes accepts his punishment.

Though I'm annoyed by each of them, I send my glare Locke's way. He should have known better. He's only been in my apartment once before, when I had a delayed flight after visiting my family in Toronto and needed someone to check on Percy. "What are you doing here? *All* of you?"

"Uh, we're getting answers. You dropped a bomb on us last night, then bolted. You didn't even stay for your midnight kiss. I'll give it to you later." Lawson presses his finger to the tip of my nose, and I blame my lack of sleep for not moving in time. "Boop."

He grins, and if he weren't holding caffeine, which I'm in desperate need of, I'd sock him right in the gut. Instead, I take the drink, then slam the door closed.

Or at least that's the plan, but a giant foot stops that from happening.

"Not a chance."

This time, it's Fox who speaks, and it stuns me so much I don't even have time to react to Lawson barging into my apartment. He lets out a low whistle as the rest of the guys pile in behind him.

"Holy fuck, this is swanky!" he says as he takes in the expansive space.

"It's basically identical to Locke's. Stop acting surprised."

"I've never been in Locke's apartment," he tosses back, his nose now pressed up against the photos lining the bookshelf I have up against the wall. He points at a picture. "Is this her?"

I don't answer. I'm too busy throwing daggers Locke's way.

"You brought him *here* before letting him into your apartment?"

He at least has the decency to look apologetic about it as he says, "We need to talk about last night."

"What about last night?" I pretend not to know what he's talking about as I make my way to the kitchen to fix my coffee the way I like it.

My eyes drift over all the junk I have on the front of the fridge, including the invitation to Hutch and Auden's wedding next month. They land on a business card that's been up there for three years now.

It was late at night at Top Shelf after I'd just moved to Seattle by myself, and I was drinking far more than I should have been. Some schmoozy lawyer guy got me talking, and by the end of the night, I was walking home alone, his card advertising that he's the best divorce attorney in the city gripped tight in my hand. I should have thrown it away, but I tacked it to the fridge. At the time, I wasn't sure Chloe would ever come back to me. And truthfully, after last night, I'm still not.

I snatch the card down, tossing it into the junk drawer to deal with later, and pull open the fridge.

"Holy shit." Lawson's voice makes me jump, especially since it's so close. I didn't even notice he came into the kitchen, and I definitely didn't notice him standing right behind me. "You're a creamer guy? And a lot of it too, I see." He tsks. "I don't think our nutritionist would approve of that."

I replace the carton of butter pecan goodness, then

turn around and shove him—*hard*—before taking a drink.

"Hey, rude. I brought you coffee." He pouts, rubbing at his chest as if he doesn't take bigger hits on the ice.

"Fuck off, Lawsy."

"Nah." He grins, then practically skips through the open-concept apartment to the living room, where he plops down on the sofa. He grabs the TV remote before kicking his feet up on the coffee table and turning the big flat screen on.

Hayes rolls his eyes and pushes off the wall he's been leaning against, snatches the remote from his hands, and shoves his feet off the table. He mutters something that sounds a hell of a lot like, "Quit being a fucking idiot, you idiot," but I can't be certain.

I'm distracted by three sets of eyes watching me closely. I fucking hate it. It makes my hands feel all tingly, and not in a good way.

"What?" I finally snap at Locke, Hutch, and Fox.

They all exchange glances, probably silently wondering who is going to be the one to ask the question they're all dying to know the answer to. After several quiet moments, it's Hutch who steps forward, which I guess makes sense with him being the captain and all.

Thumbs hooked into the belt loops of his jeans, he asks, "Why the hell didn't you tell us you're married?"

I shrug. "Didn't seem important."

I lift my coffee cup to my lips, taking a sip and

ignoring the heated stares I'm receiving from each one of my teammates. Predictably, Lawson is the first one to say something.

"Not important?!" He explodes off my couch, his arms rising in the air. "How the hell is you being *married* not important, Keller?"

I shrug again. "It's just not."

"Bullshit."

Fox says the single word so sharply it almost scares me. *Almost.*

I narrow my eyes at the usually overly nice goalie. "Excuse me?"

He shrugs, unbothered by my deathly stare. "You heard me. That's bullshit, and you know it. We know it too."

"Yeah," Lawson speaks up, always needing to butt in.

"So maybe try that again," Fox continues. "And maybe don't fucking lie to people who consider you a brother."

"I already have a brother. I don't need more."

"You have a brother?!" This is from Lawson again.

I ignore him, then take another drink, needing a moment before I try to explain to them something I can't even explain to myself. To their credit—even Lawson's—they wait. They give me time, letting me gather my thoughts the best I can.

I don't know how long it has been before I finally

speak, but I can tell it's long enough, because Lawson is practically bouncing on his heels.

"I got married when I was twenty-one."

"Shut the fuck up."

"Quiet!" Hayes barks, and Lawson mimes zipping his lips, as if that's ever kept him silent before.

I continue. "After being drafted by New York, I committed to playing in college in Denver, which is where I met…"

Her name dies on the tip of my tongue. Just thinking of her and how happy we were back then makes my chest ache. I reach for the chain around my neck, fingering it through my shirt. What happened to us? What happened to those kids who were so fucking in love we got married when we were barely even old enough to legally drink at our reception? Where did that go, and when did I miss their exit?

I think about my in-laws, whom I haven't seen since my wife told me she wouldn't be coming back from London, and I wonder if they know Chloe is here in Seattle. They always had a hold over her that I couldn't explain, and I'd bet anything they have big feelings about it.

"Keller?"

I snap my attention to Hutch, who is staring at me with a soft, worried gaze. He's not the only one. All the guys are looking at me in the same way—with pity.

I don't fucking want it.

"Anyway, we got together in the second semester of freshman year, and when I finally signed a contract with New York just before my senior year, we got married. We've been together ever since." I swallow the sudden lump in my throat. "Well, I guess not technically. We, uh, we separated when she went to London."

"When?" Locke asks.

"Huh?"

"When did you separate?"

I'm not entirely sure how to answer his question. It wasn't like it was one moment. It was a lot of little ones that led to it, and Chloe was already away when it became "official."

"I guess it was shortly after I moved to Seattle to join the Serpents. Things were already rocky before then, but we didn't make it official until…"

She'd already been gone for almost three months at that point, living abroad doing her internship. It happened over a phone call, one of the few we had exchanged. We always said it was because of the time zone difference, but it was an excuse to not face things head-on.

I shake away the memory, taking another long pull from my coffee before continuing. "Anyway, we've had little contact since then."

"Why aren't you divorced?"

"Dude," Hayes hisses at Lawson with a glower. "Do you have no filter at all?"

"What?" He lifts his shoulders. "I'm just asking what everyone else is wondering."

"It's okay, Hayes," I say, surprising everyone, including myself, by defending Lawson. "It's a valid question, but I don't have an answer."

Or at least not one I'm willing to share. I know why *I* haven't started the process for a divorce, but I don't know why Chloe hasn't, especially since she's the one who has insisted on staying away.

Fox clears his throat. "So, uh, what is she doing here in Seattle, then?"

"And who was that guy at Top Shelf last night?"

"Lawson!"

There's a loud smack, then an equally loud *oof* as Hayes lays into him. This time, I don't defend him.

"Your guess is as good as mine," I say to Fox, finishing off my coffee. I set the empty cup aside to worry about later.

"You didn't talk last night?" Hutch asks.

I shake my head, crossing my arms over my chest. "Wasn't really in the mood."

That's the truth. I *had* to walk away. I was angrier than I've ever been, and I didn't trust myself not to hurl hurtful words at her that I wasn't so sure I would be able to take back.

How can she show up here without any preamble? How can she expect me to be okay when she walked in the door on another man's arm, then tried to placate me with some bullshit reasoning? I didn't want to hear it then, and I don't want to hear it now.

I drop my arms, flexing my hands, which are suddenly feeling tight. I need to hit something. Or better yet, someone.

"What time did Coach Smith say practice is this morning?" I need to relieve the tension building in my shoulders, and smashing people against the boards sounds like the perfect solution.

"You didn't get the text?" Locke asks.

"My phone is off," I explain, having powered it down the second I tipped the Uber driver who dropped me at my apartment. Not that it mattered. It's not like my wife bothered to try to call or text me after I left her standing there.

The veteran player—and the oldest guy on the team—exchanges a glance with the captain at my answer. If I were up for more conversation, I'd ask what the hell that's about, but right now I just want to skate and work out my frustration on the ice. It's always been my favorite outlet, so why not use it now, too?

"We got the day off. Guess the old man stayed up too late last night or something," Lawson says, opening a cabinet. He pulls out a box of cat treats and shakes it my way as if I don't know what's inside my own apartment. "Uh, no judgment, Kells, but I'm like ninety-nine percent sure you're not supposed to just casually snack on cat treats. Look, it even says *Not for humans*."

I grab the box out of his hands, pop it open, grab a few, and set it back down. "They aren't for me, dumbass. They're for my cat."

"You have a fucking *cat?*"

Just then, Percy comes running out from his favorite hiding spot, otherwise known as the spare bedroom, and gives each of the guys standing around my apartment a dark look. I'm sure he's confused considering I've only had a handful of people at my place over the years and it's mostly been the pet sitter.

"Yes," I answer Lawson. The mostly white cat trots up to me and launches himself into my arms like we've practiced it a hundred times, and we might as well have. "Now stop yelling before you scare him."

I cradle Percy as I feed him his favorite treat. He knows exactly what the box sounds like, so it's no surprise he decided to make an appearance when I opened it.

"Where the hell did you get a cat? *When* did you get one? Holy shit! He only has three legs! And how did we not know you're married?"

The guy is crashing out, and while some of it is valid, I don't have the patience for it, so I ignore Lawson's questions and look at my captain. "Since there's no practice today, can we conclude this little intervention you've staged? I could use a few more hours of sleep. It was a long night."

Locke rolls his eyes, and Fox sighs.

"Keller, man—" Hayes starts, but I shake my head, cutting off his words.

"No. Don't *Keller* me, okay? I want to be alone." Fox opens his mouth to speak, but I keep going. "I don't give a shit if you guys think that's a good idea or not. It's what I want. So—and I say this with all the respect in the world, except for you, Lawson—get the fuck out of my apartment and lock the door behind you."

Then I push between them—Percy still curled in my arms—and I walk into my bedroom, slamming the door shut behind me. I rest against the door, listening as they poorly whisper at one another.

"What the actual fuck?" Hayes asks.

"Are we seriously just going to let him walk away? He's clearly not okay," Fox says, concern lacing every word. I'm sure this is killing him. He's a fixer, always stepping up to help when people need it.

He can't fix this though.

"It's what he wants. We need to respect that." Hutch has always had a good head on his shoulders, but he's become an even better leader since the birth of his daughter.

"The captain is right. We need to respect it."

"It was your idea to come here, Locke. And I have more questions," Lawson argues, and I'd bet my left nut they're having to push him out of the apartment.

Ten heavy feet stomp through the living room to the

door, and just before it clicks shut, I hear Lawson say, "I can't believe he has a fucking cat. Did you guys know he has a cat?"

Then silence. I'm relieved by it and hate it all at the same time.

Meow.

I look down at Percy, who is licking his lips and staring up at me, hoping for more snacks.

"I'm all out, little man. Sorry."

Meow.

He wiggles in my arms, trying to squirm free, and I let him go. He trots across the room to my bed, curls up on my pillow—his second favorite spot in the house— and closes his eyes like he's exhausted from his excursion.

I have to agree. I'm exhausted too. I spent most of the night tossing and turning or lying awake replaying every second of last night, from the way that navy dress clung to Chloe's curves to the way her face fell when I yelled at her on the sidewalk.

So, I do what any sensible person would do when their estranged wife comes barreling back into their life— I crawl into bed and close my eyes, pretending it was all just a bad dream.

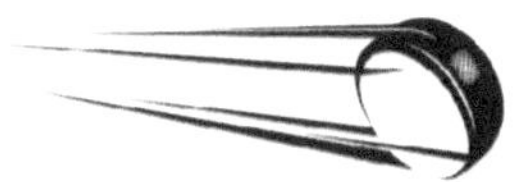

For the second time today, I'm awakened by a loud knock on my door.

"Ugh!" I grit my teeth together, then grab my pillow —now cold and empty—and put it over my head to try to drown out the noise.

It doesn't work.

"Go away!" I yell at my teammates, then peek at the clock on my bedside table.

It's almost eleven, which means I've been sleeping for just over two hours. Based on how heavy and tired my eyes are, it's not enough, and I guess my words aren't enough either because they knock again.

"That's it," I grumble as I jump out of bed. It's quick enough to scare Percy, who goes running as fast as his three legs can carry him, darting off to I don't even know where.

I wrench open my bedroom door and stomp through the living room to the door just as he raps his knuckles against it again.

"Back off, you fuckers. Don't you get that I don't want to talk? Fuck!" I growl as I fling open the door.

Only it's not Locke. Or Hutch, Hayes, Fox, or Lawson.

No.

It's simultaneously the last person and the only person I want to see right now.

"Clover."

The side of her mouth rises ever so slightly. "Callum."

And just like that, I'm transported back to the first time my name dropped from her lips.

Chapter 4

CHLOE

Twelve years ago

"Then I said to him, *Dan, you cannot drink two Red Bulls* and *have a quad espresso and expect* not *to have heart flutters. It's just creative writing. It's not* that *serious.*" Talia huffs. "Like, come on. We're freshmen. We're supposed to be having fun, not staying up and slamming caffeine all night for a paper that's not even worth five percent of our final grade. He needs to chill."

I want to remind my best friend that our parents aren't paying an arm and a leg for us to party, but I fear that would be a fruitless endeavor, so I smile and nod as we make our way to the very course she's talking about. We may only be a few weeks into school, but it's already my favorite class, though that's really no surprise. Writing has always been my outlet. It doesn't matter what I'm doing—journaling about my day, making up a short story, or even writing a research paper for school—it's like my brain comes alive when I put pen to paper, and all my insecurities and worries fall away. If I had my way, it's what I would be focusing on for my studies. But, since my parents are paying for my education, they felt they had a say, so biology major it is, just like them.

"I mean, we're in freakin' *college*, Chlo. We got out of our tiny Tennessee town. That calls for some fun."

It's funny to me how much a person can change once they leave their hometown. Just a few short months ago, Talia was the biggest bookworm I knew. Her nose was always stuck in a textbook, and I used to have to beg her to leave her house on Friday nights, even just to head to the theater to catch the latest movie. Now, I can't seem to keep her in our room for more than five minutes before she's running off to whatever new activity or boy has sparked her interest.

If I'm being honest, I'm jealous. I wish I had the luxury of having more fun, but school has never come as easily to me as it has to her. Where she's always barely had to study for a test, I was that kid who was up cramming all night and the morning before. The only subject I never had to try so hard in was science, and I'm pretty sure that was because my parents shoved it down my throat since I could barely walk.

Sometimes I wonder if that's why I'm planning to major in biology instead of pushing back against my parents' wishes and fighting to get a creative arts degree —it's easier to give in.

"Does that mean things between you and Stan are fizzling out?"

"His name is Dan, and eh. He's so-so. But"—she sighs dreamily, then fans herself—"the things that man can do with his hands more than make up for it."

"Talia!" I chide, looking around to make sure we're not being listened to, but nobody pays us any attention.

She giggles. "What? I'm just saying, Chlo. You're missing out with your whole *no boys* rule you've imposed."

I know she's teasing, but she doesn't understand that if I want to succeed—and I really do, even if I'm not excited about my degree—I need to cut out all distractions. That means no boys, no parties, and no fun until I can make my parents proud so they stop giving me those looks, the ones that say *We want more for you, Chloe.* Since they're both big names in their fields, I'm sure they do, and I want to give them that.

"I'm just trying to focus on my studies, that's all," I counter.

She rolls her baby-blue eyes, blowing out a puff of air and pushing her tousled bangs off her forehead. She's done nothing but mess with them since she got them this past summer—another big change for her—and I want to say the words *I knew you'd hate them* so dang badly, but I keep my thoughts to myself.

"Besides," I say, "we don't all have a job with Daddy Warbucks to go home to."

I bump my shoulder against hers with a grin, which she returns, but I see how shaky it is. There's a legacy to uphold for the Stevenson family, and when Talia is finished with school, she's expected to dive right into working for her father.

We waltz into class with ten minutes to spare and take our usual spots in the back.

"Oh shit. It's him, it's him, it's him," my best friend hisses, sitting up straighter in her chair and tossing her long, honey hair behind her shoulder. She elbows me. "Sit up, Chlo!"

I know exactly who Talia is freaking out about before I even look, and though I tell myself I have no interest in him, I can't deny the way my heart rate picks up. I ignore it and her as I continue pulling my laptop, notebook, and pens from my bag, then a pair of black boots comes into my line of sight.

"Well, well, well," a deep voice says from the right of me. "If it isn't my favorite seatmate." A backpack drops to the floor, and the scent of cedar bodywash and just a bit too much cologne tickles my nose. "How are you, Clover?"

I huff, annoyed by the name he gave me during the second week of classes. I can only assume it was because I was wearing the clover-shaped necklace my dad got me.

"An actual lucky charm," he said when I opened it for my birthday, which falls on St. Patrick's Day.

Or maybe this guy gave me the nickname just because he likes annoying me. Who knows?

My tormentor laughs, and it unnerves something inside me that I don't quite understand. Or maybe it's that I don't *want* to try to understand it.

I don't have time to analyze it before he says, "That excited to see me, huh, Clover?"

I clench my teeth, meeting the amber stare I've come to loathe head-on. "For the hundredth time, it's *Chloe*. Chlo-e. It's not that hard of a name to remember."

He lets out another deep, hearty laugh. "Sure it is, *Clover*."

"I think I know my own name, *Callum*."

Those eyes—the same ones I've spent far too much time daydreaming about instead of taking notes—narrow at the use of his first name. Nobody calls him that, not even the professors. That's the kind of special treatment you get when you're a talented hockey player like him. I'm pretty sure everyone—even the custodial crew—knows who he is. Callum Keller is a god around campus, and everyone treats him like one.

Well, *almost* everyone. Not me. I am completely immune to his charms.

As if on cue, my stomach does a flip as he runs a hand through his camel-colored hair that sometimes looks blond when the light hits it just right.

Okay, I'm mostly *immune to them.*

I swallow the lump that's formed in my throat as he slides into the chair next to me and spreads his legs wide until his thigh is pressed against mine. I act like it doesn't make my palms sweat as I tighten my grip on the pencil in my hand and roll my eyes skyward.

"Aw, now come on. What was that for?"

"Because I find you annoying."

He mock gasps, then points at himself. "Moi? Are you sure?"

"Absolutely positive." I move the highlighter that got knocked askew back to where it belongs. "I know that's a shock since everyone else seems to fall at your feet, but you don't have me fooled."

"Fooled? Who says I'm trying to fool anyone?" He grins, and dammit, it's ridiculously hot. "I'm just being myself."

"Right," I mutter.

Talia pokes her head around me. "Hi, Keller."

His grin falls. "Tallulah."

"It's Talia, but close enough," she murmurs, flicking her hair over her shoulder. "How's the hockey season going?"

I fight the urge to roll my eyes yet again. She knows exactly how his season is going considering we've gone to all the games this year. They're currently sitting in second place, and word on the street is they'll be one of the teams in the finals.

A lot of that is thanks to Callum. Though he's not scoring every night, he's still making plays, and it isn't going unnoticed by anyone, including me, a casual hockey fan at best.

"Good," he answers in a tone that says he's not really interested in carrying on this conversation.

It doesn't deter my best friend. She sits up straighter, leaning across my seat even more. "Good? More like great. Chloe and I have been going to all your games, and you guys are killing it."

This perks him right back up, and he swings a cocky grin my way.

"So you go to all my games, huh, Clover?"

I groan inwardly, shooting a dirty look Talia's way. She smiles at me unapologetically, and I get the sense she might realize I don't hate Callum as much as I pretend to. Damn her for being so perceptive.

I turn back to the hockey player, who is showing off the fact that he still has all his teeth.

"Not on purpose."

He laughs. "Right. Sure. I bet you just *happened* to stumble into the arena, right?"

"What can I say? There was a crowd, and I'm a follower."

"Oh," he says, his voice dropping an octave, which seems impossible since it's already so low. "I highly doubt that's true."

"She's on the school paper," Talia says with a grin

that could rival a proud parent. "She's going to be a writer one day."

"I never said that." I look at Callum. "I never said that."

He looks like he's fighting off a laugh. "Duly noted, Clover."

The professor walks into the room, and Callum holds his finger over his lips and turns toward the front of the room, pretending to be engaged. He's not, and I'm not either. All I can think about is how hot his voice just was, and how good his hair looks today, and his lips that are *just* pouty enough.

I wish I hated him more than I pretend to.

It's Talia who finally gets me to stop staring at him, elbowing me hard and widening her eyes while nodding toward the front where the professor is already prattling on about…well, I'm not exactly sure. I was too distracted.

Focus on class, Chloe. Not some boy who is so far out of your league it's not even funny. Besides, think about how your parents would feel if they knew you were daydreaming instead of studying.

After my pep talk, I try my hardest to tune in to class, but it's nearly impossible with Callum's leg still pressed up against mine and his cologne tickling my nose.

I don't know how long it takes before I feel him move. I hold my breath.

"You know," he whispers after a while, and I jump because he's close. *Too* close. So much so that I can *feel* his warm breath tickling my ear. I want to lean into it just as much as I don't. "I've been thinking a lot lately, Clover."

"Really? That's a big step for you, Callum."

He ignores me, just like I ignore how good he smells.

"When we get married, we're going to have the same initials. Clover Keller, Callum Keller. Has a nice little ring to it, huh?"

I blink once, then twice. *Did he just say…*

I snort out a laugh, not caring if it's loud and obnoxious or that several students turn our way. I'd do anything at this point to rid myself of the flutters in my chest at the idea of being someone so important to him.

It's a fantasy, though. That's never going to happen. Someone like him could never want someone like me. He turns heads wherever he goes and is always surrounded by people. I prefer hanging out in my dorm room, my notebook and pen in hand. We're two different people. We'd never work together.

"Once again, my name isn't Clover. And that is *so* not happening."

"Are you sure about that?" He uses the tip of his pencil to poke my cheek. "You're blushing at the thought."

"Stop it." I smack his pencil away. "I am one hundred percent positive. Considering I can barely stand to be around you, I'd say the idea of us getting married is not just pure comedic gold, but it'll never, *ever* happen."

"Really? You're telling me no part of you has ever

thought about it?" He inches closer. "Come on. I know you have a thing for me."

Oh shit. How does he know that? Did Talia say something? Did someone catch me staring at him? Did he catch me staring? And why is he being extra obnoxious today? Did he make some sort of bet to flirt with me, and I'm the butt of the joke?

I swallow thickly, then force myself to say, "Dream on, loverboy."

His grin widens, those amber eyes of his sparkling as he laces his fingers behind his head and leans back in his chair.

"Whatever you say, Clover." His eyes fall shut, ready for his daily nap. "Whatever you say."

The semester passes far more quickly than I'd like, and winter break seems to go by in a flash, sending us right back to classes and focusing on the final semester of our freshman year.

"Oh my gosh. I am *so* over this weather," Talia complains as we walk into the mess hall. She pulls her thick beanie off her head, shaking out her long blonde hair, which is dusted in snow at the ends.

"But we're in freakin' *college*," I echo her words from earlier in the school year. "Snow isn't that surprising this time of year in Denver."

"Yes, but I'm from Tennessee. I'm not built for this much of it," she grumbles. "I guess it's a good thing I look cute even when I dress like a lumberjack."

I snort out a laugh, then peel off my own hat. Unlike Talia, I do *not* look good dressed in so many layers. All it does is make my already big body look bigger, and I hate it. It also doesn't help that I'm on my period and bloated as hell.

I take my coat off next, hooking it around my arm, then smooth down my hair the best I can, even though I'm sure I still look ragged. I overslept this morning, and my already minimal morning routine got even shorter as I threw on whatever I could find, ran a brush through my hair, and booked it to my eight AM class. I barely walked through the door on time.

I try not to think about how my parents would be shaking their heads if they could see me now. I bet they were never late to class, something they so helpfully mentioned over the break when they found out I was struggling with my grades.

"College isn't like high school, Chloe. You have to focus more. Have you considered quitting the paper? It's taking up too much of your time." That's what my mother said when I rattled off my grades, even though I had worked my ass off to get where I was. *Of course* she blamed the paper, even if it was the only thing about my studies that made me happy.

But she's right. College *is* harder, and I *do* need to focus more, which I'll admit has been infinitely easier this semester now that I no longer share a class with the most irritating guy on campus.

"Oh my gosh!" Talia gasps, pulling me to a stop in the middle of the room. "He's here."

"What? Who?" I follow her gaze across the lunchroom, where I soon find out exactly who she's referring to.

Well, speak of the devil…

Callum Keller sits in all his glory at a table surrounded by his teammates. Most of them are tossing what look like chips into each other's mouths, and it's clear they don't have a care in the world. And why should they? Their college experience is vastly different from mine, with them receiving preferential treatment just because most of them are hockey players on the fast track to the NHL.

But not Callum. He sits in the middle of it all, the corners of his lips tipping up every so often, but he doesn't engage any more than that.

"Ugh, seriously? Can I not escape him?" I ask quietly.

Even though we no longer share a class, it doesn't mean I see him any less. Just yesterday, I went to the library to get a break from Talia's incessant need to blast country music every chance she gets, and guess who was there? Yep, him. And last week, I stopped by the admin building to see about a meeting with a professor, and

Callum was there too, trying to talk his way out of a ticket.

Now here he is sitting in the lunchroom, and if I weren't so hungry and craving something chocolatey, I'd turn around and march right back out just to avoid him. Thing is, even though I can't stand Callum Keller, I also can't seem to get enough of him.

Though it's cold and the ground is covered in snow, it's sunny outside, and that fact is only highlighted by the glow that radiates from him at his post near the windows. The light makes his already light brown hair look almost blond, but it doesn't make him any less attractive, and neither does the way his strong forearms sit crossed over his chest. He has the lumberjack look today, too, sporting a forest-green flannel rolled up at the sleeves over a white t-shirt, a pair of jeans, and his usual black boots. It's unfair how good he looks.

As if he can feel our eyes on him, he turns my way, and I swear I stop breathing for at least ten full seconds. He notices. His lips draw up in his signature smirk, and I hate how it makes my body tingle, starting right in my toes.

"Holy shit." Talia elbows me. "I swear he got better looking over break. Looks like he got a few new tattoos, too. God, look at those arms. How can anyone not think that man is hot?"

"Stop it," I whisper harshly, and not just because I

don't want to hear the details. "He's going to know we're talking about him."

"So what? It's obvious he has a thing for you."

I laugh, then grab her arm and drag her toward the food. "He does not. Not even close."

"Oh, please. Remember last semester when he sat next to you every single class and flirted with you the entire time? Or how about at his last game, when he looked *right at you* from the ice? He is *so* into you."

"First of all…" I pick up a tray, then a bowl I'll fill with yogurt and way too many sugary toppings. "He was *not* flirting with me. He was just being annoying. Secondly, there were hundreds of students at the game. He could have been looking at anyone."

"Right. Sure. Which is why he very clearly looked right at you and mouthed *Hi, Clover*. I'm sure there are plenty of other people he calls that." Sarcasm drips from every word, punctuated by the eye roll she gives me.

"I wish he'd stop it with the whole Clover thing." But even as I say the words, I don't mean them. As much as I'm irritated by the nickname, there's a part of me that loves it.

"You do not," Talia calls me on my lie as I sprinkle chocolate chips over my yogurt, then move on to the gummy worms. "You think it's cute, and I think it's cute too. Even if boys are dumb."

Dan, the guy with the magical hands, quickly became a

thing of the past when, just before Thanksgiving break, Talia started seeing Shawn Hicks, a hockey player. Things were *very* hot and heavy between them, only for him to dump her out of nowhere before the end of the year. We spent most of winter break—including New Year's Eve—either curled up in my bed or hers as I helped dry her tears.

"You were fun for a while, babe, but it's just not that serious," he'd said to her.

Though she won't admit it, it crushed her, and I had to fight the urge to throw my first ever punch when I saw him the first day back at classes. She's been in a sour, man-hating mood ever since. Not that I blame her, of course. That guy deserves all the hate and more.

"Still, I think he's into you," she insists, grabbing an apple, then tossing it back into the bin with a grimace.

While my tray is stacked with a yogurt parfait—or at least my version of one—half a turkey club sandwich, and a bag of pretzels, she has just a pack of Oreos and peanut butter on hers.

I frown down at Talia's mostly empty tray as we reach the end. "Is that all you're getting?"

She shrugs. "Not really that hungry."

I want to tell her that's the same excuse she used last night when I microwaved us noodles during our study break, but I don't have the chance to before she barrels on.

"He's *still* looking over here, just so you know."

"Stop it. He is not," I say, but I find myself peeking in his direction anyway.

Talia is right—Callum is looking over here. Not just *over here*, either. He's looking right. At. Me.

I snap my gaze away. "Probably because you're staring at him, so stop it."

"He's staring because he wants *you* to stare back. Because he likes you." She sings the word *like*, and the guy in line in front of us turns around, brows crinkled together.

I give him a tight smile, then shoot a dirty look at Talia. "He's really not, so can we drop it. *Please?*"

She must hear the desperation in my voice because she sighs and nods. "All right. Consider it dropped. But we *will* be finishing this conversation in our room later."

I accept her answer, though I have no plans of doing so, and we continue shuffling through the line. I finish my tray off by grabbing a chocolate pudding pack for later, a bottle of water, and an apple juice before we make our way to the checkout.

"Thanks," I say with a smile as the cashier hands me back my student ID. I wait for Talia as she runs her card, then I turn to her. "Where do you want to sit?"

"How about over by the windows?"

It sounds like an innocuous suggestion, but it's far from it.

"That's where Callum is."

"Oh, is it now? I hadn't noticed," she says, but she's

already moving toward the empty table. The one right next to his.

I grit my teeth, knowing arguing with her will just cause a scene, which is the last thing I want, so I don't. I do what I told Callum I was good at—I follow, and I feel eyes on me the entire way. They don't leave me as I set my tray down on the table and slide into a chair, hanging my jacket off the back.

The feeling doesn't go away, not even as I crack open my water bottle and take a long drink, and it keeps going as the conversation at the table behind us gets louder.

"She just wouldn't stop, man," says Lewis Carlo, one of Callum's teammates, and from his tone and the slick grin on his face, I get a sense I won't like where this conversation is headed. "I tried to tell her if she didn't pull off, I would blow my load right down her throat, but no, she was insistent. She just kept sucking me, and fuck, it was incredible. Didn't even last ten more seconds. Hottest fucking nut of my life, dude."

A few of the guys laugh, some of them giving him a few pats on the back like *he* was the one who did all the work. I barely resist rolling my eyes.

"What about you, Kells? Did you get any pussy this weekend? I bet you're fucking swimming in it, Mr. Overtime Winner."

I glance over at Talia, who is already looking my way. She gives me a wobbly smile, and I can tell she feels bad for dragging me over here. We've never outright discussed my little crush on Callum, but since Talia and I have been best friends since middle school, it's safe to say we practically have ESP. I don't have to say how I feel out loud—she knows.

Stop listening, Chloe, I say to myself. *Just tune it out.*

"Um, no," he finally says after a few moments of silence.

I exhale heavily, not even realizing I was holding my breath.

"What?!" Lewis exclaims. "Even after that goal you had on Saturday? I thought for sure the puck bunnies would be all over you after that."

"They probably would have if he had actually come out with us," a new voice says, and if I remember correctly, this one belongs to Frank Hamm, another teammate. "The fucker bailed again, remember? Or you would if you hadn't been completely wasted that night."

Lewis snaps his fingers. "That's right. It's all coming back to me. What was your reasoning for ditching us this time?"

"It was my little brother's birthday, and I promised him a virtual *Shrek* marathon."

Nobody says anything, almost like they're waiting for the punchline, and when it doesn't come, someone finally speaks.

"What are you doing in my swamp?!"

All the guys laugh, and I have no idea who has just poorly imitated the ogre, but it doesn't matter. I can't stop thinking about Callum's answer. He skipped going out with friends to have a movie date with his little brother? That sounds nothing like the cocky jock I know from class. It's actually…sweet.

They start quoting more of the movie, and while I find it hilarious—how can you not laugh at *Shrek*?—I'm still reeling from learning about this new side of the jock I love to hate. Admittedly, I don't know much about him other than what I've seen in class, around campus, and on the ice. We've never truly hung out, but I always got the feeling we would have nothing in common.

I'm rethinking that now.

I'm halfway through my lunch when Talia abruptly shoots to her feet. I look up at her, puzzled as she begins stuffing her untouched Oreos and peanut butter into her pocket.

"What's going on?"

"I'm finishing this in our room."

"Wait, what? Why?" I say through a bite of yogurt. "I'm not done."

"I am." She darts her eyes behind me, and I turn to find none other than the guy who broke her heart strutting up to the table…with a new girl on his arm.

I twist my lips into a sneer. *Fucking Shawn.*

"Come on, Tally," I say, "don't let him ruin your lunch. He's not worth it."

She shakes her head, unshed tears shining in her

pretty blue eyes. "I know. I just want to go back to the room, though. Please, Chlo?"

Just as I begged her for a reprieve earlier, she's now asking me for the same. I give it to her.

"All right," I tell her, pushing to my feet, "let's go. We can skip our next class if you want."

Sure, my parents would kill me if they knew I even suggested it, but I try to push the guilt away.

"Holy fuck! That chick is on her rag!"

I pause as the loud voice booms through the mess hall, and one look at Talia tells me everything I need to know—he's talking about me. I have no doubt the color of my face matches the stain on the back of my jeans, and even if I tried, I couldn't move. I'm rooted to the spot, mortification coursing through every inch of me. I close my eyes, hoping if I do, I'll wake up and this will have been just a bad dream, but when I open them again, I'm still standing in the middle of the lunchroom with *everyone* staring and laughing.

Suddenly, two tattooed arms circle my waist.

"I've got you, Clover," Callum says into my ear. "I've got you."

"I-I-I—" I sputter. "What are you doing?"

But I know what he's doing. He's tying a shirt—the very flannel he was just wearing—around my waist.

"Come on," he says, softly nudging me forward. "Just walk. Ignore them."

But putting one foot in front of the other is damn

hard to do when all you can hear is laughter and all you can see are people pointing and judging you. Somehow, I do it anyway, hurrying out of the mess hall as fast as I can, not even bothering to look back when Talia marches past me, and I hear the unmistakable sound of someone being slapped and an uttered, "You're going to pay for that, bitch."

I don't stop for any of it. I just keep going, Callum behind me every step of the way, his hand resting on the small of my back as my heart beats harder than it ever has before. I swear all the blood left in my body is *whoosh, whoosh, whooshing* in my head and ears.

"Almost there," he says through the noise as we pick up our pace. "Just keep going."

We burst through the double doors, and I gasp out a breath for the first time in what seems like forever. Then I fall. I expect to hit the ground at any moment, but I never do. Those same arms that tied the shirt around my waist are now wrapped around me as we slide against the wall to the floor, tears now streaming down my face.

When the hell did I start crying?

It doesn't matter. I just stood up in front of the whole lunchroom with a giant blood stain on my pants, and *everyone* saw it. How could they not, with how loud Shawn yelled?

"Shh," Callum whispers. "Try to breathe for me, all right? Breathe."

His words have the desired effect, calming me enough

that I can gulp in another breath. I do it again, over and over until I'm no longer struggling.

"That's it," he says. "Give me another one."

I do, then another. Slowly, I come out of the haze, blinking hard against the bright white lights of the hallway, and the first thing I see is the most gorgeous shade of golden yellow.

"Callum."

He grins, but it's not his usual self-assured smile. It's sweet. Soft, even. And perhaps a little worried.

"Hey, Clover."

For the first time, I don't completely hate the silly nickname he's given me. I might even kind of love it.

Still, I find myself saying, "My name is Chloe."

He chuckles lightly, and it sounds familiar, like he always does—arrogant.

"Sure it is." He sweeps a strand of hair from my face, tucking it behind my ear. "Whatever you say, Clover."

I want to be annoyed. I want to tell him to go away. But none of that happens. I just sit there, staring up at him like he's not infuriating and I'm not still absolutely humiliated by what just happened.

He lets me. He doesn't rush me or ask for his shirt back. He simply sits, holding my face in his hands, watching me closely, like he's afraid I'm going to break.

I have no idea where Talia went. I assume back to our room after she saw me with Callum, but honestly, I'm in no hurry to find her right now. I'm still trying to get my bearings straight.

"Why did you do that?" I ask when I trust myself enough to speak.

He tips his head to the side. "Do what?"

"Come to my rescue. Give me your shirt." I laugh quietly, the whooshing in my ears finally subsiding. "Ugh, I don't know. Why are you sitting on the dirty floor with me? Why are you being *nice*? And why are you looking at me like that?"

As I speak, his smile grows wider, and all it does is piss me off. It shouldn't, especially given the circumstances, but I can't help feeling like this is all one big joke and at any moment, he's going to realize he's ruining his reputation by doing this.

But he doesn't say anything. He just keeps grinning.

"What?" I snap.

He shakes his head, still smiling. "You're cute when you're annoyed, did you know that?"

"I am not. And I am *not* annoyed."

"Yes, you are."

"Fine. So I'm annoyed. But I just bled all over my pants and the *whole damn school* saw it."

"It wasn't the whole school."

I glare at him, and he rolls his lips together to keep from laughing.

"Sorry, bad time to get picky with words." He brushes another hair away, and goose bumps break out over my skin. "Look, who cares if those asshats saw? It's not a big deal."

"Yes, it is!" I argue. "How are you not grossed out right now? They were."

"Because I'm not them, Clover." He leans closer, and it's too much, but I can't seem to make myself move away. "Because I'm pretty sure there is nothing you could do that would gross me out."

I wrinkle my brows, shaking my head. "What? What do you mean?"

He chuckles. "Come on. Do I really have to spell it out?"

"Yes, because I don't understand what's happening here."

He watches me carefully, like he's trying to discern if I'm messing with him or not. I'm not. I have no idea what he's talking about.

Finally, he exhales slowly, then says, "What's happening is I'm trying to tell you I like you. I have since the first day of school. I've tried telling you before, but you wouldn't listen."

My jaw drops. This is a dream. I must have fallen asleep at the lunch table. I had to have. That's the only explanation I have for what I'm hearing.

"You…like me?"

He nods. "Yes."

"Since the first day of school?"

Another bob of his head. "Yep."

"But…" I think back to that day. I spent most of the time running around campus, trying to figure out where my classes were because I was so anxious that I forgot the entire route I had mapped out ahead of time. I don't recall seeing Callum at all, and I really think I'd remember him. "We didn't even talk that day."

"We didn't have to, Chloe."

Chloe.

Not Clover. Just Chloe.

I don't know what it is about hearing him say my name, but it rattles something so deep inside me that I do the craziest thing I've ever done in my life.

I kiss Callum Keller.

Chapter 5

KELLER

"What are you doing here, Chloe?"

Her smile falls at the coldness in my voice, and for a second, I feel bad. But I shouldn't feel anything other than anger. I should be so damn mad at her that I shake.

I'm not, and I don't.

All I feel is…well, truthfully, want. It's all I ever feel when it comes to her. From the second I saw her walking across campus, I wanted her. I didn't know her name, but I wanted to. There was something special about her even then that I couldn't deny.

Imagine my surprise when I walked into my creative writing course and there she was. She was sitting next to the same girl she'd walked across the quad with, organizing her pens *just so* before the professor came in. It felt like fucking fate, and in some way, it still does.

It took me an entire week to work up the courage to finally talk to her, and when I did, I asked to borrow a pen. She wrinkled her brows in annoyance, then handed me one before turning back to the teacher, dismissing me. All it did was make me want to talk to her more.

So I did. I kept bothering her every class after until it became my thing. I don't know how, but I could tell she wasn't as exasperated by me as she pretended to be, and even though we're where we are right now, I'm glad I took a chance and kept at it. Even if all those years we had together were it, it was worth it.

Please don't let them be it, though.

I grip the door tighter, trying to fight off the urge to reach for her and feel her against me like I did last night. Her perfectly plump lips part, and I wait anxiously for her answer. Is she here to say we're done? Or will she tell me she missed me and made a mistake? Say she's sorry? Will she beg us to go back to what we were? And would I?

It doesn't matter, because she snaps her mouth closed again. I sigh, cross my arms over my chest, rest against the doorjamb, and try hard to ignore how gorgeous she looks. The light green sweater makes her brown eyes pop, and the jeans she's wearing are doing wonders for her full figure, which has always driven me wild.

"All right. Let's try a different question," I say. "How did you know where to find me?"

"Mail."

My brows draw tightly together. "What?"

"Um." She tucks a piece of hair behind her ear, and

for a second, I think she's nervous. But that can't be the case. What does she have to be nervous about? She's the one who walked away from me. "Your birthday card. It had your address on it, and I assumed you hadn't moved since you sent it, so I took a chance. The guard downstairs seemed very surprised to learn you were married, and I had to flash him my ID so he'd let me up."

I make a mental note to talk to him later to tell him she's always welcome here, but right now I'm focused on something else…

She got my card?

I sent it on a whim. I was at the grocery store, and they had a display for St. Patrick's Day cards. I stopped, telling myself I could just look at them and that was it, but then I was buying one, signing it, and dropping it in the mail to the last place I knew she was staying. She never responded, and I assumed it either got lost or went to an old address. I guess I was wrong.

I clench my teeth at the sting of her not responding. "Well, here I am."

"Here you are," she echoes, then swallows roughly.

We stare at one another for several moments, and against my better judgment, I move to the side, letting her in. She hesitates for a beat before brushing past, careful not to touch me, and I don't know if I'm relieved by that or disappointed.

I close the door behind her, resting against it as I

watch her walk slowly around the apartment, taking it all in. It's nothing compared to the home she would have made for us, but it's the first thing I've ever put together on my own, and I'm proud of that.

She stops at the same picture Lawson pointed to before, the one of us at our wedding. It was a small affair, and pretty much everyone believed we were foolish for getting married so young, especially her parents. It didn't matter to us, though. We knew what we wanted, and at the time, it was each other.

Standing here with her now, watching her take the photo in, I can't tell if she still feels the same way, and I hate it. I used to read her so well. It's weird not being able to now. When she finally turns back to me, there's a soft smile on her lips, and I take a breath, pushing off the door.

"Do you want something to drink?"

"Um, sure."

I nod, moving to the kitchen and pulling a Diet Coke from the fridge. I crack it open for her, just like I always used to do, before handing it her way. Our fingers brush together as she wraps her hand around the can, and I pretend the small touch doesn't send electric jolts through me.

Either she doesn't feel it, or she's pretending just like I am, because she chugs half the can in one go. She lets out a small burp, her eyes widening in surprise as she claps her hand over her mouth.

A laugh chokes out of me, because for a moment, everything feels just like it used to. Even after all our time together, she was never comfortable being anything less than prim and proper in front of me. It never mattered to me—I would have taken her any way she came—but it was always cute when she'd slip up, then freak out.

"Sorry," she mutters, dropping her hand, her cheeks stained red. "I, uh, I didn't realize you'd started drinking Diet Coke."

I don't. I can't stand the stuff, but it's always been her favorite, so I've kept up the tradition of buying it. Sometimes I'll have one just to remember what she used to taste like.

"Yeah, well, a lot can change in three years."

The words come out sharper than intended, but that doesn't make them any less true. I think she knows it, too, if the way her smile fades and her eyes darken with sadness is any indication. A wave of awkwardness falls over the room, and I don't know what to say to her. We've never had this before, not even when she used to pretend to hate me. Things have always been so easy between us, but it doesn't feel that way now.

Air gets stuck in my lungs, trying to claw its way out, and it takes all I have in me to mutter, "Bathroom," before marching out of the room. I'm sure she's confused as I close the bedroom door behind me, but that's okay, because I'm confused too. About so many things.

How am I supposed to behave right now? How am I

supposed to stand across from her and act like the last three years never happened? Is that what she expects? It must be, because she showed up here out of the blue and hasn't offered even a lick of reasoning for what she's doing in Seattle.

I march into my bathroom and turn on the faucet. I splash water over my face, needing something to cool me off since I'm suddenly feeling hot. It works, and when I'm feeling marginally better, I grab my toothbrush and get to cleaning.

Honestly, I'm stalling. For what, I don't know. Time maybe? A chance to figure out what to say to her? But I've had a long damn time to do that. Three years, actually, and I still don't fucking know. I'm not exactly sure what that means, but I do know I've been in the bathroom too long, leaving Chloe unsupervised in my apartment. I finish up and change into something I haven't been lounging around in for the last two days, then make my way back out to face my wife.

She's standing in front of the windows that give me a beautiful view of the city. As pretty as it is, it's nothing compared to having her standing here, especially since I never thought she would be. The glow of the late-morning sun radiates around her, embracing her with its warmth and giving her rich red hair an almost golden touch. She's gorgeous, even from behind.

I'm so distracted by admiring her that it takes me a moment to realize she's not alone.

Sensing me, she peeks over her shoulder. "You got a cat."

I nod, closing the distance between us until I'm standing next to her and looking at my snow-white cat cradled in her arms. *Traitor*, I think to myself, then instantly feel bad about it. He's not a traitor. I'm sure he's just as enraptured by her as I am.

"What's his name?" she asks as she runs the tip of her finger over his head. "He's adorable."

"Percy. He's a rescue."

"And his leg? What happened to him?"

"An accident when he was only a few months old. He had to have it amputated, and his original owner couldn't handle it. I adopted him about a month after surgery."

She smiles down at the cat. "That sounds about right for you. A knight in shining armor."

I'm hit with a wave of nostalgia at her words. She hasn't called me that since college. It was an inside joke between us when we began dating, after I came to her aid when she had a period mishap in the lunchroom. It only got worse when she realized I not only helped her that day but also gave my own teammate matching black eyes for making fun of her.

Outside of the ice, that was the last time I spoke to Shawn. Since he's also in the league, it's hard to avoid him completely, but whenever we play each other, I check a little harder than necessary. He's never questioned it. He knows what he did.

"When did you get him?" Chloe asks, dragging me back to the present.

"Uh…" I scratch at the stubble on my face that I should probably do something with. "Around two years ago now, I believe."

I wasn't looking for a cat, but after the Serpents had done a calendar photo shoot to raise money for charity, I didn't hate the idea of having someone else around. It was better than sitting in my apartment alone all the time. So I stopped by Rory's clinic, and Percy had just happened to come in for surgery. It felt like kismet, and he's been mine since.

Percy wiggles in her arms, and she lets him down, watching as the cat sprints through the apartment, back to the spare bedroom. She then drags her gaze over me, and for the first time, maybe ever, I feel self-conscious standing in front of her. As much as she's changed over the years, I wonder if I have too, other than the new tattoos, of course. With how hard she's looking at me, I think it might be more than that.

When she gets to my eyes and realizes I'm staring at her too, she averts her gaze and clears her throat. That same awkwardness from before permeates the room again, and I say the first thing that comes to mind to erase it.

"What are you doing here, Chloe?"

She sighs, then shakes her head, crossing her arms

over her chest as she looks out at the Emerald City. "Honestly? I'm not sure."

I try not to let my aggravation show because *of course* she's not sure. That's what she told me three years ago, too, when I asked when she was coming back.

It was the worst phone call of my life, and it's been etched into my mind ever since. Though I have more questions now than I've ever had before, I try a different approach.

"Does your *date* know you're here?"

She whips her head my way, her dark brows pulled in tight. "It wasn't a date, Callum."

I snort. "That's not what it looked like to me when you walked in with your arm around his."

For a moment, she looks surprised, like she had no idea I was watching her, then she shakes her head. "I told you last night it wasn't what it looked like."

She did say that then, and I didn't believe her. I want to now, though—more than anything. It's something I've not let myself think about, her with other men. Sure, we're still legally married, but we haven't been together for years. Even so, the thought is too much to wrap my head around.

"It was a job interview."

Do people go to bars as part of job interviews these days? I know I'm not really in a conventional line of work, but even I know that sounds like a load of bullshit.

"I know it sounds strange, but the company was…

courting me. They reached out to me, hoping to woo me into giving up my freelance status. They wanted to hire me as their new editor.”

I don’t miss her use of the past tense.

“Wanted to? What happened?”

She straightens her back, looking anywhere but at me. “Uh, it’s just not going to work out.”

“Why not?”

She doesn’t answer. Before I can think too much about it, I reach out to her, grabbing her chin and forcing her to meet my stare.

It takes her a moment, but she finally does, giving me my first close-up look at her brown eyes, which I used to love so much. She’s always hated them, said they were boring, but they’re far from it with a mix of light and dark brown, so deep it reminds me of the 70% cacao the team’s dietitian wants us to eat.

Turns out I still love them.

“Why not, Chloe?”

I feel her swallow. “Because that guy was an ass.”

My nostrils flare as anger courses through me. “What did he do?”

“Nothing.”

“What did he do?” I repeat, my words harsher this time.

“It’s no big deal. He was just, uh, a little inappropriate a few times. Looking down my dress, making comments about my weight. That’s all.”

I flex my free hand, the same urge from before, the one that said I needed to hit something, coursing through me. "What's the company?"

She shakes her head, pulling out of my grasp, and I miss her softness instantly. "No, I'm not telling you because it doesn't matter. I already turned them down and reported him. I've dealt with it."

She tips her chin up, sounding so damn self-assured in a way I've never heard before, and I realize then that it's not just her appearance that's changed. It's her. She's not the same teary-eyed girl she was when she left for her internship. She's more confident, stronger, sure of who she is. I don't know this version of my wife, but I want to.

"All right," I tell her, stuffing my hands into my pockets to keep from reaching for her again. I blow out a long breath. "So, you're here for a job?"

"Yes."

"And you didn't get it?"

"No."

"What happens next?"

She looks taken aback, like she hadn't thought that far ahead, and it confirms every fear I had. Chloe isn't back for me. She's not here to repair our marriage. She's here for herself, and that's it. Seeing me was just an unfortunate happenstance, and if I hadn't been at that bar last night, we might not have ever crossed paths. My wife doesn't want me anymore, and I'm not sure how to reconcile that.

"I want to stay."

I snap my gaze back to her. "What?"

"In Seattle," she clarifies. "I, uh, I have a few other places I'm interested in working, so I'm not ready to leave just yet."

Oh. It's still all about a job.

I nod, reaching up to rub at the back of my neck, the tension from before getting worse the longer this conversation goes on. "Well, good luck with the hunt. I—"

"I want to see you again."

I pause, unsure I heard her correctly. "What do you mean?"

"I, uh…" She huffs, then pushes a strand of hair behind her ear. "I want to talk again. I don't want to not talk anymore."

I want to remind her it was *her* decision to cease communication, but I'm so fucking happy to hear her words that I don't.

"Okay."

Her eyes light up for the first time since I opened the door, and she looks so much like she did years ago that it makes my chest ache. I rub at the spot that hurts, and she follows the movement, her eyes landing on my empty left hand.

If she has questions, she doesn't voice them. She just returns her eyes to mine as she says, "Okay."

We don't move. We don't speak. We just stand there.

Me because I'm not ready for her to leave yet, and her because…well, I'm not sure, but I'm not about to rush her away. I want to ask her so many things. How has she been? Where is she living now? Is she still at the address I sent the card to, or has she moved again? It felt like every few months, I would get a text with a new address. London, Georgia, Ireland, San Francisco, Spain, Brazil. She's been all over the place, and I want so desperately to know about her adventures, but I'm too scared to ask the wrong thing and send her running.

As if she's getting antsy too, she clears her throat, then points to the door.

"I, uh, I'd better get going. I have an assignment due and a couple thousand words to write still."

Don't go, I want to beg. *Stay. Don't leave me again.*

But I can't say any of that, so I say nothing at all. Instead, I lead her toward the door, letting the silence linger. She pauses when we reach the small entryway, turning my way, and I fight the urge to close the already short distance between us because it's still too much.

"Can we get together while I'm in town? Maybe grab a coffee?"

A coffee? Doesn't she know I want more than coffee with her?

I nod. "Sure, coffee sounds good."

"Great. I'll, um, I'll text you. Or you can text me. You're the hotshot hockey player with the busy schedule." She smiles softly, opening the door, her hand on the knob. "It was really good to see you, Callum."

It was really good to see you. It sounds like she's talking to an old friend, not the person she promised the rest of her life to, and I feel it in every word. I rub at the spot on my chest again, my fingers brushing against the ring I keep hidden beneath my shirt.

"You too…Clover."

Her breath catches. It's subtle, but I don't miss it… and it's the only thing that gives me hope that maybe this little visit of hers has affected her as much as it has me.

With one last glance backward, she leaves. I watch her go, not turning away until she's tucked inside the elevator. I close the door and lean against it. When I pull my phone from my pocket, I realize how hard my hands are shaking.

"Fuck," I mutter, dragging one over my face, trying to scrub away all the thoughts running through my mind right now.

I can't believe that just happened. Chloe was here. *Right fucking here.* Standing in my apartment with all her beauty and making my heart beat in a way it hasn't in years. My breaths come in sharp but shallow, and it feels like the walls are closing in on me. Crushing me. *Killing* me.

I need air. I need…I don't know what I need.

Somehow, I manage to swipe through my recent calls and hit the name I've called upon more times than I could count since everything went down with Chloe and me.

"Cal?" says a craggy voice. "Everything good?"

"No." There's a shuffling, a grunt, and a distinctly feminine voice asking where her companion is going. "Are you busy?" I ask, even though I can clearly hear he is.

"Nah, it's nobody important."

"What the fuck?!" the mystery woman says, and if I weren't so consumed by what just happened, I'd yell at him for that. For being so damn smart, he sure is dumb sometimes.

She slings a few hurtful words at him, and there's a bunch of other commotion before a door slams.

"Well, that takes care of that. What's going on, big brother?"

"I don't know!" I yell, raking my free hand through my hair and pushing off the door. I pace across my apartment to the very windows Chloe was just staring out of.

All it does is remind me of her, so I turn on my heel, marching back over to the door. It's pointless. I swear the space still smells like her floral perfume.

"Fuck," I murmur as I move through my apartment, trying to find somewhere she wasn't.

In the end, I wind up in my bathroom, the door locked, even though I'm the only one here. I tell myself it's to keep Percy out, but I don't know how true that is. I think I'm trying to lock my thoughts out, too.

"Cal?" my brother says again. "You okay, man?"

"I…" I gulp in another breath as I sit on the edge of the giant bathtub in my en suite. "I don't know."

"Okay, that's fine. You don't need to know. Can you tell me what's going on?"

I hate that he's so good at calming me down. I'm supposed to be the older brother, but I don't feel like it now, just like I haven't any of the other times I've called him in a panic over the years. It's probably why he's the future lawyer and I'm not. As long as it doesn't involve his love life, he's always been good at getting the facts, then tackling a problem with a level head. I'm envious, especially in times like these when my mind won't stop racing.

"Chloe."

He laughs lightly. "Yeah, man. I figured. That's usually the reason you call instead of text."

I wince because he's right. I'm horrible about calling unless I need someone to talk to. "Sorry."

"Don't be. I do the same to you with my problems."

He's right. We hardly ever talk just to shoot the shit. We do that over text. Calls are reserved for the serious stuff.

"So, what happened with…Chloe?"

There's a pause before he says her name, and I know it's because he never knows what to call her. Before we separated, it was always "my favorite almost sister" or "the wife." Now, he doesn't know what to call her, just like I don't.

"She was here."

"In Seattle?"

"No. I mean, yes." I exhale deeply again, my breaths slowly returning to normal. "Yes, in Seattle. And in my apartment."

"Shit."

"Shit," I agree.

A few beats pass. "Are you okay?"

"Do I fucking sound okay, Stef?!"

For a moment, I feel bad for yelling at him, but it goes away quickly as I remember *why* I called him.

"That's fair. I deserved that. Guess my teachers were wrong when they said there's no such thing as a stupid question." He sighs. "All right, talk to me. Tell me everything."

I spend the next ten minutes relaying everything that happened last night until the moment Chloe walked out of my apartment. When I'm finished, he's quiet, and I check the phone to make sure I didn't lose him somewhere along the way, but he's still there.

"Stefan?" I ask.

"I'm still here," he answers. "I'm just trying to process it all."

I huff out a laugh. "Yeah, me too."

"Do you believe her?"

"Huh?"

"About that guy she showed up with. Do you believe it wasn't a date?"

At first, I didn't. I thought she was just trying to save face because she got caught, but after hearing her out, I don't think that's the case anymore.

"I do."

"Good," Stefan says. "I believe her, too. That's not the Chloe I know, the one who threw me the best thirteenth birthday party there ever was. She recreated *Judge Judy*, Cal. That was fucking incredible."

I think back on the memory. It didn't take much for Chloe to become part of my family. Though my parents thought we were nuts for wanting to get married so young, they trusted me to make the best decision for my future and loved her with every fiber of their being. They accepted her instantly, and one book on LSAT prep later, she became my brother's favorite person.

Though he's as upset with Chloe as I am about her leaving, it's always been obvious he misses her as much as I do.

"You wouldn't stop banging that damn gavel and kicking people out of the 'courtroom.' You were such an annoying little twerp."

"Yeah, well, I still am."

I grin, then realize I have no reason to be smiling right now, not when I just let my wife walk away from me yet again. She says she wants to have coffee, but is that true? Will this have been the last time I see her? Or if we do sit down and have coffee, what's that going to look like? Will it be as awkward as it was having her here? I don't fucking know.

As if Stefan can sense I'm getting stuck in my own head again, he says, "So, what's the plan?"

"What do you mean?"

"I mean, what's the next step? You're going to meet for coffee, right? You want to, yes?"

"Yes," I tell him honestly, not having to think about it for even a second. I don't care how uncomfortable it felt having her in my apartment. I'd endure a thousand awkward hours with her, just as long as she's around. That's all I've ever wanted—her to be there.

"Good," he says again. "I think that's a good plan. Start small and in public so things can't get too out of hand."

"Jeez, Stef. It's not like I'm planning to unload on her."

"No, but it's clear you're struggling with your feelings toward her. And you've been bottling them up for, what, three years now? You've got some shit to work through. A short chat with other people around might be for the best."

He's not entirely wrong. I've not reacted the best the two times I've seen her in the last twelve or so hours. I could use the safety net to keep me in check.

"What was it like?" he asks quietly when I don't say anything for a few moments.

"What was what like?"

"Seeing her again, Cal. What was it like?"

Fuck. How do I explain it to him? That it was like someone stealing your favorite sweater, then giving it back a few years later? Or like getting up to the window at the drive-thru and finding out the person in front of you paid for your order? Or winning a championship you've been after your whole life? Because it was better than all of those. So much more than I could have imagined.

"Everything, Stef. It was everything."

I swear I can hear him smile through the phone. "You're still so in love with her."

I don't deny it. I never have, and I'm not about to now. But I'm also not going to offer up that info to just anyone, especially not Chloe. Not until I know what's happening with us. Not until I know I can trust her again. Not until I know she's still mine.

"Thanks for letting me freak out on you."

My little brother laughs. "Anytime. You know that. I'm always here."

"I know. Appreciate it. And, Stefan?"

"Yeah, man?"

"You should really apologize to that girl. She didn't deserve that."

He sighs, but it's one of those resigned ones because he knows I'm right. "I know. I will."

"What happened to Elijah?" I ask, referring to the guy he couldn't stop talking about when he was here visiting last month just before the Christmas break. "I thought things were going well with him."

"Eh. We fizzled," he says. I want to comment on that, but I keep my words to myself. I have no business giving out love advice right now anyway. "Text me later?"

"Yeah. Later, bro."

We disconnect the call, and I clutch my phone in my hand as I sit perched on the edge of the tub, the one I've never used, even though it was the sole reason I got this place.

It wasn't for me. It was for Chloe. Just in case.

Even while she's been gone, I've kept her in the back of my mind during every decision I've ever made. I wish I could say it's because I never doubted she'd come back to me, but that's not true. I did it because I *hoped* she would. Always, even when I was at my darkest. But now that she's here, I have no damn idea how to react to it, no idea what to do.

The one thing I do know? I'm never going to figure it out if I don't try. I swipe through my phone again, this time looking for a different name. When I stop on it, I take a deep breath, my thumbs hovering over the screen.

Then, I text my wife.

Chapter 6

"I talked to him."

"What? Hello? Chlo?"

"I talked to him," I repeat, louder this time.

Talia sighs, and I hear what sounds like a car door closing and a bunch of rustling. Then finally, she says, "Sorry. I was trying to get my life together and get in the car. Give me a second. Let me connect you to my Bluetooth."

There's more shuffling and many curse words. I grin. My best friend has always been a little chaotic, and it's comforting knowing even though she's over two thousand miles away, she's still just Talia.

"All right. I'm here. Are you there?"

"Yes. Where are you going? Shouldn't you be at work?"

"Ugh, yes." She groans. "And I have so much shit to do today that I *need* to get done or my dad is going to murder me. But noooo." She lets out an irritated growl. "I am on the way to pick up *your* nephew from school early. He allegedly threw up, but I'm like ninety-nine percent sure he's just trying to get out of taking his science quiz this afternoon."

I snicker, proud of the kid who isn't actually my nephew, but close enough that he's called me Auntie Chloe since he could talk. "Smart kid. Science is so boring."

"Says the girl who used to work in a lab."

"Exactly. I was a technician who hated my job with a passion because science bored me and made my eyes glaze over."

She laughs. "I remember when you got the job, and you cried because you wanted to do quite literally anything else with your life. Now look at you, traveling the world and writing, just like you always wanted to do."

Her words aren't entirely true. While writing was always a passion of mine and secretly what I wanted to do for a living, this wasn't how I wanted it to happen. I thought I'd maybe write a book, possibly two. Or write articles for a big, fancy paper. I had no idea I'd be traveling and freelancing my way through life, never knowing when I'd be getting paid or where my next assignment might come from. While I love it most of the time, I'm still not so sure it's everything I ever wanted, mostly because there's only one thing I've ever been absolutely certain about, and I don't even have that anymore.

"So, what's up? Why'd you call?"

A wave of unease passes through me at the mention of what happened just an hour ago. "Seattle is…okay."

"Just okay?" I can picture her wrinkling her perfectly shaped brows. "Because your voice sounds all weird. Did something happen?"

For a moment, I rethink the entire call and debate whether I should tell her I saw my husband at all. The problem is that Talia knows me better than just about anyone else, and she'll figure it out soon enough anyway. Besides, I need someone to talk to about this. I'm having far too much anxiety about it as it is. Maybe she can help make sense of what I'm feeling.

"I saw Callum."

Aside from the pounding in my ears, there's silence.

"Tally? Did I lose you? Did your Bluetooth disconnect? You really need to get a new car, you know."

"First of all, you're right about the car. I hate this old clunker. But it wasn't that. I'm just…in shock. I thought you weren't going to see him unless you got the job." She gasps. "Wait, does that mean you got it? Oh my gosh, congratulations!"

I wince at her enthusiasm. Talia's always been my biggest cheerleader. "Uh, thank you, but no, I did not get the job. If anything, I got harassed by the guy they sent to wow me."

"What?!" She screeches so loudly I have to pull the phone away from my ear. "—fucking kidding me?" she's saying when I put it back. "Give me the asshole's name. I'll take care of him right quick."

I laugh, and I realize it's the first time I've done so genuinely since I came to Washington. Leave it to Talia to make it happen. She's always had a way of breaking through whatever shit I have going on.

"Calm down. No need to go all mama bear on me."

"Um, yes, there is. Remember when you were in London, and your boss at the paper was being a total wanker? Who was it that got him fired again?"

I giggle just thinking about it. "You, my amazing queen. Even though you really didn't have to go *that* hard with it."

"Girl, he was cheating on his wife, with whom he had *three* kids. I absolutely did. Besides, if he didn't want to be found out, maybe he should have hidden his face in his dating profile pictures. Or, you know, not made the money he was stealing so easy to trace."

When I told her my former employer wouldn't allow me to cover a story on a men's football game because I "didn't have the right equipment in my trousers," she went full scorched earth and aired all his dirty laundry, leading to his removal as CEO. If Talia weren't so set on staying in Tennessee, she'd make a damn good FBI agent.

"Are you sure you're good?" she asks.

I nod even though she can't see me. "Yes. It's been handled. Plus, the paper is letting me stay in this swanky hotel on their dime, hoping I'll come around, but I don't plan to. I am not working for a company that employs people like that."

"And you shouldn't have to. I'm proud of you. But you know I'm here for you no matter what."

"I know, and it's exactly why I love you."

"Hmm, right. *So* much that you went to see your estranged husband without consulting me first?"

The look on Callum's face as I walked out of his apartment flashes through my mind, and not for the first time since I left. It's all I thought of as I walked back to my hotel, which is surprisingly close to his place, and again as I crawled into the too-hard bed and put the pillow over my face. It was all I could think to do to try to rid myself of the tidal wave of emotions attacking me.

I knew going to his apartment would bring up all kinds of feelings. I just never expected unease would be one of them. I felt it from the moment I knocked on his door, and it only got worse when he opened it.

It wasn't because I didn't want to see him—of course I did—it was because for the first time, I wasn't sure how to act around him. I haven't felt that flustered since he sat next to me in creative writing. I remember how my cheeks would get hot, and I'd shake with the anticipation of seeing him. It never mattered if we talked or not. I just wanted to be *near* him.

I felt an inkling of that today, too, even if it was awkward. And it made me realize just how far we've let our relationship fall away from us, and I don't just mean over the last three years we've been separated. It started before then. Our conversations grew stilted. We chose our words more carefully. We stopped being *us*.

"So how was it?" Talia asks, pulling my attention back to our phone call.

"Uh, it was…strange."

"Well, yeah, I bet it was. You haven't seen him in the flesh since, what, when you left for London, right?"

"Yeah, not since then."

The lie is tangy on my tongue. Callum might not have seen me since then, but I've seen him. Sure, it's been from the stands in various arenas across North America, but it still counts. Any time he came to a city near wherever I was at the time, I made a point to go to his games. We might not have been on the best of terms, but I still wanted to be there for him.

And selfishly, I wanted to see if he still gave me the same butterflies as before. He did, and they've always left me feeling just as confused as I was the day I told him I wouldn't be coming to Seattle with him and I'd be staying in London.

It was the first time in my life I had a say in where I went. My college was picked for me, based on what my parents could afford. Then, when Callum and I got married, everything was about his career. I understood it.

I accepted it. He had worked his entire life to get to the NHL, and I wanted that for him.

I just wasn't sure I wanted it for me anymore.

"So…is he still hot? I mean, in person. I see him on TV all the time."

I laugh, because *of course* that's what Talia asks about. "Yes."

"Girl, shut up. I can *hear* the blush in your voice. It's the tattoos, isn't it?"

My free hand goes to my cheek, and as my best friend predicted, it's inflamed. Because, yes, Callum still looks good even after all these years. The added tattoos have made him look darker and a little scarier, but I've always loved the edge he has. While he's been charming to me from the start, he wasn't that way with everyone else. He was personable and approachable, but always with a mysterious air around him. He still has that, maybe even a bit more now, and I would have been a fool not to notice it.

I clear my throat. "I told him I'm going to stay."

Another pause from Talia, then, "Are you sure that's a good idea?"

"Honestly?" I exhale heavily. "No. But I feel like I need to, you know? Even if it means…"

I don't say the words out loud, but she knows exactly what I'm getting at—even if it means we officially end things.

"Can I be candid with you?"

I laugh lightly. "Haven't you always been, Tally?"

"Yes, because someone needs to." I can faintly hear her blinker in the background, and based on how long we've been on the phone, I'm sure she's getting close to the school. "You know I love that you went to London. Hell, I was the one who pushed you to apply for the internship in the first place. You did the thing, and I'm beyond proud of you for it. Yes, it dredged up a bunch of other shit, and you were gone longer than you ever intended to be, which has made things harder with your husband, but…"

She drags out the last word, then sighs, and I steel myself, knowing there's a chance I'm not going to like what she says next.

"I think you're doing the right thing by seeing Keller. I know you wanted this to be a quick trip, in and out without any incidents, but I also think it's time. It's been three years. You can't run from a hard conversation forever, you know."

I *do* know. I've tried. More than once, actually. I attempted to fill it with the internship, then writing. Then again with traveling the world and exploring places I only thought I'd ever see in the movies as I wrote blogs and articles for various publications. None of it worked. It was all wrong, and it did nothing to fill the void I felt in my heart. It didn't erase him, and it certainly didn't erase how he made me feel.

I think that's the worst part of this all. Through

everything, my feelings for my husband have never wavered. It was everything else that felt off and compounded into something more. Callum was never the problem. I was.

"Chlo?"

"I'm still here," I say. "Just…thinking."

"I'm sure this is a lot to process." She has no idea. "Do you want me to come out there? I can. I could be on the next flight out."

"I love you for that, Tally, but no. I need to face this on my own. I created this mess, and it's up to me to clean it. Besides, you apparently need to take care of my sick nephew."

"I swear, if that little twerp isn't even sick, I'm grounding him for a week. Maybe even two."

Her words are nothing but a threat. They always are when it comes to her son.

Talia surprised me by announcing she was pregnant during our second semester of freshman year in Denver. In retrospect, I should have seen it coming. There were signs for a solid month before. Her eating was off, she wasn't sleeping well, and her emotions were all over the place, highlighted by the fact that she cried because she got a ninety-eight on a paper instead of a one hundred… and she still had the highest grade in the class.

Pregnant or not, she didn't let it stop her. I was sad when she transferred back to Tennessee, but I understood. She kept up with her classes, had my adorable pseudo-nephew in the fall, then picked up right where she left off. She even graduated a whole year before I did.

I asked her who the father was, but she maintained it was a one-night stand. She said after she told him about the pregnancy, he signed away all rights, and that was that. Of course, I still have questions, but none of them matter because none of them will change how good of a mother Talia is.

"I'll take your silence as you not believing me," she says, and I chuckle.

"No, I definitely don't believe you, but that's not why I was quiet. I was just thinking about college."

"College? Ugh. Why would you want to go back there?" She pauses. "Oh."

"Yeah, oh."

Thinking back on that time always brings up so many memories. While some of them suck, like that jerk Shawn Hicks making fun of my period, there are so many others I don't ever want to forget. College is where Callum and I fell in love, where he proposed, where we made promises of forever. I don't let myself slip back to those days often, but right now, I need them. I need to remember that things can be good between us again.

Talia chuckles. "Keller was so annoying, the way he used to flirt with you in class all the time. I was trying to learn, but it was hard with you making eyes at each other."

"We were not making eyes at each other, whatever the hell that even means."

"You know exactly what it means. Heart eyes. All in love and shit before either of you was willing to admit it. It was *so* gross."

Talia's half right. We were in love, but one of us *was* brave enough to admit it, and it wasn't me. Callum always told me how he felt. After that day in the cafeteria, he didn't hide his feelings anymore. He was honest about what he wanted from me. I was the one who held back.

I guess that's a part of our relationship that hasn't changed.

"Look, as much as I'd love to keep trotting down memory lane with you, I just pulled up to the school, and I'd better go rescue the nurse from my overdramatic child."

"You're going to feel so bad when you find out he's actually sick."

"I won't, because he's not. I know my son, and let's face it, you have blinders on when it comes to your nephew. He's an angel in your eyes."

"You're damn right he is," I agree. "Little Perfect."

I'd bet the measly paycheck I got for my last article she just rolled her eyes at my old nickname for him.

"This is why I'm the favorite," I remind her.

"No, you're the favorite because you send him elaborate gifts from wherever you are in the world."

"That reminds me, I need to mail you the stuff I picked up from Pike Place Market."

"Chloe…" To untrained ears, she might sound irritated, but I know her better than that. She's grateful for everything I do for her and Ian. Raising a kid by yourself is no easy feat, and it's even harder when you have a parent like Chloe's dad pulling the strings and trying to control every aspect of her life. "I love you, you know that?"

"I love you too, Tally."

"Does that mean you're going to call me before you see your husband again?"

He didn't feel like my husband when he was looking at me like a stranger just an hour ago.

"Yes, I will."

"Good. Now go enjoy a long bath in that tub you texted me about while you still can. How long are you there again?"

"They put me up through the weekend, which is good, because I looked at my bank account this morning and it just read HA."

"You know…" She tries to sound casual, but I know her better than to believe that. "If you're hurting for money, you could always—"

"Don't." I already know what her next words will be. "I'm not touching it."

She sighs. "All right. Fine, fine. I get it." But I know

it's not the last I'm going to hear about it. "Just let me know you're good, yeah?"

I promise her I will, and she lets me know she'll send an update on Ian later before we hang up. I pull the phone away from my ear, and I'm surprised when I find a message waiting for me. I expect it to be *Seattle Daily* again—they've been calling all morning since I reported Dirk for his behavior—but it's not.

It's my parents.

> Mom: I tried to call for an update on the interview. Please return it whenever you get the chance.

I want to laugh at how succinct and impersonal the message is, but that's just how my mother has always been. She's not cold or unemotional; she's just straight to the point. My father is the more loving of the two, which is why his message makes me smile.

> Dad: We love you, our little lucky charm.

I type out a quick message, letting them know I'll call later, then set my phone aside. I love my parents, and I know they love me too, but sometimes there's a part of me that blames them for where I currently am with Callum. In the end, it was all my doing, but they weren't innocent in it either, especially my mother.

I should have known that when she suddenly decided to support my writing, it was all a ploy to get me away from Callum.

"Wow. London, huh?" She hums happily. "You know, you don't seem happy in the lab. Maybe you should apply. You did always love writing. Why not give it a shot and see what happens? You've given up so much for Callum and have gone wherever he goes for years. Take a leap for yourself."

I convinced myself her support meant I was doing the right thing. We were finally on the same page, so why wouldn't that be a sign? I *did* love writing, and as happy as I was for my husband and all his accomplishments, I wanted some of my own. She just gave me the nudge I needed to make it happen.

My phone buzzes, and I reach for it, expecting a message from my dad, likely an emoji that doesn't mean what he thinks it means, but it's not him. I spring up to a sitting position, my head feeling all fuzzy from moving so quickly, but I don't care.

He texted. Callum texted.

Even after he said he would, I wasn't sure. I hoped,

of course, but I couldn't be certain. Reading him was next to impossible.

I scoot back on the bed until my back rests against the three pillows pushed up against the headboard and read the message three times.

Callum: I'm not sure how long you're planning on staying, but I could do coffee on Thursday.

Thursday. It's only Tuesday. That's too much time to imagine all the ways this could go wrong, and I have a very active imagination.

My first instinct is to tell him no, to make up some excuse and claim I have to leave early, to run…again. But Talia is right. It's time I face this thing.

Me: I'll be here still. Thursday works for me.

Callum: Is two okay? I have to sign a few things after practice.

Me: Two works for me.

God, Chloe. Works for me? Is that all you can say? Ugh.

Me: I mean, yeah, two is great.

Callum: See you then.

Me: Cool

"Cool?" I groan at my own foolishness, then watch the screen for anything else.

Little dots appear like he's typing, but after two solid minutes of staring at the screen, nothing comes through. I toss the device aside, then rub the heels of my hands over my eyes, trying to brush away just how embarrassing that was.

It's amazing how I can do so many remarkable things like travel the world solo, make connections, and write articles for prestigious papers, but the second a cute boy comes around, I turn right back into an insecure teenager.

Then again, I don't think that feeling has ever left me. Not even after Callum and I got married, or after he joined the NHL. He was...well, he was *him*—a professional hockey player with a larger-than-life career, thousands of people cheering his name in arenas all over. He was a superstar, and I was just Chloe, the girl who still blushed every time he smiled at me. I never felt like I was good enough, and in a lot of ways, I still don't.

My phone chimes again, and I rush to grab it, my heart in my throat as I read the new message.

Callum: I'm really looking forward to seeing you, Clover.

Clover.

Even over text, the nickname sends a shiver down my spine, and it's hard to imagine a time when I said I hated it. I didn't then, and I don't now.

Me: Me too.

And I mean those two words more than I've meant anything in a long, long time.

This time, no dots appear, and when nothing has come through an hour later, I accept the fact that he's not going to text again. I peel myself off the bed so I can try to get some sort of work done, but I still spend the rest of the day checking my phone, hoping to hear from my husband again.

Chapter 7

SERPENTS SINGLES GROUP CHAT

Lawson: Sooo…are we going to discuss the elephant in the room or not?

Hayes: Not.

Fox: Elephants don't get enough love in the animal kingdom. Really cool creatures. Not as amazing as turtles, but still.

Lawson: Your turtle obsession is starting to get a little weird, Foxy. Those photos of you walking into the last game wearing your Turtley Cool socks are still all over my feed.

Fox: Finally! The people need to know how awesome they are!

Lawson: Right. So, anyway…are we just not going to talk about Keller being married?

Hutch: It's none of our business. He's made that clear.

Locke: Just drop it, Lawsy.

Lawson: Come on! You guys cannot be serious! He kept this HUGE secret from us. Are you telling me you don't want to know more?

Lawson: Your silence is deafening.

Lawson: Hello?

Hayes: Shhhhh

Lawson: No.

Lawson: Come on, really? Is anybody going to talk to me?

Lawson: HELLO?

Lawson: Wow, you guys suck.

Hayes: Then request a trade.

Lawson: GASP

Lawson: I would never! I love you guys, even if you don't love me.

Hutch: Fucking hell, are you always so dramatic?

Hayes: Dude, right? I kind of wish Keller would chime in, just to tell him to shut the fuck up.

Locke: No, we need to give him space right now. We shouldn't even be blowing his phone up like this.

Lawson: I think we're all being just a little overdramatic about this, aren't we?

Hutch: I'm sorry, but did YOU just say WE'RE being overdramatic? YOU?!?!?

Lawson: Uh, yeah. Because nobody will talk about it. I mean, so he's married? WHO CARES!

Hayes: Obviously you do.

Lawson: Duh. But I mean like…who REALLY cares, you know? Why didn't he just tell us about it?

Locke: Because clearly something big went down, and that's why she's not been around, and why he doesn't talk about her. So zip it.

Lawson: But maybe talking about it will help. I'm a great listener.

Fox: He actually is.

Lawson: SEE? Foxy agrees with me!

Fox: Not about Keller, just so we're clear.

Lawson: Booooo!

Lawson: Look, all I'm saying is, I'm kind of a little hurt he didn't confide in us. We tell him everything.

Hutch: No, Lawsy, YOU tell him everything. You tell EVERYONE everything. You have no boundaries and no filter.

Lawson: And that's okay with me. What's the fun in having those things anyway???

Lawson: I just want to know why he didn't trust us, that's all.

Lawson: See, you guys aren't even responding, which tells me you agree.

Lawson: He LIED to us. He pretended he was single. He made jokes about doing my mom. And he was married the whole time!

Hayes: Did you ever stop to think it might have been his way of coping with it? He was grieving. Give him a break.

Lawson: He was actively lying to us.

Hutch: Like you lied to us about sneaking around with Rory?

Lawson: AS IF YOU HAVE ANY ROOM TO TALK, MR. GRUMBLES!

Hayes: You really don't, Hutch.

Hayes: And just so we're clear, I don't either.

Fox: Me either. Even though you guys knew I was lying, I was still doing it.

Locke: I'm not sure I even need to chime in here.

Hutch: Considering I JUST found out about you banging my stepsister and moving her into your apartment, maybe it's best to sit this one out.

Lawson: Okay, fine. So we've all lied to one another. But this just feels… different.

Locke: Which is why we should leave him be and let him work through it. Keller has always done shit his way.

Lawson: Yeah, and how's that been working out for him, huh? He's a grump, he's mean, and he keeps saying he's going to do nasty things to my mom.

Hayes: You've said you'd do "nasty things" to his mom, too. Not sure you have a leg to stand on with that one.

Lawson: Tushy

Lawson: TOOCHE

Lawson: TWOSHAY

Lawson: The fuck do you spell that damn word???

Fox: Touché.

Lawson: THANK YOU!

Lawson: Touché, Hayes.

Lawson: But I still don't think we should let this slide.

Locke: You just want the hot gossip.

Hayes: Ew. Can you please not say that again? You're way too old to do so, and that sounded creepy.

Fox: Yeah, that was weird.

Locke: Fine. You just want the tea, then.

Hayes: Okay, still weird, but continue.

Hutch: No, no more continuing. As the captain, I'm telling you all to drop it for today. Leave him alone. We'll talk to him tomorrow IF he's ready to talk. Got it?

Lawson: Ugh. Fine. Aye aye, Captain.

Hutch: No, please. Don't.

Hayes: Aye aye, Captain.

Fox: Aye aye, Captain.

Locke: Aye aye, Captain.

Hutch: I hate you guys.

Lawson: Stop flirting with me. You're almost a married man.

Hutch: Because Keller isn't here to say it, I hate you most, Lawsy.

Lawson: I love you too, Cap.

Chapter 8

"Hustle, boys! Gotta go faster because Edmonton is the absolute definition of it."

I push my legs harder, relishing the burn of my quads. It's exactly what I need after the events of the last two days.

Practice couldn't come soon enough today. Being cooped up in my apartment suddenly became my worst nightmare, and I tried everything to distract myself from texting Chloe again. I played video games, scrolled through countless streaming apps for something to watch, and even bought and assembled a new cat tower, even though Percy didn't need one.

None of it worked. I couldn't stop thinking of her, so when my alarm went off this morning—the one I was already awake for—I sprang out of bed and got dressed in record time before hopping into my Audi R8. Sure, pushing the car to the max speed limit I could manage on Seattle streets was nice, but it's nothing compared to being out on the ice and feeling that cold air against my cheeks.

Like every Canadian kid, I grew up loving hockey with dreams of making it to the show. I worked my ass off for it, so when I was passed up the first year I was eligible for the draft, I accepted that my dream would likely never come true. I made peace with it.

Then, unexpectedly, it happened the next year—I was drafted by New York. Even then, I still didn't think I'd make it. If I were lucky, I'd play a few years in the minors and call it a career. But that's not what happened. I kept working on my game. I committed to getting better. And in my freshman year, I had a breakthrough. I wasn't just racking up points for Denver, I was getting noticed. I was making a name for myself. By the summer before my senior year, it paid off.

I remember getting that call saying I'd be signing a two-year entry-level deal, and I recall the look on Chloe's face, too. She was scared. The possibility of me playing was always there, but it never felt within reach. Suddenly, it was real, more real than anything else had ever been until that point.

She thought I'd leave her and never look back. It couldn't have been further from what was going through my mind, which was exactly why I got down on one knee and proposed to her in my shitty apartment, which I shared with too many of my teammates. And it's why she said yes, too. She was afraid to lose me, to lose us.

Sometimes I wonder if everyone was right to call us crazy back then, because let's face it—we were. Then I remember how I felt in that moment, like everything I ever wanted was clicking into place, and it wasn't just because of hockey. It was Chloe, too. I still feel that way about her, and I still feel that way about hockey.

"Keller!"

I snap my head up, looking at our assistant coach, who is waiting for me to join the scrimmage. I don't bother apologizing; I just dig right in and get to work. I battle against my teammate for the puck. It might just be practice, but we still give it our all, which is why we're both cursing and sweating by the time I get it free. I zip it over to Locke, who is not-so-patiently waiting for it, and he shoots it toward Fox. He catches it easily, then chucks it to the side.

We start all over again. The team runs drills until we're all gasping for air, then gathers in a circle around Coach Smith.

"Great practice, boys," he says. "Playing hard, which we need more than ever right now. Every point before the break counts. I know some of you have big plans for it"—he looks at Hutch, who is finally marrying his billionaire fiancée—"but we can't forget about getting ready for what's to come after it. So, these next few weeks mean a lot. It's the difference between playing hard until the last game of the regular season and being able to breathe and give a couple of guys a rest. So, let's play smart, yeah? Fight hard. We fucking got this."

A few cheers go up in agreement, but I stay silent. I've been so distracted by Chloe showing up that I almost forgot how much work we still have to do to get into a better playoff spot. Sure, we're sitting pretty right now, but Coach is right—every point matters. Every shift, every game. I don't have time for distractions…but I don't think I could stay away if I tried.

"All right. Let's call it for the day. Hutch, my office in ten. The rest of you check in where needed before you leave. You know what to do to be ready to play tonight."

We acknowledge that we've heard him before he skates off the ice. A few guys break away to work on other aspects of their game, while others head straight for the dressing room, likely meeting with trainers and checking in with medical before taking off.

I stay. I spend another thirty minutes out there, pretending I don't notice the way several of the Singles are waiting around for me. I saw their texts in the group chat last night, and I know they have questions. I wasn't ready to answer them quite yet, and I'm still not.

When my legs are nice and tired and most of my excess energy is burned off, I head to the changing room. They follow, but I keep ignoring them, going to the showers after stripping off my sweaty gear. To my surprise, they give me space, but the same can't be said for when I make it back to the room to find them still waiting.

"Aw, come on!" Hayes yells when I drop my towel at my stall. "My eyes!"

"Then stop following me around like a bunch of fucking weirdos," I tell him, pulling on my boxer briefs. "And you're lucky to look at my ass. It's fantastic."

"It is. Rory keeps asking me to get your workout routine," Lawson says.

I flip him off just because I can, and he pretends to catch it, holding it against his heart.

I roll my eyes, then slide my jeans over my legs. "Can we just get this over with already?"

"Fine," Hutch says, looking genuinely concerned. "Nobody has heard from you since yesterday morning, and we're worried."

"I got your messages in the group chat. You know I have. You can see that I've read them."

They were ridiculous, and a few times I wanted to chime in, but I wasn't in the mood.

"Right, but you never messaged back. And, usually, you're like *super* annoying."

"You're fucking kidding, right?" I look at the rest of the guys, then point to Lawson. "He's fucking kidding, isn't he?"

They all shrug, likely because Lawson *isn't* joking around for a change.

I run a hand through my wet hair. "Look, guys, I am fine."

"Okay, you say that, but—"

"No, no buts," I snap, cutting Hayes off. "I am good. I talked to Chloe and—"

"Chloe? Is that her name?" Fox asks.

I close my eyes for a second before I nod. "Yes, that's my wife's name."

They all exchange glances again, and it's so damn frustrating that they keep doing it.

"What?" I bark when nobody speaks, even though they clearly have something to say.

"I don't know. It's just kind of cute that you guys have the same initials, no?" Lawson says.

When we get married, we're going to have the same initials. Clover Keller, Callum Keller. Has a nice little ring to it, huh? I remember saying that to her in college. It was a wild statement, completely out of pocket, especially for a nineteen-year-old. But it didn't mean I meant it any less. I knew even then she was the one for me.

"How come you never go by Cal—" Lawson holds his hands up before he even finishes my first name, and I can guarantee it has to do with the look on my face that says *Don't you fucking dare.* "Okay, no to the first name still. Noted."

It's not like people don't call me by it—of course they do. But most of the time, I'm just Keller. Except for with her. It's always been Callum, so when she left, I didn't want to hear my first name at all. I was simply Keller from then on out. I'd even ignore the media in pressers if they didn't call me by my last name. They picked up on it quickly.

"Moving on," Lawson mumbles. "Am I allowed to ask more questions about the cat, or not?"

"Dude." Hayes pinches the bridge of his nose like he's as tired of his teammate's shit as I am. "Come on, Lawsy."

"What? You can't tell me you're not curious about it too."

Nobody responds, which is enough of an answer to tell me that, yeah, they're curious. But I've opened myself up far too much over the last few days, and I'd rather not continue that trend.

"If you really want to know more, ask your girlfriend."

"Rory knows you have a cat?!" He throws his hands in the air. "That's it. I give up." He marches toward the door, then stops, turning to look back at everyone still staring at me. "Well? Aren't you guys coming?"

"For once, I agree with him. You guys should go, because I'm going too. I have shit to do, because in case you all forgot, we have a game to play tonight. Like you said in the chat, I need some time, okay?"

They hesitate but eventually agree, then slowly start making their way toward the door.

Well, everyone except Hutch.

"You guys go on," he tells them, and they follow his request. I wonder if it has to do with him being the captain or if they can hear the solemnity in his tone, too.

Once they all file out, I quirk a brow at him. "Can I help you?"

He doesn't seem the least bit bothered by my attitude, which I suppose makes sense for him. Before he got together with his fiancée, he could have rivaled me with grumpiness. Now that he's all in love and happy, he's still grumpy; he just saves it for the ice.

"Uh, Auden wanted to know if we need to adjust the seating chart for the wedding."

I tip my head to the side. "Not following."

He sighs, running his hand through his short, cropped beard. I can tell this isn't a conversation he wants to have. He's been asked to do this by his fiancée, and he's so in love that he'll do anything she wants.

"She's asking if you're inviting your…Chloe to the wedding."

I laugh, though there's no real humor to it. "I have no idea, man. We haven't even had a real conversation yet. We're meeting for coffee tomorrow."

His brows rise at this new information. "Are you sure that's a good idea?"

I shrug. "No idea, but it needs to happen either way, you know?"

He nods. "I get it. Sometimes you have to rip off the Band-Aid on those hard conversations."

His face darkens, and I wonder if he's thinking about the conversation he had with Vanessa, his stepsister who moved here last year and ended up in a relationship with Locke, or if he's going even further back to when he was left at the altar by his ex-fiancée. Either way, I know neither discussion was pleasant.

"Anyway," he says, "I'll make up an answer to keep Auden happy for now, but I know she's going to ask again. I mean, you know how it goes."

"Considering I've been married longer than anyone else on this team, yeah, I'd say I know."

He shakes his head. "I still can't believe you're married. I figured *something* was up since you were always so hushed about your personal life, but I didn't know it was going to be this."

"Wasn't exactly something I wanted to discuss."

"That's fair. Makes absolute sense."

Does it? Because it still doesn't make sense to me, but I don't say that part out loud.

"You sure you're good?" he asks when I don't respond.

"Yeah. I'm fine." I give him a tight smile, and I wonder if he can tell I'm trying to convince us both. "Tell Auden I'll let her know, yeah?"

"Yeah, man. Of course. No pressure either way."

I believe him when he says it. "Appreciate it."

He dips his head, then moves for the exit. But instead of walking over the threshold, he pauses and turns back to me. I brace myself, waiting for whatever he's about to say.

"Fox was right when he said we're like brothers. You might not feel it, but we do. We're only worried because we care about you. And we're here for you. All of us."

I don't know if it's because I'm a bit emotionally raw with the events of the last two days, but I'm struck with the sudden urge to hug him.

I ignore it, nodding instead. "Thanks, Hutch. You're…you're a good guy."

If he's surprised by my words, he doesn't show it.

Instead, he says, "You're a good guy, too, Keller. One of the best, even if you pretend you're not. Whatever is going on with your wife, you'll get it sorted. Love is messy. It's never perfect. And sometimes it takes giving up on it for us to find it again."

Then he walks away as if his words didn't just smack me right in the chest. I stare at the spot he occupied for a long time, trying to figure out if I'm willing to give Chloe up if it means feeling whole again.

When I still don't know the answer minutes later, I push to my feet and grab my chain from my stall. I slip it around my neck, poking my finger through the wedding band that sits on it for just a moment before tucking the metal inside my shirt. I might not know what the future holds for Chloe and me, but I do know no matter what, where we're living or if we're on the same continent or not, she's still my wife.

And I'm not giving up on that just yet.

I lied to Hutchinson. I'm not fine. Not even fucking close.

I am so damn keyed up with anxiety and uncertainty that I'm quite literally bouncing on my heels to get back on the ice. Music pumps through the speakers—a playlist curated by Lawson—and everyone is in a good mood as we prepare for battle with Edmonton.

Winning a game is exactly what I need right now. I want to smash bodies and get hit and leave everything out on the ice. I *need* it if I want to get rid of this anxious feeling that's eating me alive right now.

"You good?" Locke asks from beside me. "You're extra quiet tonight."

I huff. "I'm fine. Can you stop fucking asking me that?"

"Sure. Can you stop sighing every two seconds, unfurrow your brow, and not jiggle your knee up and down?"

Fuck, have I really been doing all that? I hadn't noticed.

"Sorry," I mumble, dragging a strip of tape around my calf. "Pre-game jitters, that's all."

"Right."

It's a single word, but it's clear he doesn't believe me.

I don't believe me either. As much as I want to be out on the ice and as much as I want to be fully in this game, I can't stop thinking about meeting Chloe for coffee tomorrow. I have no idea how it's going to go. Are we going to fight? Will we sit in silence as we have so many times before? Or will it magically feel easy, and we'll figure out all our problems with one conversation?

I finish taping, then set the nearly empty roll aside and settle back into my stall.

"I'm guessing you're distracted because of…" Locke looks around the room, making sure nobody is listening in on us. They aren't. Most of them are either off in their own little worlds, or they're watching Lawson try to chug as many bottles of Powerade as he can in three minutes. I have no idea how many he's on, but I already know he's going to sit on the bench bitching about how he has to pee. "Chloe."

I nod. "Yeah."

"That makes sense." He drags a hand through his gray-speckled hair, then shakes his head. "Shit, man. I have no idea how you managed to keep that secret for so long. I bet that had to be eating you alive."

"Nah, it was easy. I *really* didn't want Lawson all up in my business."

Locke laughs lightly. "Don't blame you there." He looks over at me. "How are you feeling now that we all know?"

"Like I still don't want Lawson all up in my business."

This time, he doesn't laugh. He just watches me carefully, and it has me squirming under his gaze because I swear he can see through all the false bravado I'm putting on.

My knee bounces hard, and this time I actually notice I'm doing it. I put my hand over it, trying to stop it, but it's pointless. It's like my body has a mind of its own. I need to relieve this anxiety I have somehow. I itch to call my brother, but I don't have time, especially not before a game. I guess talking to Locke will have to do.

I sigh. "In some ways, it's a relief. But in others, it's the complete opposite." I wait for him to react, but he doesn't. He just sits there, listening. Then so many words tumble out of me that I never thought I'd say out loud. "I didn't want you guys to know because that would have meant I'd have to explain it, and I don't know how to explain. Not just to other people, but to myself. What's going on between Chloe and me…I don't know what it is. I was happy. I thought she was happy enough, too. But now… shit, I'm questioning everything. Was she just pretending? And if so, for how long? Was our whole marriage built on her trying to make me happy? Or was there a time when she truly was? When did it change? When did *we* change?" I exhale shakily. "I just don't know."

"Have you told Chloe all of this?"

I shake my head. "No, and that's because I can count on one hand the number of times we've actually spoken on the phone since we officially separated, and I didn't think that was a conversation we needed to have over text."

"God, can you tell Lawson that, too? I swear, he texts me the most random shit. Sometimes literally. He'll just send a GIF of like Elmo on the toilet, then follow it up with ten links to random articles about retirement or 'How to Live to Be 100' or something."

"Glad to know it's not just me he does that stuff to. Minus the old-people stuff, obviously."

Locke narrows his eyes at me for the joke at his expense, but he has to expect it by now, especially since he's pushing forty and there's a good chance he'll hang up his skates sometime soon.

"No, it's not just you," he says. "But he means well, you know."

"Meaning well would be him losing my number, and since he hasn't done that yet, I really just think he enjoys being annoying."

"He likes you. He cares about you. We all do."

"Jesus fuck, you sound like Hutch now. Did you guys rehearse this shit?"

Locke laughs. "Uh, no. But it should tell you something that we're all saying the same things, eh?"

I'm about to say something snarky when his phone buzzes. His face lights up as he looks at the screen, and I know right away it's his girlfriend calling him. He eyes me, like he's afraid I'm going to break down if he doesn't give me attention, and I roll my eyes.

"Just take the fucking call, old man. I'm not *that* fragile right now. I'll be fine."

He hesitates just long enough for his screen to go black, then he's rising from his stall and marching away to call his girl back. I can't help but reach for my own phone, wanting to do just the same. Then I remember I don't have a girl, not really.

Still, I find myself pulling up the texts between Chloe and me. I scroll back through the ones we sent yesterday and bypass those that were exchanged over the last three years until I reach a time when things weren't so damn complicated between us.

There are silly pictures and emojis and GIFs…I love yous. There's a stark contrast between then and now, and I'd do anything to get back to before. I contemplate sending her a text now, but I have no idea what I would even say. Can't wait to see you tomorrow? Hope you're doing well? I wish you were here?

Fuck, that last one hits hard, probably because it's the most honest one. I *do* wish she were here. I've almost forgotten how good it feels to have someone in the stands cheering for you. I'd do anything to have that back.

"All right, boys," Coach Smith says, and I look up, surprised to find most of the room at attention, like they were expecting this.

I wasn't. I was lost in a time when things felt so much easier than they do now.

"We've got a tough game tonight. We need those two points, and we need them cleanly, you know what I mean?" A round of cheers goes up, and I hope like hell we mean it. Overtime hockey is not an option tonight if we want to take the top spot in the Pacific. "But we can do it. I know we can. I feel it in my bones, and I need you to feel it too. That means put whatever bullshit you have going on outside the rink in a locked box somewhere and focus on what's on the line tonight." He looks right at me, and though I haven't spoken to Coach since Chloe came back, I get the sense he knows exactly what's going on with me. "Let's get out there and play, huh?"

"Heard!" the room says before clapping twice.

I don't miss how Coach's eyes linger on me for another second before he leaves the room, handing things off to the captain to get us hyped. It makes me wonder if someone said something to him—perhaps Hutch—or if he's just that tuned in to us and I didn't realize.

Either way, it has me shoving all thoughts of Chloe aside and forcing myself to be in this moment right here. We have a game to win.

Chapter 9

CHLOE

Callum is late.

Or maybe he's just not coming. I'm not sure which one it is, but I am sure I don't like the voices in my head telling me it's the latter.

We agreed to meet at a shop called The Coffee Spot, which had rave reviews, but we haven't spoken since. It's odd, waiting for my husband like it's a business meeting. It all feels so…cold. Definitely not like two people who have been married for almost a decade.

Sitting in my hotel room last night, knowing he was only a few minutes' drive away, just about killed me. But he played a good game, one of the best I've seen from him in a while, outside of their game in Vegas last week, when he got the black eye that looks like it's almost done healing.

Still, I wanted to be there for him. I was *this close* to buying a last-minute ticket, then I saw the price, checked my bank account, and laughed. So I took my tablet and the bottle of wine *Seattle Daily* had sent "for my troubles" to the tub and settled in to watch the game. The Serpents won, and it wasn't by a small margin either. 5–1 was the final score, and Callum assisted on two of the goals. I'm surprised my neighbor didn't report me to the front desk for all the noise I made for each point he got.

I tap my fingers against my phone, which is sitting on the table in front of me, and check the clock for the umpteenth time: *2:10*. Callum is officially ten minutes late. *Five more minutes, Chloe,* I tell myself. *Give him five more minutes. If he doesn't show, then you'll have your answer.*

Four minutes later, I see him running down the sidewalk, and a breath of relief whooshes out of me. His long legs eat up the concrete, and that chain he's taken to wearing in the last few years bounces beneath his shirt with every step. Even mid-sprint, he looks good, and I briefly wonder if he spent as long as I did agonizing over what to wear. It doesn't look like it with his jeans and a simple light blue long-sleeved shirt.

He skids to a stop just before the door, and I smile as he runs a hand through his hair, pushing the pieces back into place as he stares at his reflection in the shop window. He's nervous too, and something about that eases my own worries.

Finally, he pulls the door open, then walks in with that same swagger he used to have when he'd walk into class. He looks left, then right, and his eyes snag on mine.

Thu-thump. Thu-thump. Thu-thump.

I give him a small wave, and he makes his way over.

"Hey." He pushes his hands into his pockets and rocks back on his heels. "Want a drink?"

"Sure," I answer, rising from the table and not telling him I've already had one while waiting.

He motions for me to go ahead of him, and I can barely feel his fingers ghosting against my lower back as he follows behind me. It's a small touch, but it feels bigger. It feels *normal.* Like it used to. I swallow down the emotions trying to claw their way up my throat and step up to the counter.

"Hi there." A beautiful dark-haired barista smiles at me from behind the register. "Ready for another one?"

I glance over at Callum, but he doesn't react to her words.

"Uh, yes, please. I'll take a decaf this time, though."

"Good call. Eight shots of espresso might be just a little too much." She punches my order into the tablet, then looks at Callum. "And for you, Mr. Keller?"

Does she know him? Does he come here often? It's a possibility since the shop is located smack between my hotel and his apartment.

"I'll do a butter pecan Americano with half-and-half. And two muffins, please. One chocolate and one blueberry."

I smile. *He remembered.*

I've always been a sucker for anything chocolate, and

I've been eyeing those muffins since I first walked in, especially since I haven't eaten anything today. I've been too nervous to do so. I grab my card from my wallet, ready to hand it to the barista as she rattles off our order, but it's snatched out of my hand before I even realize what's happening.

"Hey!" I protest, glaring up at Callum.

He doesn't spare a glance my way, instead handing his own card to the bubbly worker, who smiles through the whole interaction before returning the black card to my husband.

"I can buy my own stuff, you know," I say once she's busy grabbing our snacks.

"I know."

"So then why didn't you let me pay?"

"Because," he says, shoving his wallet back into his pocket, "you're still my wife, Chloe. You've never had to pay for anything before, and I'm not about to let you do it now."

He says it so simply, like it makes all the sense in the world. I want to tell him that's a sexist way of thinking, but I'm too busy trying to get my heart to calm down. *You're still my wife, Chloe.* I haven't felt like his wife in a long time, but hearing the words now doesn't make me feel like that in the slightest.

We don't speak again until we're back at the table, our drinks and snacks sitting between us, Callum's long legs barely fitting beneath the booth's table.

"We can sit somewhere else if that works better for you."

"I'm fine," he says, though I know he's full of shit as he shifts around, trying to get comfortable.

I let him have his lie, though. I'm too eager for my chocolate muffin. Silence lingers between us as we both dive in, and the only sounds are our forks scraping against the plates and slurps from sipping on our hot drinks. I would say it's because I'm so into my meal, but that's not true. I don't exactly know how to start this conversation we so desperately need to have.

But I guess Callum does, because he's the first to speak.

"Sorry I was late."

"It's no problem. Is everything okay?"

"Yes. Just Percy being a pain in my ass. He has to take allergy meds, and he didn't want to play nice this morning." He holds up a tattooed hand—one I used to love watching trace over my body—and shows off a fresh scrape along the back of it. "For only having three legs, he's still scrappy."

"Something you two can bond over, I suppose."

He pauses his fork mid-bite, tipping his head to the side in silent question.

"Because you fight a lot," I explain.

A grin curves his lips as he settles back against the booth, chewing his food slowly before he says, "You still watching my games, Clover?"

I couldn't hide the blush that creeps up my cheeks if I tried.

"Shut up," I mutter, balling up my napkin and tossing it at him.

It bounces off his chest, falling into his lap. He makes no move to get rid of it. He just sits there staring at me.

"What?" I ask when I'm unable to take it any longer.

"Nothing. For a moment there, it felt like…"

He doesn't finish his thought, but he doesn't have to. I know what he was going to say: *It felt like it used to.* He's right. It did. There was no awkwardness, no unresolved tension. It was just us.

I clear my throat, then take a sip of my coffee before setting it down. "I guess we should probably talk."

He gives a wry laugh. "Probably."

I shove my empty plate to the side and sit up a little straighter, pressing my shoulders back. I try to exude confidence even though I'm feeling anything but.

I've gotten good at faking it, though. I had to. I had grand ideas of how my internship in London would go. I would arrive in the UK, learn the public transportation system within a week at most, and make so many friends I could hardly keep up with my social calendar. I would be a different person. I could be cool and confident, and I'd finally feel like I belonged.

None of that happened, and all it did was create a bigger divide between Callum and me any time we spoke. He was still thriving without me while I was falling apart without him. It made me wonder what I was doing with him in the first place, made me question whether he'd be further in his career if not for me holding him back. Maybe he would already have a championship under his belt.

I know now how ridiculous I was for letting those thoughts creep in and plant roots, and what a mistake it was to water them. I wish I could take it all back, but what's done is done, and what's left are the consequences of it all.

Callum stacks his plate on top of mine, then takes a long pull from his butter pecan–flavored drink.

"How have you been?"

It's such a simple question, and I could give him an equally simple answer, but I don't think that's what we need right now. We need honesty, so I give him mine.

"I've been better."

His brows crush together. "What's going on? Is that guy from the bar still bothering you?"

I shake my head. "No, it's nothing like that. I just meant…" I release a shaky breath. "This is hard. Being here in Seattle, sitting here with you. Having coffee with you like we're two old acquaintances. It's just…hard."

He doesn't say anything right away, and even though it's early January and still bone-numbingly cold outside, sweat peppers the back of my neck.

I try to ignore it as I force a laugh. "How have you been?"

He takes another sip from his coffee, then sets it to the side. He folds his hands together, leaning his elbows on the table as he sits forward. His honey eyes meet my own plain brown ones, and I almost forgot how intense they can be.

"Sitting across from you and not being able to kiss you is the second most difficult thing I've ever had to endure in my life, Clover."

I'm almost positive I can guess what the first most difficult thing was.

"I'm not sure about us anymore. I think we should separate."

Though I'm sure he wouldn't believe me if I said so, that conversation pained me just as much as it did him. At the time, I believed it was for the best. Even though I've missed him more than I could explain, and despite it hurting him so much, I still think that.

"Do you want to get out of here?" Callum asks suddenly.

It's the last thing I expect him to say, but it's somehow exactly what I needed to hear.

"I would love that."

Callum slides out of the booth, grabbing both of our plates and his empty cup. I cradle my still half-full one in my hands, trailing behind him as he stops at the trash cans. He scrapes our scraps into the bin, then tosses his coffee cup into the recycling bin. His hand falls to the small of my back once again as we walk out of the shop, and I try not to show my disappointment when it drops away once we reach the sidewalk.

We walk for several blocks without saying anything, our shoulders bumping against each other every few steps. The urge to slip my hand against his and interlock our fingers just like we used to hits me like a ton of bricks. I wonder if he feels it too.

It's strange to be on the street with him and watch people recognize him and do double takes; I almost forgot what that was like. Callum leads us to a park without incident, and it's a small, yet beautiful space. The flowers remind me of the ones I spent so many hours walking between in London.

I tell him that, and he looks over at me.

"How was London?"

His question is simple, but I hear the unspoken words —*Was it worth giving us up for?*

We had talked about going together once upon a time, but the timing was always off. He was either busy training or doing something else for the team. A lot of people believe the work stops once hockey players leave the ice, but that couldn't be further from the truth. There's always something going on. Practices, meetings, appointments, charity events, content to create, things to sign. It's a never-ending task, and our lives were often controlled by obligations to whichever team Callum was playing for at the time.

"It was amazing."

Though he tries hard to act like my words don't bother him, I still see how his shoulders drop.

"What was your favorite part?" he asks.

"Probably the weather. You know I've always been a sucker for gray skies."

His jaw tightens as he nods, and I wonder if he's thinking the same thing I am—I would have loved it in Seattle, too. "And your internship? How did that go?"

"I learned a lot, especially in those first few months. I didn't even know how to use their layout program, and they gave me a ton of grief about it. But once I got the hang of things, it felt almost…" I try to find the right words to explain it. "I don't know. It felt right. I *loved* writing for an actual paper. I mean, not that I got to do a lot of it, but what little I did, it felt like it was right."

He smiles softly, sliding his hands into his pockets. "I remember watching you write in college. It was the funniest thing sometimes. You'd get this crease between your brows whenever you were really into whatever piece you were working on."

"And you'd try to smooth it down, which almost always led to…"

I don't have to finish the sentence for Callum to know exactly what I'm talking about. Any time we'd get together to study or do homework, it always ended in one way—us horizontal. Sometimes we'd simply kiss or cuddle, and other times we would bring each other to the most mind-blowing places. Everything felt so much simpler back then.

"That feels like such a long time ago," Callum says quietly, and I agree.

Sometimes when I'm struggling to fall asleep at night, I lie awake in bed and think back to those days when we felt so easy and free with each other. Back before we were married and before we were faced with real-world problems. Before I felt restless. Before I ruined everything.

"You know," he starts, "sometimes I wonder what would have happened if I had never gotten that contract with New York."

After he signed his two-year deal, he put his business degree on the back burner to go all in on hockey and make it to the NHL. All it did was prove to my parents how unserious Callum was, which didn't make it any easier to drop the news of our engagement.

"We're disappointed in you, Chloe. Giving up your education to follow some boy around is just absurd and irresponsible. You'll regret it one day. Mark my words."

My mother was wrong, though. I wasn't following some boy around. It was Callum. He was my whole world.

I eventually went back to school, and even though I wanted to change my major, I had already pissed my parents off enough, so I stuck with it and got my bachelor's in biology. If only that had been enough, but no. She still felt like I could be doing better. My father was just glad he didn't waste all that money.

Me? I was overwhelmed. We were in New York City, and it was officially the biggest city I'd ever been in. I felt it every time I left the house. I was exhausted by the constant hustle, and it didn't help that Callum was hardly around thanks to the demanding training schedule his agent had him on. I understood it because if he could prove to New York he was worth it, he wouldn't have to spend much time in the AHL at all.

And it worked. After just one season in the minors and a very intense summer of training, he was called up and put on the roster for opening night. It was thrilling to see him skate out on the blue line as they called out his name, hearing the crowd roar as he was introduced. Finally, he was where he had been trying to get to all along, and I was so damn happy for him.

But me? I was still struggling. I was missing Talia, who was busy with Ian and navigating single motherhood. I was missing a quieter, slower life. I was missing my husband.

I couldn't show it, though. I couldn't let Callum know how badly I was doing. What right did I have to complain anyway? We were living in a nice apartment, and we weren't eating cheap ramen every night. In our eyes, we had gotten everything we had ever wanted. *He* had gotten it. I couldn't ruin that for him.

"Do you?" he asks when I don't say anything. "Think

about how our lives would have turned out if I had never made it to the NHL?"

"Honestly? No." I shake my head. "There was never a doubt in my mind you'd make it, so it didn't make sense to imagine anything else."

"You always did have more confidence in me than anyone else."

I prided myself on that, too. If only I could have had the same confidence in myself. Maybe then I would have spoken up about my desires and dreams earlier. About my unhappiness. Maybe we wouldn't have gotten to the point that we did.

But I didn't. I kept it in, and I buried it, and I tried to be okay. I wasn't then, and I'm not so sure I am now.

"You would have made it just fine without me."

He stops so abruptly it takes me a moment to realize he's not walking next to me anymore. I turn back to look at him, and I'm surprised by the anger stamped over his features.

"What?"

The word is barely out before he's closing the distance between us, the tips of his pristine white sneakers touching my own worn-out boots. He's not touching me, but I can still feel his body heat radiating off him. He's standing so close I have to tip my head back to meet his hard eyes.

"I wouldn't have."

I open my mouth, ready to ask him what he's talking about, but he continues.

"I wouldn't have made it without you, Clover. And don't even bother trying to change my mind about it because you can't. I got where I am because of you. Because whenever I didn't believe in myself or the dream anymore, you did, and that was all that ever mattered to me." He drags his tongue over his bottom lip before adding, "It's still all that matters to me."

Thu-thump. Thu-thump. Thu-thump.

My heart hammers against my ribs, and I feel like I'm eighteen all over again, waiting for him to walk into class and flirt with me. I've tried so hard to rid myself of the butterflies he seems to conjure whenever he's near me, but it was always such a fruitless effort. Callum Keller will always make my heart beat in double time, and no matter what is happening between us, I wouldn't have it any other way.

He takes a step back, putting distance between us that I wish didn't exist in more ways than one, and I gulp in a breath, not realizing I needed it so damn badly. We walk a few more laps around the park before we decide to leave. Callum suggests we head back to his apartment and order something to eat, and though I know deep down I should say no and walk away because this day has already been emotionally taxing, I can't seem to stop myself from agreeing.

Because if I'm being honest, I missed this. I missed *him*. I'm not ready to give it up just yet.

"I know a spot that has the best dumplings and delivers," he says as we make our way back to his building, and my stomach rumbles at the thought of them.

Callum laughs at the audible noise. "I had a feeling that muffin wasn't going to cut it."

For a moment, I think of Dirk's words the other night when he poked fun at me for eating so much pasta. Then I remind myself that throughout the years, my eating habits have never bothered my husband, and I'm not going to let intrusive thoughts try to tell me otherwise.

He points out buildings and rattles off facts about the city—like how it's essentially built on top of another one—as we walk, and before I know it, he's opening the door to a modern high-rise. Suddenly, the idea of spending time with Callum in a confined space becomes very, very real, and my palms begin to sweat in a way they haven't in years.

I'm nervous. To spend time with my husband. How ridiculous is that?

He waves to the security guard—a different one than the other day—sitting behind the front desk, and they return the gesture, though I can't help but notice the surprise when their eyes land on me.

"Oh," the older man says. "Another guest, huh?"

"Yep. I'm ordering some food too. Should be around in about thirty minutes."

The guard nods. "Noted, sir."

Callum steers us to the elevators, and we step inside, where he presses the button for his floor, which I was on just two days ago. Images of various women stepping into this very elevator assault me, Callum looking at them the way he used to look at me. I hate it, and the thought of it makes me feel not so hungry after all. In fact, I feel like I want to puke.

I move to the wall farthest from my husband that I can get to. Taking my cue, he leans against the wall opposite me, crossing one long leg over the other. There's a soft smile playing on his lips, and it's one of those same grins he'd give me all those years ago—an arrogant one. It makes it that much more annoying that I like it.

"What?" I ask when he doesn't say anything.

"You're cute when you're jealous. You always were."

"I am not jealous." But I sound like what he's accused me of being. "I'm not," I repeat, softer this time. "Whatever you do and whoever you do it with is none of my business. I…I lost that privilege a long time ago."

He lifts a single brow. "Is that what you think?"

"It's what I know, Callum," I say, the bite back in my words, mostly because I can't stop picturing him with other women.

I hate it. I want to cry. I want to scream. This elevator is too small, my feelings are too big—and I have absolutely nobody to blame but myself. I slam my eyes closed, trying to block it all out, but it won't go away.

Something tickles my chin, and I jump at the sudden contact, peering up into two pools of cognac.

When the hell did he move over here? And why is he still smirking at me?

I try to move, but he blocks me in, not letting me run like I so desperately want to. Holding my chin between his fingers and thumb, he tips my head back ever so slightly, not allowing me to look anywhere but at him.

"He was talking about Stefan."

"Stefan?" I say my brother-in-law's name as if I've never heard it before when in fact I miss him dearly. He might be ten years younger than me, but we always had so much fun together through the years. Though I've thought about calling him too many times to count, I haven't spoken to him since right after I went to London. "He was here? How is he?"

Callum ignores my question. "Xander out there was surprised because I never have people over. Hell, I pretty much only leave my apartment for practice, game days, and going down to the lobby to pick up delivery."

Relief works its way through me, but just as quickly as it comes, that same sense of dread rears its ugly head. He didn't answer my unspoken question.

"There are no other girls. There never have been and never will be." He leans down, his lips dangerously close to my ear as he whispers, "Only you, Clover. Only ever you."

Then he's back on his side of the elevator just as it comes to a stop. Though the whole interaction feels like it takes hours, it's less than a minute, but its impact is going to last far, far beyond that.

"Are you coming?"

I look up to find him standing in the hallway, holding the door open with his arm, just a hint of apprehension in his gaze. He thinks I'm bailing on him, and truthfully, a part of me wants to.

I'm tired. These last few days have been a lot, and I could use a break from it all. I don't have many nights left in my overly fancy hotel before I have to move to a less expensive—and far less nice—one. Another soak in that big tub is calling my name.

But my heart? It says to stay. It says to fight. To see if, just maybe, we can come back from three years apart.

So, I nod, push off the wall, and exit the car. "Yeah. I'm coming."

Then I follow him into his apartment.

Chapter 10

KELLER

Having Chloe in my apartment is much easier this time than it was the first.

"How do you ever convince yourself to leave this place with a view like this?" she asks, standing back in front of the large floor-to-ceiling windows.

I watch her from the kitchen, where I've busied myself with grabbing us drinks—a Diet Coke for her and a cider for me. I try hard to save drinking for special occasions during the season, but after the day I've had, I need this. I ordered dinner as soon as we got back, and I expect it'll arrive any minute now.

"I told you, I'm practically a hermit. Leaving is a rare occurrence," I tell her as I step up beside her, handing over her drink.

"Guess that hasn't really changed over the years, then," she remarks, and I know she's referring to how I used to always decline invitations from teammates to hang. It wasn't that I didn't like them. I just liked being with her more. "Thanks."

She shakes the can at me, then takes a sip of her drink, her eyes closing just briefly, same as they always do during that first sip. I grin into my bottle of Stick Taps cider.

"You know, I think some of the worst parts of traveling so much are taking the gamble on whether a place will have Diet Coke or not. They kept trying to peddle Coke Zero, but they don't understand that it has a completely different taste."

"What a travesty," I say dryly.

She shoots me a dirty look, and I smile again. While today has been far from perfect and we've avoided a lot of things we need to say to each other, it doesn't feel nearly as heavy as it did on New Year's Day. It has me hopeful that, just maybe, things could be okay between us again, and that I could live with whatever version of a relationship that might be.

"Where's that adorable cat of yours? It was Percy, right?"

I'm surprised she remembers, though I'm not sure why. She's always been good with names. She didn't go to very many events with me over the years, but whenever she did, she'd squeeze my arm and push up on her tiptoes to whisper the names of a coach, GM, or whatever obscure alumnus was in attendance. It was my favorite part of those damn stuffy parties.

"Yes, Percy. And he's around here somewhere, I'm sure."

I don't mention it's likely the spare bedroom, mostly because the chances of her questioning that are high, and I'm not sure I'm ready to dig into that just yet.

Almost like he knows we're talking about him, Percy trots up between us, rubbing himself along Chloe's black tights that have been the focus of my attention far too many times today. I wasn't lying to her earlier when I said I was running late because of the cat. The three-legged monster was being particularly difficult when I was trying to feed him his allergy meds.

But it wasn't just that. I was nervous, more than I have been since I made my NHL debut. So much so that it took me four tries to figure out what the fuck to wear. That wouldn't be so embarrassing if my outfit were actually something to turn your head at, but it's not.

It's clear Chloe put more thought into her outfit, with her ivory sweater that looks so damn soft, a black skirt that barely kisses mid-thigh, and those damn black tights. It's a new look for her, minus the boots strapped to her feet. Those look familiar, which isn't surprising since they used to sit in every entryway we've ever had. Something about her still wearing the old, thrifted shoes makes me smile, like maybe things haven't changed as much as I think they have.

"Why, hello there, little man," she says, bending over to scoop the cat off the floor.

I try not to be surprised that she just called him by the very same thing I always do, but I am. How, after all this time apart, are we still so connected? Will it always be that way between us? Does she feel it too?

"Gosh, you're just the cutest, you know that?" she tells him, tickling his stomach. "I still can't believe you got a cat. You never wanted animals before."

"That's not true. I suggested we get a ferret once."

She scowls, just as she did the first time I said it, and I laugh.

"All right, so maybe I could have compromised a bit, huh?"

"Yeah, I'd say." She runs her finger down the cat's nose. "What made you change your mind?"

Because I missed having someone around. I missed being important to someone. I missed someone needing me.

Because I missed you.

I keep all that to myself and shrug. "I don't know. He seemed like he needed someone, and I had nothing else going on."

She eyes me warily, and I wonder if she can see through all my bullshit. Just when I think she's about to call me out, the intercom buzzes, saving me.

"That would be dinner. Could you grab some plates?"

"Yeah, of course."

I hurry out the door, and it has everything to do with needing a minute alone. While it's easier having her here now, it's still not as easy as it used to be, and I'm trying to wrap my head around it all.

I smash the button on the elevator and shake out my tingling hands as I wait for the car. I think about calling Stefan, then I remember it's Thursday, and he always goes out on Thursdays for boys' night with his friends. He's likely already three beers deep, and I need someone to talk me down, not hype me up.

The elevator arrives, and I step into it without even bothering to look for anyone else. Big mistake.

"Well, well, well…"

Fuck. I know that voice.

I look up to find Lawson—who is grinning like he's just caught me doing something I shouldn't be doing, even though I live in this building—and his girlfriend, Rory. She rolls her eyes at him, then gives me a tight smile, which, for her, is considered friendly. She likes people about as much as I do, and it will never not amaze me how she ended up with Lawson, who is the exact opposite of us.

"Hi, Keller," she says.

"Rory," I counter. I take in their nicer clothes. "Date night with Locke and Vanessa?"

"Yep. I forced him to invite us over to show me his apartment. You were right. It does look just like yours except it's, like, homey. Got a real lady's touch, you know?"

His girlfriend looks thoroughly exhausted by him. "How are you, Keller?"

"Is the wife here?"

Rory stomps right on Lawson's foot, and I grin when my teammate hisses in pain. "Please feel free to ignore him," she says to me. "He's obviously never been in public before."

"With pleasure," I respond, sliding back against the wall opposite them and closing my eyes. "And I'm fine, Rory. Thanks for asking."

"*Thanks for asking?* What the fuck is that?" Lawson says, and I don't need to have my eyes open to know Rory just smacked his stomach—I can hear it. "What? He doesn't say shit like that to me!"

"That's probably because you always say the worst thing possible."

"I do not!"

I peek one eye open just in time to see her shoot him a look that says *Are you serious right now?*

"Okay, fine. So maybe I do. But can you blame me? He has a *wife*, Wednesday," he says, using his favorite nickname for her. "A *secret* wife. That's a big deal. You can't fault me for being curious."

Not that I'd tell him this, but I can't fault him either. I would be just as intrigued if one of them suddenly announced they were married. I mean, we've had our fair share of surprises—like Hutch sleeping with a billionaire,

Lawson and Rory sneaking around, Hayes falling for his nanny, Fox and Lilah pretending to be engaged, and Locke apparently having a one-night stand with Hutch's stepsister —but a secret marriage? Yeah, that definitely takes the cake.

"I get that," she tells him. "But you can be a little more…considerate with your words."

"You're right." I *hear* the kiss he gives her. "Do you still love me?"

"Unfortunately. I'm not sure I could stop if I wanted to."

It's sickeningly sweet, but it reminds me of exactly how I feel about Chloe. Even if I wanted to stop loving her, it's impossible. She's embedded in my soul, and these last three years apart have only proved it to be so.

I open my eyes as the elevator comes to a stop in the lobby.

"How's Percy doing?" Rory asks as she and Lawson pass by. "Is he taking his meds okay?"

"Depends on the day." I lift my hand, showing off the scratch I have from our battle. "This morning? Not so much. But usually he does okay."

"Good. And he's still moving around all right? No limping or pain?"

I love how worried she is about him, even though she sees him regularly for checkups, being his veterinarian and all. "He's all good, Doc."

Her eyes narrow for only a moment before she nods.

"Well, you know where to find me if there are any changes." She tugs on Lawson's arm. "Come on. I need a sweet treat and bed."

"Anything for you," he responds, a lovesick smile plastered on his face.

He gives me one last look like he wants to say something, but I guess Rory's words in the elevator really did a number on him because he snaps his mouth closed and nods before escorting his girlfriend out of the building. It's weird and so un-Lawson-like that I almost wish he had said something.

I grab the bag of food from Xander at the security desk, then head back toward the elevator, which is already waiting for me to ascend. Just as I'm about to step inside, the front door of the building is flung open, and Lawson sprints inside right toward me.

"What the—"

That's all I'm able to get out before he presses his lips to my cheek in the loudest, wettest way possible, then pulls back and smiles at me.

"You almost forgot your kiss." He pokes my nose with his finger before saying, "Boop."

He races out of the high-rise, and I'm left standing there with a laughing Xander and a hot sack of food.

"Not a word," I threaten the doorman, and he tucks his lips together to hold back his laugh.

The ride back up to my apartment is quick, which is

good, because it leaves me little time to panic. In fact, I actually feel kind of…calm. I cling to that as I make my way back inside.

"I didn't realize you still had these plates," Chloe says as I slip off my shoes and close the door.

I already know what she's talking about as I enter the kitchen to find her setting the very '90s Disney dishes on the table. Back in college, whenever we were bored, we'd walk around the local thrift store to see what weird things we could find. It was a cheap date night, and it got our noses out of textbooks. One night, we found a *Hercules* plate, and Chloe got so excited about it that I spent twenty bucks on the thing, even though I'm pretty sure it's worth about five cents. I made it my mission to collect them all after that.

"Well, if that makes you happy…" I set the bag of food on the counter, then go to the cabinet and rifle through it until I find what I'm looking for.

"No," she says, and I can hear the smile in her voice as she moves closer, trying to see what I'm doing. "Tell me you didn't."

"Oh, I did."

I produce a full two sets of plates—one for her and one for me—and she squeals, bouncing on her heels as she claps like a little kid who just got told they'd have free rein in the candy store.

"Shut up, shut up, shut up!" she chants, and I can't

help but grin. Her reaction is everything I was looking for, making all the hours I spent searching worth it.

Then she does the last thing I ever expected—she throws her arms around me, and my entire world flips on its axis.

She's hugging me. Chloe is hugging me. *My wife* is hugging me.

She smells good, like rose water and lilac, and she feels even better. Her soft belly is pressed to me, her hair tickles my nose, and for a second, it feels like the last few years never happened.

Before I can react, it's over, and I feel emptier than I ever have before as she steps back. It takes everything in me to force myself to return the smile she's sending my way.

"I can't believe you found them all," she says, still marveling over the plates as if I'm not seconds away from hauling her back to me and kissing the hell out of her.

I clear my throat. "Yeah, me either."

"How? Where?"

"It was in Minnesota, I believe. I had some time before the game and was poking around a thrift shop when I happened across the last one I was missing." I grab the Pegasus plate and hold it up. "Collection complete."

She takes the dish from my hand. "It's marvelous. Perfectly scratched up and used. I love it."

I would hope so. I got it for her.

We settle into our chairs at the small dining area, and I try not to notice how we go for the same ones we used to sit in before—me with my back toward the door and her opposite me. She always wanted to be able to see if someone broke in.

"You'd still have to fight them off, but I'd be able to warn you," she tried to rationalize. It didn't make sense then and it doesn't make sense now, but I let it happen anyway. I'd do whatever she wanted if it meant spending an evening with her like this.

"Wow. You weren't kidding about this order," she says with wide eyes as I try to divvy things up.

"I got extras. I wasn't sure how hungry you were, but I'm starving. That muffin was the first .thing I had all day."

I pause, fearing I've revealed too much, but Chloe just laughs.

"Oh my gosh. Me too. I, uh, I was nervous for today."

I look over at her as I set a dumpling on her plate. "Really?"

She nods, pushing an errant strand of hair behind her ear. "Yeah, I mean, we haven't seen each other since…"

"The airport," I provide, remembering it well.

I didn't want her to go to London, but I *did* want her

happy, and if that meant a few months apart, then I could do it.

If I had known when I kissed her in the car sitting outside the airport that it would be the last time I saw her for three years, I would have put more into it, would have savored it more. I damn sure would have spent more time memorizing every little detail about her.

I give her two more dumplings, then put a few on my plate and sit back down. We dig into our meal, both lost in thought, and while it's not an uncomfortable silence that stretches between us, it's not a comfortable one either. It's just…there. And we're just here.

She picks up one of the dumplings, and I watch as she takes a bite. Her eyes roll into the back of her head, and the sound that leaves her could rival that of a porno.

"Holy shit," she says through a mouthful. "This might be the best damn dumpling I've ever had, and I've had a lot of them."

I grin. "I thought you might like them."

"I thought the ones at that little place we used to frequent in New York were the best I'd ever had, but I think I have to change my mind about that." She smiles softly. "Remember how the owner—gosh, what was his name? Anyway, he used to always put double in our bag because he knew one wasn't enough?"

"Kenny, and yes, I remember. He was the best."

"He was." She slaps the table excitedly. "And his

wives! We could never figure out which Amy he was talking about."

"I'm still convinced it was both. There's no way. They looked nothing alike, but I saw him kissing both."

She snorts, stabbing her hot and sour noodles with her fork. "You did not. You were drunk."

"It was the middle of the season. I was perfectly sober, thank you very much. *You* were drunk."

"Oh, I definitely was."

It was our dating anniversary, and we always celebrated it, no matter how many years had passed. Most people only care about the wedding one, but to us, that was just as important. It was the start of our relationship. Why wouldn't we acknowledge it?

"That was such a fun night," she says, this time softer, her gaze unfocused on her plate, and I wonder if she's thinking about how much easier things were back then, too.

There was hardly a time when we weren't laughing, hardly a moment where we didn't act like complete fools. It wasn't like we were irresponsible—we weren't—we just had fun together. We were friends, then lovers.

Now, I'm not even sure we're acquaintances.

"One of my favorites," I tell her, and she finally lifts her head, giving me a small smile.

"Mine too."

We spend the rest of dinner making light conversation, dipping into the past here and there but mostly keeping it light. I ask about her travels, and she asks me about hockey. It's the easiest things have felt between us, but we're still just scratching the surface. Honestly, though, I'm afraid to dig any deeper. This feels too good. Why mess it up now?

"Okay, I am full." Chloe pushes her empty plate away, then sinks lower in her chair. "That was officially my favorite meal I've had in at least the last six months."

"What was six months ago?" I ask, grabbing my own bare plate, then stacking it on top of hers and taking them to the sink.

"Date Night."

The plates fall straight to the floor, and Percy goes flying through the living room and straight toward the spare bedroom at the sudden noise.

"What the…" Chloe leaps out of her chair, rushing toward me. "Callum, are you okay? Are you hurt? What happened?"

"I'm fine," I manage to bite out. "Just…go sit back down."

She doesn't listen, instead dropping to her haunches beside me, reaching for the dishes and trash strewn around the kitchen. I'm careful to keep myself far away from her as we clean the mess.

Date night? She's been dating while I've been clinging to whatever scraps she's given me over the years just to get by? And for what? For an awkward dinner and no real answers? Her hand covers mine, and I couldn't hide its shakiness if I tried.

"It was with a bunch of girls I bonded with during the internship. We used to meet up every other week and go out. We'd dress up, have dinner, and spend way too much time listening to Taylor Swift. We called it Date Night because we were trying to romanticize our lives. That's it."

While her words calm some of the panic coursing through me, they don't chase away all of it, and that little thread of terror turns into anger, which bubbles right out of me.

"What the fuck are we doing?"

I look up at her to find her mouth agape, her coffee-colored eyes wide. "W-What?"

I shoot to my feet, and she rises along behind me, slower, and it just makes me even *more* mad because she's behind. We're not in sync. We're not *right*, and I want to be right again.

"Why am I here, worrying about *my fucking wife* dating other men? How is that even a possibility? It shouldn't be because you should be here with *me*. You shouldn't be halfway around the world or wherever the hell it is you're living now." I toss the plates into the sink, the clatter echoing through the apartment, and for a second, I worry about scaring Percy, but I can't care right now. I'm finally saying all the things I've wanted to say for too long. "We shouldn't be exchanging texts every month or two like old high school buds. We shouldn't have to guess about anything in each other's lives. And we damn sure shouldn't be tiptoeing around every fucking conversation. So, again, I ask—what the fuck are we doing?"

She opens her mouth, then closes it again, and it makes me so fucking mad I could scream. Is she ever going to actually say anything? Will she explain what happened? Will she ever tell me if I'm the only one still in this marriage? I'm tired of guessing. I need to know.

Chloe steps toward me, and I brace myself. I'm not exactly sure what for, but I do it anyway.

This is it. She's officially ending this.

Then she takes another step, and another, closing the distance between us until she's standing so close I can smell her floral perfume. She pushes up to her tiptoes, her fingers tracing over the stubble lining my jaw. Even though I'm angry, I lean into it. That's how desperate I am for her touch. How *starved* I am. How fucking badly I need her.

"Look at me, Callum."

I hadn't even noticed I'd closed my eyes. I don't know why I did. Maybe because I'm scared of whatever she's going to say next. As much as I want to know what's happening between us, I'm still not sure I can stomach the answer.

"Please," she begs, and I surrender.

Slowly, I open my eyes and look right into hers.

"It wasn't your fault I left."

Six words I didn't know I needed to hear so damn badly, and they're officially my undoing. I reach for her, or maybe she pulls me in, I can't tell, but it doesn't matter either way because my lips fall to hers, and all I can think is *Finally.* I'm kissing my wife for the first time in three years, and I feel fucking whole. It's like coming home after a long, long road trip—it just feels right.

She moans into my mouth as my tongue traces along her lips, and I don't dare waste the opportunity to taste her properly. And fuck does she taste good. A little like the dinner we just had and a whole lot like Diet Coke, and I love it just as much as I hate it.

She pulls me closer, almost like she can't get enough, and I feel the exact same way. I've kissed her hundreds of times before—possibly even thousands—but I don't think any of them have ever felt this good. My hands dig into her soft hips, and I pull her closer, needing to feel more of her. She lets me, running her fingertips over my scalp roughly. It hurts, but I welcome the pain. I'll take anything as long as it means I can keep touching her like this.

Without warning, I lift her, and she lets out a soft yelp as I set her on the counter. She used to yell at me when I did this, telling me she weighed too much for me to be picking her up. She was wrong. She was never too big for me. She was always just right, which is exactly what this feels like—*right.*

"Callum," she whispers as I drag my lips from hers to

trail them over her jaw, and hearing my name does nothing but spur me on.

I kiss her softly, then trace a path downward, nipping at her just because I can. She groans when I reach her favorite spot—the one right at the base of her throat. I roll my tongue over the place I've had my lips so many times before, and her nails scratch against me, letting me know she's loving this just as much as I am.

"I missed this," she says, and I needed to hear those words too.

I missed you. I love you. I still want you forever.

The words linger in the back of my mind, but I don't say them out loud, too afraid it'll ruin this moment, and I can't risk that. I've waited too long for it. So I kiss her more. I tease her with my lips and tongue and teeth and hands until I've touched every inch of her that I can get to, then I start over.

"Come to my game tomorrow," I say against her lips.

She nods. "Okay."

Then I'm kissing her again because I don't know how to stop. I never did, not since that first time she pressed her lips against mine in the hallway. I knew from that moment on, she was mine, and I was hers. There was no going back.

Here we are, all these years later, and I still feel the same. I inch my fingers under her sweater that feels as soft as it looks, and I know instantly it's a mistake. *Fuck,*

fuck, fuck, I chant in my mind as Chloe turns to stone beneath my touch.

Slowly—because it's the last thing I want to do—I pull away and take in the sight before me. Her lips are swollen from my kisses, and little red marks are speckled across her face. Her hair is messy from my hands, and she's breathing hard, like she just ran up two flights of stairs. None of it makes her any less beautiful.

"I should…go," she says quietly.

I nod, even though I don't agree. I don't want her to leave. I want her to stay, just like I did three years ago, but I get it. This is a lot to take in, and we still have so much left undiscussed between us. As badly as I want to take things further, stopping now is for the best.

I help her off the counter, and she asks to use the restroom before leaving. I tell her the way, then busy myself with boxing up the rest of the dumplings as she does her business. When she finally emerges ten minutes later, it tells me everything I need to know—it's not just me. She feels it too. She's just as affected by this as I am.

Chloe smiles softly as she rises to stand after telling Percy goodbye.

"Thank you for today," she says.

"Of course. Anytime." I hope she knows how much I mean those words, too. "I ordered you a car. It should be here in just a few moments."

"You…" She shakes her head. "You didn't have to do that, you know."

"I know I didn't *have* to, but I wanted to."

"Well, thanks," she says.

I offer to walk her to the elevators. She refuses. I do it anyway.

"I'm pretty sure I could have found these by myself, but thank you," she smarts off once we reach them.

I chuckle. "Just being a gentleman."

She tips her head to the side, a crooked grin on her lips. "You always were one. To me, at least."

That's because you're you. But we've already had a long day, so I don't say that. The car comes much quicker than I'd like, and as she steps inside, I have to fight every cell in my body to keep from reaching for her again.

"Will you let me know when you make it back to your hotel?" I can already tell she wants to argue about that too, so I add, "Actually, that's not a question. Let me know when you make it, all right?"

She closes her mouth, then nods. "I will."

Saying good night and letting her leave would be the perfect way to end this conversation, but I don't move my arm from holding the doors open. I can't. The last thing I want is for this night to end. I need more. I need her. And I need her to know I'm not ready to give up on us.

"I…want to see you again."

"You will. I'm coming to your game tomorrow, remember?"

"You mean it?"

"I mean it. I'll be there."

It's not the three words I want to hear from her, but they'll have to do for now.

"Good night, Clover."

"Good night," she echoes.

I finally move my arm, and just as the doors begin to close, she calls my name. I turn to her.

"I'm not ready to give up on us either."

Then the doors slide shut, leaving me standing there trying to figure out where we go from here.

Chapter 11

CHLOE

I've attended many hockey games throughout my life, including important ones like playoff-clinching matches and conference finals. While each has been nerve-wracking for different reasons, none has ever felt like this.

I walk on unsteady legs down the stairs, paying attention to the letters on the rows as I go.

"L, K, I, H," I murmur before turning into the row labeled G and shimmying down the aisle until I reach the tenth seat in. I stare out at the ice, taking it all in. This is my first time seeing Callum play in this rink, and I try to blink away tears as I think about all the games I've missed while gone.

I used to sit in the stands every night, cheering loudly, sometimes even yelling at the refs when they made a shit call. But I haven't been there for him nearly as much as I'd have liked since I took that internship that changed everything.

Music pumps through the speakers, and I grin up at the Jumbotron as the cameras pan to a little kid dancing with a stuffed snake in their hands. Their toothless smile grows before they suddenly get shy and hide behind their parent. The camera pans to another person holding a sign that reads *SEATTLE SERPENTS FOREVER*, and I grin. I missed seeing people come together like this for one common goal—to see their team win.

I remember the last game I was at, just before I left. I'll be the first to admit it was an awful one. We were in our third year in Chicago, the guys were already on an eight-game skid, just past the short Christmas break. Things were not looking good, and their hopes of getting a playoff spot were slim. I have no doubt it played a huge factor in Callum being traded to Seattle.

Tonight, though…it already feels different than that. The team hasn't even taken the ice for warmups, and the crowd is already electric. I'm sure it has to do with the franchise-record-breaking season they're having.

Or maybe it's because I'm still buzzing from our kiss last night. I still can't believe it happened, so much so that I didn't even bother telling Talia about it. What's the point if I can't be sure it wasn't all a dream? I touch my lips for the thousandth time since Callum last touched me, and I swear I can still feel him pressed against them.

Okay, so it did happen. I know it did. But it still feels like an out-of-body experience, almost like our first kiss all those years ago now. Even though it's shaken me to my core and left me even more confused than I already was, I think I needed it to happen. I needed to know if there was still something between us other than memories, and it's safe to say that is absolutely the case.

Kissing Callum again…having his hands on me…it was euphoric. There's no other way to describe it. Sitting up on his counter, his lips on mine, his fingers grazing the hem of my sweater…it was everything I've been missing for the last three years.

I maintain that time away was what I needed then, but I can no longer deny just how badly I needed my husband, too. It turns out Callum is just as integral a part of me as he was when we said "I do." I meant what I said to him, that I'm not ready to give up on us. It's the first time I've said the words out loud, but it doesn't make them any less true. The job with *Seattle Daily* might have been what brought me here, but I'm staying for him. I'm staying for me. For *us*.

"I'm just saying, they'd be fools not to play him tonight. He's a beast against Calgary, and they need the points to take first place in the Pacific."

I look over just in time to see a beautiful dark-haired woman come to a stop two seats down. Behind her is another girl with dark hair who looks almost identical to her. They're followed by two other women, each looking equally as shocked as the first one, who stares down at me with her mouth agape.

"I'm sorry. Am I in your seat?" I ask, even though I

checked the number on my app at least four times before sitting.

She shakes her head. "Yes. I mean, no, not technically. You're…"

"Is that her?" the lone blonde asks, poking her head around the others, trying to get a look at…well, me.

"Vanessa!" the one who looks like the girl directly in front of me chides. "That's it—no more date nights. You're starting to sound too much like my boyfriend."

"I can't believe you're admitting he's your boyfriend in public. I would never." The girl dressed like she's going to a cocktail party instead of a hockey game tosses her hair over her shoulder, earning a pinch from the lookalike who just yelled at the blonde.

"I'm sorry," I say, "but do I need to move?"

"What?" The woman in front blinks a few times. "No, sorry. And forgive me, I should have introduced myself. I'm Auden, Reed Hutchinson's wife." She smiles. "Well, technically not yet, but I will be soon."

Hutchinson. The captain of the Seattle Serpents. Whenever Callum got traded to a new team, I used to memorize the rosters. I never wanted to come off as a hockey wife who had no idea what was happening in her partner's life. That didn't change when I left.

"No, you aren't seeing double. Yes, we are twins," the one who looks like Auden says. "I'm Rory."

"Are you married to one of the players, too?"

"Um, no." She laughs. "But I am dating one. Lucas Lawson."

When I first left for London, Callum and I kept in touch. Sometimes we'd talk for whatever five minutes either of us could spare, but there were a lot of days when we went without speaking at all. At first, I missed him. How could I not? But then the not talking got easier, especially the more time I spent away. I was having some big feelings, and I couldn't hide them if he was there prying all the time.

Even still, I remember him mentioning a Lucas Lawson.

"He's annoying, Clover. Likely the most annoying person on the planet."

"You say that about everyone."

"I don't say it about you." A long pause. "Anyway, I'm telling you, I'm not sure I'll last a whole year with the guy."

"Just give him a chance. Maybe he'll grow on you."

"Oh, how I doubt that."

I never really got the chance to find out if it happened, but I assume that if they know who I am, Callum must know Lucas better than he did back then.

"Hi," I say, sounding like a total dork. "It's nice to meet you."

The woman dressed up and wearing sky-high heels that would kill my ankles waves. "I'm Lilah. I'm here for goalie stretches." She smiles. "And I guess the goalie, too."

"Vanessa," the blonde says. "I'm with the old guy."

"You weren't calling him old earlier when you wouldn't stop talking about how he went down on—" Lilah's words are cut off as Vanessa puts her hand over her mouth.

Auden chuckles at her friends, then turns back to me. "I'm sorry. You can ignore them." She sits down, and I follow her lead for some reason. Maybe it's because even though she looks about the same age, she seems lightyears older than me. Wiser, that's for certain. "You're Chloe, aren't you?"

This must be the other wives and girlfriends. Callum failed to mention I'd be sitting among them, and I really wish he had. My experiences with WAGs over the years haven't always been positive. Some of it was my fault, but it didn't change the truth—I never felt like I belonged, no matter how much I tried. Many of the women had kids they were wrangling—something I was never interested in—or were busy posting on social media and cultivating brand deals.

I wasn't anything like that. I was the girl who worked in a lab analyzing blood samples and hating every minute of it. And my parents hated it just as much as I did.

"You could do so much more with your degree, Chloe. Your father and I did. It feels like a waste of four years."

I wanted to remind my mother that it was actually nearly a six-year program after taking time off when Callum's hockey career turned professional, but I didn't think it would be beneficial for me. So I said nothing and kept plugging away in the lab.

Callum told me repeatedly that I didn't need to work—he was making good money at that point—but I couldn't imagine sitting around doing nothing all day. I wanted more, and that feeling is exactly what led us to where we are now.

"I'm sorry," Auden says, pulling me back to the arena. "I didn't mean to scare you and sound like a total stalker, it's just…" She slides a piece of hair behind her ear, the bedazzled Serpents jersey catching one of the lights and shining brightly. "Well, I could say it's because we've heard a lot about you, but that's not really the case. We didn't find out you even existed until New Year's Eve. Keller isn't exactly forthcoming with information, but I'm sure you know that already."

She laughs lightly, and so do I, even though I have no firsthand experience with that. He's never been guarded with me. He was always an open book, and it's one of the things I've always loved about him. It's why seeing him now is so hard because he *is* guarded, and I don't know how to handle it.

"It's nice to meet you all." I send a wave to the other girls, and they all grin—well, minus Rory. "Did you need me to move?"

"What? No!" Auden almost looks offended that I suggested it. "You belong here with us."

Except I don't.

"Come on, let's sit. We have *so* much catching up to do," she says, like we're old friends.

We aren't, but we settle into our seats anyway.

Lilah pulls a pack of Oreos out of her purse, then shakes them my way. "Want one?"

I smile and nod, instantly thinking about how Talia would love her. "They sell Oreos here?"

"Oh, no. I snuck these in. Have you seen the prices here? They're outrageous!"

She's not wrong there.

"I brought chips," Rory announces, lifting her jersey —sans bedazzling—and pulls a bag from her hoodie pocket. "But I'm not sharing."

"Nobody wants your gross chips, *Wednesday*." Lilah rolls her gorgeous blue eyes, and Rory retaliates by knocking her Oreos out of her hands.

Okay, they are officially nothing like any WAGs I've known throughout the years.

"Wednesday?" I ask through a laugh.

Rory groans. "Ugh, yes. That's me. Lucas claims I'm a real-life Wednesday Addams, hence the nickname."

At first listen, she sounds annoyed, but the smile at the corners of her lips gives her away. She doesn't hate it, she loves it—and she loves him too. I've seen that look before, on myself back in college when I was so damn smitten with Callum I couldn't stop grinning even just *thinking* about him.

"So, tell us about you, Chloe. We don't know anything."

"Other than you left a few years ago," Vanessa adds, earning a glower from the three other girls.

"Careful, you're almost starting to sound like the *evil* stepsister again," Rory says.

Vanessa shrugs. "Sorry. It's the truth, though." She sits forward, looking over at me. "I'm not trying to be mean, I promise. I'm just being honest—that's quite literally all we know about you. It took days just to learn your name."

"Have none of you ever heard of Google? I had that shit uncovered by the next day, before the guys got home from checking on Keller."

They go back and forth about what they found on Google as if I'm not sitting right there.

"Is it true that you've been married since you were twenty-one?" Auden asks.

"Uh, yeah. That's true."

Her eyes widen. "Wow. I… Well, no offense, but I just can't imagine getting married so young. That had to take guts."

She has no idea.

"You guys must have really been in love, huh?"

Yes.

I close my eyes against the single word. We were in love. So damn much that we didn't care how reckless it was to hinge our entire futures on a college relationship. We just wanted to be together.

Look how well that panned out for us.

A hand lands on my shoulder, and I open my eyes to find Auden staring at me with a sad smile.

"I'm sorry. I don't know what happened, but if it makes you react like that, whatever it is, it can't be good."

But that's where she's wrong—it was good. *So* good. It didn't matter, though. I still didn't feel like it was enough. I didn't feel like *I* was enough.

"So, I heard you were in London. Isn't it lovely there?" she says, changing the subject, and I'm grateful for it.

"I loved it. I take it you've been?"

"Oh, she's been," Lilah answers for her. "She has two hotels over there."

"*Had*," Auden corrects. "I had two hotels."

"They were your creations. They still count as yours," Rory says, crunching on another chip. She looks like she's barely paying attention to any of us, but I get the sense she's as immersed in this conversation as anyone else.

"Hotels?"

"Yes," Auden answers. "Have you heard of The Sinclair?"

My brows rise. "Um, yes. It was out of my budget when I lived there, but"—I whistle lowly—"it's gorgeous. The paper I worked for during my internship had an event there. I couldn't stop staring at the details on the ceiling. Truly a work of art."

She smiles, almost bashfully. "Well, I can't take credit for that—it was all a wonderful local artist—but I can say I was responsible for the rest of it."

"Like…as in the hotel itself?"

She nods, then holds her hand out. "Auden Sinclair, as in Sinclair Hotels."

"Holy shit." My eyes widen as I take her hand and shake it, but Auden just laughs it off. "I mean, sorry. It's just…wow. I can't believe it. I don't think I've ever met an owner of a hotel chain before. Especially not hotels like *that*."

"Well, I'm not the owner anymore. I sold the company a few years ago and now run a new one with Lilah over there." She points to the woman in question. "We design and build luxury homes, so not too far off from hotels, but on a much smaller scale."

I resist the urge to ask just how much she sold it for, but I can only imagine it wasn't cheap. Auden likely has more money in her bank account than I'll see in a lifetime, and I'm in awe being in such company…and trying to sort out why she's sitting down here to the left of the penalty box and not up in the suites.

Then, suddenly, the music switches mid-song, the lights brighten, and the crowd roars to life. Everyone—including us—jumps out of their seats.

"All right, Serpents fans!" A disembodied voice fills

the arena, the music cranking up behind it, but not so loud as to drown it out. "Are you ready to see your hometown team extinguish Calgary?"

Everyone cheers, and Auden sticks her fingers in her mouth to let out a loud whistle. Lilah, Rory, and Vanessa go just as wild.

"Then let's give a big, warm welcome to your Seattle Serpents!"

He draws out Seattle Serpents in the most dramatic fashion, and it does exactly what he set out for it to do—it gets me excited. The goalie takes the ice first, and Lilah screams so loudly next to me that I have to cover my ears. She doesn't look the least bit apologetic about it either. All her attention is on the ice, along with the other girls, and I swing mine back there just in time to see Callum jump onto it.

Though my heart is already in my throat, it tries to climb up higher, but I swallow it down. Yes, watching him on TV is nice, but it's nothing compared to being here in person. His brows are pulled in tight as he pumps his legs and zooms across the ice. He barrels right into the boards, the same as he's done every game since… well, for as long as I can remember. Then he zooms a lap around the back of the net, riding the blue line until he hits the wall again.

I smile, because for a second, it's like no time has passed at all. I watch as his eyes scan the arena, going seat by seat, and I know exactly who he's looking for—me.

One of his teammates—number eighteen—bumps his shoulder against him, and he snaps out of his search. He grabs a puck with his stick, then carries it toward the net, pulling his arm back and putting all his weight behind the shot. The vulcanized rubber disc flies, and the goalie snatches it out of the air.

"That's my man!" Lilah yells, hands cupped around her mouth. She looks over at me. "Sorry, Chloe."

I chuckle. "Don't be. It's his job."

And he does it well. I watch him stop several more pucks from other players before switching spots with the other goalie, moving toward the wall, and dropping down to stretch. Several women throughout the arena cheer, but nobody is louder than his girlfriend, and the other girls laugh at her.

I'm too busy being back to watching Callum, who is scanning the seats once more. This time, I hold my breath, begging for him to find me. I'm rewarded just moments later when his ocher stare meets mine. Instantly, his face transforms. His brows relax, and I swear his shoulders drop at least two inches. I lift my hand and wave.

He grins, even though I'm sure I look awkward, then mouths, *Hi, Clover.*

And I know in this moment that we're not done. Yes, the last three years have changed us in so many ways, but they've defined us. We're still us. We're still Callum and Chloe.

"Okay, that is *so* weird."

I look over at Auden, who is watching me instead of her fiancé.

"Sorry, it's just…I've heard Keller deny love and all things feelings for years now. But that right there? That was love, like soulmates type of shit, and there is no denying that."

I don't respond because I don't know how to. Warmups last ten more minutes, and before he leaves the ice, Callum gives me another smile. I spend the rest of the game with the same expression on my face, and it's not just him that has me grinning—it's the girls. They're fun, and I can't remember the last time I felt so welcome so quickly. We chat about my travels, and they tell me about meeting the guys. We spend just as much time gabbing as we do watching the game.

"That call was horseshit, and you know it, ref!" Rory yells during the third period when the officials make a bad call against the Serpents, sending Lawson to the penalty box.

He stands in the sin bin, then points our way while yelling something at the ref. I can only assume he's agreeing with his girlfriend, and I have no doubt a clip of the whole exchange will end up on social media later.

"Do these guys not have vision insurance or

something? What the hell was that? His stick wasn't even close to that other guy's skate. He toe-picked himself."

Nobody disagrees with her, but we're too focused on the teams gearing up for another faceoff with their best guy on the dot in the box. The Serpents are tied 4–4 with Calgary with just ten minutes to go. Needless to say, this is a huge penalty kill the guys need to pull off, and since it's been a back-and-forth nail-biter all night, it's a tall ask.

"Come on, guys," Auden says, taking a sip of the white wine she's been sipping on all night. "You got this. You got this. You got—fuck!" she yells when they lose the faceoff.

"It's okay," Lilah tells her, grabbing her hand and squeezing it. "They got this. They—what the hell! That was a blatant hook!"

She's not the only one complaining, but the protests of the unpaid officials go nowhere, and they remain 5 on 4. The entire arena sits on the edge of their seats as they battle their hearts out and block shot after shot, Callum taking the brunt of most of them. I wince when one hits him right in the inner leg, dangerously close to his knee, and he drops down.

"Oh shit. He's hurt," Auden says, as if I can't see it myself.

Get up, get up, get up, I silently chant as he struggles to regain his legs. *Come on, Callum. Get up. Please. For me.*

Almost like he can hear me, he stands and gets back

into the play. He's slow and wobbly at best, but he's able to get the job done. Half of the arena—me included—jump to their feet as the sound bite indicates that the Seattle Serpents are back at full strength, and it happens just as Hayes swats the puck up the ice. It lands perfectly on Lawson's stick, and he's off to the races for a jailbreak.

"Go, go, go, go!" Rory screams at the top of her lungs, and he skates harder and faster, putting distance between himself and the Calgary player.

He fakes a shot and the goaltender bites, going down, and Lawson zips it right over his glove. The crowd explodes, cheers ringing out, the goal song blaring through the speakers. Everyone is high-fiving and hugging like they were the ones who just scored. The players on the ice gather around Lawson, tapping his helmet before he leads them down the line so they can bump fists with the guys on the bench.

He stops at Callum, then throws his arms around him. Several other guys flock around to give him kudos for his big blocked shot and playing through the discomfort. I wish I could be down there too, only I wouldn't be hugging him or patting his helmet. I'd kiss him.

The arena settles down, but the buzz is still alive as the teams take the ice again. The puck is dropped at center, and this time the Serpents win the draw. Calgary is pissed they gave up the goal, which means they come in faster and check harder than before.

Though a casual fan might not notice it, I catch the laboring in Callum's strides as he takes another shift. He's not as quick as usual, wincing through a few hits he takes. When there are just over two minutes left, Calgary gets possession, and their goaltender hustles toward their bench as another player comes on.

The Serpents don't let it change their game, and they quickly get the puck, then zip it down the ice toward the empty net. The goal horn goes off again, and much to Vanessa's delight, it's Locke they're all gathering around to congratulate.

"God, I'm going to miss this when they're away," Rory says.

I hadn't even thought about Callum leaving. They're hitting the road for a 5-game trip tomorrow, and the idea of not seeing him for that long makes my heart ache, which is funny, all things considered. What's going to happen while he's gone? Will we talk? Will we put our marriage on pause again? Is that what he wants? Is that what *I* want?

No.

The word rings loudly in my head, and I realize it's more honest than I've been with myself in a long time.

"Do you want to come with us?" Auden asks, pulling me out of my head.

"Where to?"

"We're going to the green room, then meeting the

guys. It's Friday, so we'll probably end up at Top Shelf for a bit."

Though I hoped for it, Callum and I didn't discuss getting together after the game, and I have no idea what I'm supposed to say. I want to see him—of course I do—but does he want to see me? I wish we didn't have so many questions hanging between us, but I have nobody to blame but myself for that.

Auden notices me hesitating and leans in close.

"He'll want you there. I know he will."

It's all the reassurance I need.

"Okay, I'll go."

She throws her arms around me suddenly, squeezing me tightly. It all happens so fast that she's letting go before I can register what's going on.

"Ahhh! It's going to be so much fun. All the Serpents Singles and their partners who make them not-so-single under one roof. It's perfect."

She stands, and I follow behind her, Vanessa leading us down the aisle.

"Serpents Singles?" I ask when we reach the top of the stairs.

The four girls exchange looks, and it's obvious I'm out of the loop about something.

Lilah's the one to speak up. "Uh, yeah. Hutch, Hayes —whose girlfriend isn't here tonight since she's on kiddo duty, but you'll meet her eventually—Lockey Poo"—that earns her a look from Vanessa—"Lawson, Keller, and

Fox all made a…well, I think it depends on who you ask what it is."

"A club," Rory says with a secret smile, almost like it's an inside joke, but I'm not sure who it's between.

"A pact," Auden amends. "They promised each other they wouldn't start any serious relationships and would give all their focus to hockey until they hoisted the Cup together." She giggles. "It's silly, I know. Even funnier now since we know Keller has been married the whole time and so clearly head over heels for you."

"I should have known something was up," Rory says, tossing a chip from her second bag of smuggled-in snacks into her mouth. She doesn't bother swallowing before she adds, "He who doth protest too much or whatever the hell that saying is."

The other girls laugh, but I don't. Is that how Callum has been since I left? Does he no longer believe in love? Does he not believe in forever? Does he not believe in…us? He sure as hell didn't kiss me yesterday like that was the case, but maybe I imagined it. Maybe it was just a sex-starved man who was hoping for more.

Stop it, Chloe. He loves you. He's still your husband.

I try to block out the thoughts, but it's hard to as we make our way to the green room, the area designated for family. We sit in there for a bit, waiting for the guys to finish all their obligations. We watch on the screens as the three stars of the game—Locke, Lawson, and Fox—toss snakes into the crowd, then a few players address the media.

We make our way to the hallway just outside the locker room, and finally, after what feels like hours, the Serpents file out. Callum is staring at the ground, his brows pulled in tight, and his shoulders dropped low.

"Oh shit," Lawson says, and his girlfriend hisses his name. "What? The dude has been sulking in the locker room since the game ended. He's going to be so happy. Right, Kells?"

He lifts his head at his name, and that's when it happens—his eyes lock on mine, and all my worries from earlier vanish.

"Clover." His smile is so wide it's almost disarming as he walks toward me. "I was worried you left."

I thought about it, I want to tell him, but I don't.

"I didn't. I'm right here."

"Good, because that's exactly where I want you."

Then he kisses me in front of everybody.

Chapter 12

KELLER

If I thought it was strange to have Chloe in my apartment, it's nothing compared to having her in my car.

"Well, this is certainly new," she remarks as she runs her hand over the dash. "When did you get this?"

"When I got to Seattle. In retrospect, it was a terrible idea given how hilly this damn place is, but it sure is fun to drive when I find the right routes to take."

"It's beautiful," she says. "I remember you used to always talk about getting a sports car. I'm glad you finally made it happen."

I bought it to fill the void she left behind, but I'm afraid if I say that, I'll ruin the good mood I'm in. Despite my leg burning from that slap shot I blocked, I'm happy. We won tonight, securing two more points we really needed, and Chloe is in my passenger seat. How could this night get better than that?

"That was a good game tonight. Thank you for the tickets."

I'm taken aback by her words. She never used to thank me for them before. They were just there, waiting for her, and she was always in the stands waiting for me.

"It's no problem. I'm glad you came."

"Me too."

I want to reach over and hold her hand just like I always used to when driving, but I keep my hands on the wheel.

Having her back there tonight after so long felt like the beginning of so many pieces clicking into place. I'll admit I was bummed when I saw she wasn't in her seat after the final horn sounded, but all that changed when I stepped out of the dressing room and she was standing there. I even kissed her; I just couldn't stop myself. I'm sure the guys will give me crap about that once we reach the bar, but I'm willing to take it tonight. I'm riding a high I haven't felt in a long while.

"Want to see something fun?" I ask.

"If it involves you speeding down a city street, then no."

I frown. "Boo."

She giggles, and it reaffirms that it's my favorite sound in the world. We ride the rest of the way in silence, and I pull the car into a parking garage that charges an exorbitant price, but I pay it anyway. She meets me at the front of the car after I back into a spot, and I try not to let it bother me that she didn't wait for me to open her door like she used to. At some point, I need to stop comparing our past with our present, and I might as well start tonight.

This time, I do grab her hand as we make our way to the bar up the street, and I don't bother to hide my grin when she leans into me.

"It's about time! We were ready to send the cavalry!" Lawson shouts as we walk into the bar. "Were you guys making out again?"

I steel myself, waiting for the rest of the guys to join in and give me grief for kissing her, but they don't. Before I can tell him what a dumbass he is, Chloe speaks up.

"We weren't even making out before, but it's lovely to officially meet you, Lawson."

His brows rise in surprise. "I like you." He looks at me, then points at her. "I like her."

I squeeze her hand. *I like her too.*

"All my friends call me Lawless, just so you know."

"Oh my god! Nobody calls him that!" Rory calls out as she makes her way over to us from the bar, two drinks in her hands. She stops next to Chloe. "Please, feel free to ignore my boyfriend. He nicknamed himself and won't let it go."

"That is not true! Nessa over here calls me it."

"She only did that *once*, and it was because she was new and didn't know better. We're teaching Chloe right." Rory looks at me and nods. "Keller."

"Rory."

Chloe laughs. "You two are a lot alike, aren't you?"

"Aw, come on, Chlo," Lawson says, slinging his arm around her neck, causing her to drop my hand. I miss it instantly. "Don't say things like that. It makes it sound like I'm dating the lady version of Keller, and that's just wrong."

"I happen to think it sounds nice," she tells him, and pride swells in my chest. "He's not so bad."

"Nah, you're right. He's pretty cool, even if he does make fun of me. Say, did I tell you about that time I forgot my underwear during a road trip? Picture this," he starts, waving his hand as if he's painting said picture, "there we were, six days in and…"

I don't catch the rest of it since he drags Chloe away, but it's probably for the best, or else I'd have to yell at him all over again for asking to borrow my boxer briefs. I stand with my arms crossed as I watch him take her over to the group at our usual table and introduce her in a way only Lawson could.

"Guys, this is Keller's wife. The *secret* wife."

"That's quite a mouthful. Chloe is fine," she says, holding her own, then she greets everyone individually.

I smile as I watch her integrate herself into the fold with ease, like she's always been here. There's an ache in my chest thinking about all the times like this that we've missed out on, but then I remember there's a chance I wouldn't even be here if she hadn't left. I joined their "club" because she was gone.

Would I have done that if she hadn't walked out? Or would I have spent my time at home with her and missed getting to know my teammates as I do? I think there's a good chance it would be the latter, and surprisingly, I don't like that answer. I like spending time with her. It's my favorite thing in the world, but is there such a thing as being *too* attached?

I look over at Chloe, who is laughing at something Lilah is saying. Is that…is that what broke us? Was it too much? Was *I* too much for her?

"How's the knee?"

I glance up to find Hutch standing beside me. "Good," I tell him.

"Liar."

I give a low chuckle. "Yeah, probably. But I'll live."

"Good." He looks over to Chloe, who is now chatting with his stepsister. "Seems like she's fitting in nicely."

He has no idea how much I need to hear that. "Yeah, she does."

"You look happy."

His words shouldn't rattle me, but they do. Am I happy? In ways, yes. Having Chloe here feels like a dream come true. But am I also trying to temper all expectations and remain cautious, mostly because I'm afraid the rug will be ripped out from beneath me at any moment and she'll leave again? Definitely. It's a shit way to live, but it's all I have.

Hutch's big hand lands on my shoulder, and that's all he says before he makes his way over to them, introducing himself to my wife.

My phone buzzes in my pocket, and I pull it out to find a text from my brother.

Stefan: THAT BLOCKED SHOT HOLY SHIT MAN

Stefan: Your knee okay?

Me: Hurts like a motherfucker, but I'll be all right.

Stefan: Fuck yeah man

Stefan: How's it going with YOU KNOW WHO

Me: She came to my game tonight.

Me: And you can say her name, you know.

Stefan: WHAT THE FUCK

Stefan: Who are you and what have you done with my brother????

Me: Fuck off

Stefan: Luv u bro

Stefan: I'm still here

Me: I know. Love you too.

"Hey."

I look up to find Chloe striding toward me. "Hey. You want a drink?"

"Actually, a Diet Coke sounds perfect."

"One Nasty as Hell coming right up."

She gives me a side eye, which might be effective if she weren't smiling as she does it. I lead her to the bar and place an order for a Diet Coke and a Sprite.

"You got it," the bartender says.

"And put it on Lawson's tab," Chloe tells him. I raise a brow at her as I lean against the bar, and she shrugs. "What? He said drinks were on him tonight."

I have a feeling he never uttered those words, and I can't help but laugh.

"Glad to see you're learning already."

She smiles. "Your teammates are really nice. The girls are, too."

"Yeah?" I ask, and even I can hear the excitement in my voice.

Though she always tried to hide it, I knew Chloe had trouble fitting in with the wives and girlfriends of my past teammates. It always seemed like they had nothing in common, and they couldn't connect no matter how many times they tried. I hated it. I wanted her to feel that same sense of camaraderie I did. She deserved that, and she definitely deserved a closer friend than Talia, who was all the way in Tennessee and could only visit every so often since she was busy being a single mom.

"Yeah," she confirms. "We had a lot of fun during the game. And I got to learn what a grump you're known to be."

I've never been the best with people, but something certainly changed when Chloe left, and I became an even worse version of myself than I'd ever been before. I knew it was a problem—hence the Serpents Singles vow—but I was too pissed off at the time to care. I care now, though, and that has everything to do with Chloe being back.

"Yo!" Two hands land on my shoulders. "What a block, number 10! What a fucking block!"

The overwhelming smell of booze tickles my nose, and since we're standing in a bar full of it, that says something. I try to shake the unfamiliar meaty palms off me, but they're strong, and the person they belong to is obviously drunk as he tries to shoulder in between Chloe and me.

"Excuse me. Can't you see I'm trying to talk to my man? Get lost, lady."

I push off the bar in a flash, and the guy—whoever the fuck he is—goes stumbling backward. He trips over his own feet, barely catching himself on a table to keep from falling to the sticky floor.

"What the…" His features darken. "What the hell, man? I was just trying to talk!"

"No, you weren't. You were invading my space." I take a step toward him. "And you were being an asshole."

He scoffs. "What? To her?" He waves Chloe's way. "Who fucking gives a shit about her?"

"Considering she's my *wife*, I do."

His eyes widen, and he holds his hands up. "Shit, man. I-I-I'm sorry. I-I-I had n-no idea. I didn't mean anything by it, bro. Swear." He looks at Chloe. "I'm sorry, Mrs. K-Keller. Trul-ly."

"Yeah, well, you can be fucking sorry outside. Get the fuck out."

"I—wait, you can't kick me out!"

"Yes, he can," the bartender says, pointing toward the door. "Now get out before I call security and have you removed."

The guy starts to say something else, but I take another step toward him, and he thinks better of it. He turns on his heel and practically runs out of the bar, or at least the best a drunk person can.

I swing around to Chloe. "Are you okay?" I ask her, cupping her face. "Did he hurt you?"

"No, no. I'm good. Are you okay?"

"Huh? Yeah, I'm fine. Don't worry about me. I can hold my own."

"Oh, I'm aware, Mr. Leads the Team in PIMs."

I wince. I'm usually proud of that title because my not being afraid to drop the gloves gives my team an advantage, but I know she always hated it when I fought. She used to fret over me, panic about the bruising. She would—*wait a minute.*

"How do you know that?"

"What?"

"How do you know that? How do you know I lead the team in penalty minutes?"

"Oh." She shrugs. "I, uh, I watched your games. It was a real pain to keep up with them with the time zone differences, but I always tried or watched replays the next day."

"I was only teasing you at the coffee shop, but…you really watch my games, Clover?"

She nods. "Yeah, I really watch your games, Callum."

I don't think—I just act. Not caring about waiting for our drinks, I grab her hand and pull her to the only private place I can think of in this damn place. I don't stop, even when people cast curious glances our way. I keep going until we're tucked safely into the dark corridor leading to the bathrooms, then I back her against the wall and press my body against hers.

"What are you—"

"I want to kiss you again. Can I?"

She laughs. "Why are you even asking? You didn't earlier when you kissed me in front of your teammates."

"That was different. I was…"

"What?" she pushes when I don't finish my sentence. "Claiming me?"

"Yes," I practically growl. I know how ridiculous that is, given that they're all in committed relationships, but it's true. I want everyone to know she's mine…while she still is.

I slip my hand over her cheek, loving how she presses into my touch like she can't get enough of it. I can't get enough of her either.

"Tell me yes, Clover."

"Of course you ca—"

I devour the rest of her words with my mouth, slanting my lips over hers, and she melts into me. This time, I don't hesitate to slip my fingers beneath the Seattle Serpents shirt she's wearing because I need to touch her right now, or I might just die.

She groans as I do, and her soft curves feel like heaven under my fingers as I wrap my hands around her hips. I tug her to me, all while pressing into her, because no matter how close we are right now, it's not enough. She must feel the same, because she grabs my arms, her nails digging into me like she's silently begging for more.

I give it to her. I tilt her head, pushing inside her mouth, and our tongues slide together in sync like they've done this before—and they have. My cock grows hard against the zipper of my jeans, and there's no way she doesn't feel it pushing against her. She lets out a soft noise and sinks her nails in even deeper. She's as eager for more as I am.

I trace my fingers along the waistband of her jeans, wanting so desperately to dip them inside and see if she's wet for me, but I don't. Not here. Not now.

Not *yet*.

"You're perfect," I tell her as I pull away, my lips barely grazing hers. "I missed this."

"Me too." She runs her hands higher, slipping them into my hair and pulling me back down to her. "Kiss me again."

I do. I've never been able to resist her, and I don't see the point in trying to do it now. Just like I'm not able to resist touching her.

Maybe just a little bit, I tell myself as I slide my hands higher.

She shivers under my touch as I cup her heavy tit, loving how the lace of her bra feels against my hand. I can feel her pert nipple under the material, and I brush my thumb over it just because I can. Chloe hisses, and I grin against her.

"Callum…"

"Yes?"

"Do you want to—"

A loud, booming laugh cuts her words off, and I wrench my mouth from Chloe's to find Locke standing ten feet away. I move in front of her, making sure she's covered up even though things hadn't even gotten that far.

"I'm sorry, but this is just too fucking funny."

"Can I help you, *old man*?" I practically spit at him.

He laughs, unfazed by my ire. "Say, remember a few months ago when you walked into this very hallway and found Vanessa and me in a compromising situation? Ironic now, no?"

"First of all, nobody says 'compromising situation.' This is exactly why Lawson makes fun of you for being old. Secondly, she's not my captain's stepsister. She's my wife, so can we have some damn privacy, please?"

"Callum?" Her hand lands on my arm, and she squeezes. "It's okay. We, uh, we should probably stop anyway."

But I don't want to stop. Kissing her last night was fucking magical. It shook loose something inside me that's been festering for far too long, and kissing her now feels just as good. I want to do it more, but with her brown eyes pleading for me to let it go, I do. With a sigh, I push off the wall and step aside, but not before checking to make sure her shirt is back where it needs to be.

Locke laughs.

"What?" I snarl with a glare.

He only laughs harder. "Just never thought I'd see the day Callum Keller lets a girl talk him off the ledge."

It's fair for him to say that, but what he doesn't know

is she's not just any girl. She's *the* girl, and I'd do anything she asked of me.

"Mind if I take a piss?"

I step aside with an eye roll. "Be my guest, old man." But my words have no real bite to them, and Locke doesn't miss it.

He brushes past us, shaking his head with a smile, and I turn to Chloe once he disappears into the bathroom.

"Are you okay?" I ask.

"I'm good. Are you?"

"Yeah. Why?"

"Uh, that was…intense. What happened?"

I lift a shoulder. "Nothing I don't deserve. After I caught him with Hutch's stepsister, I gave him a lot of shit about it. Like, *a lot*. It's retribution for that."

"This team has a lot of secrets, huh?"

I laugh quietly. "You have no idea, Clover." I take her hand in mine, tugging her closer. "Come on. Let's get out there before Lawson skulks back here and I have to beat up my own teammate."

"I've heard it work before. Teammates scrap at practice, then they end up winning the Cup. Could be a good idea."

"I'm sorry, do you *want* me to fight?"

"Uh, no. Or maybe. I don't know. It's been a while since I've seen it in person." She lifts her brows up and down. "Could be hot."

"As tempting as that sounds…" I grin and pull on her hand again. "There are other things I want to be doing right now."

"Oh? Like what?"

You. I want to be doing you. I want to kiss you and touch you and remind you that you belong to me.

"What do you think about coming home with me?"

I wish I didn't notice how much she hesitates, but I do. Her eyes, which were just so bright, dim, and she sinks her teeth into her bottom lip.

"You know what? Never mind. Forget I said anything. I—"

"Yes."

I tip my head to the side. "Yes?"

"Yeah. Let's go."

I've never claimed to be a smart man, but I know when to leave well enough alone, so I don't question this and proceed to drag her out of the darkened hallway. We say goodbye to everyone, which takes way too long, then we slip into my car and head back to my apartment.

We're quiet on the ride, and the silence isn't nearly as easy as it was on the drive to Top Shelf. I wonder if she's thinking about the implications of inviting her over. If so, she has nothing to worry about. I have no expectations of what's going to happen. I simply don't want this night to end.

When I pull into the parking garage and shut off the rumbling V10, she doesn't make a move to exit the car.

I turn toward her. "Clover…"

It takes longer than I'd like for her to return my stare, and when she does, I wince internally.

"I just want to spend more time with you. I'm not asking for anything else. And if you want me to take you back to your hotel, I'll do it. Just say the word. I won't be mad, I promise."

Her shoulders sag in relief, and I'm unsure if I should be offended or glad. I want to ask her if she's scared of me, us, or letting herself get close again, but I don't. I just wait for her, which is exactly what I've been doing for the last three years.

"I want to stay."

They're the exact words I want to hear. I waste no time helping her from the car, and we make our way up to my apartment. Percy meows loudly as soon as I push the door open.

"Hey, little man," I say, bending down to give him attention, but he goes right past me and jumps into Chloe's waiting arms.

"Hi there," she coos, nuzzling her nose against his. "Did you miss me, Percy?"

Meow.

He snuggles into her more, and the scene makes my heart ache because we could have had this all along. We could have been a family. We—*no.* I have to stop thinking about the what-ifs. That's not our reality, and it doesn't matter anyway. It's not like we can get those years back. All we can do is move forward.

I shove all those thoughts away as I take off my shoes, then move to the kitchen. I grab Chloe the Diet Coke she never got at the bar and a water for myself. I take an ice pack from the freezer, and without even having to ask what I need, Chloe makes her way to the couch. I join her there, noting that Percy sits in her lap instead of mine, and I cue up something on the TV just for background noise.

"Oh my god, are you seriously still watching this show?"

"What?" I ask innocently, setting the ice pack against my knee, and though it's cold, it feels damn good against the bruise that's already formed. "It's a comfort."

"How many times have you seen it now?"

"I'm not sure you want to know the answer." I hit play on the last episode I was watching, and the faces of Claire and Phil Dunphy fill the screen. "I love this one."

"Is it the one where they catch their parents doing it?"

I grin at her phrasing. Even after we were married for many years, Chloe was still always so nervous when it came to talking about sex.

"Yep. 'Caught in the Act.' An absolute classic."

She rolls her eyes, but she wiggles down further into the couch, getting comfortable. Out of habit, I reach over and grab her legs, pulling them onto my lap.

"Oh, that feels so good," she says as I press my thumb into the arch of her left one. "I can't remember the last time I had a foot rub." Her eyes fall closed. "I forgot how exhausting games can be. I don't know how you do it all the time."

"Because I love it, Clover. Now rest."

She doesn't argue, and that's how we stay—me rubbing her feet, *Modern Family* playing in the background, and Percy purring away. It's the perfect night, and I wouldn't trade it for anything.

"No, no. Don't. Please. Stay. Just stay," I beg, reaching for her.

She shakes her head, backing away until she's just out of my reach. "I can't. I have to go."

"But…why? I don't understand why. Just tell me."

"Because—"

A loud roar, almost like a train going far too fast, rushes through my head, and I can't hear anything else she says, even though I'm desperate to.

"Chloe?" I call out as the distance between us grows. "Chloe!"

But it doesn't matter how many times I shout her name. She slips farther and farther away, everything behind her falling into shadows and darkness until there's nothing left at all, and it's just me staring into the abyss.

"Chloe!" I yell again. "Come back! Please! Clover!"

"Callum!"

My eyes fly open, and Chloe stands over me, her eyes wide and filled with worry. It's dark, and it takes me a moment to realize where I am and why my wife is hovering over me, why my heart is hammering inside my chest harder than it ever has before, all playoff games included.

"I was dreaming."

Chloe frowns. "I kind of figured. Are you okay?"

"I…"

But I don't finish the sentence. I can't. The words aren't there, and even if they were, how am I supposed to explain to her that I was dreaming about her leaving, and it's not the first time?

So, I say nothing. I just reach for her, pulling her down onto my lap. She gasps as she falls against me, but I don't pay any attention to that. All I care about is holding on to her, so that's what I do.

I wrap my arms around her, pulling her tighter against me. At first, she sits there stiffly, likely trying to figure out what the hell is going on, then finally, she relaxes, sagging against me. I sigh in relief as I bury my face in her neck, inhaling her perfume and coasting my hands over her body.

She's real. She's real, and she's here.

I repeat those words over and over as I work to draw in deep breaths and calm my racing heart. I'm not sure how long it takes, but the pounding in my ears finally subsides, and I feel like I can breathe without having to think about it. Chloe must feel the tension in my shoulders release, because she pulls away, and the look she gives me is enough to send me into another panic attack.

She's scared. Terrified even. Me fucking too.

Her soft hands slide over my cheeks, and I lean in, savoring the heat and the familiarity of them.

She's real, and she's here.

"Are you okay?" she asks softly.

I nod, then swallow the lump that's settled in my throat. "I'm okay."

"What just happened? That feels like more than just a dream."

"It felt like more to me too."

Her lips pull down again. "What were you dreaming about?"

I shake my head, not wanting to tell her. We've had such a good night together, and I don't want to ruin it now.

"Please," she asks. "Tell me. Don't shut me out. We've—*I've*," she amends, "done that enough. We need to talk, no matter how badly it hurts."

I want to point out that just like in my dream, she's yet to explain exactly what caused her to walk away from me, but I don't. I'm not sure that's a conversation we should have tonight. We aren't ready. Not yet.

But she is right that we need to talk. We used to be so good at it, until…

I run my tongue over my dry lips. "Water?"

She nods, then reaches behind her to the coffee table where we set our drinks before falling asleep. I take the bottle from her hands and down the rest of it in less than five seconds. It's not enough, but it'll do for now. I run the back of my hand over my mouth, then meet her worry-filled stare.

"You left me again."

Everything about her changes in an instant. Her shoulders slump forward, her eyes are no longer filled with concern, and she tries to scramble away. I don't let her, grabbing her hips and holding her still on my lap, a place she used to spend a lot of time.

"Hey, hey," I say, pulling her chin my way and forcing her to look at me. "Don't run. *Please.*"

It must be just the word she wants to hear, because she stops fighting me and settles back on my lap. That's when I see them—tears.

"Come on." I brush away the wet streak running down her cheek. "Don't cry. You know I've always hated it when you cry."

Her soft laugh is cut off with a sniffle. "I'm sorry. I just…" She exhales shakily. "I'm sorry, Callum. I'm so fucking sorry."

Shit. The sadness and pain in her words damn near break me, and I wrap my arms around her, pulling her against my chest, where she starts to cry even harder. I hate it so damn much, but there's nothing I can do. I can't tell her it's okay because it's *not* okay, and *I'm* not okay. And I can't tell her it's not her fault because, in a way, it is.

So I don't say anything at all. I just hold her and rub her back, and I fight the tears stinging my eyes. When she's finally calmed down, she pulls away, wiping off the wetness on her cheeks.

"I'm sorry."

"I know," I tell her. "I know you are, Clover."

Her lips rise just slightly at my nickname for her, and it's enough for me for right now.

"Does this…" Another trembling breath. "Do these dreams happen often?"

"Yes." Even though she looks like she's about to cry at my answer, I don't try to change it. "And sometimes it's not just when I'm dreaming. I…" I run a hand through my hair. "I've had a few panic attacks too."

She closes her eyes, her bottom lip trapped between her teeth so tightly they lose their usual blush color and turn white. I pluck it free, and a lone tear falls as she looks at me again.

"I haven't handled them alone. Stefan's helped me."

She nods, her chin wobbling. "I'm glad he was there…and I'm sorry I wasn't."

"I know," I repeat. "But there's nothing we can do about it now. So no more tears, all right?"

Another nod, and I tug her to me again just because I want to. Because I *need* to. We sit like that for a long time, so long I fear she's fallen asleep again.

"Hey," I say, and she stirs. Her face is red and splotchy, her eyes still glossy as she peers down at me. "It's late. We should probably get some sleep. Road trip starts tomorrow, remember?"

"Right." She pushes off my lap, and I miss her heat the second she slips away and stands. "I should go."

"Go? What? No. It's"—I grab my phone from the table and check the time, ignoring the waiting text— "damn near three o'clock in the morning. You're not going anywhere."

"But I—"

I shake my head. "No. No buts. You're staying."

She wants to argue but thinks better of it. "All right," she concedes. "I'll take the couch."

I give her a look that says *Be so fucking for real* just before I swoop her up into my arms.

"Callum!"

She protests, trying to wiggle free, but I ignore her.

She blows out a puff of air. "I think you somehow managed to get even more annoying while I was away."

"Yeah, well, maybe you shouldn't have left, huh?"

She gasps, shocked as hell that I just said that, and honestly, I'm shocked too. It's the most raw and honest thing I've said to her since she got back. But maybe that's just what we need—to be brutally truthful with each other.

Once the shock wears off, a laugh bubbles out of her, then another and another until she's giggling uncontrollably. It makes me laugh, too.

"You're ridiculous," I say as I carry her into my bedroom, glad I left my bedside lamp on before I left. I drop her onto the bed ungracefully before going to the dresser.

"Here." I pull out a t-shirt and chuck it at her. "You can sleep in this."

True to her unathletic skills, she misses it, and it lands right on her face. She giggles as she peels it away, and even though it's been a heavy night, it's still my favorite sound in the world.

"Am I allowed to use the bathroom on my own, or are you going to carry me in there too?"

I move like I'm about to do just that, but she darts off the bed, locking herself in my en suite. The second she's gone, the smile fades from my lips, and I scrub my hand over my face.

"Fuck," I mutter to myself as I sit on the edge of the bed, exhaustion setting in. From the game, the last few days, the dream…everything.

I'm tired down to my bones in a way I haven't been since before Chloe left, back when things between us felt…off. I could never put my finger on what it was, but

I knew we weren't one hundred percent. I didn't think it would lead to what it did, but I guess all the signs were there. I just never thought to look at them.

I press my fingers around the bruise on my knee, checking it out. It hurts like a son of a bitch, but it's nothing I haven't been through before. I'm sure it's going to suck for a few days, especially being on the road, but I'll pull through. Speaking of going on the road…

I pull my phone from my pocket and check the text from earlier.

"Is everything okay?"

I whip my head up to find Chloe standing in the bathroom doorway. The Seattle Serpents t-shirt I gave her hugs her in all the right places, clinging to her plush curves and soft belly rolls and hitting just under her ass cheeks. She's fucking gorgeous, and I have to fight the urge to march across the room and fuck her right where she stands.

"Callum?"

I give myself a shake. "Huh? Oh, uh, yeah. Well, no." I hold up my phone. "My pet sitter won't be able to cover Percy for a few days. Apparently, their whole house is sick."

"Oh no. That sucks."

I nod, my eyes falling to where the t-shirt sits tight against her thighs. I swallow roughly. "Yeah, it does."

"I can do it."

I force my stare back to hers. "What?"

"I can do it," she repeats. "I can take care of Percy for you."

"Are you…sure?" She's already nodding. "He's a pain in the ass and requires allergy meds daily. It can get a little dicey sometimes."

She laughs, crossing the room and stopping right in front of me. I squeeze my phone in my hands to keep from reaching out and checking to see if her thick thighs are as soft as I remember. "Oh, I know. How is your cut, by the way?"

"Doesn't even hurt," I tell her. I completely forgot about my scuffle with Percy while trying to give him his meds until just now. "Are you sure you don't mind taking care of him?"

"Are you kidding me? I'd get to hang out with a three-legged cat and get covered in cat hair. It sounds like the perfect day to me."

"All right. But only if you really don't mind."

She lifts her eyes skyward, then circles her arms around my neck. "I don't. Let me do this for you. *Please.*"

It's the same word that undid her earlier, and it has the same effect on me now.

"Okay."

"Good." She presses a kiss to my forehead. "Now that that's settled…"

Then she practically skips to the bed. She pulls up the blanket and slides into the side farthest away from the door, and the familiarity of the scene almost knocks me down.

"I can't sleep next to the door. What if someone comes in and…and…I don't know! What if they try to touch my butt?"

"Then they're going to get a handful with that big thing."

"Hey! I thought you liked my big butt!"

"No, Clover, I love your big butt." I kiss her cheek. "Now go to bed."

From that day on, even in hotel rooms when I was alone, I slept nearest to the door.

"Callum? Are you okay?"

I look over at her, the comforter already pulled up to her chin as she snuggles into the bed.

"Yeah. Sorry." I point to the bathroom. "Be right back."

I hurry away before she can say anything else and lock myself inside. I stop in front of the sink, resting my hands on the countertop as I pull in breath after breath. I'm about to sleep next to my wife for the first time in three years. I shouldn't be nervous. I shouldn't even be thinking twice about it, but here I am.

It's just sleep. You'll be fine. You'll be gone tomorrow, and you'll have some space to sort out everything you're feeling. Just get through tonight. I tell myself that—or a version of it—over and over until I start to believe it.

I quickly brush my teeth and throw on the same sweatpants I wore to bed last night before padding back out to the bedroom. Chloe's eyes are still open, and she's staring at the door, almost like she's afraid I wouldn't come back. I give her a soft smile, then make my way to my side and flip the bedside lamp off. I slide into the bed beside her, and almost instantly, she scoots closer. I lift my arm, and she fits herself against me like it's exactly where she belongs.

Her hand lands on my chest, close to the chain I have dangling around my neck, but she never touches it. I get the sense she wants to ask questions, but I'm grateful when she doesn't. We lie there in the dark for so long I think she's fallen asleep.

Then she says, "I'm still sorry, Callum."

I squeeze my eyes closed, then hold her closer. "I know, Clover. I know." I press a kiss to her forehead. "Get some sleep."

She sighs but nestles deeper beneath the covers, her grip on me tightening, almost like she's scared I'm going to slip away in the middle of the night. I'm just about asleep when she says three soft words.

"I missed you."

It's the last thing I remember before drifting off into slumber.

Chapter 13

"Ugh." I groan, pressing the heels of my hands into my eyes. "Did I ever tell you how much I hate learning science-type stuff? It is *so* boring."

We're sitting on Callum's bed, me on my stomach and him resting against his pillows at the other end, three textbooks spread out between us. Even though we're studying, it's our date night, something we don't get to do often now that his hockey schedule is ramping up like it is. He's been working hard this season, and the right people are taking notice. If he keeps this up, his dreams of playing professional hockey could happen sooner than he expected.

I couldn't be happier for him, but I also can't help but worry about what it could mean for our future. Even though Callum and I have been dating for almost a year now, I'm still not used to it. We're two different people on very different paths, but so far, things have been working well between us. *Really* well, actually—so damn well it kind of scares me. Are you supposed to find your person so young like this? According to my parents, no. To say they weren't happy when they found out I was dating Callum would be an understatement.

"You're there to focus on your studies, Chloe. Not boys."

This was from my mother, who has always hated the idea of me dating while still in school.

"Your education is more important than a college fling. Did you read that article in The New York Times*? It says we're on track to finding a cure for cancer in the next twenty years. A miracle!"*

While I'm proud of his research and what he's doing to advance medicine, I didn't have the heart to remind my dad of the number of people who will still die from the disease between now and then. Or that what I have with Callum is far more than just a fling. I don't think he would have taken that well.

They want me to focus on school, which makes sense, since they didn't meet until way after college. They're why I declared my major in biology. It felt like the natural path, but now that I'm almost a year into my studies, I can firmly say this is not what I want to be doing the rest of my life.

Callum laughs as he rests his hand on my ankle, almost like he can't *not* touch me. "You've mentioned that a time or two. Remind me again why you're majoring in biology and not writing? You're killing it on the paper."

I *am* killing it on the paper. I've had the most front-page stories out of anyone else on the team, and there's been some talk of making me editor next year, a position a junior hasn't held for a long time.

But that doesn't matter in the long term, so I shrug and flip yet another page I briefly scanned over, not comprehending a single letter of it. "Both of my parents are scientists."

"So?"

Of course he doesn't get it. His focus is on hockey. He says all the time that he doesn't think he'll get offered a contract, even though he was drafted by New York, but I think he's wrong. Sure, my opinion might be a bit biased, being his girlfriend and all, but I thought Callum was a good player well before we started dating. It's going to happen for him. It's just a matter of when.

Instead of answering his question, I close my heavy textbook and shove it aside, rolling onto my back and propping myself up on my elbows.

"Let's take a break."

He raises a brow, a smile playing at the corner of his lips. "We just took a break twenty minutes ago."

"And now I've worked for twenty minutes. That deserves another break, doesn't it?" I pout, pushing my chest out a little more.

Callum growls lowly, then tosses his business law textbook to the floor before crawling on top of me and burying his face in my neck. I howl with laughter as he alternates between wet kisses and gentle bites.

"Shhh," he says into my ear. "Do you really want my roommates to barge in here?"

"You did lock the door, didn't you?"

He pulls away to look down at me, and I miss him instantly. "Yeah, but those knuckleheads will just see that as a challenge."

I giggle because he's not wrong. They've already had to call maintenance to replace a smashed door once because one of the guys was drunk and thought there was a bear inside. I don't think they're looking for a repeat of that incident.

"Guess we'll just have to make out quietly, then, huh?" I tease, and he launches at me once again.

His lips go from the crook of my neck to the spot at the base of my throat that always makes me ticklish before he drags them up and over my jawline. Then, finally, my lips. I've kissed Callum a lot since that day in the hallway, but somehow, every time feels like the first time all over again.

Right now is no different. His lips move over mine as if they're memorizing my mouth, and I slide my hands through his hair, tugging him closer like I'm unable to get enough.

And honestly, I'm not.

"Fuck, Clover," he says as he pulls away. "You taste so good, you know that?"

"I taste like Diet Coke."

He grins against me, nuzzling his nose to mine. "I think you might be turning me into a fan."

I laugh. "That's a lie, and we both know it."

"No, it's true. It's growing on me."

"Hmm. Is it that or do you just really like kissing me?"

"I just really like kissing you, Clover."

Then he does it again, this time his tongue sweeping into my mouth. I get lost in him, forgetting about everything else, like the biology test I'm supposed to be studying for and the article I still need to write for the school paper. I forget it all and allow myself to relish the feel of his body pressed against mine and his tongue doing things that have no business feeling so good.

I slip my hands under his shirt, loving the way his skin prickles beneath my touch, and lightly drag my nails up his back. He groans into me, and I do it again. Then he's gone, wrenching his mouth away, his forehead pressed against mine.

"You're killing me," he says, his breath coming in sharp. "You feel good."

"Me? You feel good."

I reach up, needing to kiss him again, but he pulls away.

I frown. "What's wrong?"

"Need a minute," he says like he's barely holding on, which sounds ridiculous since we're only kissing.

But that's just how things are between us. Even kissing can feel like so much more. I'm sure it doesn't help that we've not had sex yet.

Yes, we've been together for nearly a year, but we've been content to take our time. And, okay, maybe it also has to do with the fact that every time we get close, he pulls away. There's always an excuse, and in the moment, they sound like good ones, then later, when I'm lying in bed, frustrated and needing relief, I can't seem to find an actual reason we don't go through with it.

Other than me.

"You know," I say, trying to keep my voice light, "you could give a girl a complex if you keep holding out on her like this."

Callum opens his eyes, pulling his head back to look at me. "Are you trying to pressure me into sex, Clover?"

"What?" I laugh. "No. I mean, yes. I mean no. *No.*" I say it more firmly this time, then shake my head. "I guess…I don't know. I'm just trying to find out *why.*"

"Why what?"

"Why won't you…you know, go all the way with me?"

His whiskey-like eyes darken just a shade, but it's enough to have me swallowing roughly. Still, I push on.

"Is there…something wrong with me? Something wrong with us?"

"Is that what you think?" His voice is barely above a

whisper and hoarse, like he's been screaming at the top of his lungs for hours.

He pushes away from me, and I miss his heat so much I wish I had never said anything at all. He resumes his spot against the headboard, running his hands through his hair before adjusting his very obvious boner. I sit up, putting my own back against the wall and picking at a spot on the blanket that could probably use a wash.

"I mean, yes? What else am I supposed to think?"

He doesn't say anything right away, and I try hard to pretend I'm not dying on the inside over his lack of answer.

"Clover."

I don't look up. I can't. I'm too afraid to.

"Clover," he says again.

I keep picking at the blanket, blinking away the tears threatening to spill down my cheeks.

"Chloe."

It's my undoing. I pull my head up, meeting his stare, and I'm surprised by what I see in it—fury. He's…mad? At me?

"It's not you." He says each word slowly, like he's begging me to actually hear them. "It's not you, Chloe."

A breath rushes out of me, and I had no idea I was even holding it in.

"Then what is it?"

His brows inch inward, then he's moving before I can

even comprehend what's happening. Suddenly, I'm moving too, right into his lap, my legs on either side of his as he cups my face with his hand. He opens his mouth, then snaps it closed again. I have no idea what's happening, but I'm too afraid to move as he traces his thumb back and forth like he's memorizing the freckles that dot the tops of my cheeks. Then finally, he speaks.

"You deserve better than a quick fuck in my room, okay? Especially when I constantly have people going in and out of my apartment. When we have sex for the first time, I want it to be special. Because *you're* special to me, Clover. In a big damn way."

While Callum hasn't shied away from telling me how he feels about me, we've still never uttered those special three words to each other. This is certainly the closest we've gotten. There is no part of me that doesn't believe I'm in love with him, but I'm far too afraid to say it out loud and make it real.

What if he doesn't feel the same? What if I'm lightyears ahead of where he's at? Yes, he says I'm special to him, but that doesn't automatically equal love. What if this isn't the start of forever like I thought?

"Hey," he says softly, tucking his finger under my chin and forcing me to meet his eyes again. "Where'd you go?"

"I'm right here."

His eyes fall to slits, like he doesn't believe me, but there are no follow-up questions, and I'm thankful for it.

Thinking all those things is one thing, but putting a voice to them gives them power, and that's the last thing I want to do. So, I tuck all the thoughts away deep inside my brain where I can analyze them and replay them later.

His lips pull up into a sly smile. "You know, Clover, I hadn't realized you were so eager to get in my pants."

My eyes widen. "That is *not* what I said!"

"No?"

He squeezes my hips, his fingers inching under my shirt. While we still haven't had sex, we have fooled around a little, mostly just Callum putting his hands under my shirt and a hand job in the dark of night. So when he drags his hand up and cups my breast, it doesn't surprise me, but it does stir something inside me that's been building over the last several months.

"It might not be what you said, but it's what you want, isn't it?" He flicks his thumb over my nipple that's already hard, and I gasp. He laughs darkly. "That's what I thought."

"You're so mean." I groan when he shoves my bra down and does it again, this time with the pad of his digit against my bare skin.

"Maybe. But you like it."

"Shut up," I grumble, but my words have no venom behind them, especially not when my hips involuntarily move, my body seeking friction of some sort.

Callum notices, just like I notice how hard he is.

Feeling brave—or maybe just needy—I swivel my hips, and this time it's him gasping.

"Fuck. *Shit*," he curses, his hand that's still on my hip tightening. "Do that again."

I do. Then again and again. His thumb brushes against me with every move, and it feels so damn good I might just burst if something else doesn't happen soon.

"Fuck," he mutters. His eyes are glassy as he stares up at me, and his cheeks are getting redder than I've ever seen them before.

No, that's not true. I've seen him like this one other time, when we were in his car and I had my hand wrapped around the hard member pressed between my legs. I want to make him feel as good as he did then. I grind against him again, and this time he lets out another string of cuss words. I'd laugh if I wasn't feeling the exact same way.

He yanks me to him, his lips finding mine as he rolls my nipple between his fingers, his tongue plunging into my mouth. I roll my hips against him as he kisses me like he never has before, and he plays with my nipple. It's so simple yet so damn good, and I teeter closer and closer to the edge of an orgasm.

"You're killing me," he says again when he pulls away. "I'm so damn close."

"Me too."

"Then get there. Do what you need. Come on my

lap, Clover. I can't think of anything else I want more." He chuckles lowly. "Well, I could think of one thing…"

I want to tell him he could have that *one thing* right now if he wanted, tell him I'd lie back on his twin-sized bed and let him have his way with me until the wee hours of the morning, his roommates be damned, but I'm way too chicken to actually say it.

So, instead, I get brave in a different way. I slide my hand between us, right into the waistband of my leggings, and I press two fingers against my clit.

He inhales sharply, his nostrils flaring. "Holy fuck." He snaps his eyes to mine. "Are you touching yourself right now?"

I nod, drawing a small circle around the sensitive bundle of nerves.

"Shit." He drags his teeth against his bottom lip. "What does it feel like? I need to know how it feels."

"It's…good."

He laughs. "I know that, but I want more. I need details." He kisses me hard, then pulls away just as fast before dragging his lips to my ear. "Tell me what your cunt feels like, Clover."

He sinks his teeth into my neck, and I gasp. Not just because he's being far from gentle and I like that much more than I could have anticipated, but because I've never heard anyone utter that word in real life before. I've read it in a book, and it was said once in a video on a website I had no business being on, but never in person, and certainly never from Callum.

"Say that again."

"What?" he asks, licking across the spot where he just had his teeth.

"That word."

He pulls back and looks up at me. "Cunt?"

I groan, and his eyes spark with something I can't quite name.

"Oh, Clover," he murmurs, laughing lowly again. He ghosts his lips against mine. "I want to hear how your cunt feels. Can you tell me? Can you tell me how wet you are for me? Can you tell me how your fingers feel pressed against you?" He spreads his legs more, and my thighs go along with him. "Can you slide inside that pretty little pussy of yours and finger yourself until you're making a mess all over?"

I nod and do just that, my eyes closing as I dip two fingers into myself.

"Ah, ah, ah," he says. "Open your eyes. Look at me. Talk to me."

I run my tongue over my lips and draw in a deep breath. "I… It's warm."

"Warm. Mmm. What else?" He kisses the corner of my lips. "What else does it feel like, huh? Is it as tight as I imagine?"

"Yes," I gasp out. "It's so tight. I can barely fit two fingers in there. I don't…" I moan as I grind my hips against my hand, my palm brushing my clit. "I don't know how you're going to fit down there. You're so… big."

"Oh, don't you worry about that. I'll fit, I promise you." He kisses the other corner of my mouth. "What else does it feel like?"

"Wet. I'm *so* wet. It's kind of embarrassing."

"No, it's not. It's beautiful, Clover. Don't ever be embarrassed about that. Not with me. Understood?" I nod, and he kisses me again, this time on my chin. "Give me another one. Tell me more."

"I…" I groan when he pinches my nipple again while biting at my neck. "I don't know. It's hard to concentrate when you're kissing me like that."

"*You* think it's hard to concentrate? You're in *my* lap right now, and you're fingering your sweet little hole that I can't wait to stretch around my cock. I think I win in the 'hard to concentrate' competition."

His words light a fire inside me, and I pump my fingers harder and faster. I need to come. *Now.*

"Callum…I'm close."

"Good. Me too." He kisses my favorite spot. "So come on. Make a mess."

It's all the permission I need. In an instant, I'm spasming around my own fingers as I work them in and out, my orgasm racing through me so hard my legs begin to shake. Callum lets out a loud groan, and it's all the warning I have before I feel the wetness seep through his jeans. There's an obvious wet spot on them when I look down, and it's all I need to see to know he's just as satisfied as I am right now.

We untangle ourselves, Callum putting my bra back in its place, but I don't move off his lap. Not yet.

He cups my face, holding my hair off my sweaty neck. "How was that for a study break?"

A laugh bursts out of me. "Not too bad. Want to take another?"

He grins, then kisses the tip of my nose. "Go study for your biology test, Clover."

In all the fun, I almost forgot about the exam I'm supposed to be cramming for, the one for the class I don't even want to be in.

His finger finds the wrinkles between my brows, and he tries to smooth them. "You know you don't have to follow in your parents' footsteps, don't you?"

"You try telling them that."

"Okay, I will. They already hate me, so it's not like I have anything to worry about."

While they haven't met in person yet, only via video chat, it's safe to say my parents aren't too fond of my boyfriend.

"They don't hate you. They just don't understand you. You're a hockey player, and that's not their thing. They're…"

"Super smart and I'm just a big dumb jock?"

I scowl at him. "No. You're just from two different worlds, that's all."

"Well, it's okay if you're from two different worlds, too. If you don't want to study biology, don't. Be a writer. That's what you really want. Chase it."

I've thought about it more times than I can count, but that's the exact reason I can't do it. What if I try, graduate, and am not good enough to get a job in the real world? Or what if I don't even make it through my first year as an English major? Or what if it ends up taking me away from Callum? We already have so much stacked against us with his hockey career taking off like it is. I don't want to get a job across the country and lose him entirely.

"Biology is what I want," I assure him.

He frowns but doesn't argue. Instead, he pats my butt and says, "All right. Then I guess you have a test to study for. And I have a mess to clean up."

Reluctantly, I climb off his lap, laughing as he grimaces at the wetness and awkwardly walks to the bathroom across the hall. I lie back on his bed with a smile, trying hard not to let all my doubts ruin the high from my orgasm, but it's a pointless effort.

They're there, and they're there to stay.

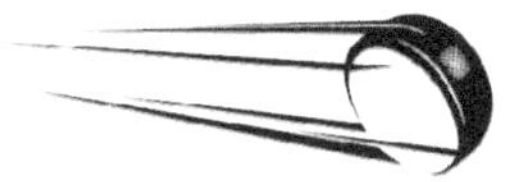

I hug my jacket around me for at least the fifth time tonight, then pull my dress down, but it doesn't budge. I silently curse Tally for making me wear the damn thing, but that's what I get for asking my best friend for help picking an outfit for my date tonight.

"Stop showing me jeans. You're not wearing them," she said as *I held up the eighth option of our video chat.*

"Uh, yes, I am. I'm going to a hockey game."

"You're not getting banged for the first time in jeans, Chlo. Wear the skirt. Or better yet, the dress."

"Oh my god, we are not having sex tonight!" I insisted.

"Yes, you are. I'm telling you, I have a feeling."

I huffed. "You're ridiculous."

"So? Now go shave your legs."

I rolled my eyes and told her she was being preposterous, but the truth was, I had hoped she was right. I even let myself get all worked up over it as I got ready for our night out. I felt so silly getting dolled up for a hockey game, and now that I'm sitting in the bleachers, I know I was right to feel that way.

A group of girls sitting two rows below me turned around and snuck a glance at me. I've officially lost count of how many times they've done it.

"Is she seriously going to come to all *his games? Like, can she not take a hint? He plays so much better when she's not in the stands."* That wasn't true. He's even said he plays better with me here.

"I bet she's wearing the biggest size jersey they sell." I wasn't,

not that it should matter if I were, but their words still hurt because it was just another reminder that I wasn't good enough for Callum or his world.

"He's just fucking her because he feels bad for her. That's all." Considering my virginity was still intact, that one made me laugh.

I pretend I don't notice their stares and snickers and focus on the ice, where Callum just jumped over the boards for his shift. He pushes his legs hard, catching up with the play easily, and I hold my breath as he checks an opponent hard into the glass. The guy doesn't take too kindly to it, and he gets right in Callum's face. I can see their mouths moving, but I can't make out what's being said.

It doesn't matter, though, because suddenly Callum shoves on his back, and the other player goes sprawling to the ice. The rink explodes, half the people cheering, the other half wanting a penalty as the training staff runs over to check on him. It takes a few minutes, but he gets up on his own, and the away team gets the call they were looking for. The home crowd boos as they announce that Callum has to sit in the box for five minutes.

"I'm telling you, she's a curse on him," one of the girls from earlier says loud enough for me to hear.

But that's not what has my attention. I'm too busy watching my boyfriend in the penalty box, his head hanging low as his team goes down a man and has to fend off a five-minute power play. Much to the team's dismay, it's a brutal five minutes, with the other team scoring twice and officially taking the lead. They're unable to recover, and the game ends 5–3 with the win going to the out-of-towners.

I can tell Callum's mad as he skates off the ice, and I try to rack my brain for what could have happened while I wait for him outside the building. I watch his other teammates leave as I stand there, a few of them sending me glances, but nobody says anything to me. They hardly ever do.

When he finally comes walking out thirty minutes after the game ends, his hockey bag slung over his shoulder, he spots me immediately and walks my way. He moves in to kiss me, but I turn my cheek. I have way too many questions to let myself get distracted by his kisses.

"Everything okay?" he asks.

"Um, no. What the heck happened out there? What was that?"

"It was nothing," he says, grabbing my hand and tugging me toward the parking lot. "Are you ready? We don't want to be late. The restaurant won't hold our table much longer."

"Okay, I know, but, Callum…tell me what happened. You didn't cross-check him like that for no reason."

"It wasn't a big deal, Clover. Just hockey stuff."

Except he's not looking me in the eyes as he says it. He's lying. I stop, and since he has his arm slung around me, he stumbles, barely catching himself.

"Shit, Chloe." He moves to stand in front of me. "Are you okay? What's wrong?"

But I don't say anything. I don't need to. Callum knows.

He sighs, pressing his fingers to the bridge of his nose. "Come on, Clover," he begs quietly. "Can't you see I don't want to rehash it? I just want to move on and have a good night. We have reservations, remember?"

I know we do. It's our first anniversary. How could I forget marking the best day of my life so far? But in this moment, I don't care about it. I just want to know what was so bad that he took that penalty.

"What did he say to piss you off?" I ask him. "Was it…" I gulp. "Was it about me?"

He closes his eyes, and it's all the answer I need. It's just like those girls who were whispering about me earlier. I had really hoped bullying would be left behind in high school, but that hasn't been the case since we began dating. At first, I thought I could handle it. It was a few comments here and there, usually about how "he could do so much better." But as the months went on and people realized it wasn't just some fling, things got worse.

I think the worst part was that while I *knew* it was because the girls were jealous that I was Callum's girlfriend and they weren't, it didn't matter. The words still stung and planted themselves in my brain to the point that I almost started to believe them. Then he would give me one of *those looks*, and everything would be okay.

Right now, though, it doesn't feel okay.

"What did he say?"

Callum closes his eyes. "Please don't make me repeat it."

"Why not?"

"Because it's not true!" he explodes, tossing his hands into the air. "It's not fucking true, and I don't see the point in discussing it anymore. Now, come on. I want to go to dinner with my girlfriend."

He reaches for me again, but I sidestep him.

He growls. "Clover…"

"No, don't *Clover* me. If you're going to speak, you had better be telling me what was said out there that was so awful you got a five-minute major and cost your team the game."

"I should have done more to him than just cross-check him. I should have beaten his skull in. I should have killed him. I should have…"

He closes his eyes again, working his jaw back and forth, and I wait. I'm not going anywhere with him tonight until I know what has him so mad. If I'm going to be the reason he loses a game, I want to know what was said. Then he opens his mouth, and I hold my breath.

"He said…" He opens his eyes, then sighs. "He said,

'She must give one hell of a blow job because I wouldn't be caught dead with a girl like that.'"

A girl like that. He doesn't have to elaborate on what that means—I know.

A girl who is good enough for him, who fits the standard for hockey girlfriends of tall, blonde, and slim, which is the total opposite of me.

He looks sick repeating it, and I feel sick hearing it. It's somehow exactly and not at all what I was expecting at the same time. I hate it. I hate this moment. I hate that my eyes are burning with unshed tears, and I really hate that Callum lost a game because of me.

This is all my fault. I knew I wasn't good enough for him from the start, and now I've cost him a game.

"No, no," he says, dropping his bag and taking my face in his hands. "Don't cry, Clover. Please. I can't stand to watch it, especially when that fuckhead isn't worth your tears." He swipes his fingers under my eyes, catching the ones that have already fallen. "Especially when it's not true. Okay? It's not true. Don't listen to him. Don't listen to any of them."

It's the first time he's ever acknowledged the whispers I've been hearing for months. I had no idea he knew about them. Why has he never said anything before? Or has he, just not to me but to them? He's been hanging out with his teammates and roommates less and less. Is that…is that because of me?

"Come on." He picks up his bag, grabs my hand, and pulls me toward his car.

"Callum…" I tug on his hand, but he doesn't stop. "I know you were excited for tonight, but I really don't feel like going to dinner right now."

"We're not going to dinner."

"Then where are we going?"

He doesn't answer, just opens the car door, and because I feel so wrung out right now, I climb in without question. We don't talk as he drives to I don't even know where. I don't have a car, so I haven't explored Denver much since moving here, and I'm surprised when he pulls into a hotel parking lot and backs into a spot.

"What are we doing here?" I ask as I unclick my seat belt.

"I'm proving to you just how much it's not true."

He helps me out of the car and leads me into the hotel lobby, and in a daze, I let him. He checks us in—he apparently already had a room reserved—and we make our way to the elevators. We stand inside the car in silence, our hands linked together, a soft jazz song playing overhead. I want to ask him so many questions, but I don't even know where to start.

When we arrive on our floor, I let Callum pull me out and into the hall, which feels so small as we make our way down it. He stops in front of room 1010 and holds his keycard up to the scanner. It turns green, and I expect him to rush inside, but he doesn't.

He pauses, exhaling a long breath before he turns and looks at me—*really* looks at me—for the first time since he finished his game.

"We were supposed to come here after dinner, our bellies full of pasta and dessert. I was supposed to hold your hand on the drive over, and I was going to kiss the hell out of you in the elevator, Diet Coke breath be dammed." He smiles softly. "But I ruined that."

I open my mouth to argue with him, but he shakes his head.

"I did. It was my fault." He points at his chest, then takes a step toward me. "I shouldn't have taken that penalty. I shouldn't have let him get to me. I shouldn't…I shouldn't have listened to him."

He closes the last of the distance, one hand landing on my hip, the other cupping my face as he turns my eyes up to his. I blink back the tears that haven't let me alone.

"What that prick said…ignore him, Clover. You're perfect. Fucking gorgeous. Your curves"—he squeezes my hips that have always been a bit too big for my liking, like he's trying to make a point—"they're one of my favorite things about you. They have never bothered me, and they never will. My other favorite things? One, you're smart."

I'm not, though. He knows how hard I have to work to get the grades I do.

"You're smart," he repeats, as if he knows I need to hear it again. "You're kind, even when you really don't fucking need to be. You're funny but never on purpose. And you're…you're…" He laughs. "Fuck, you're *you*. Do you have any idea how special that is? How special *you* are?"

You're special to me, Clover. In a big damn way.

I remember his words from before. Hell, I've stamped them onto my heart, clung to them whenever I needed a reminder that he chose me and not one of those other girls.

"I love you, Chloe. Okay? I fucking love you. More than I've ever loved anyone or anything in my life. I've never felt like this before. My heart races whenever you're near, and sometimes even when you're not, just because I've thought of you. My entire body tingles whenever I touch you, even if our hands barely graze. And whenever I see you enter a room…" He grins, almost like he's picturing just that. "Shit, I don't know. It's like time slows down, you know what I mean? Like one of those cheesy scenes from those rom-coms you've made me suffer through. You make me want to jump on top of tables and serenade you in the middle of the cafeteria to a really bad song, and we both know how awful I am at singing. You make me want to be a better person, and I've never really cared about doing that before."

He bends down ever so slightly, until our eyes are level and he's not looking down at me and I'm not looking up at him. We're on the same level. The same page, even.

"You are it for me, Chloe. From the second you rolled your beautiful brown eyes because I called you that nickname you hate, you were mine. And even though this night didn't go how I planned, if I'm lucky, you're going to follow me into that room and let me prove to you just how much I mean those words. Just how much I love you."

I don't know what to say. Or maybe that's not true—I do know what to say. *Of course* I do, but it doesn't feel like enough. Not in this moment. This moment needs more. It needs action. It needs *me* to make a decision—and I'm ready to do just that. With shaking hands, I take the keycard from Callum and hold it up to the scanner.

This time, when it turns green, I push on the door handle. I reach back, taking my boyfriend's hand, and I lead us into the room.

Chapter 14

KELLER

I've always hated road games for as long as I can remember. I hate hotels, I hate sitting on planes, and I hate trying to coordinate everything else in my life around them.

That hasn't changed in all my years playing hockey, and now that we're on the last leg of a nine-day trip, I am more than ready to get this final game over with and go home. Sure, it's not like Chloe will be there waiting for me in my apartment, but at least she'll be a lot closer than she is now, and that'll have to do.

Despite how heavy the last night we spent together was, the next morning, it almost felt like it had before. *Almost.*

Usually, we'd spend the last few hours in bed, me buried between her legs, but that wasn't the case this time. Instead, we had coffee at the table while I explained to her how to get Percy to take his meds with the least possible chance of bodily harm. Then I kissed her—without asking permission this time—and I left.

I had hoped we would talk while I was gone, but I didn't expect to be spending so much time on the phone with her.

"How was the morning skate?" she asks after we get our daily Percy chat out of the way.

My pet sitter ended up being sicker than she thought, so I told her to take this road trip off with pay, and she was more than happy to do so. Luckily, Chloe didn't mind stepping in and taking care of the cat full-time. I was glad to have her there…and to have a reason to talk to her.

Our calls started because of him, but they soon blossomed into more, which turned into texting, too. Aside from sleeping and games, I'm not sure we've gone more than a few hours without talking.

"Not bad. We'll need to move a little quicker if we want to beat the Carolina Comets, though. They're too damn good on the puck. They never sit back, so that means we'll need to think faster."

"Isn't that the team Lawson's brother plays for?"

I'm surprised she knows that. "Did Lawson tell you that?"

"Yes, but so did Wikipedia."

I chuckle. "That's fair. Wait, what does Wikipedia say about me?"

"Nothing I don't already know. Though interestingly enough, it mentions nothing about us."

"Hmm," I say, though I'm not entirely shocked by that. I've never been interested in sharing personal details and always try to keep interviews about hockey or keep my answers light enough that people aren't asking follow-up questions.

"I'm guessing that's why your teammates never knew you were…"

She doesn't say the word married, and I try not to read too much into that.

"Probably. Though I expected Lawson to do a deep dive and find it out. He's nosy as hell."

"I don't think he's that bad. He's clearly smitten with you."

"He would be smitten with a damn banana if it gave him enough attention."

She laughs loudly, and I *hear* her clamp her hand over her mouth. "Oops. I definitely got stares for that one."

Stares? Is she not at her hotel?

"Where are you?" I realize quickly I'm not automatically privy to that information anymore and backtrack on my question. "I mean, if you want to tell me, of course."

"I'm at The Coffee Spot. I'm meeting Auden and Lilah for lunch."

It's the last thing I expected her to say. "Oh?"

"I know, I know. Me, hanging with WAGs—can you

believe it? But they were so nice that night at your game and when we went out, so…" I picture her shrugging. "I don't know. We kept in touch, and they invited me out today."

Her words ease a worry I hadn't realized I was carrying around. I'm glad she has someone there for her. She needs it.

"That is okay, right?"

Her words snap me out of my head. "What? Yeah, of course it is. Why wouldn't it be?"

"I don't know…because this is your world and not mine? I don't want to step on any toes."

I want to tell her it's her world too and always has been, but that's not exactly true. Sure, she cheered me on at my games and went to a handful of stuffy events with me, but she was never really *in* my world.

And I think that might be my fault. After what happened in college, when people would treat her like trash just because she wasn't who they *thought* I should be dating, she took a step back. I allowed that. Yes, I reassured her that I loved her no matter what, but maybe that wasn't enough. Maybe she needed more.

Is that the reason she left? Because she didn't feel like she belonged? I don't know, and I want to ask, but things are just starting to feel right with us again, and dredging up the past isn't what I want to do right now.

"My toes are fine, thanks. Though if you had a foot kink, you could have told me."

She lets out another loud laugh and says, "Shut up."

It makes me grin. *That's* normal. *That's* right.

"So are you ladies just grabbing coffee or doing something else too?"

She doesn't answer straightaway, and I wish it didn't set me as on edge as it does. Will it always be like this? Will I always be waiting for that other shoe to drop? Will I always be waiting for her to run?

"Just coffee, but afterward I have…an interview."

I stop breathing.

I wait.

"Callum?"

"Where?"

"Sorry?"

I clear my throat. "Where is your interview?"

"Here. In Seattle. It's, uh, it's for a paper. I'm not entirely sure it's in my wheelhouse since they mainly focus on sports, but apparently the owner wants to expand and mix in more lifestyle articles. He thinks I'll be a good fit to possibly run the editorial department for it, so I'm going to hear him out."

Holy shit. Could she…could she stay in Seattle? Could she build a life here? Could she come back to me after all?

"Cool," I say, trying to keep my composure and not let myself get too excited. I have no idea if I'm even a thought in all of this. I'm probably getting way ahead of myself.

Still…the idea of having Chloe so close again…of being able to see her before, during, and after games… having her to myself on off days… Fuck, the whole thing sends a rush of excitement through me.

When she doesn't say anything, I worry maybe I'm being *too* chill about the whole thing.

"Are you still there?"

"Huh? Oh, yeah. Sorry. I was just…thinking."

Fuck. She sounds off.

"I think what I should have said is, *That's amazing, and I agree that you'll be a good fit. This is really great news, and I'm proud of you, Clover.*" I pause. "Is that better?"

"Yes." This time, I can hear the smile in her voice. "But the first answer was okay, too. Truly. You don't owe me anything, Callum. Not after…"

I want to say she doesn't need to keep blaming herself like that, tell her perhaps her leaving had something to do with me, too, even if she says it doesn't, but she speaks before I'm able to.

"Wait, aren't you supposed to be napping right now?"

I check the time on the bedside clock. Normally, this would be my nap time, but I gave that up a while ago.

"My, uh, pre-game routine has…changed a little."

Truthfully, it didn't feel the same after she left, especially not when the routine typically included her, and since I wanted to get as far away from all reminders of her as possible, I changed it. I guess, given where the

Seattle Serpents are at now, it might not have been such a bad idea.

Chloe is quiet on the other end of the line, so quiet I start to question if we lost connection, but then she speaks.

"Can you tell me about it? Your new routine, I mean."

I grin, even though she can't see me. "You want to hear about my pre-game routine?"

"Yes."

She never had to ask about it before, having been there for it since college.

"Okay," I tell her, wiggling down in the hotel room bed more. "What do you want to know?"

"Everything."

I smile. "Well, it starts with a bit of meditation."

"Shut up."

There are those words again.

My grin grows wider. "I swear it's true. Can you believe it?"

"No." She laughs. "You drop the gloves far too often to be a person who meditates regularly."

It's my turn to laugh. "All right, that's fair. Okay, so maybe I don't meditate. But I do like sitting in silence for a bit, then I put on my headphones and blast all that screamy music you hate."

"I just don't get it. How the hell do you understand what they're saying?"

"Then I usually have a plate or two of pasta," I continue, thinking of all the times she used to complain about my music tastes, not that hers are any better, usually putting on some bubblegum pop that I can't stand. "Then I'll do a quick two miles on the treadmill, then three to five on the stationary, whatever I'm feeling that day."

"You really lost me at all that cardio," she says. "Hmm. So no nap?"

Curling up with her used to be my favorite thing, but after she left, nothing I tried felt right, so I gave up the naps completely.

"Not anymore."

"That's a shame. I miss taking naps."

I miss taking naps with you.

I don't give that thought a voice and instead change the subject.

"When is your coffee date?"

"Right now, actually. I can see Auden and Lilah walking toward the shop."

My shoulders deflate. I'm not ready to let her go. I want to keep talking to her, even if it's about boring stuff like my pre-game routine, which could probably use a little work. Honestly, I'll read her a grocery receipt if it means we're talking.

"I'd better let you go."

"Yeah, I guess so."

She sounds sad, and it comforts me knowing she doesn't want to get off the phone either.

"Oh!" she says. "Percy keeps pawing at the spare room door, and since I'm not trying to snoop around your apartment, I haven't opened it for him. Should I?"

I think about what's hidden behind the door that was intentionally closed before I left, despite Percy's pleas for me not to. It's not that I don't trust Chloe in my home when I'm not there. I just don't want to answer all the hundreds of questions I'm sure she'll have if she enters that space.

"Uh…no. He'll be fine until I get home."

"Oh." And just like that, the excitement is gone. It's on the tip of my tongue to tell her to go ahead and let him in there, but I don't. "All right, then. No problem. Um…guess I'll see you tomorrow to give you your key back?"

Keep it. It should be your place too, I want to say.

I don't.

"Yeah, I'll see you tomorrow."

"Good luck at your game tonight, Callum."

"Thanks, Clover."

We hang up, and we're only off the phone for a minute when I remember I forgot to tell her something.

Me: You're going to nail your interview.
I'm proud of you.

．　．　．

She never responds, but she does read it, and I tell myself that's enough for me.

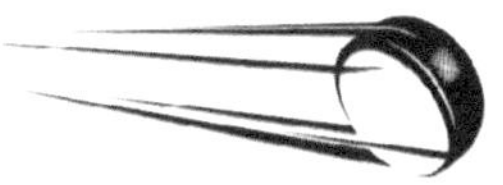

"So, how's it going with the wife?"

I glower over at Hayes, who has dropped down in the seat next to mine. While a lot of teams tend to have a certain spot they'll sit in or try to keep lines together to promote team bonding, the Seattle Serpents plane is a free-for-all more often than not.

I guess tonight it's Hayes I'm stuck beside. Could be worse. It could be Lawson.

"Fine," I tell him, just to get him to stop staring at me expectantly, and I close my eyes as I pull my eye mask down.

I'm not typically so pretentious, but there's just something about sleeping on a plane with one that feels right.

"Quinn is super bummed she hasn't gotten the chance to meet her yet, but she's looking forward to it at the wedding."

Right. The wedding. Hutch has asked about it only once more since the first time, but I haven't given him an answer yet. Mostly because I haven't asked Chloe to go with me. At first, I told myself it was because I wasn't sure she'd be staying in Seattle, but she's making plans to. I mean, she wouldn't be applying for jobs if that weren't the case, right? That has to be the case… doesn't it?

The uncertainty isn't the only reason I'm stalling. I'm scared she'll say no, worried it'll be too much, too soon. I don't want to lose my wife again, not when I just got her back.

I don't feel like spilling my guts to Hayes about it, so I say, "It'll be a hoot."

He reaches over, lifting up the sleep mask, but when I open my eyes, it's not Hayes. It's Lawson. He's turned around in the seat in front of us, practically hanging over the back as he holds my eye mask off my face.

"Hi."

I swat at him, but unfortunately for me, he's quicker than I am and moves out of the way before I can make contact.

"Can I help you, Lawson." It doesn't come out as a question, not really, but that doesn't bother him at all.

"I don't know. I was missing you."

Even Hayes sighs at him. "You literally *just* saw him on the ice. You know, where we beat your half brother 3–2 in overtime?"

"It was a beauty of a goal I had on him, no?" Lawson grins proudly. "And yes, of course I miss you, Kells. We didn't share any minutes together."

"Thank fuck too," I mutter, yanking my mask back down.

He pulls it up again.

"What the fuck?" I yell, and to absolutely nobody's surprise, it doesn't scare him off one bit. "Can I get some damn shut-eye?"

"No. Not until you tell me why you just lied to Hayes."

I glance over at the man in question. His brows are raised, a very dad-like look on his face, and it's wild to me to see his transformation over the last year and a half or so. He went from being a rowdy young guy who destroyed a hotel room to being a father to his niece and settling down with Quinn. Sure, she used to be his nanny, which isn't the best example to set, but who cares? It doesn't make his accomplishments any less impressive.

"Did you, Kells? Did you lie to me just now?"

"What? No." But even I hear the uncertainty in my voice.

"Is Chloe not coming to the wedding?"

It's still so strange to hear them say her name, especially when Lawson says it like he's an old friend of hers. Part of me loves that they've accepted her so damn easily, but also…well, I'm still cautious of what her being back could mean, and I don't want them to get their hopes up that she'll stick around.

I don't want to get mine up either.

"I never said that."

"You didn't have to. Hutchy told me."

"I didn't tell you shit," the captain says from the seat behind me.

Goddamn, is the whole plane listening in on our conversation right now?

"Did too," Lawson argues. "You said you asked him twice, but he didn't give you an answer. That means she's not coming."

"Or it could mean he didn't ask her," Fox pipes up, joining the discussion.

I sit forward and look around Hayes to the seats next to ours. "Anything to add, Locke? Seems everyone else has an opinion on this."

"Oooh, this would be *perfect* for the group chat. Quick—someone type exactly what we're saying."

"Please shut up, Lawson," Hayes says.

"Yeah, what he said," I agree. "Locke?"

"Nope. I got nothing." He holds his hands out, the cards he and Fox are playing something with—probably poker—gripped tightly. "Just waiting to see how this plays out is all."

I sigh, then settle back against the seat and pull the mask down again. "Well, since we're done discussing it…"

Lawson snatches the mask up again, this time removing it completely and stealing it away.

"Hey!"

"Shhh! Some of us are trying to sleep, you know!" someone from up front hollers.

"Well, maybe if he didn't have ten gremlins running around his house, he'd get a little more sleep, huh?" Lawson says to us with an eye roll. He spins my mask around his finger by the strap. "Anyway, did you ask Chloe yet?"

"No," I say through gritted teeth. "Are you fucking happy? Is that what you wanted to hear?"

Lawson frowns. "Uh, no, buddy. That is *not* what I wanted to hear. Why haven't you asked her?"

I shrug. "I don't know. I just haven't."

"Maybe he's scared," Fox says. "And I hope you brought some good bait, because go fish, Lockey Poo."

Huh. Guess I got that game all wrong.

And how the fuck did Fox know that's the reason? Am I easier to read than I like to think?

"Guys, come on. Let's leave him alone. If he asks her and she says yes, great. Auden will find a way to fit her in. If he doesn't want to ask her, he doesn't have to. Auden was just being nice and wanted to make sure Chloe felt included."

"That's because Auden is, like, the sweetest ever."

Everyone looks at Lawson.

"What? She is, and you guys know it. Were you expecting me to say that about Rory or something?" He laughs. "She'd tear my balls off if she heard me talking so nicely about her. She'd want me to say she's a blackhearted evil queen. Mostly because she'd wear that name with pride."

"Yeah, all right, that's fair," Hayes says. He pokes me with his elbow. "For what it's worth, I don't think you should be scared to ask her. I mean, shit, she's your wife, right? I know you guys have had your problems, but there must be a reason she's still around, yeah?"

It's the same thought process I've had, which makes me feel a little better about hanging on to that very thin thread of faith.

"Yeah, and if she says no, it's okay. I'll slow dance with you, Kells."

This time, Lawson isn't too quick for me, and I flick him right between the eyes before he ever sees it coming.

"Hey! Ow!"

He tries to smack me like this is some playground fight, but I grab his wrist, practically hauling him over the seat and snatching my eye mask out of his hand in the process.

"Think you boys can maybe keep it down back here?"

We all look up to find Coach Smith hovering at the end of our aisle, one of his dark, bushy brows quirked high, the gray in his beard and the wrinkles around his eyes extra noticeable tonight. You'd think he'd be happier that we just beat the team he was once a member of before retiring, but he looks exhausted. We all are at this point in the season. We've been playing hard, fighting every night to get as many points as we can to put us at a better advantage to open the playoffs at home.

But I'm also certain a little bit of his tiredness is from us.

"Sorry, Coach," Fox says, and *of course* he's the first to apologize.

Coach Smith doesn't look his way—his eyes are locked on me, where my hand is still wrapped around Lawson's wrist.

"Want to let go of my leading goalscorer, Keller?"

I drop his wrist instantly, and Lawson cradles it, even though I wasn't holding him that tightly. I shoot him a dirty look, and he grins at me in a way that says, *Ha-ha. You just got yelled at by Dad and I'm innocent.* I give him one back, promising he'll regret that. He looks scared.

"Keller, you got a minute?" Coach Smith asks.

"Yeah, sure."

I squeeze past Hayes, flipping Lawson off on my way, and follow Coach back to the front of the plane. We settle into two seats, separate from everyone else.

"What's up, Coach?" I ask once we're comfortable.

"I just wanted to check in with you. I've heard rumblings that you're dealing with some stuff at home."

He doesn't mention my game or say that's what he wants me to focus on. He's genuinely looking out for me, and that's what sets him apart from all the other coaches I've had. He cares. Not just about our play, but about us as people.

So, I decide to be honest with him.

"I am dealing with some…things. My, uh, my wife is in town visiting." I pause, giving him a chance to ask questions, but he doesn't. "But I'm handling it. *We're* handling it. I've been able to compartmentalize and play, so we're good there."

"That's good," he says with a nod. "But I really wasn't worried about that. I know you have a good head on your shoulders. I know you'll do what you need to in order to give this team the best chance they have at the Cup. I was just worried about you."

I don't know why, but his words have my throat tightening in a way I'm not expecting, and I have to push down all the emotions threatening to bubble out.

"I'm not okay, Coach, but I will be."

He studies me for a moment, looking for any inkling of dishonesty in my words, but there is none. When he sees that, he nods once again.

"All right. I'll take that answer for now."

I sit there a moment, unsure what to do next. When he doesn't ask me to leave or say anything else, I ask, "Uh, is that all you needed?"

"Yeah, that was it."

"Should I…go back to my seat?"

"If you want. Or you can sit up here with me and avoid Lawson for the rest of the flight, maybe actually get some sleep. Your choice."

I slip my eye mask around my head, ready to pull it

over my eyes, then Coach Smith decides to add one last thing.

"You know, Keller, I've never really been in the position you're in before, so I can't pretend to know exactly what you're going through. But what I can say is if, for some reason, I ever found myself right where you are, I would fight. I wouldn't give up. Even when it's hard—which I'm sure it is most of the time—I would be right there in the thick of the battle, and I'd come out swinging every time. I wouldn't let anything get between my girl and me, even if it was myself." He clears his throat, then folds down his table. He grabs his notebook, the one he's always walking around with, and opens it. "Anyway, that's all. I won't get in your business any more than that. Just thought you might want to hear a little from someone who has had to make hard decisions for the woman I love before."

He tilts his head down, pen already in hand, and begins to scribble on the page. I don't say anything, not because I don't have anything *to* say, but because I already plan to do just what he said.

I plan to fight.

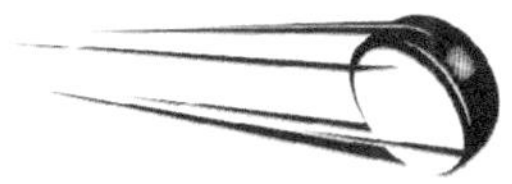

By the time we land in Seattle, deplane, and grab our stuff, it's one in the morning, which means by the time I get home, it'll be around one thirty…and that's if I'm only counting West Coast time and not all the hours I've been up on East Coast time. Even though I was able to get some rest on the plane after moving away from Lawson, I'm still bone tired, and I cannot fucking wait to crash the moment I get home.

I wave goodbye to the team, letting Lawson know if he even thinks about bothering me on our off day tomorrow, I'll castrate him with a rusty spork, then I hop into my R8 and smile at the sound the V10 makes when I fire it up.

Since it's so late—or early in the morning, whichever way you look at it—the streets are empty, and I make it home ten minutes earlier than I thought I would. The night security guard looks up at me as I enter the building but doesn't say anything, and I'm okay with that. I just want to get upstairs, give Percy a few back scratches, then crawl into my bed and sleep well past when I should tomorrow.

The second I push open my door, I know something is off, and not just because of the extra set of worn-out boots lying by the door. It's Percy. He's meowing loudly, like he's been forced to eat hard food for six days straight, and I race toward where the sound is coming from without even dropping my bags.

I skid to a stop when I find him.

Well, *them*. With tired eyes, Chloe looks up at me from her spot on the floor. Much like Coach Smith looked earlier, it's clear she's exhausted. Under her eyes are puffy, and her hair is a mess like she's been brushing her hands through it all day. Next to her sits a can of Diet Coke and what looks to be a half-eaten chocolate pudding cup, which has always been a favorite of hers.

She smiles softly. "Hi."

Fuck, even her voice sounds tired.

"Hi, Clover," I reply, dropping my bags and crouching down next to her. Percy darts over to me, rubbing against my legs, still meowing. "What are you doing here?"

She winces. "I'm sorry. I didn't mean to overstay my welcome, I swear."

She tries to stand, but I push her back down gently.

"No, no," I say, brushing back some of her messy red locks. I let my touch linger, enjoying how they feel between my fingers a little too much. "That's not what I meant. I'm glad you're here."

"You are?"

I smile. "Yeah, I am."

If I'm being honest with myself, there was a part of me that had hoped she'd be here. I didn't expect it, because what real reason would she have, but I did wish for it. I wished for her.

Meow.

I reach down and pet Percy. "Hey, little man."

Chloe gives a breathless laugh. "You call him that, too?"

"Yeah, and you stole it from me." Percy pushes into my hand, meowing again. "I take it he's why you're here?" She nods. "What's going on?"

"I don't know. Remember how I told you earlier he keeps pawing at the door?"

I look over at the spare bedroom she's just pointed to with her thumb. "I remember."

"When I came to check on him and give him a few treats after my interview, he was just meowing his head off. It didn't matter how many snuggles or snackies I gave him, he wouldn't chill. I finally got him calm after a while, but he started up about an hour ago and hasn't stopped since. I was going to text Rory, but I was worried it was too late, and you were coming soon, so…" She lifts her shoulders and hands in an *I don't know* kind of way, then slumps back down. "I'm sorry."

"You have nothing to apologize for. I *should* apologize. I should have just told you to let him into the room."

"Is that what he wants?"

I nod. "It's his favorite spot."

"Oh." She wrinkles her brows. "Why?"

"Because of you."

She jerks her head back. "What?"

I push to my full height, then stand over her, holding my hands out. "Come on. Up."

Chloe lets me pull her up, and I wrap my arms around her when she stumbles backward a bit.

"Sorry," she says sheepishly.

"Stop apologizing to me, Clover." I hold her steady. "You good?"

"I'm good." She looks over at the door, where Percy is scratching and begging to be let in. "Want to fill me in on why that's my fault?"

I sigh, then dip my chin and step away. "I'll do you one better and show you."

I close my hand around the cool knob and push the door open. Percy is inside before I even move it three inches, and I don't have to flick on the light to know where he's gone. I do it anyway, then step aside to let Chloe see.

To most, it probably doesn't look like much. In fact, it might even look a bit disappointing, but not to her.

She gasps. "Callum..." Her eyes scan the room and the boxes stacked haphazardly across the floor. "Is this..."

"Everything you left behind? Yeah."

She runs her hand over the dresser that used to be in our bedroom, the very one I fucked her on multiple times over. Then she moves to the box labeled *Chloe's clothes* and peers inside.

"Holy..." She reaches inside and pulls out a dress I haven't seen her wear since... "I haven't seen this since that last New Year's Eve."

I give her a tight-lipped smile. "I remember."

It was the night everything changed, and when I saw that she had left it behind and didn't pack it for her

London trip, I didn't think anything of it at first. But then she never came back, not really, so I packed it away along with everything else.

"I can't believe you kept everything," she says, taking in all the rest of the boxes.

Some contain things from our first apartment together in New York, then our second place in Ottawa, and our third in Chicago. A few hold items from her life before me, back when she lived with her parents in Tennessee, and a few are ones she doesn't know about, filled to the brim with stuff I found over the years, trinkets I thought she might like or that reminded me of her.

Then she walks over to our bed, the one we took with us everywhere, even after we could afford a much better one. The one where I made love to her on our wedding night, then as often as I could afterward. It was the first thing I got rid of when she left. I couldn't stomach sleeping in it alone. It smelled like her and reminded me far too much of everything I had lost, so I ditched it and slept on the couch for a solid six months before I got a new one, only because the team chiropractor threatened to tell Coach if I didn't start sleeping in a real bed.

It's where Percy is curled up, right on her side.

"I told you it was his favorite place," I say as she approaches the cat, who looks entirely too happy right now. "He comes in here all the time."

I used to as well, but now I only come in to collect

Percy and get out. This space holds too many painful memories for me to spend time in here.

Chloe stands in the middle of the room—as close to it as she can get—and looks around. "I can't believe you kept all this. I thought…I thought my parents came to collect it."

I remember that day well. It was the second worst day of my life, right after the one where she told me she wasn't coming back. They showed up on a game day, and though I knew they were coming, I still wasn't ready to sit there and watch them pack up our life together.

"They did, and they were pissed as hell when I sent them packing."

Her eyes widen. "You did what? They never told me that. They said it went fine, and we never really spoke of it again."

I shrug, not the least bit sorry about it, then tuck my hands into my pockets. "I told them to get lost. I mean, I was a lot nicer about it than that, but I couldn't do it. I couldn't let them take all this away and pretend we never happened. Not when I believed you'd come back."

It's the first time I've said it out loud, the first time either of us has acknowledged that I never gave up hope. The room is quiet, and only the soft sounds of Percy's snores echo through it.

"Look," I say after a few tense moments, taking a couple of steps toward her. "I'm sure you're mad at me for telling them to leave after they drove all the way to

Chicago from Tennessee, but I just couldn't, Clover. Okay? I couldn't. I—"

My words are cut off by her lips, and I'm so stunned that at first, I don't move. Chloe is kissing me. *She's* kissing *me*. It's the first time she's made the first move since she's been back, and I'm so fucking elated by it that I forget how to function. How to breathe. How to simply exist.

Then she runs her tongue against the seam of my lips, and it all comes flooding back to me. I open for her but take control of the kiss, sliding my hands into her hair and tugging her closer. Her arms go around my neck, and she pulls at me just as hard as I pull at her. We're pressed so close together, but it still doesn't feel like enough.

I need more. I need *her*.

But first, I need to know if we're on the same page. I can't keep doing this. I can't keep being taken to the edge and never fall over it. I wrench my mouth away, and she whimpers at the loss.

"Clover…" I whisper. "Tell me you want this like I do. Tell me you want more. Tell me…"

Tell me you love me still. I want to scream those words out loud, but I can't.

"I do. I really do."

"Yeah?"

"Yes."

Then I kiss her again, just because I can't stop. She tastes too sweet, and I know it's because of that damn soda she loves so much, but I can't even complain about it. I'd take this over her leaving any day of the week.

"Fuck, I missed this," I say against her lips between kisses. "I missed *you*."

She pulls back, her lips swollen, eyes glassy like she's a little drunk. Then slowly, she drops to her knees in front of me, and it's not until she reaches for my belt that I realize what's happening.

"Whoa, whoa…" I grab her hands, halting her movement. "You don't need to do that."

She looks up at me. "I know, but I want to. I want to show you how much I missed you, Callum."

Chapter 15

His eyes widen, and at first, I worry that maybe I read this situation wrong. Did I mess up? Is this not what he wants right now? Is it…me?

He releases my hands, then nods once. "All right. Then show me."

It's all the permission I need. I was tired before he came home, all thanks to Percy, but now I've never felt more awake. I make quick work of undoing his belt, then free the button on his pants. My hands are shaking, and every move is jerky, but I'm so eager to prove my words to him that I don't care.

I missed him, and not just these last nine days either. Over the last three years, I thought of him every minute of every day. I thought of our lazy mornings on his off days, of quiet dinners and every joke we ever shared. I missed my partner, the man I promised so much to. I missed my husband, and I already know that whatever happens next won't be enough.

I try not to let myself think of that as I push his boxer briefs down and get my first glimpse of my husband's cock in years. He's long and thick and just as perfect as I remember, and I cannot wait to taste him. I lean forward, pressing a kiss to his right thigh, above the tattoo of a polar bear playing hockey. He has many silly tattoos like this, and I couldn't even begin to count the hours I've spent trying to trace each one with my fingertips.

"Shit," he mutters when I press my lips to his skin again.

I always loved this part of being on my knees for him, teasing him and seeing him looking down at me like he is now. His eyes are dark, almost like a thick maple syrup, and his lips are parted ever so slightly. His cheeks are stained pink, and he's swallowing hard, like he's desperate for something to quench his thirst.

I move my lips from the polar bear to the tattoo on his other thigh, this one an abstract sort of design. I never quite understood what it's supposed to be, but it doesn't make it any less beautiful.

"I'm not sure I can handle this," he says through clenched teeth, and I look up to find his shirt pulled up and balled into his fist as he stares down at me. It's almost like he's barely hanging on when I haven't even started.

I smirk. "I'm just kissing you. Getting reacquainted with old friends, that's all."

His eyes narrow. "You're being a tease is what you're doing, Clover."

"Me? I would never."

But I would, and I am. Seeing him come undone like this…it's worth it, even though I'm just as needy for this as he is. When I kiss his tattoos again, he growls in frustration, and I grin.

"Chloe…"

It feels like a warning, or maybe a promise of retaliation later, but either way, it's enough to spur me on, and I finally drag my tongue over his length.

"Fuck, fuck, fuck," he whispers as I let just the tip of him rest against my lips. "Shit. Do that again. *Please.*"

I do, but only because *I* want to. With Callum being my first everything, it took me a while to work up the courage to do this. But once I felt his heavy cock in my mouth, I knew I'd never grow tired of it, and every chance I got to suck him, I took it.

Which is what I do right now—I take him to the back of my throat, pulling him deep until I can't anymore, and my eyes water as I try to breathe. I back off once I can't take it anymore, running my tongue around the head of his hard length, and I do it again. I keep it up, alternating between sucking him deep and just teasing the head, my nails dragging along his thighs in light touches.

He groans, his knuckles turning white as he watches me, holding himself back from doing what I know he wants to. I discovered early on that not only did I enjoy sucking his cock, but I loved it even more when he took control and showed me what he wanted.

It's exactly what I'm after right now. I grab his hand, moving it to the top of my head, and I wait. *Eagerly.* Right away, Callum knows what I want.

"Are you sure?"

I nod around him, sliding my hands up his thick thighs and grabbing on to him to keep me steady.

"Jesus, Clover," he says, trailing his finger down until he's cupping my jaw. "Do you have any idea how beautiful you look right now? With my cock sitting in your mouth, waiting for me? Fuck, you're drooling. Did you know that?" He swipes at my chin. "So fucking stunning."

Even though I'm fully dressed and sitting on my knees in a small bedroom that's packed with all my favorite things, I *feel* beautiful right now. More than I have in a long time. And it's purely because of the way Callum is looking at me, like he's never seen a prettier sight.

"Are you ready? Because I don't think I can hold back."

I nod again, and it's the only warning I have before he surges to the back of my throat, filling my mouth with him entirely. He stays there, unmoving. I try to swallow, but it's nearly impossible to do.

I love it.

"Holy shit," he murmurs. "Again."

I heed his request, and he inhales sharply. Then he finally moves, pulling out just enough that I can catch my breath before pounding back in. It's bordering on being uncomfortable, and my jaw is already hurting, but I chalk that up to not doing it in so long.

The ache between my legs? That's all right now, this moment, where my husband is using my mouth for his own pleasure. Callum's hold tightens on my hair to the point of it being painful, but I don't want him to stop. I've dreamed about this so many times since I've been gone, and I'm not about to interrupt it now.

His movements grow jerkier and more chaotic as we go on, and I take it all, savoring every moment of it. When the throbbing between my legs gets to be too much, I have no choice but to relieve it. I slip my hand into the leggings I threw on before coming over, sighing when my fingers collide with my clit.

"Yes, Clover. That's it. Play with yourself while I fuck your mouth."

I moan around him, and it prompts him to pump into me harder and faster. I move my fingers right along with him, and I'm hoping he's getting close, because I am, and I'm not sure how much longer I can last.

"Do you want to come?" he asks.

I nod the best I can as he slides into me again.

"Don't. I want your first orgasm of the night, you hear me?" Another rough thrust. "I want to feel that sweet cunt of yours squeezing me when you come."

When his thigh tenses under my hand, I know he's close. I look up at him, my mouth tired and my knees burning from the carpet. I wouldn't be surprised if they're bruised tomorrow, but I don't care.

I dig my nails into his leg, and his nostrils flare. "Chloe…"

It's all he says before he spills into my mouth, filling me up with his cum. Spurt after spurt hits the back of my throat, and it's so much so fast that it leaks out of the sides of my mouth. I can't even begin to imagine what a mess I must be right now.

When he's emptied himself, Callum releases me, tucking his cock back into his boxer briefs, and I fall back on my heels, trying to catch my breath. It's pointless, because suddenly he's grabbing me, hauling me to my feet. He wastes no time sealing his mouth over mine, and I groan into the kiss. He doesn't care that my tongue is still coated in his cum, and it's clear I've awoken a long-sleeping beast. He swoops me into his arms, and I let out a soft squeal.

"What are you doing?" I ask, but it comes out garbled.

Callum is still trying to kiss me, but he understands anyway. "I'm taking you to my room so I can fuck you properly."

He says it so simply, as if I'm a fool for even asking. Maybe I am, because even though I wanted it and started this whole thing, I still wasn't expecting tonight to lead here. I'm certainly not mad about it.

His still hard cock is pressed between my legs, and it hits all the right spots as he carries me out of the spare bedroom and to his. He drops me to my feet at the end of the bed, and his hands instantly go to the hem of my shirt, lifting it over my head and tossing it aside in a flash.

Growing up, I was always bigger than the other girls my age. My thighs are thick, my ass and hips wide, my boobs always a bit too big, and I've never had a flat stomach in my life. I never thought it was a problem until they did, then it was all I felt like people cared about.

Until Callum. He's never said a mean thing about my body. In fact, it's always been the opposite, which is why I'm relieved to see him raking his eyes down me with nothing but admiration. There's nothing fancy about the simple black cotton bra I'm wearing, but it doesn't matter. Callum is still looking at me like I'm wearing a Valentino gown walking a red carpet.

"Fuck, you're gorgeous."

Then he's closing the small distance between us and kissing me again, and when his hands curl around my bare waist, I sigh. *This. This is what I missed.* Dying to feel his skin on mine, I tug at his shirt, and he understands what I want straightaway. He pulls the material over his head, tossing it aside.

Just like he did a moment ago, I take the time to appreciate him. He's always been in good shape thanks to hockey, but he looks even better than he did before. His body is all hard edges and muscles, covered in tattoos. Aside from the lamp on his bedside table, it's dark in the room, but I can still see that he has new ones, though I can't make them out clearly.

What I can see uninhibited for the first time is the chain that dangles between his pecs, and it takes me no time at all to recognize what it is—a ring. The very one I slipped on his finger when I said "I do" all those years ago.

He still has it.

I don't know why I thought differently. I still have my ring, even though I haven't worn it. It was too hard to look down and see it, so I took it off and stashed it away in an old jewelry box I kept with me through all my travels.

When I first came to Seattle and saw he wasn't wearing it, I wondered what he did with it, but I didn't feel like I had the right to ask anymore. Seeing it now, even if he's not technically wearing it, I don't know…it's doing something to me that I didn't expect.

"Fuck, Clover," he mutters, and his thumbs swipe under my eyes, catching tears I wasn't aware were falling. "Why are you crying?"

Instead of answering him, I reach out and trace the metal resting against the smattering of hair on his chest. He sighs, but it's not with dejection. It's understanding.

He leans forward, resting his forehead against mine

as I keep my fingers on his chain. "I took it off after you told me you weren't coming back," he says quietly. "I'll be honest and say I didn't wear it for a long time. Hell, I didn't look at it. I was angry. So fucking angry, Chloe. But then one day I stopped being mad, and I just started missing you. More than I already did. So, I took it out of the box I'd put it in, got this chain, and wore it. It wasn't the same as having it on my finger, but it made me feel closer to you, and that was all I really wanted. I just wanted to know you were still out there and we were maybe still an option, to know even though we were miles apart, you were still mine."

I am yours, I want to say. *I've always been yours.* But the words won't come. They're stuck in my throat, and I can't force them out.

So I don't. I take the ring in my hand and tug him to me, pressing my lips against his in a long, hard kiss. It's slow at first, then it's not, and it's like everything I've bottled up for the last few years comes spilling right out of me, and I *need* him. I want to touch him and taste him, and I want to feel him inside me more than I've ever wanted before.

"Callum…" I say between kisses. "I need…"

I don't even need to say it, because he already knows. He slowly backs me to the bed and pushes me down gently. I fall to the mattress, then scoot my way up, Callum stalking me the whole way. I settle against the pillow, and he hovers over me, his eyes dark.

"You know," he says, a wolfish smirk on his lips as he watches his fingers tracing along the waistband of my leggings. "Part of me is saying to tease you as you teased me earlier, and I have to admit that retribution sounds nice. But what I want even more is to taste you." He flicks his gaze back to mine. "Can I taste you, Clover?"

I nod before he's even finished asking, and he chuckles darkly as he leans down and fits his mouth against mine. The kiss is lazy and, quite frankly, rude. How can he ask me what he just did, then kiss me like this?

Sensing my frustration, he moves on from my lips, but just to my chin, peppering kisses there over and over. I groan, and he laughs.

"Oh, I'm sorry. Do you not like being messed with?"

"No, and I know now how mean I was earlier. So can we pretend I've apologized, and you can get on with…"

He pulls back, looking down at me with one lifted brow. "With what?"

I roll my lips together, shaking my head.

"Oh, no, Clover," he says, trying to pull away entirely, but I quickly wrap my legs around him, holding him to me.

"No, no. Don't go. Please. I'll…I'll say it."

His grin grows wider.

I slide my tongue over my dry lips. "Can you get on with…going down on me?"

Both brows rise, and I know it's not the words he's

looking for. I grit my teeth. If I weren't so damn turned on right now, I'd be annoyed.

"Well?" he prompts when I don't say anything.

I sigh. "Can you get on with…eating my pussy?"

The request is barely audible even to me, and I'm the one who spoke the words.

He leans closer, tipping his ear toward me. "I'm sorry, what was that? I didn't quite catch what you said. Something about…"

"Eating my pussy!"

The words are loud and filthy, and I hate saying them, but right now, I don't care. I just want to feel his tongue on me in all the best ways.

I look at my husband. "Please, Callum. I want you to eat my pussy."

His eyes darken even more, and he says, "Well, since you asked so nicely…"

Then he's kissing me again, and this time, I'm not even mad about it. I just need him so badly that I'll take whatever I can get right now. Just like before, it's soft and slow, but he doesn't linger nearly as long. He trails his lips down my chin and the column of my throat, paying extra attention to the spot at the base that I love. Then he's going down, down, down until he's kissing the tops of my breasts. His finger slides under the cup of my bra, pulling it aside until I'm exposed to him and he can clamp his mouth around my already pert nipple.

"Oh god," I cry out when he flicks his tongue over it. "Yes, please, yes."

His laughter feels good as it vibrates around me, and I want to cry when he releases me. Then I realize where he's going as he kisses a wet path down. He traces his tongue over the stretch marks that fan out across my belly. I've always hated them, but Callum made sure I knew he didn't.

"Fuck," he says, his lips ghosting against my skin. "You're still the most beautiful woman I've ever known, you know that? I don't give a shit if we're living on different continents, you're still going to be the prettiest thing in the whole damn world, and I could spend an eternity worshipping you like this."

I'd let you.

It's too much too fast, which sounds ridiculous given that we've been married for nearly a decade, but we're not there. Not yet.

When his lips meet the top of my leggings, he yanks them down and off my legs in a flash, taking my panties right along with them. I have no time at all to worry about feeling awkward or insecure because Callum is *right there*, his warm breath tickling me.

"I've waited so long for this," he says, his eyes on mine. "I don't think I'm going to be able to stop if I start."

"Then don't stop."

It all happens so fast, and I arch off the bed as he

drags his tongue up my slit, then back down again before he latches on to my clit and sucks me hard.

"Holy…"

But nothing else comes out. I'm too busy getting lost in the feel of his mouth on me for the first time in so many years. It's perfect. Pure fucking bliss. I'm not sure I'll ever come down from this, and I don't think I want to.

"Fuck," he murmurs against me. "Fuck. You have no idea how much I missed burying my tongue in my wife's cunt."

As embarrassing as it is, the one word is all it takes to set me off, and I'm coming way sooner than I ever wanted. My orgasm slams into me, and I squeeze my thighs together, even though I'm not sure if I'm trying to get him to stop or keep him there.

I guess Callum decides for me. He continues to eat me, his tongue switching between fast and slow strokes as he builds me right back up after breaking me down. He adds a finger into the mix, then two, his mouth never leaving me as he pumps his digits into me in short strokes.

He knows it'll never get me off, and I think it's what he wants—to keep me teetering and at his mercy. I can't continue on like that, though. I need a reprieve, or I fear my heart might burst out of my chest with how fast it's beating.

"Callum…" I plead. "Please. I need to come again."

"Then let go, Clover. Let it all go."

He presses his fingers into me deeper, then hooks up, hitting that perfect spot right in tandem with him wrapping his lips around my clit and sucking hard. And I'm a goner. I soar right over the edge, and I'm flying high in the clouds. My body tingles from head to toe, and everything feels as if it's been imbued with just a little bit of magic.

Only then does my husband relent on his torture, kissing his way back up to my lips, giving me a taste of what he's just enjoyed. He kisses me slowly, then hard, and I'm a drunken mess with a strong pull in my lower belly because, somehow, after all that, I still feel empty. I need him.

"Do you remember earlier when you said you were going to fuck me properly?"

"Of course I do," he says, his mouth kissing along my jaw.

"Now would be a good time to do that."

He pulls back ever so slightly, staring down at me like he's trying to get a good read on me.

"Are you sure? I know I said I was going to, but that was before…"

"Before you ate my pussy and brought me to two mind-blowing orgasms?"

"Well, look who has no problem saying it now."

"Callum…"

"Clover…" he mocks, then laughs. "All right. I guess if I have to."

"Look, if you don't want to, then—"

"No, no, I want to. I really do. I was teasing. It's just…"

But he doesn't make a move or say anything else, and I start to worry that maybe this was a mistake. Maybe we aren't ready for this.

Then he speaks.

"I'm nervous."

It's the last thing I expected him to say.

"You're…nervous?"

He nods, and I can just barely see the pink at the tops of his cheeks. "Yeah, I am. It's, you know, it's been a while. I know we've done this a lot before, but this is…"

He doesn't need to finish because I already know what he's going to say—different. He's going to say it's different, and he's right. I'm not the same girl I was three years ago, and he's not the same guy. And even though we're still married, taking this next step changes things.

But I'm okay with that, and I need him to know it too.

"I'm nervous too," I admit, cupping his face and running my thumb over the worry lines by his lips. I see the instant relief in his eyes. "But as you said, we've done this before. And yes, while it'll be different, we're still us —Callum Keller and Chloe Keller, remember?"

He smiles. "It does have a nice ring to it, but I'm pretty sure I said Clover Keller."

This time, I do roll my eyes, but only a little.

"Shut up and fuck me already."

He laughs. "As you wish." Then he grimaces. "Shit."

"What?"

"It's just… Look, I know we didn't use them before, but if you want me to wear a condom, I'll do it. I mean, I don't have any, so we'll need to put a pin in this, but I'll—"

"No."

He tilts his head. "No? You don't want to do this?"

"No, no." His brows draw inward. "I mean, yes! I want to do this." I laugh. "I meant, no condom." His shoulders drop in relief. "I want to feel you, Callum. Every bare inch."

He swallows once, then twice. Then he's moving so fast I can't help but laugh.

"Shut up and take your bra off," he tells me as he shoves his pants down his legs.

When he fits himself back between my legs, he's bare, and so am I. He doesn't take his eyes off me as he drags the tip of his cock against my soaking core, nor when he presses just the tip of himself inside me. He pauses, waiting for me to change my mind, but I don't. I was never going to. I've been looking forward to this for far too long to do so.

He inches in even more, going slow, giving me time to

adjust to his size until he's completely bottomed out and there's nothing else to give. We stay like that for a long minute or two, Callum just resting inside me, not moving, and I appreciate it as much as I hate it.

Then he's moving, and I don't hate it at all. I tug him down to me, needing to feel his lips on mine, and he comes willingly, slipping his tongue into my mouth and kissing me the same way he's fucking me—slowly.

He was right—it is different, but it's not a bad kind. Even when we were struggling and things felt tense between us, we still had a healthy sex life. But this? It's nothing like it was before. It's unhurried and tender, almost like our first time all over again. I think back to that night and how Callum told me he loved me for the first time, and how I couldn't say it back. Not yet, anyway. I felt it, though. With every touch and stroke and kiss, I felt it, just like I feel it now.

Tears prick my eyes, and I'm glad we're kissing because I don't want him to see me crying. He'll panic and think it's bad, but it's not. It's good. Really, really good, and so is this moment. I don't want to ruin it.

He rocks into me with a measured pace, yet my body doesn't get the memo. It races right back to the brink of release and teeters there until he's shaking because he's holding back so much.

"Callum…" I say, tearing my mouth from his, and just like before, he understands what I'm after.

He pushes onto his knees, his hands on my thighs as

he picks up his pace. He sets his hand on top of my pubic mound, his thumb reaching down toward my clit while his palm presses into just the right spot. I don't know where he learned the trick, and I never asked, but it does what he intends, bringing me moments away from coming all over again.

"You're close, aren't you, Clover?"

I nod, barely able to keep my eyes open.

"Ah, ah," he says. "Look at me. You asked for this, now look at me."

I do.

"I'm going to let go now, okay? I've been trying to hold back, but I can't. Not anymore. It's going to be hard and fast, and I can't promise it won't hurt, but I'll make it up to you later. Deal?"

I nod again.

"Say it."

"Deal."

He holds true to his promise, and he fucks me, completely unrestrained. He thrusts into me hard, and there's no real finesse, but I don't need it. He's barely three pumps in before I'm coming apart around him in a way I never have before. It's like every stifled orgasm I gave myself in the last three years times a million. I'm officially spent. Wrung out. Totally done for.

Callum's orgasm isn't long behind, and he comes with a roar of my name and a sigh on his lips. He collapses on top of me, and I welcome the heavy weight of him, wrapping my arms around him and holding him close. So many emotions whirl inside me—bliss, sadness, confusion, and anger. They're all there, so many of them pointed at different things. But there's one that's the loudest, and it's also the simplest—love.

While I've always loved Callum, I think I just fell *in* love with him all over again, and I have no fucking idea how to handle it. What does this mean for us? What does it mean for our future? *My* future? Am I ready to be an us again? Am I ready to go back to how things were? Can we? And if we do, what's to say it won't lead us right back down this very same road?

I don't know, and I'm too tired to think about it now, so I don't. I push it aside, burying it just like I've been burying it for the last three years.

Just when I think he's fallen asleep, Callum stirs, pulling back and giving me a lazy smile.

"We still got it, Clover."

A loud laugh bubbles out of me, and it's just the icebreaker I need to rid myself of all the worry that's brewing inside me.

"We still got it," I agree.

He rolls off me, then waves his hand toward the bathroom as if to say *Ladies first.* I take advantage of his chivalry and shimmy out of bed to race over. I take care of business, then wash my hands, and I'm stunned at what I see in the mirror. I'm a complete wreck. My red hair is messier than ever before, and I'm flushed everywhere I can see. There are a few bite and kiss marks along my breasts and neck that I pray don't leave a mark tomorrow. But the biggest change of them all? My eyes.

I lean closer to get a better look, taking in how bright and clear my usually dull brown eyes look. If I didn't know better, I'd say I was wearing contacts, but since the evidence of what just happened is all over me, it's definitely not that.

It's all Callum. My husband. My partner. The man I've loved since I was eighteen. The one I *still* love but am too afraid to tell.

Later, Chloe, I say in my head. *Your husband is waiting for you. Deal with it later.* I smooth down my hair the best I can and squirt a bit of toothpaste on my finger for a quick brush before padding back out to the bedroom. Callum's sitting up in bed, looking sinfully hot with the sheet draped over his lower half.

"What?" he asks with a grin when I stand and stare for far too long.

"Nothing." I shake my head, forcing myself to move and crawl into the bed and under the sheet beside him. "Just looking at you."

"Like what you see?"

I nod, resting my head against his chest, loving how he wraps his arm around me instantly. "Very much."

I play with the ring around his neck, and he rubs my back softly, lulling me to sleep. My eyes are nearly closed when something catches my attention from the corner of my eye. I sit up, looking down and squinting at the ink dotting Callum's chest.

"What?" he asks, but I ignore him.

I need a closer look, a better one. I reach over and turn on the lamp on my side of the bed, then turn back to him. This time when I look, it's perfectly clear. There, above his heart, sits a new tattoo. It's small and, among the mass of other designs, hard to notice, but I know that shape. I *am* that shape.

I look up at him to find he's already staring down at me as I roll my tongue over my lips. "You got a clover."

He pauses, almost like he's waiting to see if I'll say anything else. When I don't, he exhales slowly, then nods.

"I got a clover." A gulp. "Actually, I got three clovers."

I pull my brows in. "Three?"

"One for each year you were gone." He points to a small one I hadn't noticed on the inside of his bicep. It's brighter than other tattoos around it. "I got that over Christmas break because I knew you weren't coming back." He gives me a rueful smile. "I guess I was wrong about that one."

A small part of me wants to tease him for being wrong, but an even bigger part of me wants to kiss him for being so damn sweet.

That part wins. I launch myself at him, not caring that I'm still naked or that he is too. I kiss him because I have to, and I can't wait another moment to do it.

I pull away, nuzzling my nose against his, his fingers tangled in my already messy hair. "You got a clover."

He laughs lightly. "Three of them."

"I can't believe you did that."

"I can't believe you came back to me." His words are soft, almost whispered. He sighs. "I love you, Chloe."

I freeze. It's the first time I'm hearing him say it since I left for London that second time. It was hard then, and it's hard now. And just like then, I don't know what to say or do.

"You don't have to say it back," he says, "but I wanted you to know. I love you. I never stopped loving you, and dammit, Clover, I never plan to either."

He kisses me slowly and sweetly until my lips are numb, and it's far too early in the morning. We finally part, and Callum takes his turn in the bathroom before climbing back in bed beside me. He wraps himself around me and tugs me close, fitting his body around mine like a second blanket.

"Good night," he says, pressing his lips to my bare shoulder.

"I love you, too," I go to say, but instead it comes out, "Good night."

He never asks me to say it back, and I never do, but it's still somehow the best night of sleep I've had in years.

Chapter 16

KELLER

Last night was heaven, but waking up this morning feels like I'm in hell, and that's solely because I'm so damn hot I can hardly breathe. I peel my eyes open and am unsurprised to find Percy curled up in the crook of my neck. Next to the bed in the spare bedroom and my pillow, it's his favorite place to sleep.

What I wasn't expecting was to have Chloe wrapped around me on the other side. For as long as I can remember, we'd always fall asleep with her head on my chest, but sometime during the night we would roll away from one another and not touch again until we were both awake.

I guess that's not the case anymore.

I push her deep red hair out of my face and look down at the woman who is draped around me like she's afraid I'm going somewhere. I'm not. For the first time in years, I am right where I want to be. Unable to stop myself, I drag my finger down her nose, tracing the small freckles dotting it. She crinkles her brows but doesn't open her eyes, and I take the opportunity to admire her.

I wasn't lying last night when I told her she is the most beautiful woman I've ever seen. I thought so the day she walked right past me on campus, and I still think it over a decade later. Seeing her last night, on her knees, staring up at me with my cock in her mouth… It was like a fucking dream come true, one I've had many times over the last few years.

It wasn't just that or the sex, though. It was all the little things. Her sighs, her moans, the way she's able to laugh even during an intimate moment like that. It was how soft she felt beneath me, the way she asked for what she wanted, and it was how she looked at me like she used to—like she loves me. It's been so long since I saw that look in her eyes that I almost forgot what it felt like, and dammit, I want to feel it again.

I run my finger down her nose once more, that crinkle deepening and her lips twitching. I do it again and again until she begins to stir. Her eyes flutter open, and Percy goes scurrying away, hopping off the bed and trotting out of the room.

She blinks a few times, then rears her head back like she's trying to get me to come into focus or figure out just where she is. I should feel bad for waking her up, but I don't. Even though she's scowling at me, I got exactly what I was looking for. There, in her sleepy gaze, is that look I've craved for so damn long—love. She never said the words back last night, but she didn't need to. I could see it all along, just like I see it now.

"Was that Percy?"

I nod. "Sure was."

"He's doing better?"

"Didn't meow all night."

"Good," she mumbles, closing her eyes again.

"Hi," I say quietly, tapping the end of her nose. "Good morning."

"Hmm," she responds, and I laugh. She was never a morning person, and there's comfort in knowing that hasn't changed.

"How'd you sleep?"

"Like I had three orgasms."

"And here I was thinking it was four."

She opens her eyes again and blows an errant hair out of her face. "Sorry, loverboy, but not this time."

I chuckle at the nickname she hasn't called me since before we started dating, back when she was still trying to deny her feelings for me. I guess that hasn't changed either, because she's doing it even now, even though I can see it.

I let her have it. Maybe it's for the best. Yes, we might have broken down walls last night, but there's still so much we have to work through, and it's probably best I don't let myself get too attached until I know just where it is that we stand.

"Practice?" she asks, rolling away and stretching her arms above her head. The borrowed shirt she put on while I was in the bathroom rises with the movement, giving me a look at the very spot I was buried in last night.

She notices.

"Oh, oops. Sorry," she says, tugging the material down and trying to cover herself back up.

"Don't." I still her hands. "Don't be sorry, and don't hide."

She opens her mouth like she wants to argue, but she snaps it closed just as quickly and nods. I remember when we first started sleeping together, how she would always want to keep her shirt on or would cover up the second we were done. It always bothered me that she felt the need to do it. I wanted to see her—*all* of her—and that's still the case today, just like I still want to touch her and kiss her and make her sigh my name.

I roll over on top of her, loving the little squeal and giggle that leaves her when I fit myself between her legs and press my nose into the crook of her neck.

"What are you doing?" she asks with a smile.

"I was thinking about kissing my wife. Is that okay?"

"Tempting, but I have morning breath."

"Okay, and?" I press my lips to hers in a quick kiss. "Considering you were begging me to eat your pussy last night, I think we're beyond worrying about morning breath at this point."

She gasps. "I did not beg!"

"Bullshit. I believe your exact words were, 'Please, Callum, I want you to eat my pussy.'"

"You made me say it! You wouldn't do it unless I asked."

I shake my head, our noses brushing together. "I don't recall this at all."

She growls in frustration, and I laugh again. I don't remember the last time I woke up this happy. Maybe it was after that game where I assisted on every goal *and* we got Fox a shutout? But even then, I don't think it was *that* good of a morning. Not like this.

"To answer your question, no. I don't have practice this morning. I'm off today and tomorrow."

She nods. "That makes sense after being on the road for so long."

"Yep, and I think Coach Smith needs a break from us. We might have gotten a little rowdy on the plane last night."

"Let me guess—Lawless Lawson?"

Not even mentioning him and the ridiculous nickname he gave himself is enough to shake my grin. "Always." I nuzzle my nose against her cheek, inhaling that floral scent she always seems to have. "You know, I never did thank you for taking care of Percy for me."

"That's not true. You thanked me on the phone every day when we talked."

I did do that, but I pretend I didn't. "Nah. I don't recall that either."

"Then it sounds like you need to get your head checked with Doc." She raps her knuckles against my temple. "Maybe you hit it against the glass one too many times."

"Or…" I kiss her lips softly. "I'm just looking for an excuse to say thank you again."

"Okay. Then say it."

"You know…I was kind of thinking of saying it in a different way…"

She lifts a brow. "Such as?"

But I don't answer her with words. Instead, I kiss my way down her chin and neck, sliding my tongue over the spot she likes. A breathless sigh leaves her, and the sound is like a short song written only for me. I do it again, and I'm rewarded with another verse.

I pay attention to the spot for a few more moments before slipping lower. I want so damn badly to push her shirt up and kiss every inch of her, but I don't. If I did, there's no way I'd be getting anything else done today. I'd spend the entirety of my off day worshipping her, and as nice as that sounds, I was hoping we could spend the day together in other ways.

So instead, I kiss her thighs where the shirt meets her skin, then I push them farther apart and give myself a look at her center.

"Fuck, Clover," I say, looking at her. "You're already wet for me."

"Do you have any idea how good a kisser you are?"

I chuckle. "I wasn't aware."

She peers down at me. "Liar. You know. You're just being—ahhhhh!"

Her words turn into nothing but a garbled mess as I slide my tongue over her, loving how she tastes first thing in the morning.

"Sorry, what was that?"

She shakes her head, her lips clamped tightly together, and I chuckle against her as I glide my tongue across her once more.

"Callum…" She tugs on my hair, and I force myself to stop and look up at her. "You don't have to do that, you know."

"Oh, I know. I want to. Do you have any idea how many nights I would lie awake dreaming of doing this to you again? How often I'd slip back into a memory of the time I've spent here? How I've yearned for this? I know I don't *have* to lick your pretty little cunt, Clover, but I really, really want to."

She swallows, then swallows again.

"Fuck," she mutters, her eyes closing as she sinks back against the pillow, and it's all the approval I need.

I slide my tongue over her again, and the soft moan that leaves her eggs me on, so I do it again. Over and over until she's writhing beneath me, and fucking hell, I missed this. I missed watching her come undone. I missed teasing her. I missed lazy mornings like this. And I fucking missed bringing her so much goddamn pleasure. She's given me so much of it by just being her, and returning it has always been my favorite thing to do. I'm glad I get to again.

When I suck her clit between my lips, she bucks off the bed, and I know I've got her right where I want her. My face is a mess as she pushes her hips toward me, seeking more, and I give it to her, grinding my own hips down in an attempt to relieve the throbbing between my legs. My cock is aching, and I'm dying to fist it and get just as close to an orgasm as she is, but I want this moment to be about her. She practically fucks my tongue as I hold it steady, letting her take whatever she needs.

"Oh god," she cries out. "I'm so, so close…"

Me too, and I haven't even touched myself yet. I fear if I don't do something about it soon, my day will consist of doing laundry instead of getting quality time with her.

She whimpers when I pull away, and for once, I agree with her annoyance.

"I didn't intend for this to lead to more," I tell her, reaching out and dragging a single finger through her wetness because I *have* to touch her. "I just wanted a little taste, but I need to be inside you. Can I do that? Can I fuck you until you're begging for mercy?"

"God, yes," she practically begs. "Please. Please fuck me."

"Then roll over and put your ass in the air, Clover. I want to see all of you while you ride my cock."

It's a mad scramble as we get into position, nothing coordinated or pretty about it, but I don't care. That's just life, and it wouldn't matter anyway. Not with her.

Once in position, I push the shirt up—an old one from when I played for Chicago—and I want to cry at the sight laid out before me.

"Christ, Clover." I run my hand over her bare ass. "You're gorgeous. I love your dimples, you know that? This one right here." I bend down and poke my tongue into it. "It's my favorite. And this one"—I kiss another—"this one is my second."

She hums happily, wiggling back against me, and I get the idea to kiss her in a place I haven't in far, far too long. I pull her cheeks apart, then slide my tongue over the tight ring I've worshipped many times before.

"Fuuuuuck." She lets out a long, satisfied groan, and I push against her hole with the tip of my tongue. "Holy hell, Callum. You have to stop."

"Or what?" I ask, then do it again.

"I'm going to come."

"Isn't that the goal?"

Another low moan. "Yes, but I want you inside me when I do it."

She doesn't have to tell me again. I abandon her tiny hole, vowing to myself to come back to it later and give it proper attention, then I push my boxer briefs down and press my cock to her other opening.

"Yes," she whispers as I slide inside slowly. "Yes, just like that."

I pull out, then push in again, just as languidly as the first time. I don't do it to torment her. I do it because if I don't, *I'm* going to come, and this will all be over far too soon. I keep a steady pace as I rock into her, my movements soft and precise. Nothing too fast or wild, even though I'm quite literally shaking as I hold myself back. Chloe notices.

"Please," she says. "Just do it. Fuck me like you want to, Callum. I don't care if it's over too soon. We'll just do it again. I need to come, so I need you to move faster, harder. I just need you. *All* of you."

Who am I to tell her no? This time, when I slide my cock out, I slam it back in, and she lets out a string of undiscernible words as I find a new rhythm, one that satisfies us both. When I know I'm only moments away from blowing my load, I press my thumb against the tight hole I wish I had more time with, and that's all it takes.

Her pussy constricts around me, squeezing me so fucking tight I swear I see stars, and I'm spilling into her before I even realize it's happening. I keep thrusting, eking out every ounce of her orgasm that I can, and she takes it all, letting me get my fill, even though she's barely holding herself up at this point.

When I'm certain I've wrung every last drop out of

both of us, I pull out and collapse next to her. She grunts as she falls beside me, her hair a mess from having her face pressed against the mattress, and there's a small smile playing on her lips.

"Well, good morning to us."

I laugh, then tuck a piece of hair behind her ear. "Yeah, I'd say." I let out a yawn, the road trip, the long night, and this morning catching up with me. "What are you doing the rest of the day? Do you need to write?"

She shakes her head. "No. Much to my bank account's chagrin, I'm between assignments."

Her bank account? But she should—

"Hey!" She shoots up, and I follow along with her, her excitement palpable, though I have no idea where this is going. "Since you're off today and I am too, I have an idea."

"Yeah, and what is that?"

"Nope. Not telling." She pats my chest. "Get showered and dressed, then I'll tell you."

"Counteroffer: you take a shower with me, then you tell me while I fuck you against the glass door."

She taps her chin. "Hmm. It's tempting but… Well, I'll be honest and say I'm a bit sore between last night and this morning. I don't have the stamina of a hockey player, and it's been quite a while since I've been wrung out like that. I think I need a break, maybe some food to get a bit of energy back, and possibly an ice pack for my knees."

I glance down and notice for the first time that her knees are looking a little red, and I'm hit with the image of her looking up at me last night with my cum dripping down her chin.

Down, boy, I tell my cock when it twitches.

I press a quick kiss to her nose. "All right. Your plan it is. But…you are okay, right? I didn't hurt you? I know we got a bit carried away in the spare bedroom last night."

"It wasn't any more than I wanted you to. I'm a big girl. I'll be fine."

"Okay. Good." I climb out of the bed, then hold my hands out to her. "Come on. I'll show you where the shower stuff is."

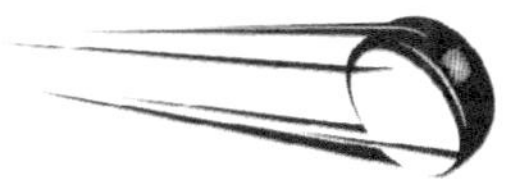

Chloe is standing at the fridge when I pad into the living room after my shower. For having spent nine long days on the road and not getting near enough sleep last night, I feel oddly refreshed, and I'm pretty sure it has to do with the multiple orgasms in the last ten or so hours.

I stop and pet Percy, who is lounging across the back of the couch, enjoying the random bit of sunshine we're having in January. The clouds will be back to covering every inch of the sky any minute, but it's been a mild winter with hardly any rain, and I'm certainly not mad about it.

"Hey." She jumps as I wrap my arms around her from behind. "Shit, sorry."

"It's okay," she says, turning in my hold. "I was just lost in my own head."

I flick my eyes to where she was looking and realize instantly what had her so concentrated—Hutch and Auden's wedding invitation. *Shit.* Fox was right last night. The reason I haven't invited Chloe yet *is* that I'm scared. I don't want her to say no. I want her to say yes and come with me to this damn thing I don't even want to attend.

Well, that's not entirely true. I want to be there for Hutch, and I guess Auden too. But it would be a lot easier to tolerate all the love and mushy shit if I had my wife by my side.

"So, um, I didn't know how to bring it up, but Auden, she…" I watch as she drags her tongue over her bottom lip. "She, uh, she asked me to come to her wedding. If I'm still in town, I mean."

Right. Still in town. I hadn't thought about that. I was so worried about her not wanting to spend time with me or hang out with my teammates that I hadn't thought about her leaving again. Is…is that what she's planning to do? Is she ready to pack up and move out already?

"I plan to be."

I flick my eyes to hers. "You plan to what?"

"Be in town. I mean, if that's okay, of course."

I'm nodding before she even finishes. "Yes, that's okay. More than okay."

"Yeah?"

"Yes, Clover." I clear my throat, pushing down all the nerves making themselves known. "Uh, since you'll be around for it, do you want to go to the wedding with me?"

She hesitates, but only for a moment, before nodding. "Yes, I would love to go with you."

"Oh, thank fuck." I gather her to me and hug her tightly.

I don't know why I was expecting her to say no, and I would have accepted it if she did, but I'm so happy she didn't.

I pull back, then kiss her just because I can. It's quick and over far too soon, but if we have any chance of getting out of the house today, it has to be. Even though she said she wouldn't take a shower with me, it didn't stop her from sneaking into the bathroom while I was in there and taking me to the back of her throat. It was a quick blow job, not nearly as messy as last night, and she refused to let me return the favor, but I promised her I'd do so later.

"How are your knees?"

"They'll be fine. I'll ice them later tonight back at the hotel."

I'm not sure what I thought she'd say, but I didn't plan on her going back to the hotel tonight. Actually, not ever. Or at least not while she's still in town. I want to offer to let her stay here, but she's already twisting out of my hold and moving away, and it just doesn't feel like the right moment anymore.

"So," I ask as I pull open the fridge and grab a bottle of water. "What's on the agenda?"

"Thrifting."

"You…want to go thrifting?"

She nods. "Yes. I haven't been in ages, and remember how we used to go in college all the time, and we loved it?"

Of course I remember. We spent hours in various shops picking through all they had to offer. We would find the weirdest shit and laugh so hard we'd earn dirty looks from the sales associates. It was simple but fun. I remember we used to have a lot of that before things got complicated.

"I want to do it again. Can we?"

If she looked like she does now, I'd say yes to anything she wanted. It wouldn't matter if she asked me to go rob a bank; I'd run to the nearest store for a ski mask and drive the damn getaway car. Whatever she wants, I'll give it to her.

"I think thrifting sounds perfect. I mean, we can definitely afford new stuff, but why the hell not? Maybe we can find another set of Hercules plates."

"Yay!" She claps her hands together excitedly. "Percy, we're going thrifting!"

Meow.

"Percy, you're staying home!"

Meow.

"Boo," Chloe pouts, and I laugh.

"Sorry, Clover. He's an indoor cat. He's only got three legs, remember? He's not equipped for the outside world."

"All right. Fine. Maybe we can find a treat or two to bring back for him?"

I try not to let myself get excited that it sounds like she's planning on coming back here and agree to grab treats for the cat. We finish getting ready, grab our jackets to shield us from the late-January wind, and head out for our adventure.

Our first stop is coffee and food, and I have to grip the table's edge to keep from hauling her across it and fucking her in front of the entire coffee shop as she moans through eating her breakfast. I fear that might always be the case with her, me just barely able to control myself. If these years apart proved anything, it's that she means just as much to me now as she did when I first met her, and that'll never change. She can go wherever she wants in this world and run from whatever she needs to, but I'm going to love her the whole damn time.

"Hey, how'd your interview go?" I inquire when we walk out of the shop, our nearly empty coffees in hand. "I forgot to ask last night."

"Well, we were a bit preoccupied, no?" She smirks,

then her crooked grin falls quickly. "Uh, the interview went well. *Really* well, actually."

Pride balloons in my chest because I expected nothing less from her.

And maybe a little excitement too, because it would mean she'd be staying here even longer, and I really want that, even if the reason isn't for me.

"That's amazing, Chloe, really. But how come you're not smiling?"

She lifts her shoulders. "I don't know. I just try not to let myself get too excited, in case it doesn't pan out, you know? I've learned over the years that it's best to go in with low expectations, then be wowed later if something good happens."

I can't say I blame her. I've adopted that same mindset, even if it is likely unhealthy.

"How's Talia doing?" I change the subject, since it's clear she doesn't want to talk about it.

"Oh, you know Tally. The same but different. Still amazing though."

"Bangs or no bangs?"

She smiles. "Bangs. I think. She's always flip-flopping."

"And Ian? How's he doing?"

"He's great. He misses his uncle, you know."

A pang of guilt moves through me. When Chloe left, I didn't feel like I had a right to talk to Talia or Ian anymore, even though I'd been part of their lives for so damn long. I realize now that probably wasn't the best move.

"I miss him too. It's been a while since I called. I should do that."

"You should. You're missing out. He's *so* smart, Callum. It's almost scary sometimes how much he knows already. But the one thing he can't stand is science. Talia was convinced he faked being sick to get out of a quiz, but it turned out he actually was. I'm pretty sure he'll never let her live that one down."

"Well, if he needs a science tutor, I think he'd have a pretty good candidate in you."

It's the first time I've referenced her old job, and it can be felt instantly. Her shoulders stiffen, and she walks just an inch farther away from me.

"I mean, I know you're no longer a lab tech, and I know you hated it, but you were good at it."

She smiles softly. "Thanks. And I didn't *hate* it. I just… I don't know. It didn't feel like *me*, if that makes any sense. But maybe not. You've always known what you wanted to do with hockey."

"Not always," I tell her. "When I didn't get picked for the draft that first year, I thought for sure my dream of playing professionally was gone, and I was ready to go all-in on business management. Hockey is part of me, yes, but it's not all I am."

"No, no. I know. It's just…maybe I'm not describing it right."

I don't point out the irony in the writer not having the words. That little wave of awkwardness has passed, and I don't want to ruin the moment again.

"I was good at biology. It was easy for me. But in many ways, it was *too* easy. I never felt a real challenge with it, and I think that's part of the reason I ended up not liking it. I wanted to be tested. I played it safe for a lot of my life, and I was tired of it. I wanted adventure. I wanted to find out who *I* was. Writing allows me to do that."

I want to tell her I've always known who she is, but I can understand where she's coming from. She needed to discover it herself. Slowly, the reasons she left are starting to make sense, but I've yet to get the full picture or learn why she chose the moment she did, why she stayed away. Why did she decide *I* couldn't be part of that journey with her?

I have so many questions I want to ask her, but they're all cut short when she grabs my arm and lets out a loud cheer.

"This one! Let's go in here!"

I let her pull me into an old thrift shop that looks like it has seen better days and grin as she all but skips down the aisles that are stocked full of every odd and end you can imagine.

"Oooh," she says, lifting up a wooden pelican holding a bowl of what looks like ramen. "This is just exquisite. The details on the feathers. Magnificent."

I laugh, knowing exactly what she's doing. It's a game we used to play when thrifting. We'd pick up the strangest thing we could find, then compliment it with a straight face. Whoever laughed or broke first would have to ask the cashier if they had another one just like it. It was *so* ridiculous and probably really annoying for the employee, but it was harmless fun, and I could use a bit of that right now.

"Yes, it truly is, but is it as magnificent as this?" I pick up an ashtray shaped like a sleeping raccoon—or at least that's what I think it's supposed to be. It's beyond misshapen, and I'm fairly certain it has two extra legs, but who cares?

"Ah, yes, the six-legged trash panda," she says with a blank face. "Explorers thought it was a myth, but behold —it is true!"

I hold it in the air. "Huzzah!"

"Huzzah!" she cheers, then immediately breaks character, doubling over in laughter.

"Um, sir?"

I turn to find the cashier standing a few feet away. "Yes?"

"Could you please put the sleeping chupacabra down?" *Wait, what? This looks nothing like a chupacabra.* "It's a very unique item, and we have a strict do-not-touch policy for this case right here." He points to the sign I completely missed. "If you'd like to purchase it, we ask that you let us know and we'll take care of it for you."

I roll my lips together, looking back at Chloe as she continues to laugh, then turn back to the cashier.

"Then we'll take it."

His eyes widen, surprised. "Wonderful. I'll get it wrapped up right away."

"And the pelican too."

He frowns. "That's an ostrich, but yes, we can get that boxed up as well."

I hand him the statue, then grab Chloe's hand, who is mouthing *Ostrich?* I shrug and drag her to the front, shooting her looks to try to get her to stop laughing, but it's pointless. By the time we spill back out onto the street, we're both snorting from laughing so hard.

"I cannot believe that's an ostrich!" she says once we've finally calmed down.

"I can't believe I just bought it."

"It's going to look so good next to your door. Oh! Oh! You could put it on the shelf next to our wedding photo. It'll be perfect!"

Just the mention of our wedding has the air around us shifting, and suddenly, we're not laughing at all anymore. It's not awkward, but it's not easy either.

"So, uh, where to next?"

She yawns, covering her mouth with the back of her hand. "Yikes, sorry. I guess I'm a little more tired than I thought. Would you be mad if I suggested a nap?"

"Not at all. A nap sounds perfect."

"Great, my hotel is just a few blocks over."

Oh. She doesn't mean a nap with me. It's not what I expected, but I guess I should have.

"Lead the way," I say, waving her on.

The walk is quiet, and more than once, I get the urge to reach for her hand, but I don't. I can't understand how we can go from mind-blowing sex last night—and this morning too—to her going back to her hotel like it's nothing. I fucking hate it. She should be in my apartment. It should be *our* apartment.

"I'm just up here," she says once we've walked for a while.

I glance around the unfamiliar area we're in. I haven't been over here, and I'm starting to understand why. It's old, which is most of Seattle at this point, but I get a bad feeling in my gut that I can't shake. It feels like we're being watched, but I can't tell from which direction.

Chloe pushes open the door I hardly even realized led to a hotel, and we step into a lobby. Or at least I think it's a lobby. There are desks stacked two high, blocking off the elevators, and an old lady sitting behind the front check-in who looks like she might be falling asleep.

"This is where you're staying?" I look up at the ceiling of the old building that's in obvious need of a renovation.

There are cracks every few inches, and I'm surprised it's still intact at this point. An older gentleman sits in a corner and tips a brown bag up to his lips, loudly slurping back what I assume is a beer before belching, the noise echoing through the mostly empty area.

"This is where I'm staying," she confirms, pulling a set of keys out of her coat pocket.

I work my jaw back and forth. "Why?"

"Excuse me?"

"Why? This place… Fuck, it's a piece of shit, Clover."

I don't bother keeping my voice down. There's no point. Everyone can see that what I'm saying is true. She tips her chin higher like she's offended by my words, but I don't care. She is *not* staying here another night if I have anything to say about it.

"It's perfectly fine, and I like it here."

It's like she forgets how damn well I know her and that I can read her better than anyone else. She's lying. She doesn't like it here, not one bit.

"Well, tough. You're not spending another night here. Give me your keys. I'll go get your bag."

She gasps, clutching them to her chest. "No! You can't just boss me around and *demand* that I leave. I'm an *adult*, Callum. I can make my own decisions."

"Yeah, and you're my fucking wife, too, and my *wife* is not going to stay in some run-down, shady-as-hell hotel." I take a step toward her, leaning in closer. "Now, give me your damn keys before I break down every door in this godforsaken place until I find your room. And trust me, Clover, I'll do it. You know I will."

She stares up at me with wide eyes, and because I know her so well, I know she's debating telling me to fuck off. It's right there on the tip of her tongue, and if I'm being honest, I almost *want* her to say it. Then I'll have an excuse to hit something, and I really want to right now.

I can't believe she's been staying here. I figured she was someplace much nicer than this, or else I would have insisted she stay at my place while I was on the road.

Picturing her here makes my stomach sour. Have these people been harassing her? Has she felt secure for even a moment? Does she often stay in areas like this? And how bad of a husband am I for not knowing the answer to that? We might not have talked often while she was gone, but when we did, she always reassured me that she was being safe, and I trusted her. Maybe I shouldn't have.

After several tense moments, she relaxes, and I know I've won. It doesn't absolve me of the guilt, but at least I'll know she's someplace safe tonight.

"Fine," she says. "I'll go with you."

She holds the keys out to me, and I snatch them away before she can change her mind.

"Thank you. Now, which room is yours?"

She opens her mouth to tell me, but I shake my head.

"Not out loud. Show me, Clover."

She nods in understanding and leads us up to the third floor. If I thought the lobby was rough, it's nothing compared to the rest of the areas. There are doors that can't even close all the way, held in place by a chain, and more than one room has piles of trash sitting outside. There's a housekeeper's cart, but given the state of the hotel, I'm not sure it's ever been used.

We're in and out of her room in a flash, then we stop at the front desk. After having to ring the bell three times to wake the old lady up, we get Chloe checked out early, and then we're on our way back to my apartment, her measly two bags of luggage in my hands.

"What the hell were you doing there?" I ask once I've calmed down a bit. "That place was a shithole."

"It wasn't that bad," she says quietly, but she can't even keep up the pretense. "All right, so it was. But I don't know. I was trying to save some money. I wasn't sure when I'd get my next paycheck, hence the whole me-applying-for-a-job-with-a-paper thing. I was looking for something a bit steadier than freelance."

"What about the money I send you every month?"

When she doesn't answer, I look over at her. Her gaze is trained on the ground, and I already know her answer is just going to piss me off more.

"You are getting the money, aren't you?"

She nods. "I'm getting the money."

"Okay, and what? I mean, it's okay if you're blowing through it. I know you're traveling a lot, so it would make sense. But if that's the case, all you had to do was ask for more, and I would have gladly sent it. You know that, right?"

"I know," she says quietly. "I, uh…" She scratches at her nose. "It's not that I was running out of *your* money. I was running out of mine."

"But…my money *is* your money. It always has been. That didn't change just because…"

You left, I want to say, but I leave the words unfinished.

"I know. But… Ugh, I don't know, Callum. I just didn't feel right spending it, okay? I left you. I walked out with a promise to come back, and I didn't. And still, you took care of me. You sent me money and cards and gifts, and I…I…I just couldn't do it. I-I'm s-sorry."

She's crying, and right there in the middle of a busy Seattle sidewalk, I drop the bags and gather her in my arms.

"Hey, hey," I say softly, stroking her back. "It's okay. It's okay. You don't need to be sorry. I get it, all right? I get it." I pull back, running my fingers over her cheeks to wipe away the tears streaking down them. "I get it. I'm sorry I got upset. I just… Shit, I wanted to take care of you, that's all. I love you, and you're my wife. It only felt right to be helping you in some way. Do you know what I'm saying?"

She nods. "I do. I understand, and I appreciate it. I truly do. I just needed to do it on my own terms. I needed to do it alone."

I want to scream and tell her she wasn't alone, I was

always there, always in her corner, even when I was mad at her, but it's been a long day. Hell, it's been a long three years, and I'm tired. All I want to do is take her back to my apartment and hold her. That's it.

"Come on," I say, pressing a kiss to her forehead before releasing her. I grab her suitcases, one in each hand, and nod in the direction of my building. "We're this way."

I lead her back to my apartment, and after ordering a pizza and devouring the entire thing, we crawl into my bed, and I hold her the rest of the night. It doesn't make up for everything I want to say to her, but it's all I can give her right now.

We'll deal with the rest later.

Chapter 17

"You did what?!"

Talia's screech is so loud I wince. "Uh, I moved in with him."

"And…" my best friend prompts. "Say that other part again, too."

"Slept with him."

"Holy shit!" she screams, then continues to do so for a solid minute.

It's loud and annoying and way overdramatic, but I find myself smiling anyway. I think that has to do with how good I've felt ever since we slept together earlier this week. While our conversation after leaving that seedy hotel was hard, things have actually been great since then. Sure, it's only been five days—a fact I didn't mention to Talia since she'd kill me for not telling her earlier—but it's a start.

"Well, how was it?"

"I only had two bags, Tally. It was a very quick move."

"Oh my god." She groans. "You know exactly what I'm talking about. The sex! How was the sex?!"

"Ew, Mom!" Ian yells in the background.

"That's what you get for listening in! You're supposed to be doing your homework."

"It's a Saturday!"

"Well, that's what happens when you decide not to do it during the week." She rolls her eyes. "Hang on. Let me deal with him."

She sets the phone down on her bed, and I'm left staring at her ceiling fan as she wrangles her son back to the kitchen table to work.

"Okay," she says a few minutes later, picking the phone back up and putting it way too close to her face. "Tell me *everything*."

"I am not detailing sex with my husband for you."

"Ugh, boo. But I'm, like, horny for it. It's been too long."

Talia hasn't seriously dated since Ian came along, and while I wish she would put herself out there more, it's not like I have any room to talk. I married the only man to ever be inside me.

"Can you at least tell me if you came?"

"Talia!" I scold.

"What? It's an important question."

I chuckle at her, shaking my head. "Fine, yes. I came. Are you happy?"

She squeals again, then shimmies her shoulders. "I'm very happy, but it sounds like *you're* happier." She wiggles her brows up and down.

"You're ridiculous," I tell her, but it doesn't stop my face from getting hot.

"Girl, you are ridiculously giddy and blushing, and it's so cute. You are *so* falling in love with him again."

Her words shock me. "What do you mean by 'again'? I never stopped loving him."

"So you *do* know that, then."

"What? Of course I know."

"Well, you could have fooled me sometimes, like when you decided to come back from the London internship."

My jaw slackens. "You were the one who pushed me to do it!"

"Yeah, but I didn't tell you to stay gone for three years. That was your call, and I was shocked as hell when you did because it was obvious to everyone how much you missed him. Even your mother was urging you to go to Seattle for that interview."

Shit. She has a point, and it's a big one too. While my dad eventually warmed up to Callum, my mother never did. It was like she held some sort of grudge against him for "stealing my youth" or whatever. It didn't matter how many times I tried to tell her it was my decision to marry him and he wasn't pressuring me; she didn't care. She blamed him.

I was surprised when she approved of the internship to write, but for some reason, I didn't bat an eye when she pushed me to go back to Seattle. Maybe I should have. Was she trying to tell me something? Was she trying to tell me to get my husband back?

I don't know, but I do know I'm here now, and I'm not going to waste it. Callum and I still have a lot to work through, but I'm ready to roll up my sleeves and get right in the thick of it. But, like, maybe after this wedding.

"Okay, okay, enough sappy talk," Talia says, reading my mood perfectly. "Your text mentioned a wedding. Does this mean dress shopping? Because I know you didn't pack any wedding guest attire."

"Ugh. Don't remind me. The closest thing I have is that dress I wore on New Year's Eve, and I really don't want to be reminded of handsy Dirk the Dick all night long. But I also don't want to go shopping. You know I hate it with a fiery passion."

I was never a fan, mostly because finding something that fits my hips *and* short legs is nearly impossible. Throw in my big boobs, bigger butt, and my belly, and it's damn near impossible.

"You do, but I have an idea…"

Talia keeps talking, and I halfway listen, but my eyes drift to the clock on the microwave. I try my best not to smile when I see that Callum should be getting back at any moment. My body buzzes with excitement at the idea. I can't recall the last time I felt like this. Maybe five years ago? More? I'm not sure, but one thing I do know is I can't wait for my husband to walk in the door.

"Um, hello? Did you hear me?"

I give Talia my attention. "Um, no. Sorry."

Her eyes narrow. "Just because I want to acknowledge it: rude. However, I will let it slide because I know you're daydreaming about your steaming hot sex with your husband." She starts kissing the air, pretending to be us making out.

"It's times like these I cannot believe you're raising a kid."

She laughs. "Yeah, me either." The phone jostles as she moves around. "Anyway, as I was saying…as jealous as I am that you're out in the gorgeous Pacific Northwest making friends with hot hockey wives while I'm stuck in Snoreville, Tennessee, I think it might be a good idea to ask one of them to go shopping with you. As you said, you hate shopping, so why not take a buddy?"

I consider her suggestion, but those same old feelings from before I left creep in. All the doubts and worries and voices telling me I'm not good enough to be friends with successful women like that scream so loudly I barely remember promising Talia I'll think about it and getting off the phone with her.

It's only Callum's key turning in the door that rattles me from my stupor.

"There you are." He smiles at me, kicking his shoes off and crossing the apartment in a flash. He bends and presses a kiss to my lips. "Mmm. I missed that."

I giggle. "I just kissed you like three hours ago."

"Three hours is a long time when I've missed you for three years."

I don't have time to process his words before he's kissing me again, this time longer and harder. I fist his shirt, ready to pull him right on top of me and let him have his way, but my growling stomach ruins the moment.

"Good thing I ordered us lunch on the way up here, huh?" he says when he pulls away. He pets Percy, who is lying right beside me and has been all morning as I work on a new piece. "Extra dumplings, and it should be here in about thirty minutes."

"You're amazing, you know that?"

"I'm aware." He nods toward my laptop. "Work?"

"Yes. Just a freelance job. Working on a piece for a small press in Tennessee. Nothing too wild."

"How's it going?" he asks, moving to the kitchen and pulling a bottle of electrolyte water from the fridge. He gestures, silently asking if I want one, and I shake my head.

"So-so," I tell him, but honestly, it's a mess, and I'm struggling to come up with anything of substance. I have a feeling that has a lot to do with me wanting to spend all my time with Callum instead of working.

"Need to talk through it?" He hands me a Diet Coke, then settles onto the couch next to me while Percy gets up and heads to the spare bedroom. "What? Why are you looking at me like that?"

I hold up the drink I didn't ask for. "This. Be honest with me—did you keep these around for me?"

He pauses, then sighs, running a hand through his hair that's looking extra light today. "Busted."

I grin, set the opened drink on the table, climb onto his lap, and kiss him.

He smiles as I pull away. "Well, hi to you too."

"How was practice?"

"Good. The guys are trying to sort out a new power play with Thomas going down, but I think we'll figure it out."

The Serpents are still in a really good spot for the playoffs, but last night, one of their players got hurt battling one of the league's best teams and is expected to miss at least the first round of the postseason. It was hard to hear the news of losing a teammate to injury, especially in the first intermission, but they went back out and played like they had something to prove and won the game 4–2 in regulation.

He squeezes my thighs. "Did you do anything other than work this morning?"

"I talked to Talia."

"Yeah? And how did she react to the news of you staying here?"

I tip my head. "How did you know we talked about that? Is there a camera in here?" I look around, glancing at the empty corners. "Are you spying on me?"

He laughs. "No, I just know you, Clover."

He's not wrong. Callum has always understood me in a way that was almost scary. It was as if he saw right through me, down to my soul, and I felt safe with him in a way I've never felt with anyone else.

"I mean, you did tell her, didn't you?" he asks when I don't say anything.

"Yes."

He grins smugly. "I knew it."

"Shut up." I glare at him, but all he does is continue to smile. "Anyway, she, uh, she actually suggested I ask the girls to go dress shopping with me. You know, for the wedding."

"Okay, one: it's really weird to hear you say 'the girls.'"

I don't even bother arguing. It is weird. I've only ever had one true friend in my life—Talia—so having a group of women who actually *want* to hang out with me and that I want to hang out with is…odd.

"Two: I think that's a great idea. I know how much you hate shopping."

Talia said the same thing. It's so nice having two people in my life who know me so well, but it's strange because there are so many moments where I feel like I don't even know myself. How can they and I don't?

"You getting lost in that head of yours, Clover?" He taps my forehead lightly.

"Maybe a little."

"Anything I can help with?"

"No, I'm good." The response is automatic, and the second I say the words, I want to take them back, especially when Callum's jaw tightens, like he was hoping I'd take him up on the offer.

I should have, but it's too late now, and I hate that I just ruined the moment. I want it back. I want his smiles, his easygoing laugh. I want happy Callum, not the one frowning at me now.

"How long did you say until lunch gets here?"

"Uh, about twenty minutes now. Why?"

"Oh good. We have time."

I slide my hands beneath his shirt, dragging my nails up over his hard abs, and he shudders under my touch.

"Time for what, exactly?" he asks, his words coming out in a hiss as I do it again.

I grin. "For you to show me where that other clover tattoo is…"

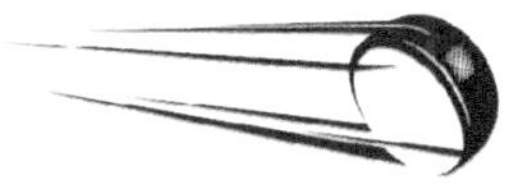

I took Talia's advice and asked the girls if one of them could go shopping with me. Imagine my surprise when they all responded with a *very* enthusiastic yes, aside from

Rory, who just sent a thumbs-up. According to Callum, that meant she was excited.

So, we made a plan to meet up that worked with everyone's schedules, and now we're shopping with just four days to go until the wedding. The guys are golfing, enjoying their All-Star break and time away from the rink. Callum left in the wee hours of the morning, and since there was no way I was getting up that early, I stayed in bed an extra hour before getting ready to meet the girls for brunch prior to hitting the shops.

But now I'm running late.

"Hey, I am *so* sorry to be bothering you on your Boy Date, but I think Percy might have stolen the key you left me, and now I can't find it, and I'm going to be late for the dress shopping date with the girls."

"First off, do *not* say Boy Date. If Lawson hears that shit, he will *never* let it go. Second, I am still not used to hearing you say that."

"What? Girls?" I growl. "Really, Callum? I'm running late. Help me!"

He laughs. "All right, all right. Did you check the spare bedroom?"

"Yes, but that room is a mess. I've been going through boxes and trying to sort through things, and I think I made it worse. Percy barely even goes in there anymore because it's so cluttered."

"It's cluttered because I've awakened a beast, and you won't stay out of the thrift shops."

"Hush! You love that Canadian whiskey lava lamp, and you know it!" Okay, so maybe I went a little overboard with that one, but I'm not admitting that to him. "Can you think of anywhere else? I've checked the living room and our bedroom already."

There's a pause on the other end, and it takes me a moment to understand why. *Our.* I said *our* bedroom, not his. It just slipped out, and I didn't even notice it. I think it was because it felt so natural to say. It's funny how, after all the time and distance between us, we so easily slip back into who we were before everything fell apart.

"Come on," I say, moving on and acting like it's no big deal. "Help me, or I will accidentally let it slip to Rory that you wish you could go on more Boy Dates with Lawson—*just* Lawson."

I swear I can hear his teeth grinding.

"You are an evil, evil woman, Chloe Lynn Keller."

I smile at hearing my full name. "I always liked it when you called me Chloe."

"You like it better when I call you Clover."

He's right. I do.

"I do not. Now, where's the key, *Callum*?"

He laughs at the emphasis I put on his name, likely thinking back to when I used to do it all the time in college. "I don't know where the little weasel put it, but I think there's a spare in the drawer next to the fridge."

"Please be there, please be there, please be there," I chant as I make my way across the apartment.

"You okay?"

"Huh? Yeah, why wouldn't I be?"

"I don't know. You sound a bit nervous."

"I do?"

I hadn't realized I did, but it's not surprising. My stomach has been in knots all morning, and I couldn't pinpoint why. Being nervous for today makes sense, and of course Callum would catch on to that.

"I guess I am a little," I admit. I don't know why, though. I've hung out with them before, and they've all been so nice. Maybe it's me hanging on to some old feelings from a long time ago.

"Don't be. You're going to have fun, and you're going to look gorgeous in whatever dress you buy."

"You want me to send you a picture?"

"Nah, surprise me. Plus, I fear if you send me a photo, I'll get a boner, and I really don't need that to happen on the golf course."

"Dude! Keller just said he has a boner! It was that last swing, wasn't it?"

The unmistakable voice of Lawson in the background makes me laugh, and I can just picture Callum dropping his head back on a sigh and giving his teammate a murderous look.

"Shut the fuck up, Lawsy! I swear I'll club you with your putter!" He lets out a slew of cuss words before saying, "If the Serpents weren't playing so damn well, I would request a trade."

His words are nothing but a lie. He loves his team and Lawson, too, even if he won't admit it.

"Did you find the key, Clover?"

Oh shit, I almost forgot about looking for it. I yank open the drawer, and items go flying. He wasn't kidding about it being a junk drawer. There are so many random things in here, from chargers to batteries that probably aren't even good, a pocketknife, and so many restaurant menus it's not even funny.

But no key.

"Anything?"

"No. Not yet. I just…" My fingers collide with something cold, and I pull free a key that looks almost identical to the one Percy stole. "Does it have a blue piece of tape on it?"

"Yep, I marked it so I didn't throw it out."

"I found it! Ah, thank you, thank you, thank you. I appreciate it so much. I'm sorry to bother you again."

He laughs lightly. "You're never bothering me, Clover. You can call me anytime."

I smile at his words as I work to shuffle things back around so I can close the overstuffed drawer, and my eyes snag on a card lying under a piece of paper with a few scribbles on it. At first, I think nothing of it, but then I read the words in small print at the bottom.

Seattle's Best Divorce Lawyer

It's not at all what I expected, and I pick it up with shaky hands, hoping like hell I just really need to get my vision checked. I don't. There, on the card I can see *very* clearly, is the information for a divorce lawyer, and the words *Nice chatting with you! Looking forward to working together!* are scrawled in nearly illegible handwriting.

He's divorcing me. Or he was planning to. It doesn't matter which one it is, because both mean the same thing —he gave up on us. My breaths come in short, and I have to work for each and every one. I hate it, but mostly because this shouldn't be a surprise. *Of course* he would seek a divorce. I left him, for crying out loud. It makes perfect sense, and I wouldn't blame him one bit.

But holding this card in my hand…it makes it all too real just how close I came to losing him, and just how badly I don't want to.

"Clover? Are you still there?"

I give myself a shake, forcing my voice to come out evenly and praying I sound unbothered as I say, "Sorry, I'm here. I got the key. Thank you so much."

"Of course. Have fun with *the girls*. I'll see you tonight."

"Yeah, see you tonight."

He pauses, and I close my eyes, readying myself to hear those three words he's uttered only a few times since I've been back. They never come, though, and I wish they had.

The line goes dead, and I let the phone slip away from my ear. I look at the card again, then decide it's better to deal with it later. I don't have time for a spiral right now. I stick it back where it came from, careful to place it just so, and head toward the door.

I'm just about to open it as my phone rings again, and I answer it without looking, assuming it's probably Callum calling because he forgot to tell me something.

"Did you forget something?"

"Oh, I'm sorry. I must have the wrong number."

It's not Callum. It's a woman, one whose voice sounds vaguely familiar.

"No, no, I'm sorry. I thought you were someone else calling. Who are you looking for?"

"Chloe Keller. This is Avery Danes calling from *Sports Action News*."

Holy shit, holy shit, holy shit.

My heart begins to pound, and I try my best not to make it obvious. "Um, this is Chloe Keller. Hi, Avery. How are you?"

"Chloe!" I can hear her smile through the phone. "I'm doing well, thank you for asking. I hope I'm not catching you at a bad time."

I look down at the key dangling out of the knob. "No, not at all. How can I help you?"

"Well, I was hoping you could help me by coming in for another interview. We would love to chat with you some more about what you could bring to the new position."

Oh my god, they want a second interview? That's huge and likely means I'm on their shortlist for editors. My eyes drift back to the drawer, the one housing the card for the divorce lawyer. I don't know what it means. It could be everything, and it could be nothing at all. Whatever it is, I shouldn't let it dictate my career. I've wanted this for so long, and I've worked damn hard for it. If things with Callum and me are meant to be, we'll work it out.

"I would love that, Avery."

"Perfect! I was really hoping you'd say that," she says cheerfully.

We make a plan to meet two days from now, and Avery tells me she's looking forward to seeing me again before we hang up. I stand there for a long moment, Percy meowing at me for not leaving yet, and it's not because I don't want to leave—I am *really* going to be late now—but because I can't. My mind is spinning with so many scenarios that I can't even begin to sort through them.

Callum telling me he wants a divorce. Me walking out once again. His heart breaking all over again. *Mine* doing so too.

It's all too much, and just like the card sitting in the drawer, I don't have the time to deal with it now. So, I don't. I take a steadying breath, shove all the thoughts into a box, and tuck it into the back of my mind, then push my shoulders back.

I have a dress to find.

Chapter 18

KELLER

"May I have this dance?"

"No."

"What? Come on! Just dance with me!"

"No."

"Please? Please, please, please?"

"I swear to fuck, Lawsy, if you don't walk away from me in the next five seconds, I *will* break your kneecap, and you'll be the next member of the Seattle Serpents who misses playoffs."

"Pfft. You would never do that. You love me, even if you won't admit it. You—hey, hey, hey!" he says as I push out of my chair and move toward him. He holds his hands up and backs away slowly. "I was kidding, I was kidding. Mercy!"

He looks over at Chloe like he's looking for help, and I step into his line of vision.

He laughs. "Oh, jealous Keller is a fun Keller."

"Get lost, Lawson."

"Fine. But only because I spy Rory, and I'd much rather dance with her than you."

"That's a lie," Fox says into the water he's been sipping on all night. I think most of the players here are doing the same thing. We might be on break, but nobody is risking everything we've worked so hard for with a hangover.

"It is not!" Lawson looks at me. "Okay, so maybe I *do* want to dance with you, but only because I bet you're secretly really good at it."

"He is," Chloe says, and I shoot her a dark look as I settle back down beside her. She laughs and shrugs. "Sorry, but it's true. Remember our honeymoon?"

Between school and hockey, we weren't able to take a trip until our fifth wedding anniversary, but fuck, it was worth the wait. And I don't just mean because of the lounge chair we broke when she rode my cock.

No, it was the dance we had at sunset, in a little secluded spot I found one afternoon while she was taking a nap. I wrapped her tight in my arms and kissed her, and we swayed back and forth for what felt like hours. We didn't take it any further, and I don't think we even fucked that night, but it was easily my favorite of the trip.

Before I can respond, Hutch says, "Fuck, I can't wait for our honeymoon."

With the season resuming in just three days, it's no surprise the newlyweds are waiting until later this summer to celebrate their nuptials. I always wondered what made them want to get married in the middle of the season, but Hutch just kept saying it had to happen because, when he won the Cup for the first time, he wanted to hand it to his wife. He's that convinced it'll be ours this year.

"I can't either. Where are we going again?"

Hutch glowers at Lawson. "*We* are not going anywhere. My wife and I are going to Barbados."

My lips twitch at the two words he's uttered at least fifty times tonight since they said *I do*. I get it, though. After Chloe and I got married, I couldn't stop saying wife because I couldn't believe it had happened. In a lot of ways, I still can't believe it.

"Boo," Lawson says, jutting out his bottom lip. "I was going to invite you to mine, bro."

Hutch sneers. "We are *not* brothers. Go find Rory or something."

"I'm going, I'm going…*bro*."

And that's how Hutch ends up chasing his own groomsman through the reception hall.

"What the hell!" Lilah shrieks, kicking off her heels and chasing after them, likely trying to stop Hutch from committing murder and leaving his new wife without a husband.

"They'd better watch out. She's fast," Fox remarks, grinning after his girl.

It's strange because it doesn't feel like we're at a

wedding at all. Sure, we're all dressed up, and there are several people I've never seen before in my life, but it's almost like we're just sitting at Top Shelf, having a few drinks, and shooting the breeze.

It's still miles better than the reception Chloe and I had. Our parents—mostly hers—were still upset about the wedding, and her mother sat at their table all night, pouting. It was already done, though. We were married, and that was all that mattered to me.

It's still all that matters. I lay my hand on her thigh, almost like I need the reminder that she's here, and she puts her palm on top of it without breaking conversation with Quinn.

I was right—Chloe looks gorgeous in her dress. It's floor-length, satiny copper, and fucking stunning with her dark red hair swept up in an elegant bun. Her makeup is heavier than usual, but it doesn't make her any less beautiful. Actually, it makes me want to take her by the hand and lead her into a dark closet where I can have my way with her.

I squeeze her thigh, and she returns the gesture, still locked in conversation. I have no idea what they're gabbing about, but I'm glad she has someone to talk to. She was different the other night after coming home from dress shopping, and I can't quite place my finger on what it is, but I'm guessing it has a lot to do with "the girls," as she called them.

I'm happy she's finally found friends outside of Talia.

No offense to her, of course, but I always hoped Chloe would find someone closer than Tennessee. I always had my teammates for connection, but who did she have besides me?

The tempo of the music slows down, and the deejay comes over the PA system.

"All right, guys, gals, and pals. It's time to invite all the couples on the floor. We have a special request from —hang on, I want to make sure I'm reading this right." He squints at the napkin in his hand. "Looks like it's from Lawless. He says this one is for Cal. You know who you are, with a heart drawn on it. So, Cal, if you're still out there, this one is for you!"

I groan, tossing my head back as the chords of "At Last" by Etta James flow through the speakers.

"I hate him."

Chloe laughs from beside me. "You wish you did."

"No wishing, Clover. It's true."

She presses her lips to my cheek. "Liar. Now, are you going to ask me to dance or not?"

I quirk a brow at her. "Do you want to?"

We've been to many weddings over the years, being on so many different teams with guys in various stages of life, so this isn't our first reception together. As such, I can perfectly recall how I always had to coax her to dance, and most of the time we'd end up just sitting in one spot all night, never once setting foot on the floor.

She lifts a shoulder. "Yeah, why not?"

"How many white wines have you had, and what have you done with my wife?"

A giggle bubbles out of her. "Only two, and you know it takes far more than that to get me drunk. Let's dance, loverboy."

I grin at the nickname, then rise to my feet and hold my hand out to her. "May I?"

She grins as she slips her palm against mine, and I sweep her away from the table just as Hayes does the same with Quinn. I wrap Chloe in my arms, looking around to find that all the Serpents Singles are out here. It's funny to think we ever made that little promise in the first place. Funny that *I* did, especially since I was well aware that love doesn't always wait. Sometimes it finds you in the least likely of all places, like a creative writing course you were wrongly assigned to and had to fight to stay in after the error was discovered.

"I forgot how good a dancer you are," Chloe says, her fingers tangling in the ends of my hair, which I cut just for this occasion. "Remind me to thank your mother again for forcing you into those lessons."

My parents were pleased when I told them Chloe was moving in with me, even though I have no idea how permanent it really is. All they wanted to know was if I'm happy, and when I told them yes, they didn't care beyond that. They still love her just as much as I do.

"She misses you, you know." I brush a hair out of her

face, then put my hand back on her hip. "You should call her."

"She's not…mad at me?"

"What? No. Why would she be mad?"

"Because…I left you."

Her words are like a punch to the gut, even though I've been telling myself I'm over it. I'm not, and I don't know if I ever will be. Even so, the last thing I want to do is ruin this dance by digging into the past, so I pull her closer, letting her fall against me as I bury my face in her neck and inhale her floral perfume.

"No, Clover," I say after the next verse of the song. "She's not mad at you, and I'm not either."

I feel her sigh rather than hear it and hold her tighter. It's a mistake, because even though we're in the middle of a crowded room, having her pressed against me, swaying like she is, is sending my body all the wrong signals, and I'm soon popping that boner Lawson screamed about days ago.

Chloe notices.

"Is that…" she asks, pulling back and looking down.

I grab her chin, forcing her eyes back to mine. "Yes, but don't look at it."

Her nostrils flare, and her brown eyes look nearly black. "But what if I want to?"

It's a statement that shouldn't do a damn thing to me but does. Without another word, I grab her hand and push through the crowd of couples. A few people give us weird looks—and some knowing ones—but I ignore it all, trying to get as far away from prying eyes as possible. We hit the hallway, and I look left, then right, but there are people everywhere.

Fuck, how many people did they invite to this damn wedding?

I usher Chloe past them, giving a nod to Poldzkin, who is rocking a brace on his knee, his crutches leaning against the chair he's sat in. We turn a corner to find several doors, and I know one of them has to lead to somewhere secluded.

Perfect.

I try the first. Nothing. I grab the handle for the second, and it's locked too.

"Motherfucker." I gnash my teeth. "Do none of these doors open?"

"Try that one."

She points to one farther down the hall, and we race toward it. It opens.

"Callum, are you sure we should—"

I cut off her words with my lips as I pull her inside, and she doesn't seem to mind, sinking against me and wrapping her arms around my neck. Because yes, I am sure. I am so fucking beyond sure that my cock is quite literally leaking inside the damn tuxedo pants Hutch had us all wear.

I feel my way through the dark room, searching for a light, because if we're going to do this, I want to see it. I'm rewarded when my fingers graze across the switch, and I flick it on. The room comes into focus, and though it's not the closet I wanted to pull her into earlier, it'll have to do.

"Is this a bathroom?" she asks, looking around.

"I think so. I wouldn't be surprised. This place is huge."

She palms me through my pants. "Speaking of huge…"

I growl, then practically throw myself at her, and all she does is laugh as she kisses me back. I'm not sure who removes what, but I find myself with nothing but my unbuttoned dress shirt on and Chloe on her knees, taking me to the back of her throat. She always loved doing this, and I wasn't about to complain. I'm not going to now, either.

"Fuck," I mutter as she takes me deep. "I swear your mouth is magic."

"Kind of like your cock," she says as she pulls off with a loud pop.

I'm already on the brink of coming, and while I'm desperate to do so, I don't want to just yet. I want this to last just a little longer. I tap her head, and she peers up at me with glossy eyes.

Fuck. She's perfect.

It takes everything in me to say, "You have to get up. I won't last long, and you don't want to wrinkle your dress."

She releases me, her lips glistening with spit. I'm sad when she drags her hand across them, wiping it away.

"Fine, but I want to finish that later."

"You can. I promise. But for now, I want you up on the counter. And spread your legs. I want to see you."

I grip my cock as she hoists herself up onto the counter I think is supposed to be used for doing your makeup, but right now, it's being used to put my wife on display. She hikes her dress up, then opens her thighs.

"More," I tell her, still jacking myself slowly.

Chloe pulls her panties to the side, revealing herself to me fully, and I drop to my knees like I'm begging for mercy. And maybe I am.

"What? No, no. If I don't get to have fun, you don't either. You—"

Her words die a slow death as I drag my tongue over her wet slit, and I smile as her legs slide even farther apart. I inch closer, pushing into her cunt, and she cries out.

"Oh god, Callum." Her fingers slip through my hair. "That feels so good."

"Tastes good too," I tell her, then dive back in for more.

I've loved eating her out from the start, and I think it's one of the things I missed the most about her being gone. I missed spending time on my knees, feeling her thighs pressed against my ears, and hearing the low whimpers she elicits every time I suck her clit between my lips.

Which is exactly what I do next.

"Yes," she mutters. "Please, yes."

I continue to lap her, dragging my tongue over every inch, paying extra attention to her clit every so often, then starting over again.

"You're killing me," she complains when I do it for the fifth time. "If I don't come soon, I might cry."

It doesn't matter that her words remind me of Lawson's—I'm so damn into tasting her that it doesn't even bother me. When I pull off her little bud for the eighth time, she groans, and it's clear if I don't stop messing around soon, she won't be fulfilling her promise to finish the job she started.

So I slip a finger into her, then another. It's when I add the third and put my lips back to her clit that her orgasm finally rolls through her, and she comes with a shout. She's not even done shaking before I'm pushing to my feet. I drag her off the counter, then turn her around.

"I thought you were worried about wrinkling my dress," she says as I push the satiny material up.

"Right now, I'm just worried about how good your cunt looks stretched around my cock." I arrange her how I want her—one leg up on the counter, the other foot on the floor—and drag my finger under the sliver of material that's hidden between her bare cheeks. "Do you know how fucking hot this thing is?"

"I hate it."

"Well, I don't." I push the underwear aside and swipe my thumb over her hole. A shiver rolls down her back, and I swear I feel her legs shake. "I could fuck you here instead, you know. If you wanted me to."

"Yes," she whispers with a sigh of delight. She always loved it when I took her ass. "I want."

As tempting as it sounds…

"I will, Clover," I promise her. "But not now. Tonight, I want your pussy."

"It's yours, Callum. Take it."

I slam into her without another word, loving the cry that leaves her as I bury myself until I can't anymore. I drag my cock back out slowly, then thrust in again.

"I think you got bigger," she says, her breaths uneven. "It certainly feels like you did."

I didn't, it's just the angle, but my stupid chest puffs up anyway, and I rock into her again.

"Callum…people are probably looking for us, you know."

"Are you saying you want me to speed this up?"

She peeks at me over her shoulder. "I'm saying I want you to fuck me like you mean it."

She doesn't have to ask me twice. I give in to what I want, and I pound into her with abandon. Over and over, loving how her ass shakes with each thrust, showing off the dimples I want to drag my tongue over.

And she takes it all. Every hard thrust, every squeeze

as I grip her tight, and every damn grunt as I get closer to my release. If someone were to walk past this room right now, there's no way they wouldn't hear our skin slapping together or our harsh breaths filling the otherwise quiet room.

I'm not sure which of us gives in first, but suddenly I'm erupting into her, coming so damn hard my knees buckle, and it takes all I have to remain on my feet as Chloe shakes around me. Once the aftershocks subside, I pull out of her and help her off the counter. She holds on to my shoulders as I tug her dress back down, smoothing out the wrinkles that are *very* obvious. Her hair is no longer in a clean updo, many pieces sticking out, and her makeup is smudged from having her mouth on me.

"You're gorgeous," I tell her.

"I'm sweaty and a mess."

"Still gorgeous."

She smiles, then wraps her arms around my neck, but I grab her hips and hold her away.

"No," I say. "You can't touch me right now. If you do, I might have to fuck you again, and then everyone will *definitely* know what happened in here."

She looks down at her dress. "Uh, I think they're already going to." She takes a step back. "But I understand. We probably should go back out there before someone comes looking for us."

"You can say Lawson's name."

She laughs and leans in for a kiss, but I shake my head.

"Really? You don't trust yourself with just a kiss?"

"When it comes to you? Not at all."

She tucks her lips together, trying to hide her grin, but I see it anyway.

"I'll see you out there?"

I nod, hating when she takes a steadying breath, then pulls open the door. She's just stepped through it when I grab her wrist, and she stops, turning toward me.

"Don't even think about cleaning that up, Clover. I want to spend the rest of the night knowing my cum is drying on my wife's legs, got it?"

She gulps. "Got it."

I pat her ass and send her on her way. I spend the next five minutes trying to talk my cock back down, and when it doesn't work, I go back to the reception and pray nobody notices. Thankfully, nobody seems to pay me much attention as I make my way back to the party. I slip into the crowd like I never left, nobody the wiser to what just transpired.

"Chloe!"

I turn at the mention of my wife, but I don't see anyone I recognize. Then someone moves, and I see her. I smile and move to walk toward her but stop when I notice she's not alone. There's a woman talking to her, and I recognize her instantly. She's the wife of the Serpents' first captain, who is around here somewhere.

"Wow, I was not expecting to see you here," Avery says. "How do you know Reed and Auden?"

"Uh, Hutch—sorry, *Reed*—is my husband's teammate."

"Your husband? You're married to a Serpents player? How come I didn't know this? We should have met way before now."

"I've been out of the country on assignment," Chloe tells her. "I'm here with Callum Keller."

"Oh! I know him. He's grumpy, no offense, but still very kind."

Chloe laughs. "None taken, though that's not the Callum I know."

"Well, anyway," Avery says, "I'm glad I ran into you. I've had a few drinks, and I probably shouldn't be saying this, but…you're it. We absolutely *loved* the second interview on Wednesday, and we plan to officially offer you the position once we get our ducks in a row."

She had a second interview? She didn't tell me. It must have happened when I was doing that event at the middle school that I agreed to months ago. Is there a reason she hid it from me? Was she afraid to say something to jinx it? Or is she planning…

No.

I don't let myself think. She couldn't be leaving again. Not after everything…right? My breath disappears, or at least that's what it feels like, because suddenly I'm struggling for air and can't seem to get enough of it.

Fuck, not now. Please not now.

This is the last place I want to have a panic attack, but I feel it coming on. Even though I'm dying to hear what Chloe's response is, I need to leave—*now*. I push through the crowd once again, keeping my eyes downcast because I really don't want anyone to try to stop me. I don't think I could handle it if they saw me like this.

When I finally clear the room, I burst through the front doors of the swanky hotel and gulp in breath after breath of February air. Is she leaving me again? Is my wife walking away from us? Does what we're doing here not mean anything to her? Or the last ten years we've spent together?

I try to tell myself I'm making a big deal out of nothing and maybe what I heard wasn't true. Avery did admit to having too much to drink. Maybe she has Chloe confused with somebody else.

But even as the thought flits through my mind, I know it's not true. Chloe had a second interview, and she didn't say a word to me about it. She's making plans for our future again and leaving me out of the decision-making process.

I pull my phone from my pocket, swiping my thumb across the screen and pulling up my texts with Stefan. I'm typing out an SOS message when I hear her.

"Callum?"

No, please no.

"Hey." Chloe sets her hand on my back. "I was wondering where you went. Everything good?"

I close my eyes, willing myself to remain calm and act like everything is normal. If she didn't tell me about the second interview, there must be a reason.

She's staying. She's not going anywhere. It will all be okay. I repeat the words to myself as I peel my eyes open and look over at her. She looks much more put together than she did when I watched her walk out of the bathroom, but if I look closely, I can still see the smudge of her lipstick from my kisses.

"Callum?" she says when I don't respond.

"Yeah." I clear my throat. "Yeah, sorry. Just got a little hot in there. Too many people for me."

She smiles. "You always did hate crowds."

"I did. But I'm good now. Want to head back in?"

There's a pause, and for a moment, I think she might tell me about the offer from Avery. It seems like for the first time, we'll lay it all on the line.

But she doesn't. She just nods, and I lead her back inside, where we spend the night laughing and dancing and pretending everything is okay.

When we crawl into bed several hours later, I pull her close, holding her tight because even if I'm not sure what the future holds, there's one thing I am certain of—I'm not ready to let her go.

Chapter 19

Lawson: What do you guys think about me starting a love advice podcast?

Lawson: I could call it Lawless Lawson's Love Languages.

Lawson: You're right. I should do it. I'm doing it.

Hayes: Are you just not going to wait for anyone else to chime in?

Lawson: Nah. It's a fantastic idea.

Lawson: Besides, I don't need your permission. I just didn't want to keep it a secret from all of you.

Lawson: Because, you know, LIKE SOME PEOPLE, I don't keep secrets from my FRIENDS.

Me: Are we really still going on about this?

Lawson: Um, yes. You lied to us for years. YEARS, KELLER!

Me: Has there ever been a day in your life when you're not dramatic?

Lawson: Yes.

Lawson: No.

Lawson: YES. Because I am not dramatic. I'm passionate.

Me: I think the word you're looking for is annoying.

Lawson: That's not what your mom said.

Lawson: Wait, seriously? No comeback, Kells?

Me: Not really in the mood.

Lawson: What's wrong? Is Chloe tired of you already?

Me: Shut up, Lawson.

Lawson: Aw, come on, Mr. Secretly Married. I was only teasing.

Lawson: Speaking of being married, how's the wife, Hutchy?

Hutch: Perfect. Now shut up.

Hayes: I'm trying to take a fucking nap, so can we not do this today?

Locke: What they said.

Me: Looks like I'm not the only one who hates you today, Lawsy.

Lawson: Jeez, is everyone in a bad mood?

Fox: Uh, we're in the middle of a horrible road trip. I'd say the chances are pretty damn high.

Lawson: You know what's not high? Your save percentage.

Hayes: You know, I think it really might actually be time to delete this group chat.

Lawson: WHAT

Lawson: NOOOOOOOO

Lawson: I was kidding. I love you guys. Please come back.

Lawson: Hello?

Lawson: Foxy Baby?

Lawson: I'm sorry! I was teasing. I'M A FUNNY GUY. HA HA!

Lawson: This is totally going to ruin the podcast. I was going to have you all on as guests. We were going to talk about our club and everything.

Me: We aren't a fucking club.

Lawson: You can't see me right now, but I'm pointing to the group chat name.

Me: Uh, it literally just says SERPENTS SINGLES GROUP CHAT.

LAWSON HAS CHANGED THE GROUP CHAT NAME TO "SERPENTS SINGLES CLUB GROUP CHAT"

KELLER HAS CHANGED THE GROUP CHAT NAME TO "WE'RE NOT A FUCKING CLUB. ALSO, SHUT THE FUCK UP, LAWSON."

Lawson: Wow. Rude.

LAWSON HAS CHANGED THE GROUP CHAT NAME TO "KELLER WOULD LICK HIS OWN BALLS IF HE COULD, AND WE ARE SOOOO A CLUB, BABY"

Me: I really hate you.

Lawson: Liar.

LAWSON HAS CHANGED THE GROUP CHAT NAME TO "KELLER LOVES LAWSON"

Lawson: Awwwww, Kells. That is SO sweet. I love you too, buddy.

KELLER HAS LEFT THE GROUP CHAT

LAWSON HAS ADDED KELLER TO THE GROUP CHAT

Lawson: Nice try, buddy. But you're stuck with us.

KELLER HAS CHANGED THE GROUP
CHAT NAME TO "LAWSON CRIES
EVERY TIME HE CUMS"

Lawson: I'm quitting the team.

Me: Don't tease me like that.

LAWSON CHANGED THE GROUP CHAT
NAME TO "KELLER IS A BUTTHOLE
AND A DIRTY LIAR AND HE EATS HIS
OWN BOOGERS"

Hayes: Okay, this is just getting really
sad at this point.

Hutch: It really is. And annoying.

Locke: Seriously. I need my pre-game
nap. I'm old, remember?

Lawson: At least you've finally admitted
it!

FOX HAS CHANGED THE GROUP CHAT
NAME TO "WHY CAN'T WE ALL JUST
GET ALONG?"

Lawson: Okay, that's too cute, Foxy.

Fox: Thanks, but also…and I say this
with respect…shut up.

Lawson: BUDDY!

Lawson: But okay. I get it, I get it. I'll let
you guys sleep now.

Lawson: I love you, Hutchy.

Hutch: ARE YOU FUCKING KIDDING ME????

Lawson: I love you, Lockey Poo.

Locke: 🙂

Lawson: I love you, Foxy Baby.

Fox: Love you too, buddy.

Lawson: I love you, Hayesy.

Hayes: …

Me: Don't. Just fucking don't.

Lawson: I LOVE YOU, CALLUM KELLER, YOU BEAUTIFUL GRUMPY FUCK!

Me: Please, someone delete me. I'm begging you.

Lawson: Not a chance.

LAWSON CHANGED THE GROUP CHAT NAME TO "SERPENTS NOT-SO-SINGLE CLUB"

Lawson: Sleep tight, boys. 😴

Chapter 20

Something changed after Hutch and Auden's wedding.

I'm not sure what, but the days leading up to him leaving for the road trip felt like they did before I left. We talked, but not about anything significant. We had sex, but it wasn't as passionate as before. It's like a switch got flipped, and we're back to where we were three years ago. I hate it, and I really hate that it's the only thing I can focus on as we watch the guys play their last road game.

"Come on! Get it together!"

Lilah and Rory nod at Auden's words, and I share their sentiments. The Serpents have been playing like trash since they left. Every game is a nail-biter, and not in a fun way. They've given up multiple leads, and not a single sports network can figure out what's happened with this sharp drop-off.

I've tried asking Callum about it a few times, but each time I do, he shuts the conversation down or tries to distract me. I let him have it because I have no business prying when I'm hiding such a big secret from him.

Avery's drunken words at the wedding haven't left me. I've tried not to put too much stock in them with her being inebriated, but I would be lying if I said I wasn't hoping they're true. A job in Seattle would mean being with Callum again, this time for real. It wouldn't be what we're currently doing, which is just pretending everything is okay. A part of me wishes we could do that forever, because man, does it feel good, but I want to get back to who we were. Before the NHL. Before I got so in my head I didn't know who I was anymore.

I can't do that until Callum knows about the offer… and until I tell him I know about the card. I've opened the drawer every day he's been gone, have stared at that little rectangle so many times I have the phone number memorized. And yet, I still can't figure out what he's doing with it if he doesn't intend to use it.

Yes, he's told me he loves me and it's forever, but people say those things all the time. Meaning them is a whole different story. I once told him I'd stand by him until my dying day, and look how that turned out—I left when I couldn't handle it anymore.

It's why I haven't mentioned the job and why I still haven't uttered those three big words to him. I'm too scared if I do, it'll all get ripped away when he wakes up and realizes everyone else was right all along—I'm not good enough for him.

"Fox, what the hell are you doing?!" Auden screeches at the TV, drawing my attention, and though the sound is loud, it's just what I need to get out of my head. She looks at her best friend. "Sorry, but *please* text your man and tell him to keep his ass in the net during the third."

"He's great at playing the puck, and he knows what he's doing. Chill, mama."

"Don't you *mama* me, Lilah Jane."

I look at Rory, who is completely unbothered by their exchange, and she shrugs. Auden continues yelling at the TV, and Lilah keeps trying to get her to relax. Vanessa interjects every now and then whenever someone says something about Whitlocke slowing down and his age, but it's pretty much how the rest of the period goes.

"I'm going to check on the baby. I can't watch this anymore," Auden announces when they give up another goal after they were up 3–0 at one point. As she leaves the room, I swear she mutters, "Why can't I be a smoker? I could use a cigarette right about now."

"How are you handling all of this, Chloe?" Quinn asks. "You're a seasoned WAG, right? You've been with Keller since before he was pro."

"Since college, but as cheesy as it sounds, it doesn't get any easier to watch. My stomach is in knots right now."

"Mine too," Rory agrees, then she shakes the bowl of chips she's been snacking on. "Hence the stress eating." She holds the dish out to me. "Want one?"

"I'm good, but thank you. I'll settle for my emotional support Diet Coke."

"Cheers."

She taps her water bottle to my can, and we settle in for the third period. Yet again, the Serpents give up their lead and end the game with a shootout win. It's a big positive getting the two points, especially since they dropped so many during this trip, but you can tell just by looking at the guys that they aren't happy with their performance.

"Well, that was…a night," Vanessa says dejectedly.

"Even *I* could use a hug after watching that," Rory comments.

Lilah nods. "Same. I'm ready for them to be home. Ten days is too long."

Even though things are a little rocky with Callum right now, I'm ready too. I forgot how much I missed him when he was on the road. Even when things don't feel right between us, I still want him there.

We bid each other good night, and I climb into the car with Vanessa, who is giving me a ride home since we're going to the same building.

"So," she starts once we're halfway there, "how are things going with Keller? Are you settling in okay?"

"Seattle has been great. And you ladies have really welcomed me into your group, which I appreciate."

She twists her lips, then slides her eyes my way before looking back at the road. "And with Keller?"

Shit. I was hoping she wouldn't catch on to the fact that I didn't answer that part of the question.

"Uh, they're good."

"Yes, because you sound *so* sure about that," she deadpans.

She's right. I didn't sound sincere at all, and that's mostly because I'm not. Things aren't okay, but I don't know why, which makes it hard to explain. How familiar does that sound? I had no idea three years ago what was making me so unhappy, but once I had space, I could pick out what it was—me.

Now, I feel like I'm right back at square one, and I don't *want* space this time. I want to stay. I want to work it out with my husband. That starts with being honest—with myself and Callum. I need to tell him about the second interview and the conversation I had with Avery at the wedding. Unlike with London, I want him to be involved in the decision-making process this time. He's my husband, and he has a right to know.

"You don't have to tell me," Vanessa says when we pull into the garage. "But just so you know, I'm here if you need an ear. We're *all* here. I might be new to the group, but we've all been through some rough times, some more than others, so there won't be any judgment if that's what you're worried about. Or if you're still trying to figure it all out yourself, that's okay too. But you're not alone. Just remember that."

I tell her I appreciate it and will let her know if I

want to talk, and I'm surprised by how much I mean it. I try not to think about the fact that if I lose Callum for real this time, I'll lose these new friendships too, or how I *really* don't want that to happen.

I wave goodbye to Vanessa as I exit the elevator, and as I push into the apartment, exhaustion takes over. All I want to do is take a long bath and lie down, so that's exactly what I do. I fill Callum's big tub—one I highly doubt he's ever used since he thinks baths are like swimming in your own filth—then climb inside. I don't get back out until I'm wrinkled like a raisin.

After, I take my time applying lotion and moisturizing all the places that need it. Then I put on the coziest pajamas I can find and head toward the bed. But the second I look at it, I know it's not what I want right now. I want familiar. I want comfort. I want our old bed.

I pad into the spare room, where Percy is already curled up on my destination. "Hey, little man," I say to him as I approach. "Mind if I get in there too?"

Meow.

I take his answer as a yes and settle in next to him. He gets up and lies back down against my neck, a place I've seen him sleep several times now on Callum. I'm not sure how long I stay there like that, but it's long enough that I fall asleep, only to be awoken by two strong arms lifting me up.

"Callum?" I ask, trying to blink my eyes open.

"Yep, just me. Not a stranger trying to touch your butt."

I smile, then snuggle against him, loving how warm he is and how good he smells—like home.

"I miss you," I say, the words slipping out easily.

He chuckles lightly. "I missed you, too, Clover." I want to correct him, but I'm too tired to do so. "What are you doing sleeping in there?"

"I don't know. I just wanted to feel close to you again."

He doesn't say anything, but I still get the sense he understands exactly what I mean. He sets me on the bed, then shuffles me around until I'm tucked tightly under the blankets. I protest when he moves away from me, but he promises he'll be back, and I take him at his word as he shuts the door to the bathroom.

Five minutes later, he returns and slips beneath the blankets beside me. His hand lands on my hip, and his touch is completely innocent, but I don't *want* innocent. I want him. I scoot back, rubbing against him until I feel his cock stir to life and hear his unsteady breaths in my ear.

He squeezes my waist. "Clover…it's late."

"Please?" I ask, rolling toward him, suddenly *frantic* for his touch. "Please, Callum. I want to feel you inside me."

He stares at me—*hard*—and I worry he's going to tell

me no, or worse, break up with me in this moment. But he doesn't.

"Fuck it," he mutters, then he kisses me, and I sigh because everything feels right again.

I don't know exactly how we get undressed or how we end up with me straddling him, but it's happening, and I groan when I slide onto his hard length.

"Fucking Christ," he grates out. "Fuck, you feel so good."

I nod, because he feels good too, and I let myself get lost in a steady rhythm and his hands roaming over every inch of me. He traces the paths my stretch marks make, then cups my breasts, running his thumbs over the stiff peaks of my nipples. His hands feel like paradise, like every incredible vacation or perfect sunny afternoon. It's euphoric, and exactly what I needed.

But it's when he presses against my clit that I truly come undone. I shudder around him, riding him through every wave that crashes into me, and Callum follows right behind me, bucking up into me like a wild animal.

Once the high wears off, I climb off him, curling into my favorite spot next to him, and he pulls me even closer. There's so much I want to say to him, so many words sitting on the tip of my tongue, and the urge to lay it all out there right this instant overwhelms me.

"Callum?"

He doesn't answer, and I look up to find him fast

asleep. I sigh, then press a soft kiss to his lips. He doesn't even budge.

"I love you, too," I whisper to his sleeping form, and I follow him into slumber.

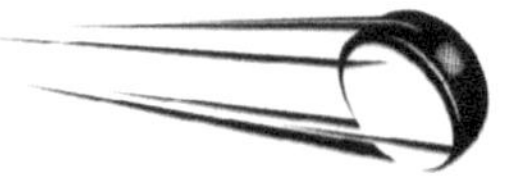

The call comes on a Monday in the second week of March.

I chickened out the next morning after Callum came back from his last road trip. I had been so ready to tell him everything the night before, but he was in a good mood the next morning, so I thought it best not to ruin it.

If only I had known the good mood wouldn't last. He's been sulking around the apartment since then, and this time I can't even blame hockey for the sour mood he's in. Once they got back on home ice, the Serpents returned to their dominating play and have gotten eight of their last ten possible points. They're right back where they were before, and they're officially the top team in the Pacific by a cushiony five points. They've still got work to do, but they can breathe a little easier now.

I just wish someone would give my husband the memo.

"Uh, I'm going to take this outside."

I don't know why I bother saying it. Callum doesn't even look up from the TV he's been sitting in front of since he got home from practice. He's playing some video game where he runs through what looks like hell on earth with a chainsaw shield.

I hit save on the article I'm working on, then step out onto the balcony, shielding my eyes against the bright midday sun.

"Hello?" I say, holding the phone up to my ear.

"Chloe!" Avery's cheerful voice comes over the line. "I'm so glad I was able to catch you."

"Avery, hi. How are you?"

"Doing well. Gosh, that was a fun wedding, huh?"

"Yeah, it was great." I glance inside to see where Callum is, but he hasn't moved. I step farther away from the door, keeping my voice low as I say, "I assume you're calling about the editor position?"

"You assume correctly." She imitates a drumroll before announcing, "Welcome to *Sports Action News*, Chloe!" She laughs. "Well, not technically. It's more like welcome to *Seattle Life & Leisure*, a subsidiary of *Sports Action News*, spearheaded by yours truly and hopefully —our new editor-in-chief, you."

I smile, loving the sound of it. *Chloe Keller, Editor-in-Chief.* It's everything I've been working toward, and the title sounds just as amazing as I always thought it would. Even so, I can't help but feel like something about it isn't right, and I have a suspicion it has to do with the man sitting roughly thirty feet away.

"Chloe? Did I lose you?"

I give myself a shake. "No, sorry. I'm still here. I'm just…I guess I'm just trying to wrap my head around it."

"I know! It's amazing, isn't it? My husband and I are excited about this new venture. And we're both *very* excited to have you on board. I mean, I know I gave you a heads-up about it"—she laughs, remembering her drunkenness at the wedding—"but this is the official offer. All you need to do is say yes, and we'll take care of the rest."

Yes! I want to shout, but the word doesn't come as easily as I hoped it would, and I know it's because of the tension I feel with the person on the other side of the glass. The one who has been cranky the last few weeks but is still somehow so good to me. The one who has been patient for far too long and the one who has loved me since I was eighteen. The one I love too.

"Chloe? You are still interested, right?"

"Sorry," I say again. "Yes, I'm interested. I just… Would it be too much trouble if I asked for some time to think about it?"

"Oh." She sounds just as surprised as I expect, especially given that I've had a month to think this over. "Um, yes. I can do that. I mean…are you sure you're still interested?"

"Yes, I swear I am, Avery. I, uh, I just need to discuss it a bit more with my husband."

"Ah, right. I completely understand. It's a big decision. I was never truly a hockey wife since we were only together for a short time while Emmett was playing, but I'm sure it's a lot to try to manage a career *and* the NHL schedule."

She has no idea.

"Yeah, it's definitely a lot," I say. "Could I let you know soon?"

"How soon? We're hoping to launch the new paper this summer, and there's still so much to do to get ready for it. We wanted to get the ball rolling sooner rather than later."

"A week?"

She pauses, and I can tell she doesn't love the request, but she grants it anyway.

"Thank you," I tell her. "I appreciate it. One week, and I'll have your answer for you."

"Good. And, Chloe?"

"Yes, Avery?"

"I hope it's a yes because I'd really love to work with you. You're very talented, and I can't believe another paper hasn't snapped you up already. I want to be the one to do it. So, get back to me soon, even if you don't need the full week. Heck, *especially* if you don't."

"I will," I promise her.

We end the call, and I clutch the phone in my hand like it's a lifeline. Right now, it feels like one.

Chloe Keller, Editor-in-Chief.

I smile again, but it fades almost instantly, and I look back into the apartment. The game is paused, and a heavy knot settles into my gut. With a long inhale and an equally long exhale, I walk back inside. Callum is sitting up, and as I pad closer to him, I can see that his head is tilted down, his shoulders damn near his ears. I don't have to question why.

"You know."

He closes his eyes, then nods. "I know."

I drop onto the couch next to him, trying hard not to be offended when he scoots away.

"When?" I ask.

"The wedding. I guess congratulations are in order."

Ah. That explains why things have felt so off between us since then, why he changes the subject whenever I mention work, even if it's his work. He's been avoiding this just as much as I have.

He turns to me, and the hurt in his eyes is evident. I wish more than anything I could wipe it away.

"I think the better question might be why."

"Why? What do you mean?"

"Why didn't you tell me?" He explodes off the couch, and Percy goes running into the spare bedroom.

I don't blame him. I wish I could run too, but I don't. It's time I face this.

You can't run from a hard conversation forever, you know.

Talia's words ring loud in my head, and I already know she's going to be so mad when she finds out I've been hiding this from her too, but I had to. I had to make this decision on my own. For too long, I've let others dictate so much, and I wanted as little outside influence on this as possible because this is for *me*, not anyone else.

"I found the card."

He tips his head to the side. "What card?"

"The one in the drawer. For the…" I swallow, not wanting to say the word but knowing I need to. "For the divorce lawyer."

He doesn't move. Doesn't even blink. And it tells me all I need to know—he kept it on purpose. I close my eyes, all my worst fears slamming into me at once.

This is it, I say to myself. *We're over.*

"I wasn't going to use it."

I pry my eyes open and look up at him. "What?"

He crosses back toward me and sits on the coffee table. His long legs barely fit between us, his knees pressed firmly against mine, but I don't care. I'm still reeling from what he just said.

He…wasn't going to use it? Relief rushes through me, but it doesn't quell all the chaos still happening inside me.

"I wasn't going to use it, Clover. I swear I wasn't."

"Then why did you keep it?"

"Why did you leave?" He counters my question so effortlessly, and it makes sense. I'm sure those words have been sitting on the edge of his lips for years, begging to be set free.

They're free now.

"You said before that it wasn't my fault you left." He

scratches at the stubble lining his face. "Then why did you leave?"

"Because I needed to."

He shakes his head. "I don't get it. You're going to have to spell it out for me a little more than that."

I sigh, trying to sort out where to even begin. For the millionth time, I wish there were an easy answer to what led to the decision, but there isn't. It's as complicated as all the feelings I have swirling within me.

"What happened to us?" he says, his voice breaking on the last word, and I can feel my eyes begin to sting. I blink it away, refusing to cry. "Where did everything go wrong?"

"I don't know. I think it might have been broken from the start. I think *I* was broken."

His jaw slackens, like he can't believe what he's hearing, then he shakes his head. "But you're not. Don't you get that? You're not broken. You're just…" He sighs. "Fuck, Clover, you're just mine."

I smile softly, picking at an invisible piece of lint on my leggings. "You never could pick out any of my faults."

"That's because to me, you don't have any."

"But how is that healthy, Callum?" I ask, looking at him. "How can you say there isn't anything about me that you don't like?"

"Is that what you want me to do? You want me to pick you apart? Want me to tell you you're not good enough?

Confirm all your worst fears?" He scoffs, shaking his head. "I'm not doing that. I'll *never* do that because it's not true. None of it is true. All those voices you hear in your head saying you're not good enough? They're fucking lying. You *are* good enough. You don't need to change yourself. You don't need to 'be better,' whatever the hell that means. And you really don't have to do *anything* you don't want to. Not for me and sure as hell not for anyone else."

He doesn't have to clarify that he's talking about my parents deciding my future for me all those years ago. I hear him loud and clear.

"So, no, I'm not going to sit here and let you tell me all the things I'm not supposed to love about you because those things don't exist, not to me."

"But they exist to *me*, Callum. Just because you tell me you love me doesn't mean I automatically love myself. Just because you say I'm smart, it doesn't mean I don't feel like the dumbest person in every room I walk into, because I know how hard I had to struggle to keep up in school. It doesn't mean I don't know I'll never be as clever as my parents, and just because you say I'm beautiful, it doesn't mean I'm not aware of what other people say about me when they see someone like me on your arm."

His eyes flare at the reminder of the words uttered about me so long ago, the ones I've never forgotten, not for a single second.

His knuckles turn white as he grips the table. "Fuck, I wish I could bash that guy's face in."

"I know. I know you do, and you have no idea how much I love it. When you stuck up for me back then, I should never have been mad at you for losing the game. I should have thrown my arms around your neck and told you right then that I loved you. But I didn't. I was so damn embarrassed and scared, and all I wanted was to be worthy of you. To be worthy of my parents. To be *enough*."

His face crumples, and he slides off the table, dropping to his knees and pushing between my own. He cups my face, wiping at the tears I feel rolling down my cheeks.

"Is that what drove you away? Not feeling like you're good enough?"

"Yes. No. I'm not sure." I take a deep breath. "All I know is that I felt...I felt stifled. I felt like I was looking through a glass window, watching my life pass by. I was living it, but I wasn't really in it. And that would have been such an easier pill to swallow if you weren't so amazing."

"But I wasn't amazing. I should have—"

"No." I shake my head. "Please, don't. Don't try to make it so you're at fault. You're not. I'm the villain in this scenario."

"You're not," he says, pushing my hair out of my face as I wipe my nose with my shirtsleeve. "You're just...shit,

I don't know, Clover. I just wish you had said something to me. I wish you had told me how you were feeling. Because I would have given it all up in a fucking heartbeat—hockey, the chase of lifting the Cup, the long weeks away—all of it. I would have walked away if it meant keeping you."

I scoff. "And that's the problem. You would have, and I would have let you. I'd let you make sacrifices for me because I'm selfish. Because I'm insecure. Because I need reassurance. I would have let you. But in the end, I wouldn't be able to live with myself, and eventually I'd resent you. I don't want that. I never want that. I can't ask you to give anything up for me. I never could. So, I left. I needed space. I had to figure out who I was beyond being a hockey wife, beyond what my parents expected of me, and beyond you. I needed to learn to love myself without your love attached to it. I needed to know *myself*."

"And do you? Do you know who you are now? Do you love yourself now?"

I exhale heavily because that's the million-dollar question, isn't it? *Do* I love who I am now? I got everything I wanted. I was just offered an incredible position as editor-in-chief. I have a husband with a successful career who could easily take care of me so that I'd never need to work a day in my life. And I have friends who love me and cherish me. Sure, some of them are new ones, but I know they're there for me.

I have it all, yet if I walked in the bathroom and

looked in the mirror this instant, I still would feel like I wasn't enough. I thought running away and becoming a new, better me would change that. I was wrong. So fucking wrong.

"No," I tell him honestly. "But I've made peace with that. I've accepted that I'm still learning every day, that it's not a destination, but a journey."

He blinks, and I realize how red the whites of his eyes are and how so damn close he is to crying. I hate seeing him like this, and I hate being the cause of it even more. He doesn't deserve it, and I don't deserve him.

He drops his forehead to mine, exhaling heavily as he whispers, "Fuck, Clover."

And yes, fuck indeed. We sit like that for a long time, Callum holding on to me, breathing me in, and me trying to wrap my head around what's happening.

"So what about us?" He pulls away, moving back to the table, and I tuck my hands beneath my legs to stop myself from reaching for him. "Where does that leave us now?"

I rack my brain, trying to find the perfect answer, but nothing comes.

I lift a shoulder. "I…I don't know."

He sighs, dragging a hand over his face, then through his hair, leaving it messy. I so badly want to reach over and fix it, but I'm not sure I have the privilege to do so right now.

When he looks at me, my heart beats overtime.

Thu-thump. Thu-thump. Thu-thump.

"I love you, Clover. I always have. That's never changed, no matter what."

I smile softly. "I know."

"I'll wait. If that's what you want from me, I'll do it." He rolls his tongue over his lips. "I'm…I'm not going to stop loving you, okay? No matter how long it takes, I'll be here."

I choke back a sob. Asking him to wait is wrong. I shouldn't do it. He deserves someone who knows who they are. Someone who doesn't let so many other people have a say in their life. Someone who is…well, enough.

And I really want to be that person.

"You don't have to say anything now. Just…think about it, okay? Think about what you really want, and don't make the decision for anyone other than you. Not your friends, not your family, and especially not me. Just you, Clover, okay?"

But doesn't he know he is my friend and my family and the one person I want more than anything in this world? I can't say that, though, not until I figure out *me.* So I don't.

"Okay," I say.

Callum gathers me into his arms, holding me tighter than he ever has before, like he's afraid he's about to lose me, and I'm gripping him just as hard for the very same reason.

We stay like that a long time, and I never do decide who is holding up who.

Chapter 21

KELLER

Three years ago

I've seen Chloe wearing my number too many times to count over the years, and no matter how many times I do, it still makes my heart beat just a little faster.

She cups her hands over her mouth and yells. I might not be able to hear her, but I still smile. We're losing this game, down 5–1 with four minutes left to go in the third, but that's just how it's been in Chicago lately, and I've accepted that. It doesn't make seeing Chloe cheer for me any less sweet.

The game concludes, and though we should all be bummed about yet another loss and where we're currently at in the standings, there's a buzz, and it has to do with the date. It's New Year's Eve, and just about everyone in this room has plans tonight, including me.

I quickly shower, then I'm one of the players stuck addressing the media. I keep my answers short and to the point, sticking to the usual hockey script of "get pucks in deep," "go hard at the net," and "we just have to keep going down the stretch here." I sound like a broken record, but even that's not enough to sour my good mood.

"Hey," Chloe says as I walk toward her once I'm released for the night—after a rousing speech from Coach about staying on the straight and narrow, of course.

"Clover." I grin, pressing my lips to hers.

She's the first to pull away, and I pretend it doesn't sting. Things have been…off between us lately. I kept telling myself it was because of the stress of the holidays, but now it's New Year's Eve, and it still doesn't feel normal. I have no idea what's wrong, but I'm hoping we can get back on track tonight. This has always been her favorite holiday, so maybe that will be on my side.

"How was work?" I ask her.

"Fine."

Fine. It's her go-to answer whenever I ask about it, and I gnash my teeth to keep from sighing. She hates her job. I know it, and she knows it too, but for some reason, she won't do anything about it. She thinks she's betraying her parents if she decides she no longer wants to work in a lab, and I hate that she's resigned to being unhappy just to please them.

Don't they know their daughter is miserable? Don't they see she wants something else? Can't they just let her off the hook? Can't she let *herself* off the hook? I love my wife, but I wish she would stand up for herself a little more sometimes. She doesn't even have to work if she doesn't want to, so making herself so damn unhappy makes no sense to me.

"Are you ready to go, then?" I ask because I know she's not going to offer any more.

"Yep."

We make our way to a local bar we've gone to a few times, and I'm unsurprised to find it's packed. I would personally rather be at home, but this has always been the one night a year Chloe likes going out, so I suck it up and push through for her.

We order drinks—a beer for me and a Diet Coke for her—then find a spot in the back where it's not as packed and just a smidge quieter. When I look at her across the tiny two-person table, I can't help but smile. Even after all these years together, she's still fucking gorgeous, and I still want her. I never gave much thought to finding true love or getting married or anything like that, but the moment I saw her, I wanted it all.

That hasn't changed.

"Have I ever told you how hot you look with my last name across your back?"

"Hey, that's *my* last name too." She smirks at me over the rim of her cup. "But thank you."

I laugh, take a drink, and set it back down with a loud smack of my lips. "So, New Year's Eve."

"New Year's Eve."

"Any resolutions you want to share?"

I don't know what's so wrong about what I've said, but it's clearly the wrong thing, and almost instantly, Chloe's entire mood shifts. I watch as her shoulders slump forward and she folds into herself. Her eyes darken so much they look black beneath the bar lights.

"Um, actually…" she starts, wrapping her hand around her soda. "I, uh, I wanted to talk to you about something…"

My stomach drops right to the sticky, dirty floor of the bar, and a shiver rolls down my back. Something isn't off with us. Something is *wrong*.

I force my voice to remain neutral. "Sure. What's up?"

"I, um…" She looks around the bar, squinting. She leans in closer. "Do you mind if we talk somewhere quieter?"

No. I want to talk right here, right now. I want to know why you're pulling away from me in more ways than one. I want to know how to fix it. I want to know that we're okay.

But I don't say any of that.

"Let's go up to the roof."

It's freezing out, which is why it's much less crowded up here than inside, but I'm so hot and clammy trying to sort out what it is my wife could possibly want to talk to me about that I don't even notice the bite of cold.

We find a corner away from the other people

scattered about, and I stand as close to her as possible. I don't know why, but I feel like I *need* to be near her right now, like whatever she's about to say…it could change everything.

She takes a drink of her Diet Coke, then sets the glass on the railing before turning out to look at the city. I don't miss how she inches away, either. She's quiet for a while, and I let her take her time, and not just because I'm not so sure I'm ready to hear what she has to say.

When she shivers, I tug off my jacket and drape it around her shoulders.

She smiles up at me softly. "Thank you."

"Of course. Anything for my girl."

Her eyes flit away from mine, and I push down the vomit that threatens to make itself known.

"So…"

"So…" she repeats, then sighs. "I applied for an internship."

I'm not sure what I was expecting, but it certainly wasn't that. She applied for an internship? When did she do this? I try to sift through all our conversations over the last few months, but I can't, for the life of me, figure out when she may have mentioned an internship. Did I miss it somewhere? Did I not pay attention?

"An internship? For another lab?"

She shakes her head. "Uh, no. If I have to spend another three months in one, I might scream."

My brows furrow. "What's the internship for, then?"

What I really want to ask is *Why didn't you tell me? I'm your husband!* But I don't.

"Writing."

It's the second time tonight she's surprised me. "Writing? What? Since when?"

"Um, I don't know. For a while now, I guess. I, uh, I've been blogging. I don't know what possessed me to do it, but one night when you were on the road and I couldn't sleep, I grabbed my laptop and wrote something about it. You know I've always loved journaling and getting my thoughts out."

"I know. I remember watching you all the time in college. I haven't seen you do it lately, though."

"I do. I just use my computer now instead."

Am I just not as observant as I thought? I had no idea she was still writing…or that she still wanted to. I know I've been wrapped up in hockey, especially lately, since I'm about ninety-nine percent sure I'm on the chopping block as Chicago looks to revamp their roster yet again, but I didn't realize I was so distracted I didn't even know what was going on in my own home.

"Anyway," she says, "I found it online and applied on a whim. With Talia's encouragement, of course."

Her best friend knows about this, yet she didn't think it was important to tell her husband? That's fucked up in so many ways I don't have the words for.

"I wasn't expecting to get accepted at all since I have no real formal practice in writing, which is why I didn't say anything," she continues. "But I guess they liked my samples so much they decided to take a chance on me, and I…" She shrugs. "I don't know. I really want to do it. I don't love the lab, but you know that already. Maybe this could be something new for me, you know?"

But it's not new for her. It's new for *us*, and I don't think that's something she's taken into consideration. I can understand being worried she wouldn't get it, but to not even mention to me that she applied? Then spring this on me tonight of all nights?

Well, I suppose that part makes sense. She always saw this holiday as a chance to start over.

"Callum?"

"Hmm?" I give myself a mental shake. "Sorry. Yeah, that's amazing, Clover. I'm happy for you." I mean it too. Sure, it's not at all what I was expecting, but it doesn't make me any less thrilled for this opportunity she has. "I know you'll be great at it. When does it start?"

"Um, soon. Like in two weeks."

Two weeks? What the fuck?

"I know that's not ideal," she continues. "I know your agent mentioned a possible trade, but this is really important to me. It's a great writing program, and London—"

"London? The internship is in London?"

How could this even work out? Would we just go long distance, then pick back up when she returns? And then what happens? Does she leave again? Does she pursue writing? Will she be happy? And if I *do* get traded? Then what?

She pauses, her brows furrowed. "Yeah. Did I not mention that?"

I scoff. "No, Clover, you didn't."

I take a healthy drink of my beer. It's not nearly strong enough for this conversation, but I'm not about to go back inside before I find out more about how my wife is going to fucking London without me.

"Oh, well. I'm sorry but…" She wrings her hands. She's nervous telling me this, and I hate that she is. "Yes, it's in London."

"And I'm guessing it's for three months? That's why you said that about not being able to work in a lab for that long, right?"

"Yes."

Fuck! The single word rings in my head, and I know it's unfair the moment it does. I have no room to be upset right now. *Of course* she wants to go do something for herself, and she should. She's followed me around for years now, bouncing from city to city every time I get traded. She's put up with canceled plans due to injuries and adjusted schedules because of obligations.

She *deserves* this. I just wish she had told me about it before now.

"Well, that's amazing. I'm happy for you."

"You said that already." She purses her lips. "Look, if you don't want me to do it, I won't. I know it'll suck being apart, but it's only for three months. We can do that."

But…can we? I've felt her slipping through my fingers for a while now, way longer than three months, and I've done nothing but hold on tight. Maybe it was *too* tight, though. Maybe…maybe she needs to do this, and maybe I need to let her.

"I want you to do it," I tell her, and she relaxes instantly, which doesn't make me feel any better. Did she really think I wouldn't support her? Wouldn't sacrifice for her like she's done for me so many times before? Is that how she views our relationship?

"Are you sure?"

"Yes, I'm sure. Come here."

I pull her to me, holding her close, and it's not just for her. It's for me too. I need it. I need this. I need *her*.

"I'm sorry I didn't say anything before. I was just… nervous. But I'm excited now. It's a really amazing program, and I swear I'm not going to go over there and squander this chance I'm getting."

I don't care if she goes over there and tap-dances in the streets. I just want her to be happy, whatever that means.

"The three months will be up before we know it," she says.

"Yeah, it'll be like a blip in time. No big deal."

Three months. Ninety days. I can do that. We can do it.

I'm certain of it.

Chloe has been gone for almost three months, and my life feels so fucking empty that not even hockey is filling the hole she left behind. I was traded to the Seattle Serpents a month and a half after she left, and I thought it might fix things, thought maybe it was just Chicago she hated and she would be elated to come back to a new city and we'd start fresh.

But considering we haven't spoken in days, I'm not so sure that's the case anymore.

"Clover? Are you there?"

"Hello? Callum?" She sighs when someone shouts something in the background. "Sorry, the pub is loud. Let me step outside a moment."

A moment? I haven't talked to her on the phone in three days, and she wants a *moment* with me? I push down the anger that courses through me.

"Sorry," she says again, and it's much quieter now.

"It's all good. I just wanted to check in with you. It feels like it's been ages since we talked."

"We've texted."

We have, but that's not what I mean, and she knows it, which tells me she's okay with us not talking. Maybe that is for the best. We've been attached at the hip since we were in college. We can manage a few days without talking. Who knows? Maybe it could bring back that spark that's been missing for so long.

"How are things going?" I ask, not wanting to get into it now. "How's the writing?"

"It's…" She sighs dreamily. "It's amazing, Callum. I can't remember the last time I had so much fun working. It's like every day is a new one, and there's always something new to learn. I feel so…refreshed."

The giddiness in her voice is almost infectious, and I find myself smiling as I stare out of my apartment window. It's some fancy place another teammate suggested. I'm sure it's not where I'll end up staying whenever Chloe comes back, but it'll be fine in the interim.

"You sound happy, Clover."

"I am. I really, really am."

Then she's quiet. *Too* quiet. I try not to read too much into it, but it's nearly impossible because that's all I have these days—silence. Our texting has been sporadic at best, and whenever I do get a message, it feels half-baked and without any real substance. I've gotten the sense she's avoiding me, but I can't seem to figure out why.

"So, are you getting excited about coming home? Seattle is great. You're going to love the weather here. And the apartment. The tub is massive, and I know you love a good bath."

"I do love a bath."

But there's next to no emotion behind her words. It's like she's a robot I'm trying to form a connection with, and nothing is going as planned.

"Listen, Callum…" she says, but I don't want to listen at all. Her tone is off. It's wrong. And there is no doubt in my mind I'm not going to like what comes next.

"I was thinking of staying a little longer."

"S-Staying?" I hate how shaky the word comes out. "In London?"

"Yes. At least for a while. I just need…I don't know. I need more time, I think. There's still so much I want to learn."

"Oh."

It's a stupid thing to say, but it's all I have because I don't know what else to do in this situation. She wants to stay? Thousands of miles away? Hours and hours of time difference? An entire fucking continent? And for how long? Weeks? Another month? A *year*?

An ache I've never felt before forms in my chest, and I rub at the spot that burns as if I've eaten way too much red sauce.

"Uh, how long were you thinking of staying?"

"I'm not sure."

"Are you sure about anything?"

I say it before I can think about the consequences of the words, and they fall heavily between us, like a bomb dropping from the sky. What's even more devastating is her silence. It's fucking deafening, and I wish more than anything I could rewind the last thirty seconds and take it all back.

"No," she finally says after what feels like years. "I'm not."

I squeeze my eyes shut. Not even the picturesque view of the city can save me now.

"What does that mean, Clover?"

"I…"

But she doesn't finish her thought, and it pisses me off. I've been sitting around waiting for her for *three months* now. I've given her the space she obviously wanted. I've stepped back in so many ways. But if she won't tell me what she wants, what the hell am I supposed to do next?

"Do you mean with your career or…us?"

"Us." She whispers it, but it certainly doesn't feel like she does. "I'm not sure about us anymore. I think we should separate."

She…wants to separate? Isn't that what we're doing right now? There's a fucking ocean and more between us —we *are* separated, in more ways than one.

"Do you mean…a divorce?"

"What?" She sounds panicked. "No, no. I just mean taking some time apart. Like, trying to live on our own for a while, you know? You do your thing, and I do mine. But we stay married."

I want to tell her she sounds selfish, like she's trying to have her cake and eat it too, but I'm too fucking stunned by what I'm hearing to say it at all.

"Look, it's late, and I've had a few beers."

I wish I had a fucking beer right about now.

"Maybe I don't know what I'm talking about. Can we…can we talk later? Maybe tomorrow? Or the next day? Please, Callum?"

"Yeah," I say, my voice scratchy. I clear my throat. "Yeah, tomorrow is fine."

"Or the next day," she says.

I grit my teeth. "Or the next day. Just call me whenever you get the chance, okay? If I don't answer, I'll call back as soon as I can, all right? Just keep trying."

"Okay." But she doesn't *sound* okay.

"I love you, Clover."

A pause.

"You too, Callum."

We disconnect the call, and I throw my phone right into the glass window I was staring out. It doesn't shatter, but I wish it would. It would be so fitting for how I feel right now. My wife just asked me for a separation, and even though I don't want it, I think I might give it to her.

It just might be the only way to save our marriage.

Chapter 22

CHLOE

I haven't been back to Tennessee in at least two years, and I can safely say I didn't miss being here one bit. It might be March, but it's somehow in the upper seventies, and I'm already dying in the sweater I put on this morning before taking the first flight out of Seattle.

Callum fell asleep around ten, but no matter how hard I tried, I couldn't get my brain to stop spinning. It was like every bad thought I ever had about myself or my writing or my marriage just kept coming and coming. I could hardly make sense of any of it.

But there was one thing I could understand: I wanted to talk to my mom. I don't know why. We've never had the kind of relationship where I just call her up and chat, but something told me to do it, and to do it *now*.

So, I got on my phone and booked a very expensive last-minute flight, then crawled out from under Callum's hold and packed a bag. Now that I'm here, standing in front of my parents' front door, sweltering, I have no idea what convinced me this was a good idea. It's too late now, though.

I raise my fist and rap my knuckles against the giant white door that could use a new coat of paint. This is the same house I grew up in, and I don't think anything has changed over the years. Hell, the mailbox is still crooked from when Talia backed into it a month after getting her license.

I hold my breath, waiting for someone to answer. I release it when I hear shuffling inside, and I smile, imagining my father pushing out of his old recliner with a curse. But when the door swings open, it's not my dad at all.

It's been a long time since I've seen her and *truly* looked at her. Her hair, which has always been a few shades of red lighter than mine, is now white around the temples, showing her age. And her brown eyes—the same boring shade as mine—look tired, like she's been up working since the wee hours of the morning, and knowing her, she probably has. She was always an early riser, even when we had nothing going on. Give her five minutes, and she could fill a day with activities.

"Chloe? What are you…" She shakes her head like she can't believe her eyes. "What are you doing here?"

"Surprise," I say, but there's no real enthusiasm behind it.

"Well, I'd say." She smiles, then opens her arms. "Come here."

The second I fall against her, something inside me breaks, and all the tears I've been holding back since I walked out of Callum's apartment fall like a levee breaking during a raging storm.

"Oh, Chloe girl," she says as she rubs my back, and I can't remember the last time she called me that. Certainly not since I married Callum, that's for sure. She's been mad at me since then. "What's going on?"

"It's…everything."

I feel her nod, then she's ushering me inside.

"Honey?" she calls to my father. "Chloe's here!"

"What? My little lucky charm?"

I hear my father push out of his chair, then the string of cuss words follows, and I smile. I try to wipe my tears before he makes it into the foyer, but it's pointless. The second he sees me, he knows something is wrong.

"What did that boy do to you?"

I huff out a laugh. "No, Dad. I promise. It wasn't him. It was me."

My mother puts her arm on my shoulder. "We're going to go out back and talk. Bring us some iced tea, will you?"

Dad nods, not taking his eyes off me, and I bet he's already thinking of a medicine he could create that would kill Callum in an instant. But it's not my husband's fault I'm crying. It's my own, and that's the exact reason I'm here.

My mother leads us out back, and I realize right away I was wrong about the house not changing. Instead of the old, rickety porch they had, there's now a full patio complete with comfortable-looking rocking chairs and a table that has an umbrella poking out through the middle of it. There's even a firepit, which is the most surprising of all, considering my parents never used to like building fires when we'd go camping.

We settle onto two chairs, but we don't say anything right away. My mother just lets me sit there, taking it all in. I watch the clouds move across the sky and listen to the birds chirp without a care in the world. Dad brings us two teas, and I wish it were Diet Coke, but I take a drink anyway.

"So," my mother says, rocking back in her chair, cupping her hands around her glass after he leaves. "I'm guessing you're not here because you have good news."

"Actually, I do. I got a job offer. A paper in Seattle is branching out and starting a second paper. They want me to be the editor-in-chief, and I plan to accept their offer."

"What?" She grins. "That's incredible, Chloe!"

She sounds genuinely happy for me, and I can't help but be a little suspicious of her reaction. She pushed me to take the internship to get me away from Callum once.

Is that what she wants to happen now? Is that what *I* want to happen now?

No.

"I'm proud of you, you know," she says, and my jaw slackens.

"You…are?"

"Of course. Why do you seem so surprised by that?"

"Because it's not biology. It has nothing to do with the degree you and Dad paid for. Because it would mean I stay in Seattle with Callum. I don't know. A whole myriad of reasons."

She flattens her lips. "I suppose that's fair." She takes another sip of her tea. "I don't hate Callum, you know."

"Mom…"

"No, let me get this out, okay?"

I sigh, then nod. "All right. Say your piece."

"I don't hate him, Chloe. That boy has been nothing but good to you, and if I did hate him, that really wouldn't be fair. Yes, I pushed you into biology because it's a much more stable career than writing. I felt you needed that. Plus, I knew how much you struggled in your studies except for with that. I thought it might be the safer choice, easier." She taps her wedding ring against the glass. "I was wrong for doing that, but I was not wrong for pushing you to take that internship and sending you to London."

I open my mouth to argue, to tell her if she hadn't, maybe I wouldn't be in this position with Callum now and we wouldn't have lost three years of our marriage—but she holds her hand up to stop me, and I clamp my lips shut.

"I was married before your father."

I shoot forward in my chair. "What?!"

"Shh!" she says, looking back into the house, where my father is focused on the news. He's not paying us any attention at all. "Don't be so loud."

"Sorry." I sit up straighter. "But what the hell do you mean you were married before? Does Dad know?"

"Of course he knows." She leaves off the *duh*, but it's still implied. "I tell your father everything."

I snort. "But not your daughter."

She gives me a hard look. "Now, don't be like that. It's not like I was *trying* to hide it from you. That was just a part of my life that happened a long time ago, way before you were ever even a thought. I didn't feel like it mattered." She sighs quietly. "Clearly, I was wrong about that."

I tilt my head. "What do you mean?"

She doesn't say anything right away, and for a moment, I worry she won't elaborate at all.

Then she speaks.

"I was eighteen when I got married."

Holy shit. That's younger than I was!

"I met a boy in high school, and it took all of one month for him to become my whole world. I'm talking about applying to every college he applied to, canceling plans with friends in favor of being with him, breaking curfew for the first time in my life, and arguing with my parents when they tried to keep me away from him. I was in love. Truly, wholly in love."

I can hear it in her voice. It's almost wistful, like maybe a part of her misses him, whoever he is.

"So when he proposed just after we graduated, I said yes. It was the easiest decision of my life at the time. My parents tried to talk me out of it, much like your father and I did with you, but I wouldn't hear it. It didn't matter what they thought—I wanted to be his wife more than anything in the world. I wanted to be his."

I know exactly what she means. When Callum dropped to his knee and proposed after he was offered that first contract, all I wanted was him. It didn't matter that I was scared or what everyone else thought. I was determined.

"I was…for, oh, about four years."

"Did he…cheat on you?"

She laughs under her breath. "No, but it would have been a lot easier if he did."

The number of times I thought that myself…it's far too many to count. Of course I didn't want to think of Callum with other people, but I didn't want to think about him with me either, especially when I didn't feel worthy of his love in the least.

"But the problem wasn't him. It was me." She points at her chest. "I soon realized that while I loved him, I wasn't aware where I ended and he began. We became one, and while that doesn't sound like a bad thing straightaway, it gets very stifling after a while. You start to wonder whether you like things because *you* like them or because they do. You think about every choice you've ever made, and you consider if you made them because you were worried about how your partner would feel or if they truly were what was best for you. You question everything, even yourself." She gives a resigned smile. "*Especially* yourself."

I understand what she means more than she could ever know. It's exactly how I began to feel with Callum, and it was hard, because through it all, I truly loved him. There wasn't a second that I didn't. I just didn't know how to love myself too.

"What did you do? When you were feeling like that, I mean. How did you handle it?"

"For a long time, I didn't. I buried it. I tried to be happy because I truly didn't have any reason not to be. I had a husband who loved me, and I had a good life. We were living in an apartment that was nice enough, my in-laws adored me, and we were *good*." She shrugs. "But I wasn't happy, and it took me a long time to figure out why."

"How did you figure it out?"

"I left."

It's like I've been punched right in the gut. Not only is this all a lot to process, but for all my life, I thought my mother spent her early twenties with her nose in a book. I was wrong about that, and I think I might have been wrong about her, too.

"I packed a bag in the middle of the night and took off. It was cowardly, I know that now, but at the time, I didn't know what else to do. It's really hard to try to explain to someone you love that it's not their fault you're not happy."

I nod, understanding her in a way I never have before.

"What happened after that?"

"Well, I went back. A lot sooner than three years." She gives me a pointed look. "But the damage was done. He was upset—and rightfully so—and we tried to work things out, but we couldn't. In the end, we wanted different things, and neither of us was willing to compromise on it."

Fear zings through my body. I don't want that to be Callum and me. I don't want to lose him over my own insecurities and fears.

"You said it took you a long time to figure out why you were unhappy, so I'm assuming you did."

She rocks back and forth for a long time, and I worry for a moment maybe she *didn't* figure it out. Maybe she's still unhappy.

"Yes, and no. Honestly, I think a lot of it is just that I was young, and I didn't know who I was. I never got the chance to figure it out. I went from high school to being a wife. I didn't get to go to college or meet new people or find new hobbies. So, I felt like I was missing out on some formative years. And the other part of it…" She weighs her words carefully. "Well, it was just me. I just wasn't okay, and that's okay. Does that make any sense?"

"Yes, but I guess…" I turn toward her. "Why us? I mean, I know of plenty of couples who got together young, got married young, and they're fine. They never went through what we did."

"Remember: everyone goes at their own pace, Chloe. Maybe those people understood themselves better. Or maybe they worked through it with their partner. Or perhaps they're just really, really good at pretending. Sometimes things aren't as magical as they appear."

I pretended for a long time, and it was because I felt like I had to. I didn't want to rock the boat, not when Callum already had so much on his plate with hockey and worrying about contracts or being sat out of games. I didn't feel as if what I was going through was big enough…until it was.

"Are you happy now?"

A wide grin stretches across her lips. "Yes, very much so. After things fell apart, I took time to get to know myself in every possible way. I spent time alone. I made new friends. I went to school, and I got a job that worked for me and me alone. It didn't matter if my choices made sense to anyone else. They were right for *me*, and that was all I cared about."

I can hear the unspoken words loud and clear: *Don't take the job for Callum. Take it if it's what you truly want.*

Honestly, it *is* what I want. I haven't doubted that at all. My ability to do the job? Yeah, I question that all the time. But the position itself? No, it's everything I've been working toward, and that goal hasn't changed, even with Callum knowing about it now.

"And things with Dad? They're good?"

Her smile grows even more. "Yes, very good. Your father and I talk about everything. There are no secrets between us. Every little good and bad moment…we share them all. It's the only way we're able to work through our problems when they arise. If one of us ever feels like we aren't happy, we tell the other person, and we put in the work. I know marriage sounds fun, and a lot of people think you'll never have any issues again once you slip those rings on, but the real relationship has only just begun. You have to keep showing up for your partner every day, as well as yourself. It's exhausting, but it can be so rewarding too."

I think that's where I made the biggest mistake with Callum. I stopped talking to him, and I bottled everything up. I tried to shoulder it myself. I forgot I was supposed to be a partner, and not just a wife.

We sit in silence for a while. My mother sips on her tea, and I do the same.

"Do you still talk to him? Your ex-husband?" I ask

when the ice in my tea is melted and the glass is sweating all over my sweater, which is still way too warm.

"Not anymore. We stayed friends for a long time, though. He helped me apply to school, and I helped him set up his handyman business. I even helped him hire his future wife." She laughs. "I don't have any regrets, aside from hurting him the way I did. I'm glad I went through it. I needed it, or else I wouldn't have gotten here. I wouldn't have your dad, and I wouldn't have you. In the end, it all worked out just as it should."

I hope it works out for me, too, even if that does mean a future without Callum. I don't want it to, but I now know sometimes life doesn't turn out the way you plan it to, and maybe that's okay.

"Any other marriages I should know about?"

Mom lets out a loud laugh. "No. Just the two."

"Good. I was worried I might have another almost dad out there."

She rolls her eyes, but I see the way her lips twitch. A few more minutes go by before she says something else I wasn't expecting.

"You know, I think I might have made a mistake with you."

I pause. "What do you mean?"

"Well, I pushed you. First, into biology, then away from me because I thought I knew best when it came to you and your relationship with Callum. You were young, but you were an adult too, and I should have respected that more. I just didn't want you to go through what I did, but I should have let you figure it out, just as I needed to. I'm sorry for that, Chloe. I truly am. I don't know what this means for us or if you'll forgive me, but please know that your feelings right now…they're valid. Even if you don't understand them, they're still allowed to exist."

I swallow roughly, and this time when my tears fall, I don't bother trying to wipe them away. I want her to see how her words have affected me, and just how badly I needed to hear them.

She gets up and wraps me in her arms, holding me tightly as I work through everything we just shared. It's far more than I was expecting to get when I hopped on the plane to come here, but it's somehow everything I was looking for too.

When she finally releases me, I feel lighter in a way I haven't in a long, long time, and I feel ready to do the work, as she said. With myself, and with Callum too.

"Can I ask you something else?" I ask once she's settled back into her rocking chair.

"I think at this point, I'm an open book."

"Callum mentioned that he sent you and Dad packing when you went to get my stuff in Chicago. Is that true?"

She grins, nodding. "Yes, it's true. I was pissed, especially since we drove all that way, but deep down, I was proud of him, too. It was actually the first indication that maybe… Maybe I didn't make the best choice with you. He loved you so fiercely."

"He still does."

"I know, Chloe girl. I know."

"Is that why you never told me about it? Because you had regrets?"

"Yes, but also no. You were happy in London, and even though I was conflicted about my involvement in the whole thing, I really did want you to experience it. I thought if I said something, you'd come running back, so I kept quiet and made your father promise to do the same."

I'm not pleased that she made that decision herself, but it was so long ago that I'm not sure if I have any room to actually be mad, especially when I'm glad I stayed in London, even if it did lead Callum and me here.

"What did you and Dad do with my old bedroom?" I ask instead of laying into her about it.

"We turned it into a sewing room. Typical old-people stuff." She winks. "Why?"

"Do you think I could stay here tonight? And maybe tomorrow too?"

"Oh, my little lucky charm, you can stay as long as you need."

I do.

Chapter 23

I'll be back. I promise.

I read the note for the hundredth time, my eyes lingering on the words that have been underlined three times: *I promise.* But the thing is, she's said that before. She's made other promises, too—*vows.* Look how well she's upheld those.

I crumple the paper and toss it across the room into the trash can by the door. Then I get up and grab it, smoothing it out and putting it back on the bedside table I found it on four days ago. Luckily for me, I've been sufficiently distracted with hockey. We had an event the day I woke up to a cold spot beside me, and then back-to-back games here at home. I've not had any time to think about my wife leaving me yet again.

Until now.

"Please tell me we're getting together after practice. Rory is busy in the clinic all day, and I really don't want to just be a couch potato," Lawson says, even though he's supposed to be running drills.

"Dude, go. You're up."

Hayes shoves him forward, and the Serpents' leading goalscorer takes off toward the net, the puck on his stick. He rears his arm back and swings, sending the frozen puck right past Fox's shoulder.

"Fuck!" the goalie yells.

He's been extra hard on himself since that road skid we had, even in practice. We all have been. We've worked too damn hard to get where we are to even think about letting it all slip through our fingers now.

The assistant coach blows the whistle, then Hayes takes off. He tries the same move as Lawson, and this time Fox catches it with ease.

"That's what I'm fucking talking about!" Lawson says to him, racing over to knock his fist against his helmet.

"Kells, you're up."

The whistle is blown again, and I take off toward the net, much slower than either of the other guys. When I drag my stick back, trying to shoot it over Fox's left pad, I miss by a mile wide, and I don't even care. I don't care about much right now, actually.

"Well, that was shit," Lawson remarks when I skate back over to the squad we've been broken up into. "You're bad, but not usually this bad. What gives?"

I ignore him.

"Hello?" He taps on my helmet with the knob of his stick. "Anyone in there?"

I smack at him. "Fuck off."

"Not until you tell me what's wrong."

"What's wrong is that you're breathing. Mind stopping?"

"Damn, dude," Hutch says. "A bit brutal, no?"

"He's still here, so apparently not enough."

"*He* can hear you, and *he* is getting pretty damn tired of being your punching bag, you fucking dick."

Even my eyes widen at his words, because I've never heard him sound so serious or hurt before.

Fuck, Callum, what are you doing? He's your teammate. Apologize, you ass.

But I don't. I just let him skate away to the other end of the ice.

"Hey." Hutch grabs me by my practice jersey, pulling me so close our noses are almost touching. "I don't know what the fuck your problem is, but whatever it is, leave it at home. Don't bring that shit to the ice and don't treat your fucking teammates—*especially* the ones who give a shit about you—like trash. That Cup is within reach, and the last thing we need is to be at each other's throats. We need to be a unit right now. Think you can manage that, *Callum?*"

Callum. Just hearing my name drop from his lips has me clenching my hands at my sides because all I can think of is Chloe. Chloe, who hid a job offer from me for weeks. Chloe, who fell asleep in my arms. Chloe, who walked away from me again.

"Everything okay over here, Cap?" Locke says, his eyes flitting between Hutch and me.

The captain drops me back to my skates. "Yeah, all good." Then, without another glance backward, he skates away.

Locke doesn't. He looks at me, his lips pulling down in a frown.

"What?" I bark, and from the corner of my eye, I see several people look our way.

"Nothing, man. Nothing at all."

He skates away too, leaving me all alone, just as Chloe did. We finish practice with no other incidents, and I speed through my shower and meetings. Being on the ice is usually my solace, but I need out of here, and I need out *now*.

When I slip behind the wheel of my R8, I don't steer toward my apartment building. I take a detour, heading toward Top Shelf. It's been a long fucking week, and a drink sounds like exactly what I need right now. I wave to the bartender when I walk in, then slide onto a stool.

"Hey, Keller. Your usual?"

I shake my head. "Shots. Tequila. Six of them."

I can tell he wants to say something, maybe try to talk me out of it, but I raise a brow, and he thinks better of it.

As he moves to ready my shots, I pull my phone out and call Stefan. I need to talk to someone, anyone at this point, but I really want to talk to my brother.

When he doesn't answer, I assume he's in class. That would make the most sense, considering the time of day. That's fine. I'll just drink alone.

The bartender drops a tray in front of me, then takes the black card I slide his way. I nod at him before grabbing the tray and carrying it over to the booth the Serpents Singles usually occupy. I stare at the shot glasses for a while, debating whether it's really a good idea to take them.

Hutch was right—the Cup is right within reach. We have just a few more weeks of the regular season, and we need to be ready for a deep run. Everything is on the line. We can't slip up. None of us.

I flip my phone over and open my texts, clicking on Chloe's name. I read through the last messages she sent me, which are from before she left this second time.

Clover: I didn't forget to take the chicken out. YAY!

Clover: I'd better get a reward for that tonight. 😉

I did reward her. Over and over with my tongue lashing against her clit, if my memory serves me well, and it does. I want that again, and I don't mean the sex. I want simple. I want domestic. I want flirty texts and fun nights.

I just want my fucking wife.

I pick up the first shot of tequila, toss it back, and swallow. Then I do it again. And again. The booze hits me quick, and I suspect it has to do with the fact that I can't remember the last time I ate. Maybe it was last night? Who knows? Better yet, who cares?

I sure as hell don't. My wife is gone. *Again.*

"Well, aren't you just a fucking sight for sore eyes."

I close my eyes, hoping if I don't see him, he's not really here. But the bench across from me squeaks under his weight as he slides into the booth, and I know he's not just a figment of my imagination.

When I open my eyes, Lawson sits across from me looking like…well, how I usually look: grumpy.

"What the hell are you doing here, Lawsy?"

"Honestly?" He runs a hand through his hair, then rests his elbows on the tabletop. "I don't fucking know. You're a dick, Keller. A real goddamn prick, if you ask me."

"I didn't."

"But," he continues, "for some reason, I care about you. So, I followed you here. I was hoping you might walk inside, realize what a bad idea this is, and come right back out. When you didn't, I figured it was best I come check on you." He nods toward the empty shot glasses. "Clearly, I should have come in earlier."

I grab another shot, but I don't take it. Not yet. My stomach is feeling a bit off, and I'm not sure what it means just yet, so I'm not testing my luck.

"So," he says, settling back against the booth, "what crawled up your ass today?"

For a split second, I think about not telling him. Or better yet, I think about telling him to fuck off. But that's not what I actually say. Instead, I tell him about the job offer, the fight, then waking up to a note and an empty bed.

"Shit," he says, exhaling heavily. "Fuck, I didn't know her leaving again was even a possibility. I thought you two were working things out."

"I thought so too, but I guess not."

He nods as if he understands, but he doesn't. How can he when even I don't get it? I thought when we went to bed that night, we might be okay. We'd talked a little more after our big heart-to-heart, and I even held her as we fell asleep like I always do.

Then she was just…gone.

"Can I ask you something without you trying to punch me?"

"Sorry," I say, pushing the shot glass back and forth between my hands, not caring when a bit of alcohol spills out. "I can't make any promises."

He laughs lightly. "Fair enough." Bravely, he leans

across the table again. "Why'd you let her walk away if you love her so much?"

"Which time?" I hate that I even have to ask it, but it's true.

"Both. I mean, it's clear you've never stopped loving her. Does she know that?"

I shrug. "Yes. No. I don't know. I told her before she left the second time, and every day before the first. I thought it was enough, but maybe it wasn't. Maybe she needed something else. Or maybe she just didn't need me."

Lawson shakes his head. "Nah, that's not it. It's clear Chloe loves you, too."

I laugh, and it sounds bitter to even me. "She walked away. *Twice* now, mind you. I'm not so sure that's true."

She hasn't said it, that's for certain. There have been so many times in the last two months that I thought she might, but she never uttered the words I so badly wanted to hear.

Lawson responds with a simple eyebrow raise, seeing right through all my bullshit, and it pisses me off just as much as it defeats me. I sink lower in the booth, then toss back another shot before slamming the glass to the table. I drag the back of my hand over my mouth and sigh.

"Because it was what she wanted."

"Huh?"

"You asked why I let her walk away, right?" Lawson

nods. "I let her walk away because it was what she wanted."

He tips his head to the side. "I'm not sure I'm following."

Honestly, I'm not either, but that could be the four shots I've slammed in the last fifteen minutes.

"She came to me with stars in her eyes about an internship in London. She said she felt like she *needed* to do it, and I was happy for her. Over the fucking moon, actually. But I was also confused because I had no idea she had even applied for it. I had no idea she was looking. How messed up is that? She's my wife, and I had no idea what was happening in her life. I was so damn focused on me and my own shit that I didn't think about it."

A look of pity crosses Lawson's face, and it takes everything I have not to reach over the booth and smack it away. "Come on, Kells. That's not your fault. We're busy guys. Yeah, we're playing a game, but it's still a lot to keep up with. It could have happened to anyone."

I shake my head. "No, you don't get it, Lawsy. We've been together since I was *nineteen*. That's almost thirteen years ago. Do you have any idea how long that is to know someone? To be someone's partner? A long fucking time."

But he doesn't get it. How could he? Before Rory, he wasn't exactly celibate. He has no idea what it's like to love someone like I love Chloe. He really doesn't know what it's like to build a life with someone and have it ripped away from you *twice*. He doesn't know anything at all.

"I should have known," I say, reaching for yet another shot and tossing it back. I cringe as the alcohol burns on the way down. "I should have fucking known."

"You should also probably slow down," he says, moving the remaining glass out of my reach.

I don't even bother arguing with him. What's the point? Hell, what's the point of anything anymore?

"The point is that she's here now."

Shit, did I say that out loud? Am I drunk?

He slides a cup of water my way, and I realize I must be because I have no idea where the drink even came from. Still, I take it, gulping half of it in one go. I belch loudly, and even that reminds me of her. All I can think of is how she would cover her mouth and look mortified by something natural.

Fucking hell, I miss her.

"But she's not. She's not here."

"Not technically, but you said her note said she was coming back, right?"

Fuck, did I tell him that?

"Yeah."

"Then believe her," Lawson says. "Let her show you she means it. Give her time. Give her space."

But I have. I've given her so much space and so much time, and I don't want to anymore. I told her I'd wait for her, and I meant it. I will, but I'm not going to pretend I'm okay because I'm fucking not. I'm not okay.

Lawson senses that, and as his lips pull downward, all the tequila I just downed tries to fight its way back up my throat.

"I'm—"

"Don't," I warn him. "Don't you dare tell me you're sorry, Lawson. Not you. Anyone but you."

His brows pull downward, but he nods. "All right. I won't say it. But, Keller?"

I sigh, running a hand over my face, which feels hot and a little tingly. "What?"

"You're always the first to drop the gloves out on the ice, and I've always respected the hell out of you for that. So do that this time too. Fight for her. If you love her, fight. Don't let this be the end. Just fight."

I hear his words. I really do. But sometimes, it gets to a point where fighting isn't worth it anymore. As much as I don't want that to be the case with Chloe, I might have to just accept that I'm the only one in this battle.

She's my wife, and I love her, but maybe…maybe it's time to let her go.

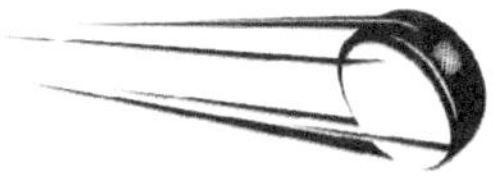

Every hockey player knows at a certain point in the season, even the most skilled and seasoned fighters decide to keep their gloves on, especially when their team is in the position the Serpents are in. Apparently, the fuckhead from Vegas didn't get the memo, and he picked the wrong person to mess with tonight. I'm hungover thanks to my little trip to Top Shelf yesterday, and I'm fucking angry because I *still* haven't heard from Chloe. I even texted her last night and got nothing in response.

"Come on, 10." He cross-checks me right on top of my pants. "I thought you were the goon. I thought it was you they sent out when they want to fire up the crowd. What?" Another shove as I battle to keep the puck away from him. "Can't get it up now that your team is down four to zero?"

Ignore him, I say to myself. *Just fucking ignore him.*

"Fuck off," I tell him, turning around and giving him a taste of his own medicine, shoving my stick against his chest.

"Nah, don't think I will. Maybe it's not just your wife you can't get it up for."

As soon as the word *wife* leaves his lips, I lose all ability to hold myself back, and I attack. The edges of my vision go blurry, but I can still see him as I grab his jersey and land a blow right to his cheek.

"Come on, you fucker!" I scream as my fist connects with his face again. "You wanted a fucking fight, didn't you?"

He stumbles, but I steady him as I lay another blow.

"You bastard!" he yells as he tries to swing at me but misses.

I laugh, and it only pisses him off more. Faintly, I can hear sticks being smashed against the boards, and I can feel the other players trying to drag me off the guy, but I fight them all.

"Hey, hey! That's enough!" someone says, but I keep going.

I *have* to keep going. I can't stop now. I'm supposed to fight, aren't I? That's what I'm on this team for, and that's what I'm doing with Chloe too. I'm fighting.

Her demons.

Punch.

Her insecurities.

Punch.

My own bullshit issues.

Punch.

For our fucking marriage.

"All right, all right," someone yells in my ear, grabbing me by the shoulders and trying to pull me off the limp player in my hands.

When did he go down? Where did all this blood come from? I blink once, twice, and the bright lights and roaring cheers come back into focus. *What the hell just happened?*

"You're good. You're good," the voice in my ear says, and they're still clutching me tight. "You're good, Keller."

I try to shrug him off, but he keeps hold of me as I skate toward the box.

"No, no. You're done for the night."

"What?" I push at him as he drags me in the opposite direction. "What the fuck for?"

"You hit him with your stick. Right to the face."

"Bullshit, I did!"

"You did. We saw it. Everyone did. You're done."

I try to scramble out of his hold, but it's pointless. I'm tired. So fucking tired. I can feel it in my bones, right down to my core.

"All right, all right," I say as he pushes me toward the door on the bench. "I'm going!"

I hop up the step, and someone pats me on the back as I head down the tunnel, ripping my helmet off and throwing it who knows where. Behind me, I can hear the crowd gasping and oohing, but I don't stop to see what's going on.

I need to sit down. Or lie down. I don't know which. All I know is I need to get somewhere else and fast. My lungs are burning, my eyes are watering, and I'm on the verge of a panic attack in the very last place I ever wanted to have one.

I make it to the locker room just as the tears begin to fall, and it takes everything in me not to drop to my knees right then. I stumble to my stall and finally collapse. Everything from the last two months—no, from the last three years—all comes out in one long wail, and if I cared at all in this moment, I would be embarrassed, but I'm not. I'm just really, really fucking sad.

I sit like that for a long time, tears streaming down my face, my heart thundering in my chest, and blood pumping in my ears. I don't know when I finally calm down, but when I do, the rest of the team is piling into the room. From the looks of it, the game didn't get any better.

Nobody speaks to me. In fact, very little is said, and most people are in and out of the showers, packing up to go home in under ten minutes.

Coach Smith claps me on the shoulder. "We'll talk in the morning."

I nod, but I don't make a move to leave. I'm not eager to go back to an empty apartment anyway. When I finally look up, I expect it to just be me, but it's not. Hayes, Locke, Fox, Hutch, and Lawson sit in their own stalls, all of them fully dressed, just like me.

I look every one of them in the eye, then say, "Well? Which one of you is going to tell me what a fuckup I am?"

"You're a fuckup," Hutch says.

"A big one," Locke agrees. "Pretty sure you're getting suspended for that one."

Hayes nods. "At least a game."

"Maybe two," Fox adds.

I drag my eyes to Lawson. "Nothing to add?"

"I mean, when I told you to fight yesterday, I didn't mean actually *fight*."

I feel the edges of my lips tip up just the slightest, but they drop as quickly as it came on. They're right. I messed up big-time. I don't even remember hitting the other guy with my stick, but I trust the ref when he says I did. And if my hand hurts as badly as it does, that means I lost control. I'm screwed.

"What happened out there, Keller?" Hutch asks.

"I… Fuck." I sigh. "I don't even know where to start."

"The beginning," Fox says. "It's usually a pretty good place."

So, I do. I tell them everything, from meeting Chloe at college to our wedding, everything leading up to Chicago, and her getting the internship. Then I tell them about the last three years and how we barely talked. About how I fucking *ached* for her. How my heart felt like it was sitting outside my chest at all times. How I've been having panic attacks. How when she finally came to me, I felt alive for the first time in years. And how when she left, I died all over again.

By the time I'm done, I'm crying again, and fuck if I give a shit. I don't care about anything at all. Not anymore.

"You know," Hutch says, being the first to speak per usual, "maybe if you had come to us before, we could have helped you through this."

They all nod.

"You wouldn't have had to shoulder this alone," Locke says.

"He *still* doesn't have to shoulder it alone. We're still here, aren't we?" Fox looks around. "I mean, I know we aren't technically a club anymore, but we're still friends, right?"

"We were never a club," I say, but the words don't hold their usual contempt.

"We were so a club. We *are* a club. We took a blood oath, remember?"

"Dude, how many times do I have to tell you nobody else did that?" Hayes says to Lawson.

They go back and forth about the oath nobody except Lawson took, and I sit there, taking it all in, thinking about the other vows I made in my life. Once upon a time, I promised Chloe forever. I meant it then, and even after everything, I still mean it. I just want her here. I want her back in Seattle and back in my bed. I want her here right now, holding me and pressing her lips to the cuts along my hand.

I just...I want her.

"Kells? You okay?"

I look up, and they're all staring at me again. For just a second, I think about telling them I am, but they're right—we *are* friends. And if, for some reason, Chloe doesn't come back this time, I'm going to need them more than I ever have before.

So, I try being honest with them for the first time in…well, maybe ever.

"No, I'm not okay. Not at all."

Hutch sighs, then sits forward. "What can we do to help?"

"I don't know," I tell him honestly. "Just…be here?"

"We can do that," Fox says with a soft smile.

I exhale slowly, sinking back against my stall, that same tiredness from before slamming into me. And if anyone ever asks, it's why I say what I do next.

"I swear to fuck, if this ever—and I mean *ever*—leaves this room, I will gladly take three hots and a cot for the rest of my life."

I look around the room, letting them know I mean it, then I suck in a steadying breath.

"I know it might not seem like it because I certainly don't act like it, but…you're like brothers to me. Ones I definitely didn't ask for, but still brothers. You're the most obnoxious bunch of assholes around"—I give Lawson a pointed look—"but I wouldn't trade that for anything. I…well, I just love you guys, okay? So, thanks for being there for me through all this shit with…"

I can't bring myself to say her name, so I don't.

"Fuck, with this whole situation. It's been a lot to deal with, and I know I've been an asshole to all of you more times than I can count. I can't believe you're still sitting here with me right now, but…I don't know. Thanks, you know. Thanks for putting up with my shit.

For putting up with me. And for being there, too. Just… thanks."

Nobody moves. Nobody says a word. It's just dead silence hanging between us. I wish I could take it all back with the way they're currently staring at me, like I've gone and grown an extra limb or some shit.

Then someone moves. I sit up straight, looking Lawson right in the eye.

"Even me?" he asks.

"What?"

"Even me?" he repeats. "Do you love even me?"

His lips twitch before he's able to get the question fully out.

Mine involuntarily do the same. "Yeah, even you, *Lawless*."

He faints—or at least pretends to—and Hutch catches him with an eye roll before he can hit the ground.

"Shut up," I grumble, already back to being annoyed with him.

Locke and Hayes laugh, helping our captain set Lawson back up straight as he is still annoyingly pretending to be all weepy.

"Can we please group-hug now?" Fox asks.

I chuckle, and it feels so foreign. I haven't laughed at all since Chloe walked away again. I wasn't sure I ever would. "Yeah, we can group-hug."

They all move toward me at once, and I hold my hand up, stopping them.

"But just this one time, okay? This does not, at all, give anyone permission to touch me otherwise, understand? I know where each of you sleeps and will make it look like an accident when I—"

But I don't get the rest of my threat out. I can't. I now have several pairs of arms slung over my shoulders, and fuck if it doesn't feel good. I have no idea how long they embrace me for, but it somehow feels like forever and not long enough, not that I'd ever tell them that.

One by one, they pull away, until it's just Lawson left. His arms tighten around me, and maybe it's just all the shit that's been piling up lately, but I find myself letting him. Hell, I even sink against the guy. I might not know what's happening with my marriage, but I do know without a doubt that this group of guys? They're not just teammates. They're my family, and they're here to stay forever, even if Chloe isn't.

I opt for getting a ride home with Locke, not entirely trusting myself behind the wheel right now, and he doesn't even ask me questions as we make the trek back to our building.

"Keller?" he says as I step out of the elevator.

"Yeah, man?"

"You're going to be okay. I know it doesn't feel like it now, but you will be. We'll make sure of it."

I don't have the heart to tell him I don't think I'll ever be okay again, so instead I tell him good night, and I watch as the doors close. My footsteps feel heavy as I make my way down the hall to my apartment. Every stride weighs a thousand pounds, and the closer I get to my destination, the harder I have to force myself to move. I stop in front of the door, staring at the plain white wood and wishing I were anywhere else right now.

Just go inside, Callum. Walk inside. You can do this. You're going to be okay.

I don't believe the words, not really, but they give me just enough fuel to keep going. I close my eyes and take a deep breath, then I push the door open and walk into my empty apartment.

Chapter 24

Callum should have been home at least an hour ago, and I've been worried as hell about him ever since that fight.

It was tough to watch. The only other time I've seen him even close to that was in college, when he had that dirty cross-check on that asshole who made a comment about me. As soon as I saw him go after that Vegas player, I worried it may have happened again, but I refused to even go down that path.

It's not about you, and even if it is, who cares? He loves you. It's all that matters.

I repeat the words to myself as I spin on my heel and walk the same line I have been for the past thirty minutes. Back and forth and back again I go. Percy followed me for a solid five minutes before realizing I wasn't playing a game, then he scampered off into the spare bedroom.

Honestly, that's where I want to be right now, too—in

bed. I want to be curled up next to my husband, my head on his chest as he tells me about the game. I don't want to be up waiting and worrying, but here I am.

When another fifteen minutes go by, I'm just about ready to pick up my phone and call him to see where the hell he is when I hear it—a key in the door. I halt my pacing and hold my breath, ready to be told to go fuck myself, but he never comes inside.

I wait, then when I can't anymore, I make my way to the door. Just as I reach for the handle, it's pushed open, and I let out a loud yelp.

"What the—"

He freezes, eyes wide. Then he shakes his head, like he can't tell if he's awake or not.

"Clover?"

I nod, lifting my hand in a wave. "Hi."

His brows furrow, his jaw tightening. "What are you doing here?"

It's not exactly the welcome I was expecting, but I understand it all the same.

"I told you I was coming back."

He huffs out a humorless laugh. "Forgive me if I didn't believe you. You don't exactly have the best track record with those words."

I wince. "Okay, so I can see you're mad. I—"

"Mad? *Mad?!*" I jump at his words, backing up as he stalks into the apartment, the door rattling against the frame when he slams it closed. "You're fucking right I'm mad, Chloe! You left me—*again*! You cut off all communication—*again*! So yeah, I'm mad, though I think that's putting it mildly."

My hands shake as I brush a lock of hair out of my face. "I left a note."

"Yeah, it was a real long one too." He scoffs, dropping his bag to the floor and setting his hands on his hips. "You know, for a writer, you'd think you'd have a few more words than *I'll be back* and *I promise*. But no, that's all I got. Five words. Five simple, unexplained words as you just took off to—well, fuck. I don't know." He throws his hands in the air. "Because you didn't tell me!"

He's right. I fucked up. *Again.* Am I ever going to learn my lesson? Am I ever going to learn that I need to communicate with him?

"I'm sorry," I say simply. "You're right. I should have called or texted. I just needed a few days to clear my head, and you said I could do that. You said I could think about what it is I want."

He hangs his head, shaking it back and forth, then he sighs. I hate the pain in his gaze when he looks back up at me.

"I did say that, but I didn't know it would mean you'd take off again. I… Fuck, I didn't know where you were, Chloe. You were just gone again, and I didn't know."

"I'm sorry," I say again, taking a step toward him because I don't think I can stay away any longer, because I don't want to stay away. "I was in Tennessee."

"Tennessee? What were you doing there?" He nods. "Oh, Talia, right?"

"No. Well, yes, but I wasn't there for her. I saw my parents."

His eyes widen. "You did?"

I nod. "Yes. I thought a conversation with them, particularly my mother, might do me some good. As I'm sure you know, we have a long, complicated history, and I figured if I was looking for answers about my future, I should face my past first."

He swallows. "And?"

"I learned my mother was married before she met my father."

He rears his head back. "What? What are you talking about?"

I tell him about my mom's first marriage…and how it fell apart, just like ours did. When I'm done, he seems like he's calmed down a little, and I dare to take another step his way.

"So, as you can see, my mother and I have a lot more in common than I thought."

"That's…wow." He squeezes the back of his neck, and I track the movement, paying extra attention to the cuts and bruises along his knuckles.

"Does it hurt?"

"Huh?" he asks.

I nod toward his hand. "Does your hand hurt? That fight was…rough."

"You watched my game?"

"Of course I did. I haven't missed one yet, and I wasn't about to start now."

His lips twitch. It's subtle, but it's there, and my shoulders relax an inch or two.

I take another step. "Does it hurt?"

"A little."

"Are you going to get in trouble for it?"

"There's a good chance I'm looking at a suspension."

Another step. He notices.

I pause, and he tips his head to the side.

"Did you find it? Whatever you were looking for there, did you find it?"

I tilt my left hand back and forth. "Sort of. She helped shed light on things I've been struggling with for a long time, feelings I kept thinking I had no right to have. She helped me realize it's okay, realize I'm allowed to not know myself and to keep searching for her."

"And is that what you plan to do? Keep searching?"

"Yes."

His shoulders drop, and fuck it, I cross the rest of the way to him. I don't stop until I'm standing right in front of him. I tuck my finger under his chin, his stubble tickling me as I force his gaze upward.

"But I don't want to do it alone. Not anymore."

He gulps. "You…don't?"

I shake my head. "No, and the worst part is, I don't think I ever wanted to. I just didn't know how to tell you that."

Suddenly, he sags against me, and I struggle to hold his full weight, but I accept it anyway, wrapping my arms around him. I don't know how I know it, but I know he's crying, and I hate that he is. But I get it. I'm on the verge of tears myself.

I can't cry, though. Not now. This isn't about me. Not really.

"I'm sorry," I say softly, and when he pulls away from me, his eyes are redder than I've seen before, his cheeks wet. I want to kiss all the hurt away, and I plan to. But first, I have some things I need to say to him.

"I was wrong to apply to that internship without telling you, and I was wrong before that too. I should have told you how I was feeling. I should have let you in and let you help me. I shouldn't have tried to bury it and pretend it wasn't happening."

"Why didn't you, Clover? Why didn't you tell me?"

"Because I didn't want to burden you with my problems. At first, it was because I felt like I was being silly. I had no real reason to feel the way I did. You treated me so well. You told me you loved me every chance you got. And you never, ever made me feel like I was less than. You were perfect."

He shakes his head. "But I wasn't. I wasn't because I knew. I fucking *knew*. I knew something was going on with you, knew you were slipping away. I knew you weren't truly happy, but I let you pretend. I let you keep me at arm's length because at least it meant I got to keep you. I was as scared to rock the boat as you were, which means I'm just as guilty."

It breaks my heart that he thinks he has any blame in all of this, but maybe…maybe he's right. A relationship is a two-way street, and we didn't communicate what direction we were moving in, so we were never in the same lane. We fucked this up together, even if we were apart.

"I wish you had said something. I wish *I* had said something too. I feel like we wasted so much time by just…not talking," he says, and I couldn't agree more.

"We did, and I don't ever want to do that again. I want to tell you everything, even when I don't think you want to hear what I have to say."

"I don't think you could ever say something I don't want to hear. You could read me the terms and conditions on the back of a receipt, and I'd still hang on to every word."

I chuckle. "That's not what I mean, and you know it."

"Then what do you mean, Clover? Talk to me. Tell me."

I sigh. "I mean telling you things like when I'm unhappy."

"Okay. I'm unhappy sometimes too. I would understand."

"Come on, Callum. You can't be serious. If I had come to you and said I was unhappy, how would you have reacted? And I want a serious answer. Don't tell me what you *think* I want to hear. Dig deep. Be *honest*."

He doesn't say anything right away, and for the first time, I'm okay with that.

Then finally, he does.

"I would have wondered what I did to make you feel like that."

"Exactly. That's my whole point. My mother said something to me. She said it's hard to try to explain to someone you love that it's not their fault you're not happy. And she's right. If I had told you I wasn't happy, you would have taken it personally, even if I had said it wasn't your fault. Because why wouldn't you? You're my partner. We're supposed to make each other feel good, and if that's true, it *must* be something we've done wrong, right?" I shake my head. "But that's wrong. Sometimes people just don't feel happy. Sometimes they don't understand themselves. And that's okay. *I'm* okay, just the way I am. It's okay that I don't have it all figured out because I know the really, truly important stuff."

"And what's that, Clover?"

I step back into him, placing a hand on his chest because I need to feel him in some way right now.

"That I love you, Callum."

His eyes flare, and he opens his mouth, but I keep going because I need to say this.

"I love you. I have *always* loved you. I loved you when you sat next to me in college and called me Clover for the first time. I loved you when you stuck up for me at that game, and I loved you when I gave myself to you later that night. I didn't say it then, but I should have. I should have told you you're it for me, too. You always have been, and no matter where I've been in this world, that hasn't changed. I know I've hurt you many times over. I know I've probably made it hard to trust me, too. But please— *please*—listen to me when I tell you this: there will never be a day in my life when I don't love you. And there will never, *ever* be a single second where I am not wholly and completely yours. I love you, Callum, and I'm sorry if I haven't said that enough, but if you'll let me, I'll tell you every day for the rest of our lives."

He doesn't move. He doesn't speak. For a moment, I worry I'm too late, worry I've broken him too many times, fucked this up beyond repair, and lost the one person who means everything to me.

Then, he says, "You have no idea how long I've waited to hear you say that, Clover."

And he kisses me. It's soft and slow, then hard and fast. It's messy and uncoordinated as we pull at each other until I'm not sure where the other starts and ends, and I'm okay with that. For the first time, I truly am. Even though I still have a lot of work to do with myself, I know the one thing that doesn't need work is how I feel about the man kissing me right now.

When we finally break apart, we're both gasping for air, and I've never been so happy to struggle to breathe before.

"I love you, Chloe Keller."

I smile. "And I love you, Callum Keller."

"That has a nice little ring to it, huh?"

I laugh, and he swallows the sound with his lips.

At some point, we come up for air, and his hand goes right to my left ring finger.

"I missed seeing this on you, you know."

I smile, looking down at the gorgeous 2-carat set that was my gift on our five-year wedding anniversary. "I missed wearing it. I'm never taking it off again."

"Good. Let's keep it that way."

Then he's kissing me again.

I'm not sure what's next for us. I still have work to do on myself, and we have a hell of a lot we need to work through together, too. Maybe we live apart for a while. Maybe we can pick up right where we were before that damn job offer. Or maybe…maybe we do one even better and we come back from this stronger than we've ever been.

Whatever we decide, we're going to do it together.

Forever.

Epilogue

KELLER

I don't know how, but I walked away with only a one-game suspension after the fight with that douchebag from Vegas. I'm damn glad because otherwise, there's a chance I wouldn't be sitting on this bench with my teammates during Game Seven of the Finals. Coach wouldn't have trusted me to help carry the team through the playoffs if I couldn't keep myself in check.

"We can do this," Hutch says, his eyes locked on the ice as Lawson passes the puck to Hayes. "I'm sure of it."

I'm glad he is. We're down one goal with just under seven minutes to go, and I have the worst feeling we might be fighting a losing battle. It's been a hard-fought series with New York. At first, I found it fitting that we were playing them given they were the ones who drafted me, but then we went down two games, and nothing felt good anymore. We managed to come back and bring it all the way to seven, but now there's a chance we'll walk away with nothing but disappointment.

"Fuck yeah, we can," Locke agrees. He sits forward, then holds his hand out. "iPad me."

He's not usually one to review plays in the middle of a game, so I'm surprised he's asking for the device. I hand it to him anyway, then track the puck as my teammates dump it in deep.

"Come on, come on, come on," I repeat as Lawson battles for it. The guy pinning him up against the wall is much bigger than he is, but who cares? This is playoff hockey. It's a whole different beast than the regular season.

"He's got this. We're good. We're—fuck!" Hutch shouts as the puck squirts out of the zone.

I feel the exact same way.

Fox comes out of his net to play it, likely telling the defenseman who goes back for it that we should work up the ice the other way, which is how we get right back into the play after a partial line change.

"Fucking hell! I was so damn close!" Hayes bangs his stick against the boards, clearly frustrated, and I don't blame him. We've had to work hard for every damn goal this series, and it's a tough pill to swallow knowing we sit here so close, yet so far away from winning this game.

"We can do this," Hutch says again, trying to calm him, but as the seconds tick by, I'm feeling less and less hopeful that he's right.

Then suddenly, the puck is in the back of the net, and we're jumping off the bench in joy.

"Fuck yes, baby!" Hayes screams.

"See?" our captain says, grabbing me by the shoulders and giving me a shake. "We fucking got this!"

We bump fists with Frederic as he skates by, and if we somehow win this thing, that guy is getting *all* the free drinks for the rest of his time as a member of the Seattle Serpents.

The clock winds down, and we're officially headed to overtime.

"Holy shit! What a thrill!" Lawson says through labored breaths just before guzzling half a bottle of sports drink once we're back in the locker room.

"What a fucking goal!" Poldzkin adds.

Similar sentiments go up throughout the room. Everyone is buzzing with energy from the game-tying goal, several people patting Frederic on the back, me included.

But as soon as Coach Smith walks in, the room falls silent. He stands in the middle of the space, his hands on his hips, the gray at his temples more obvious than ever before. Though we just tied the game, he's not smiling, and that's because he knows better than anyone else that the hard work isn't over yet.

"I know we went down for a bit in the third, but that might have been the best sixty minutes we've played this season, fellas. These next ones… Well, shit, they just might be the most important." He lifts his head, locking eyes with every single player. "Frederic, that was a hell of a goal and good job getting us back in the game, but I want to make myself clear when I say this isn't just one man's game. This is *everyone's* game, and if we're going to win this, we have to fight as a unit. As one. *Whole.* Not a piece of a puzzle, the entire fucking thing, all right?"

"Heard," we respond as he walks out of the room.

It's the last thing anyone says. We don't even look to Hutchinson to make a speech. We all know what we need to do to win.

When we finally get back out on the ice, we're locked in completely. There's hardly any conversation on the bench, but there doesn't need to be—we know.

I take the ice for my first shift, tapping my stick for the puck. It's shot over to me instantly, and I take it toward the net, hoping for an opening, but there's nothing. I drag it around back, making sure to box out the opponent, then I zing it over to my teammate, and it lands right on his tape. He zips the puck toward the net, but the New York goalie is faster than him, and it bounces off his pad as I take a cross-check, a warning to get out from in front of their net, though I don't heed it.

We scramble for the puck, and it eventually pops free. We try to get it past the goalie again, but he snatches it up this time, flashing his glove to show the ref he's got it.

The whistle is blown, and the play is officially dead. We get set again and win it back, but it takes a weird bounce and goes out of the zone. We take the chance to get some fresh legs on the ice and make a quick change.

"Go high," I say to Lawson as I skate past him.

He nods, then flies onto the ice, jumping into the play. Another whistle is blown when Fox snatches the puck out of midair, and there's another faceoff. Even though he's usually on the wing, Lawson is the one on the draw because we need our best man right now, and it's no surprise he wins it back.

It *is* a surprise that he plays it off the boards and right to himself. He then smacks it over to Hayes, who skates it up the ice, pushing harder than I've ever seen him do before. It's still not fast enough, because New York is *right there*, ready to snatch the puck back.

What they don't count on is Lawson's skating abilities, a skill that is severely underrated, and soon he's not only flying past the New York players, but ours too. When Hayes passes him the puck—a beautiful tape-to-tape play—it's no wonder New York's goalie ends up sprawled on the ice and the puck lands in the back of the net.

"Holy shit!" Hutch explodes beside me, grabbing me and hauling me to my feet.

"What the fuck just happened?!" Locke yells, then he's hopping over the boards just like the rest of our team.

Helmets go flying, and so do sticks as we all skate across the ice and crowd around Lawson and Hayes, who are hugging and celebrating. Fox crashes into us, jumping as high as a goalie can in all that gear, and screams happily.

"We did it! We did it!"

He's right—we did do it. For the first time in my career, I am a Cup champion, and there's not a better group of guys out there to win the damn thing with. I hug every one of my teammates, some of them longer than others, and when I finally make my way to the game-winning goalscorer, he's grinning ear to ear, his arms stretched wide.

"Kells! Come here, you beautiful fuck!"

For the first time, without any protest, I do. I wrap Lawson in my arms, then plant my lips right against his cheek. He's finally getting the kiss he's been teasing me about for years, and if it means getting to lift that trophy, I'd do it again, too.

"I knew you loved me!" Lawson yells once I set him back on his skates.

"Right now? Fuck yes, I do."

He grins, then we hug again, because that's just how damn good I feel right now. We're handed champion-branded hats and shirts and towels, and I hug more people than I have in my entire life, even if there's only one person I want to share this with.

Once the trophy is presented and Hutch takes a

photo with it, he lifts it into the air, and the entire arena erupts in cheers once more. The next several minutes are a blur, even as I lift the thirty-plus-pound trophy and take my lap with it. I'm too preoccupied with thoughts of something else. *Someone* else.

I don't know how long passes or really what's said or happens until finally, there's a part in the crowd, and I see her. My cheeks hurt, that's how wide I'm smiling, and while I'm sure it's a strange sight to some, it feels natural to me. It always has when it comes to her.

Chloe stands with her hands tucked into her back pockets, her teeth worrying her bottom lip as her eyes dart all over the place, searching. She's fucking stunning in her WAG jacket, her dark red locks up in a half ponytail, those same worn black boots she's had forever strapped to her feet.

My favorite part, though? The ring sitting on her left hand. To my knowledge, she hasn't taken it off since that night she came back to me, and if I have my way, she never will again.

In addition to a grueling schedule and working my ass off through the playoffs, I've been attending counseling sessions twice a week—one for myself to help work through my panic attacks, and the other with Chloe as we tackle the issues putting a strain on our marriage. It's not like we've fixed anything overnight—we still have a long way to go—but it's been a little easier to breathe lately without having to worry if I'm going to lose everything in one fell swoop.

I still cling to far too many fears, but losing Chloe isn't one of them. She's here, she's staying for good, and it has nothing to do with her job at *Seattle Life & Leisure*. It's for her. For me. For *us*, which is exactly what we feel like now.

When her brown eyes snag on mine, I see the sigh of relief she lets out, and I go to her. She meets me halfway, throwing her arms around my neck, and I lift her into my arms. I hug her tightly, my face buried in her neck, just breathing her in. When I finally come up for air, she's grinning at me.

"You did it."

"I did it," I echo.

Then I kiss her—*hard*. There's nothing slow or sweet or gentle about it. It doesn't matter that we're standing on the ice surrounded by my teammates and Serpents staff and far too many reporters. All that matters is having her in my arms and my mouth on hers. She tastes like Diet Coke and chocolate, a combination that's abominable, but I love it anyway because I love *her*.

We break apart, and I'm still smiling as I set her on her feet, loving how her body slides against mine the whole way down.

"I'm so proud of you, Callum," she says, her finger slipping into the ring around my neck. Though it's always on my finger off the ice, it still stays on the chain when I'm playing. I've gotten used to keeping it there, and honestly, it makes me feel closer to my wife, even when she's not around.

"I couldn't have done it without you." She opens her mouth to refute that, but I shake my head. "No, I'm serious. I wouldn't be standing here without you. You gave me a reason to fight, even when I didn't want to. You believed in me every step of the way, even when you weren't here. I think somehow, someway, I felt that, and I needed it. I needed you."

"You have me, Callum. I'm not going anywhere," she promises.

"I know. Because you're going to marry me."

She laughs, her eyes sparkling under the arena's bright lights. "We're already married."

"I know, but I want to do it again. Marry me with all my friends there—my family, *your* family. Marry me so I can show the entire fucking world how madly in love with you I am." I bend at the knees until we're eye level. "Marry me again, Clover, because I can't imagine my life without you."

Her mouth hangs open, then closes again, only for it to float back open. She looks like a fish, but I don't care. All I care about is the single word she utters.

"Yes."

There's one thing I'm absolutely sure of: it's better than winning the Cup.

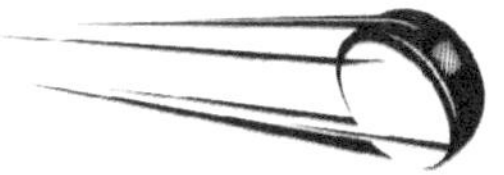

When I was younger, I never really thought much about marriage. I figured it was something that might happen one day, and I'd cross that bridge when it came.

Then I met Chloe, and for the first time, I *knew* it was inevitable, and I also knew I would only get married once. So why I'm shaking from head to toe as my bride walks down the aisle to me at my second wedding is beyond me, but here we are. Sure, I'm not *technically* getting married again, but I am saying my vows knowing their full weight in a way I never have before.

A hand lands on my shoulder, and I don't have to turn back to know it's my brother. "She's a vision, bro."

"Yeah, she is," I reply, unable to take my eyes off Chloe.

Her dress is simple, almost understated, but it's in no way any less stunning as she makes her way toward me. Her hair is swept up in a fancy updo, and the only piece of jewelry she's wearing is a necklace that's shaped like a clover. There's a bouquet clutched tightly in one hand, and she's holding her father's arm with the other. Even *he's* smiling, but that's not my focus right now. It's her.

If you're lucky, you get to marry the person you love once, but if you're *really* lucky, you get to do it twice, and I feel really fucking lucky right now.

Hi, Clover, I mouth, and she grins.

Her father "gives her away," and after shaking his hand, I can't stop myself from leaning in and kissing Chloe right on the cheek. Several people snicker, and her mother sighs dramatically, but I don't care. All I can focus on is her.

"Thank you all for coming today," Lawson says. "You may be seated."

When he came to me with the idea of being our officiant, I gave him a fifty-item list of things I'd rather do than have him at my wedding. But Chloe loved the idea, so here we are.

"Today, we're here to celebrate the vow renewal of Chloe—shit, I probably should have gotten your middle name, huh?" Lawson laughs uneasily. "Chloe Keller and my best friend, Cal—Keller!" he amends when I glare at him.

Chloe giggles, and I think if she weren't here holding on to me, about to say *I do* all over again, I *might* be jealous, but I can't find it in me to be.

"My mother, who Keller is a *big* fan of, used to make me watch cheesy Hallmark movies with her. I hated it, naturally. It was pure torture for a young kid who just wanted to be out in the backyard playing hockey. But I did it because it made her happy, and to me, that was all that mattered."

Several people in the crowd laugh and *aww* over his story.

"Then one day, I found myself watching them when

she wasn't around. Unknowingly, I had fallen in love with them. There was a sweetness that I enjoy, and they're a comfort, because no matter what, you know the couple will find their way back to each other and they'll live happily ever after. I felt that the second I saw Chloe and Keller together for the first time."

I look over at Lawson, and I'm surprised there's no smirk on his lips. He means it, and it's the first I'm hearing this.

"You see, sometimes we meet people who are just supposed to be part of our lives. Sometimes it's a teammate who claims to hate you but secretly loves you so much he trusts you to officiate his wedding."

"Or is coerced into it," I murmur, which earns me a glower from Lawson and a laugh from Chloe.

"Or sometimes it happens in a college classroom. Life might try to tear you away from that person on many occasions, but no matter what, you make your way back to each other. That's what happened here with Chloe and Keller. Life tried to stop them from being together, but they told life to kick rocks, and they fought for their love, just like those folks in the Hallmark movies. It's why I'm standing here today as they say their vows once more. Because that's what marriage really is—showing up every day, even if you don't want to. It's about being there not only for your partner, but for yourself too. It's fighting, and not just in the traditional sense either. It's fighting yourself, your doubts, and your assumptions of what the other person should be. It's just being there, and that counts a hell of a lot more than most people realize."

Lawson's words are true in more ways than one, and I never thought I'd see the day when he brought tears to my eyes, but it's exactly what happens. I blink them away, not missing how Chloe squeezes my hand with hers because she knows too. She feels the weight of his message just as much as I do.

Fighting is exactly what we've done over the last few months. Between coming back together, the Cup run, winning, and everything that came after, we've had to do just what Lawson's said time and time again—show up, and it's exactly what I plan to keep doing. I almost lost her once, and I'll be damned if I ever let it get that close again.

Not that I'll tell him, but Lawson wraps up the ceremony beautifully, and soon Chloe is slipping my ring onto my finger, though it's pointless since I got it tattooed on me last week. I wanted it to be a surprise, but I couldn't wait a second longer. I needed her to know just how serious I am when I take these vows.

We're forever. The good, the bad…all of it. I'm going to be here, and I know she will be too.

When Lawson finally announces us as husband and wife for the second time, I dip Chloe back and kiss her long and hard and way past appropriate because I can't help it. I've always been a little out of control when it comes to her, and I don't see that changing anytime soon.

We hold on to each other as we make our way down the aisle, and I don't let her go as we take photos or even when we walk into the reception, all of our friends and family cheering for us. Not until we break for dinner do I finally let her go, and only after she promises to come right back.

"Dude, I don't think I've ever seen you smile so much, and it's freaking me out a little," Hayes says.

"He's right," Fox chimes in. "But I'm happy you're happy, man. Truly."

"Me too," Locke adds.

Hutch pats me on the back. "I knew you two would figure your shit out."

I roll my eyes, but secretly, I'm glad too.

"My boy! He did it!" Lawson slings his arm around me, squeezing my neck tightly, and I try to push him off, but it's no use. He tips a beer to his lips, taking a swig. "All right, who's next?" He looks at Locke. "You and Nessa getting hitched anytime soon?"

The veteran grins, shoving his hands into his pockets. "We'll just see, won't we?"

I watch him carefully, getting the sense there's maybe a little more truth to his words than he wants to admit, but I let him have his secret for now.

"Still bummed you and Chloe moved out of the

building," Locke says, changing the subject. "How's the house?"

As if we didn't have enough going on this summer, we added buying a house together for the first time to our plates. I'm not sure if we'll be staying in Seattle forever, but for now, it's home. It was high time we made it so and got a place that's truly *ours*.

"Great. Auden and Lilah did a fantastic job on it."

Fox and Hutch bump fists, clearly proud of their partners.

"And it's still close to Rory's clinic, which is nice for Percy."

"And me," Lawson says, clinging to me. "You're even closer to me now."

I groan. "Don't remind me." I finally shake him off. "And get the fuck off me."

"Aww, come on. Just love me! Remember when I scored the game-winning goal and you kissed my cheek? Why can't you love me like that all the time?"

I roll my eyes, ignoring him.

"Well, how about it, boys? We fucking did it. We won the Cup *and* we got the girls," he says, lifting his beer in the air. "To the Serpents Singles!"

We all look at each other, then laugh before holding our own drinks up and clinking them together.

"Serpents Singles!"

"Best fucking club there is," Lawson adds before taking his drink.

We groan collectively, and I swing my gaze across the room, right to Chloe, who is huddled in a corner, holding Talia.

"Uh, I'll be right back," I say to the guys, breaking away from them and heading toward my wife.

"You still owe me a kiss!" Lawson calls to my back.

I flip him off, smiling when I hear Hutch, Locke, Hayes, and Fox all laugh. I have a feeling I'll be doing a lot more of that, but only after I sort out why my wife's best friend is crying at our wedding.

Everything okay? I mouth to Chloe as I make my way over. She shakes her head, then holds Talia closer.

"Hey, Tally," I say to the small blonde woman. "You all right?"

She looks up at me, her eyes red from crying, and she bursts into tears again before brushing past me and running toward the bathroom.

"What's going on?" I ask Chloe.

She shakes her head, working her jaw back and forth.

"Talk to me, Clover. Tell me what happened."

"It's…" She sighs. "It's not my story to tell, but I feel like you need to know this. Do you remember that guy you were teammates with at college? Shawn Hicks?"

My fists clench at my sides just thinking of the prick. Things were never the same between us after that day in the cafeteria, and they've remained so, even with us being in the same league.

"Yeah, I remember. Tally 'dated' him for a while,

right?" I use air quotes around dating because nothing that guy did should have been considered that. He was always so shitty to the girls he brought around, and Talia was no exception.

"Yep. And remember how Talia has never told me who Ian's father is? Always claimed it was a one-night stand who didn't want anything to do with the baby?"

I close my eyes, knowing exactly where this is going.

"He's the father, isn't he?" My wife nods, and I scoff. "Fuck, I knew I should have taken another run at him last time we played against each other, just for good measure."

She laughs lightly. "Yeah, probably, especially since she wasn't lying about him not wanting anything to do with Ian."

"What a piece of shit. So, what's going on now? Why is she crying? Did something happen?"

"He just got traded."

"Okay…trades happen all the time. What is she—oh god."

My eyes widen, and Chloe nods, confirming the worst news possible for my wife's best friend.

"Please tell me it's not…"

"Tennessee," she says quietly. "Talia's secret baby daddy is the new star for the Tennessee Twisters."

**

. . .

THANK YOU FOR READING!

I hope you loved Callum, Chloe, and the rest of the Serpents Singles! If you enjoyed this book, I encourage you to leave a review on your favorite platform.

Want more?
Keep reading for a bonus scene!

Bonus Scene

KELLER

"Callum, where are you taking me?"

"You'll see," I tell her, tugging her forward and down the stone path I traveled earlier while she was taking a nap back in the hotel room.

Chloe giggles, and I can't help but grin. It's easily my favorite sound in the world, even topping a goal horn going off. While I love to score, I would go the rest of my life never putting a puck in the back of the net if it meant I got to spend every day listening to my wife's laughter.

My wife.

We've been married for five years already, but I don't think I'll ever truly get used to calling her that. How could I when every time I look at her, it still feels like we're a couple of kids in college, falling in love for the first time?

Her hand is grasped tightly in mine as the sun dips

lower in the sky. The deeper we go into the overgrown trees, the darker it gets, but I know what's lies ahead.

"We're almost there," I promise her.

Less than two minutes later, we step into the clearing I found, and Chloe gasps at the sight before us.

"Holy…" she whispers, her eyes wide as she takes in the sun glistening off the waves. "Callum, this is… gorgeous."

Maui *is* gorgeous, but it's nothing compared to her.

Her deep red hair is swept up in a messy bun, and there's not a lick of makeup on her face. A floor-length lemonade-colored dress hugs in all the right places, and there's a bit of pink to her cheeks that wasn't there when we first began our two-week honeymoon.

I wish I could have swept her away the night we got married and spent the next month buried inside of her, but thanks to signing the contract with New York, I had obligations I couldn't put off.

It doesn't matter now, though. We're here. We're together. Nothing can beat this.

I step up behind her, wrapping my arms around her waist and tugging her against me. I press a kiss to her exposed shoulder, reminding myself to rub a little extra sunscreen on it before hitting the beach tomorrow, and rest my chin on the top of her head, loving how she sags against me with a happy sigh.

"I found it earlier," I tell her as she rests her hands on top of mine.

"I was wondering where you snuck off to. I woke up at one point, and you were gone. I thought you had maybe come to your senses and had taken off."

I frown. This isn't the first time she's made a comment like this, and I hate it just as much as all the others.

We've been married for five years. Is she ever going to believe she's enough for me?

"I'm not going anywhere, Clover. You couldn't get rid of me even if you tried."

She squeezes my hand, and I try not to overthink the fact that it's the only response I get.

We stand like that until the sun dips below the horizon, and I know if we don't make our way back to the hotel soon, we'll be trying to navigate the rocky path in the dark.

"We should probably head back," I tell her, even though I don't want to leave this spot any more than she does.

"Five more minutes?" she asks.

I don't dare deny her.

"Five more minutes," I agree.

Chloe wiggles back against me, and swaying softly back and forth to a song that only she can hear.

It gives me an idea.

She whines when I pull away, and I grin to myself as I slide my phone from my pocket and navigate to my music app.

"What are you doing?" she asks, trying to peek, but I hold the device closer to my chest, trying to keep it a surprise.

"I found a song that made me think of you, and I want to play it for you."

"Of me?" she asks excitedly, then huffs. "It's not one of those screamy songs you love so much, is it?"

"No. It's a romantic song, believe it or not."

She lights up again. "Really? My, my. Are you going soft on me, Callum Keller?"

"I'm always soft when it comes to you." I scrunch up my face. "Wait. That didn't sound right."

Chloe laughs. "No, it didn't, but I know what you mean. You act so tough on the exterior, but I know deep down, you're a secret romantic."

"Only for you, Clover," I tell her, meaning every word.

She blushes as I set the song to repeat after it's done, because I already know I'm going to want her in my arms for longer than the music lasts, and hover my thumb over the play button before looking at her.

"May I have this dance, Mrs. Keller?"

She giggles, and I wish I could bottle up the sound and keep it for all time. I'd use it for lonely nights in hotel rooms when I'm on the road. Or listen to it on repeat on the long flights. Honestly, just whenever I need a pick-me-up, because that's what being around Chloe feels like to me.

"Yes, Mr. Keller, you may," she says as she slips her hand in mine.

I press play on the song and put the phone into my pocket before dragging her to me, loving how she falls against me effortlessly.

My arms go around her, and she presses her head to my chest, almost like she's listening to my heartbeat instead of the building melody.

"Sometimes I forget what a good dancer you are."

"Shhh. Listen to the song, Clover. And I mean *really* listen."

"All right, all right," she says, sounding exasperated, but she does as she's told.

We stay pressed together like that for another play through, and just when I think she's going to pull away, she tugs me closer, her fingers digging into me as she grips me tighter, and I don't dare try to move.

I couldn't even if I wanted to.

I'm rooted to this spot. To *her*. It's been that way since the beginning, and if luck is on my side, that'll never change. *We'll* never change.

Her shaking shoulders pull me from my thoughts, and I lean back, looking down at her.

"Clover?"

"I'm sorry." She wipes away the tears beneath her eyes. "That was just… Gosh, that was beautiful, Callum. Is that…" She gulps in a breath. "Is that really how you feel about me?"

"Yes. Is that so surprising?" She nods, and I hate that she does. I tug her closer, tracing my palm over her back in soothing circles. "Yes, Clover. That's really how I feel about you. You're…everything to me. You always have been."

I feel her smile against me. "You're everything to me, too, Callum."

We stay like that for a long time, swaying back and forth to the same song over and over. The sun is long gone, and we'll definitely be walking back in the dark, but I don't care, not if it means getting to hold her like this.

"We should probably head back," she says after a long while, and I nod, even though I don't want to let her go.

"Yeah, sure, let's go back."

She slides her hand against mine, twining our fingers together. "Want to order room service? I'm thinking a brownie sundae and a long, hot bath sounds really nice."

"Of course you do, my little chocaholic."

"Hey! It's not an addiction. I can quit whenever I want. Maybe."

She's lying, and we both know it.

But I don't call her on it. I love that she loves chocolate so much. Hell, I'd love it even if she didn't, but that's just because everything about her is my favorite. She might be addicted to chocolate, but I'm addicted to her, and I don't see myself ever quitting.

"Hey," she says when we're halfway back to the hotel.

"What was that song we just danced to? I want to make sure I add it to my playlist. I mean, I'll probably be a sobbing mess every time I hear it while you're on the road, but I still want to know."

If she only knew the number of times I've been in that exact spot.

"It's called 'You in January' by The Wonder Years."

"It was really beautiful. Thank you for sharing it with me."

I squeeze her hand. "I'll share everything with you, Clover. Always. Let's promise to never stop sharing."

"Deal." She squeezes back. "Race you back to the hotel? First to the room gets the last bite of brownie?"

"You're on."

The words have barely left my mouth before she's sprinting ahead of me, laughing and smiling over her shoulder as I chase behind her.

She's the first to reach the room, and I'll never tell her, but I let her win.

Because for her, I'd do anything.

Forever.

Thank You

Well, we did it. We made it to the end of the Seattle Serpents. I dreamed this series up waaaaay back when I was writing book five of the Carolina Comets series, Scoring Chance. Keller came to me first, so it feels fitting to be ending the series with his book.

If I'm being honest, this book hit a bit close to home while writing it. I've been with my husband since I was fifteen, so I related to how Chloe was feeling a bit too well. There were a lot of pieces of me within her, and while I struggled with that at first, I've made peace with it, even knowing there will be some who don't understand her. That's okay. That's life, and that's what I wanted to show with this book. Not everyone has the same experiences. Not everyone feels and processes things the same. We shouldn't be ashamed of that. We should embrace it. It makes us who we are. And we *are* loveable, even when we don't feel like we are.

With that said, this book wouldn't be possible without the following people:

My husband, Henry. Nearly twenty years together and you're still my favorite person. I don't always like you, but I do always love you, and at the end of the day, that's what matters.

Laurie and Kristann. You're always there for me whenever I need to crash out and complain, and I love you for that.

My editing team. Caitlin, Julia, Judy… As usual, you ladies whipped this manuscript into shape and turned it into something amazing. I owe so much to you.

Kim, Nina, and the VPR team. I cannot imagine this journey without you. Thank you, thank you, thank you.

Tidbits. Thanks for always having my back.

And you. This whole writing thing is scary. Putting pieces of yourself into the universe for others to judge is truly terrifying, but I'm grateful to have you there with me through it all. See you in Tennessee.

With love and unwavering gratitude,
Teagan

Other Titles by Teagan Hunter

TENNESSEE TWISTERS

Line Change

SEATTLE SERPENTS SERIES

Body Check

Face Off

Delayed Penalty

Empty Net

Top Shelf

Match Penalty

STICK TAPS SERIES

Grumpily Ever After

Grumpily Yours

CAROLINA COMETS SERIES

Puck Shy

Blind Pass

One-Timer

Sin Bin

Scoring Chance

Glove Save

Neutral Zone

ROOMMATE ROMPS SERIES

Loathe Thy Neighbor

Love Thy Neighbor

Crave Thy Neighbor

Tempt Thy Neighbor

SLICE SERIES

A Pizza My Heart

I Knead You Tonight

Doughn't Let Me Go

A Slice of Love

Cheesy on the Eyes

TEXTING SERIES

Let's Get Textual

I Wanna Text You Up

Can't Text This

Text Me Baby One More Time

INTERCONNECTED STANDALONES

We Are the Stars

If You Say So

STANDALONES

The DM Diaries

Best Friends for Never

Stay on top of my new releases, cover reveals, sales, and more by visiting:

www.teaganhunterwrites.com

TEAGAN HUNTER writes steamy romantic comedies
with lots of sarcasm and a side of heart.
She loves pizza, hockey, and romance novels, though not
in that order. When not writing, you can find her
watching entirely too many hours of *Supernatural,*
One Tree Hill, or *New Girl.* She's mildly obsessed with
Halloween and prefers cooler weather.
She married her high school sweetheart,
and they currently live in the PNW.

www.teaganhunterwrites.com

9 781965 946770